Also by Angela Davis-Gardner

Plum Wine

Felice

Forms of Shelter

Butterfly's Child

Butterfly's Child

A Novel

Angela Davis-Gardner

THE DIAL PRESS | NEW YORK

Copyright © 2011 by Angela Davis-Gardner

Published in the United States by Dial Press, an imprint of
The Random House Publishing Group,
a division of Random House, Inc., New York.

DIAL and COLOPHON are registered trademarks of the Random House
Publishing Group

LIBRARY OF CONGRESS CATALOGING-IN-PUBLICATION DATA
Davis-Gardner, Angela.
   Butterfly's child: a novel / Angela Davis-Gardner.
      p. cm.
   ISBN 978-0-385-34094-6
   1. Illegitimate children—Fiction.   2. Illinois—Fiction.   3. San Francisco
(Calif.)—Fiction.   4. Japan—Fiction.   5. Identity (Psychology)—Fiction.
6. Psychological fiction.   I. Puccini, Giacomo, 1858–1924. Madama
Butterfly.   II. Title.
   PS3554.A9384B88 2011
   813'.6—dc22   2010005562

Printed in the United States of America on acid-free paper

www.dialpress.com

9 8 7 6 5 4 3 2 1

First Edition

Book design by Virginia Norey

For Evangeline McLennan Davis

Synopsis of Puccini's Opera
"Madama Butterfly"

ACT I. On a hill in Nagasaki, Japan, U.S. Navy Lieutenant B. F. Pinkerton inspects the house he has leased from a marriage broker, Goro. Goro has arranged a wedding between Pinkerton and Cio-Cio-san, known as Madama Butterfly. When the American consul, Sharpless, arrives, Pinkerton describes his carefree life; he is a sailor roaming the world in search of pleasure. At the moment, he is enchanted with Cio-Cio-san, but his 999-year marriage contract contains a monthly renewal option. When Sharpless warns that the girl may not take her vows so lightly, Pinkerton brushes aside such scruples, saying he will one day marry a "real" American wife. Cio-Cio-san is heard in the distance, joyously singing of her wedding. As she enters, surrounded by friends, she tells Pinkerton that when her family fell on hard times she had to earn her living as a geisha. Her relatives bustle in, noisily expressing their opinions on the marriage. In a quiet moment, Cio-Cio-san shows her bridegroom her few earthly treasures and tells him of her intention to embrace his Christian faith. The imperial commissioner performs the wedding ceremony, and the guests toast the couple. The celebration is interrupted by Cio-Cio-san's uncle, a Buddhist priest, who curses the girl for having renounced her ancestors' religion. Pinkerton angrily sends the guests away. Alone with Cio-Cio-san in the moonlit garden, he dries her tears, and she joins him in singing of their love.

ACT II. Three years later, Cio-Cio-san waits for Pinkerton's return. As her maid, Suzuki, prays to her gods for aid, Cio-Cio-san stands by the doorway with her eyes fixed on the harbor. When Suzuki shows her mistress how little money is left, Cio-Cio-san urges her to have faith: One fine day Pinkerton's ship will appear on the horizon. Sharpless brings a letter from the lieutenant, but before he can read it to Cio-Cio-san, Goro comes with a suitor, the wealthy Prince Yamadori. Cio-Cio-san dismisses Yamadori, certain that her American husband has not deserted her. When they are alone, Sharpless again starts to read the letter and suggests that Pinkerton may not return. Cio-Cio-san proudly introduces her blond, blue-eyed child; as soon as Pinkerton knows he has a son, she tells Sharpless, he will surely return to her. If not, she would rather die than return to her life as a geisha. Moved by her devotion, Sharpless leaves without having revealed the full contents of the letter. Cio-Cio-san hears a cannon report; seizing a spyglass, she discovers Pinkerton's ship entering the harbor. Now delirious with joy, she orders Suzuki to help her fill the house with flowers. As night falls, Cio-Cio-san, Suzuki, and the child begin their vigil.

ACT III. As dawn breaks, Suzuki insists that Cio-Cio-san rest. Humming a lullaby to her child, Cio-Cio-san carries him to another room. Sharpless enters with Pinkerton, followed by Kate, Pinkerton's new wife. When Suzuki realizes who the American woman is, she collapses in despair but agrees to aid in breaking the news to her mistress. Pinkerton, seized with remorse, bids an anguished farewell to the scene of his former happiness, then rushes away. When Cio-Cio-san comes forth expecting to find him, she finds Kate instead. Guessing the truth, the shattered Cio-Cio-san agrees to give up her child if his father will return for him. Then, sending even Suzuki away, she takes out the sword with which her father committed suicide and bows before a statue of Buddha, choosing to die with honor rather than live in disgrace. Suzuki pushes the child into the room. Sobbing farewell, Cio-Cio-san sends him into the garden to play, then stabs herself. As she dies, Pinkerton is heard calling her name.

(Adapted by permission from the Metropolitan Opera's *Opera News*.)

Overture

Sharpless:
What lovely fair hair!
Dear child, what is your name?

Butterfly to her child:
Answer: Today my name is Sorrow.
But when you write to my father, tell him
that the day he returns,
Joy, Joy shall be my name!

May 1895

It is spring in Nagasaki, and the strands of silk she has set out for the mating birds are gone from the maple tree in the garden, and the mother birds are nestled in silk, but still he has not come. Lieutenant Pinkerton had promised to return to his Cio-Cio-san, his Butterfly, when the uguisu warblers nest. He is late, but he will come. His ship has been delayed—perhaps a storm at sea—but soon she will see him at the entrance to their house, his Navy satchel over his shoulder, his pale blue eyes watering a little, and when he embraces her, his mustache will prickle her mouth and he will smell of sweat and salt.

But last spring he did not come, nor the three previous springs, Suzuki-chan reminds her. Why does madame believe he will keep his word this year? Suzuki makes a sour face as she flaps at the tatami with her cloth.

Because he is a man of honor, she replies, and several times each year he has sent money through Sharpless, so he knows she is waiting. And she and the fox god have a strong premonition that this will be the year.

He will come because he must come. The packets of money are not enough; there are still large debts at the geisha house to be paid, as her geisha mother has lately reminded her. If she is forced to return to the geisha way, Benji will be taken from her and will be an orphan wandering the streets of the pleasure district, destined to become a servant, or worse. So Pinkerton will return this year. Her skin is alive with the knowledge of it. She and Benji will be saved.

She is not surprised, then, that on a warm May afternoon when the hydrangeas are in bloom all over the hills and fragrant roses spill over the gates of houses, Sharpless arrives with his news.

He is a tall thin gaijin with a neck like a crane's, and sometimes he stutters when he speaks; it amuses her to think that he is a diplomat at the American consulate, such a nervous man, but he is her friend and confidant, and her connection to Pinkerton.

He gives her the envelope of money, an odd expression on his face, not quite a smile. There is something more; she catches her breath.

"I have had a letter," he says.

"From Pinkerton-san."

"Yes."

"He is coming."

Sharpless nods.

"Soon?"

"Yes. However . . ."

She spins around the room, embraces Benji and Suzuki, and kisses Sharpless on the cheek, making him blush. Then, taking Benji and Suzuki with her, she runs to the shrine to give thanks to all the gods.

Now she is preparing, singing as she cleans the Western-style room where Pinkerton smoked his pipe and studied his Navy papers. She drags the lumpish chairs outside to beat them with bamboo swatters, dust and white hair from Pinkerton's cat flying. She freshens her summer kimonos by draping them over the shrubs as an American woman might do—this will bring her luck, she thinks; the pale yellow and lavender kimonos rise and fall in the air like butterflies. Benji has been practicing his English sentences. "Welcome home to Papa-san," she coaches him, holding up the photograph of Pinkerton for him to address, and "Benji is one smart boy." Benji resembles his father physically, with his American nose and blond hair, though his hair—the color of butter—is darker than Pinkerton's. Otherwise he looks Japanese; he has her eyes. Pinkerton will be not only surprised but deeply pleased to see such a son and will want to provide for him. She is certain of this in spite of Suzuki's pessimism.

When Pinkerton had asked to be her danna, she'd said yes without hesitation, for he seemed steady, a man who could bring her a new ease.

As she made her farewell at the okiya, she did not put red beans of uncertainty into the rice presented to her geisha mother.

Benji was born nine months after Pinkerton's departure, and these have been the happiest years of her life. In her time at the geisha house in Maruyama, she could not have dreamed of being able to care for a child of her own. There was sensual pleasure in nursing and bathing Benji when he was a baby, and in smelling his sweet feathery hair and playing with his toes. She carried him everywhere, but now he is big enough that he can walk with her and hold a parcel or two when she goes to market like a housewife. They stroll along the bay to look at the ships and the changing shades of sky and water. He knows all the colors in Japanese and English, and he asks astonishing questions: How far does the water go? What makes the waves? Where is America? She knows he is a prodigy, even though Suzuki laughs at her for saying so. When Pinkerton returns, he will marry her and give up the Navy to become a Nagasaki businessman, as he had said he would like to do, and they will raise Benji to be an educated man, perhaps a scientist or doctor. She will never again have to dress for geisha parties with vulgar men who made her tie the cherry stem with her tongue, then giggled like schoolgirls when they boldly took the cherry from her lips with their own. So when Pinkerton arrives, she will please him in every way, and she will wear his favorite kimono, black with a river of butterflies.

One morning, a thunderstorm rolled in from the bay—ink-black clouds, lightning, a heavy downpour—but then there was a sudden clearing: a brilliant blue sky, sun shining through light needles of rain. Fox wedding weather, auspicious weather. She sent Suzuki to the harbor for news, and an hour later, when she heard Suzuki's geta clattering toward the gate, she knew.

"He has come!" she cried, when Suzuki entered the room.

"Yes, madame." Suzuki gave a deep bow.

"You see?" She embraced Benji, who was sitting beside her, playing with the new string ball she had made him.

"But, madame." Suzuki came closer; her face was grave. "I am sorry to tell you that Pinkerton has come with a wife—an American wife."

She stared at Suzuki's plain face, her wrinkled eyelids. "Then it is not Pinkerton."

"I have seen them myself, entering a hotel. The owner said Mr. and Mrs. Pinkerton had registered and could not be disturbed."

"She must be his mother."

Suzuki shook her head. "She is too young. A young woman with yellow hair, fresh like a lemon."

"His sister," she said.

"I'm sorry, madame, but I have made several inquiries. There is no doubt. She is his wife." Suzuki nodded once, twice, for emphasis.

For a moment the air went black before her eyes.

"Mama?" Benji leaned against her. "Is Papa-san coming?"

She turned to him, taking his rosy, innocent face in her hands. "Yes, Papa-san is coming."

She jumped up. "Stay here," she told Benji. "Be a good boy. You will see Papa-san before long." In the kitchen, she packed some fried tofu, then hurried outdoors. The rain had ended. Pinkerton's white cat crouched below the maple tree, staring up at a nest of young wrens, his tail swishing. Bad-luck cat. She threw a pebble at him and he streaked from the yard.

She went down the hill and up another, to the pleasure district of Maruyama, passing small shops and teahouses crowded with people. A geisha she knew well, Mayumi-san, who'd had to give up her son last year, waved at her from a balcony. At first Mayumi-san had tried to disguise him as a girl, saying there would someday be a new geisha in the house. Now people said Mayumi-san was crazy.

She looked down at the street, studying the cracks in the flagstones. Some fortunate few geisha sons were adopted by wealthy parents, but this would not be the fate of a mixed-race child with yellow hair.

The plum trees around the borders of the shrine were wet, their oval leaves glistening with rain. She pulled down a branch; the fruit was still green, but she plucked two plums and took them to the stone vat of sacred plum seeds, where she made a prayer. Slowly she approached the stone fox, placed the tofu on the ground before him and bowed, then gazed at his mysterious eyes, his wise smile. "Help me, Inari-san." A breeze rustled through the leaves above them, sprinkling her with drops of rain. She closed her eyes. If she were very clever, Inari-san said, she could find a way.

As she walked out of the shrine and down the hill, a plan began to take shape in her mind. She stopped at Taiko's carpentry shop and called to him from the entrance. Once a houseboy for Americans, Taiko-san not only spoke but wrote English. Many geisha and courtesans came to him when they needed love letters for their foreigners.

He soon appeared, greeting her with a lively smile. "Ah, you have been away too long," he said. "Please take some tea." He was a winsome man of middle age, his hair still black; he had always favored her.

She explained that she needed assistance quickly, a brief note.

"Hai, hai." He disappeared into the dark recess of his shop and returned with paper, pen, and ink; they sat together on a bench.

She dictated her words and he translated, writing in careful English script: *Mr. B. F. Pinkerton: Come immediately to see your son, Benjamin Franklin Pinkerton the younger, or Benji as he is known. Sharpless-san says this knickname may sound both American and Japanese, as indeed he is by birth. That he is your son I swear by my life, my honor, and all the gods. Some few poor words of English he can speak but not many. He is very good and smart and can count to 100. He likes fresh fish but not salted ones. He must go to America with you now. Sincerely, Cio-Cio.*

Postscript: Take care of him always, American wife of Pinkerton.

Taiko-san, no longer smiling, put the letter into an envelope, hesitated, and gave it to her with a deep bow. "Please be in good health," he said. He did not meet her eyes.

She bowed and walked back up the hill, her body heavy, as if the air were pushing her back. She must be resolute.

She found Suzuki in the kitchen, boiling potatoes. Speaking in a low voice so Benji could not hear, she told Suzuki what they would do. Suzuki gasped and covered her mouth with her hands.

"First show this letter to Sharpless-san and entreat him to accompany you to the hotel. Do not return until the letter is in Pinkerton's hands." Sharpless would make certain that Pinkerton did as she asked.

While Suzuki was gone, she packed Benji's trunk, the one she had brought when she came here from the geisha house with Pinkerton. The chalky odor of the interior almost made her buckle; she would never again embrace him or cook his favorite soba noodles. He would be wild with grief at first. She could see him curled on the floor, his arms tight over his face. She took several shaky breaths. She would never see his young man's face. But Pinkerton would give him a home, a bright future in America. Her son would not live in the back alleys of Maruyama, picking through garbage, his face streaked with dirt. She could not falter. For Benji's sake, she must summon all her courage.

Suzuki entered the room and knelt beside her.

"The letter has been delivered to them privately at their hotel. At first Pinkerton cannot believe the boy is his, though Sharpless-san assured him this is so."

"He will believe when he sees him. The wife?"

"She is shocked. But she has a soft face."

"Good. Help me prepare."

In the room where she kept her kimonos, she knelt before the small round mirror to apply the makeup. She would look exactly as she had that first day when she struck his heart. She rubbed wax into her skin, then, her brush trembling, applied thick white paint over her face, covering her lips and eyebrows, leaving a subtle line of natural skin just below the hairline. Using fresh brushes, she painted the lids of her eyes a delicate pink and feathered on brown eyebrows. Bright red for the mouth. The mask gazed back at her from the mirror, her Cio-Cio face.

Suzuki painted the white makeup on the back of her neck, leaving the serpent's forked tongue of unpainted skin below the hair. Her hair was thick but for the bald spot on the crown that was caused by the tight hairstyle of her maiko days, when she was training to be a geisha. Suzuki arranged the hair on the top of her head in hills and valleys, using a swatch of yak hair at the top.

Just as she had done in the geisha house, Suzuki helped her dress: a gauzy red petticoat, a white cotton blouse with a red collar and long red sleeves, and a floor-length petticoat of white. Then the kimono, an explosion of colorful butterflies down the front, swirling around the hem and up toward her shoulder as if in flight.

In the reception room, she set a bowl of irises on the tokonoma and hung a scroll of a mountain shrouded in mist. At one side of the room was a folding screen, on it a river of plum trees; Suzuki helped her move it to the center, dividing the space. The sword—a souvenir from one of her patrons—she placed beside the tokonoma, on a fresh white cloth, then went outside.

Benji was in the garden, watching a frog in the pond. On his face was the solemn expression that she found uncanny and a little frightening: At such times he looked like a man in a child's body. He would need his wisdom now.

"Benji, Papa-san will arrive soon. Come dress in your Western clothes to greet him."

"Papa-san!" Benji jumped up and skipped into the house with her. He practiced his English phrases again as she helped him dress in the white sailor suit she had made for him.

They went to the reception room to wait.

She set the string ball before him on the tatami and put in his hand the small American flag she had bought at a shop by the harbor. "Sit here and play with your toys. Papa-san is coming soon. If you be very good and quiet, Papa-san will buy you new toys."

She wanted to grab him and run. Perhaps they could go to another city, but she had no training other than that of a geisha and no connections elsewhere; they would be paupers.

In the distance, there was a long yowl. "What is that?" Benji asked.

"Shh. It is nothing."

She embraced him as long as she could bear it, then rose and went to the other side of the screen to kneel beside the tokonoma. She stared at the scroll, the brushstrokes meaningless. Pain seared her chest. He would see her dead, lying in blood, but it was the only way. In America he would become a successful man. She must be stronger than the blade of steel.

Suzuki entered, very pale, carrying a ceramic sake bottle. She placed it beside the tokonoma, then bowed and left the room.

"Mama?" Benji called. "Is he here?"

"We must wait a little longer," she said. "We must be patient."

Benji fell silent behind the screen. She had taught him to be obedient.

She bent forward, a sob trapped in her throat. For his sake. He had been born without good fortune; she must provide it for him.

A grasshopper on the tatami, pale green as a young leaf, made a tiny clicking noise as it jumped. She closed her eyes.

She knows how it will be, like a scene from a Kabuki play. They will climb from the harbor, Pinkerton and the blond wife; already they are on the way. Suzuki will come to announce them, then begin to wail. When Pinkerton runs in, there she will be, lying on the tatami, a bloody sword loose in her hand, her geisha face turned toward the side, his Cio-Cio-san, looking just as she did the day she met him, and beside her will be Benji, staring down at her, the flag of his new country in his hand.

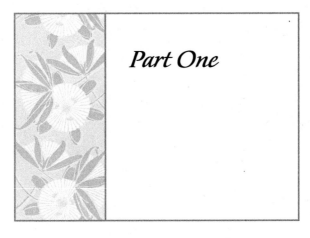

Part One

Pinkerton:
Oh, the bitter fragrance
of these flowers
spreads in my heart like poison.
Unchanged is the room
where our love blossomed.
But the chill of death is here.
My picture . . . (He lifts a photograph from the table)
She has thought of me.

Kate imagined how odd they must appear to people who strolled past them on deck, casting covert glances their way: a blond, blue-eyed man and woman sitting in silence, on the man's lap a child with a Japanese face and light hair. All three of them motionless, staring out at the sea like revenants, the boy immobile as a statue, clutching a multicolored string ball.

She drew her blanket more tightly about her shoulders. She should say something. They would look less strange in conversation.

"How can it be so cold in May?" she asked, trying to smile.

"The black current," Frank said. *"Kuro—kuroshiwo."* He made a snaking motion with one hand. "It's a mysterious, shifting current that runs along the coast of Japan and then out to sea. We should be leaving it soon."

She gazed out at the gray water, the dark line of Japan receding, then at the boy. Yesterday they had carried him kicking and biting to the hotel, but he hadn't made a sound since recovering from the sedation. The doctor said he was in profound shock—how much did the doctor know about the circumstances? she wondered. Poor child. She looked at him, his small hands gripping the ball as if his life depended on it.

"What shall we call him?" she said. They were to sit at the captain's table tonight and hadn't discussed how to introduce the boy. "He can't remain Benjamin. It would be a clear signal to the world that he's your child. Everyone knows you were named for Benjamin Franklin."

Frank said nothing. He was uncomfortable, of course, she thought, racked with guilt, but they had to discuss this bizarre situation; it was his responsibility, after all. God help me, she prayed silently. She must remember that he had married her and not that awful woman.

"It would be one thing if he looked completely Japanese," she said. "Remember your promise." The condition under which she'd agreed to take the boy home with them was that no one would know his parentage. "Frank?"

"Yes, darling." He looked at her. Today his eyes were gray, but they could be blue or blue-green depending on the surroundings and his mood. From looking at the sea so many years, he'd told her. He reached beneath the blankets to take her gloved hand. "I agree—anything you say."

"What about a simple Japanese name? Surely he has one. Ask him."

Frank spoke to the boy in halting Japanese.

"Benji," the boy said. It was the first word he had spoken.

"You could give him a Japanese name," Kate said.

"It would make life harder for him in America to have a Japanese name."

"Well . . . an American name, then."

They considered William, David, Michael, then settled on Tom—one syllable, easy for the boy to learn.

"What do you think, Tom?" Frank said, giving the boy a little shake. *"Anatano namae wa Tomu, desu ne?"*

The boy turned, holding up his ball so that it blocked his view of Frank's face. *"Watashi wa* Benji!" he screamed. He rolled off Frank's lap and went flying down the deck. Frank took off after him; Kate unfurled her blankets and followed.

She found Frank at the back of the ship, gazing about frantically. The deck was empty, the boy nowhere in sight.

Perhaps he had leapt overboard. Anything was possible; he was in a state of lunacy. She scanned the wide fan of wake behind the ship.

"Here he is," Frank yelled. He had found him squatting behind a large spool of rope. The boy was sucking on his ball, his eyes closed.

Frank lifted him out. "Benji it will have to be, for the time being," he said.

"He shouldn't get his way with tantrums," she whispered, glancing at a couple walking past. The woman, wrapped in fur, stared at them avidly; the man tipped his hat with a slight, superior smile. "He'll be spoiled beyond salvation."

"It's not just a tantrum," Frank said. "Remember what happened to this boy."

"I'm not likely to forget." She made her way back down the deck to the cabin.

Later that afternoon, the ship began to roll, rising high, slapping down hard. Kate lay in her berth, dizzy and nauseated. The cabin was claustrophobic and the motion relentless; she felt as if the pitching of the ship and her nausea and the voyage were never going to end, that she would be mired in this torment forever.

Frank opened the door to the cabin, leading the boy by the hand. "I've been mulling it over," he said, leaning down to peer at her. "What's the matter, darling? Seasick?"

"Wretched."

"I'm so sorry. Do you feel like hearing my idea about the name?"

She nodded. Frank and the boy were going up and down in her vision. The boy was staring at her with those black eyes. She shifted her gaze to the left and fixed on the sink.

"We must call him Benji, because eventually he's going to let slip that was his name. So I thought I could tell people this: The priest at a church, where we can say we found him, called him Benji after me, having no other choice at hand, and by the time we came to fetch him, the name had stuck. He simply had no other name that we were aware of. What do you think?"

"Fine," Kate said, closing her eyes.

"Sleep if you can, darling. The boy and I are going back up on deck—I'll see if I can make a sailor out of him."

The door closed.

"Benji," she said. The name was bitter in her mouth.

The name was the least of it. There was the shock of learning about Frank's vulgar liaison—and then, after the tragedy, suddenly having his child to raise.

But he was just an innocent child, she reminded herself. None of this was his doing. He couldn't help it that he had a mother so cruel as to butcher herself before his very eyes.

The American consul, Sharpless—who had insisted that the boy was Frank's—told them that as a mixed-race child he would be unadoptable. He would live on the streets, prey to disease and criminals. Frank said he would feel guilty all his life if he left the child to such a fate. He begged Kate to forgive him and to consider what he knew to be a heavy burden.

She had gone to the Oura Church to pray about her decision and afterward went to the cliff where the sixteenth-century Christians had been crucified rather than abandon their faith. It had been a fiercely beautiful day, the sea a smooth blue shroud. If those souls could give up their lives for Christ, she could make the modest sacrifice of finding room for this boy in their home.

Frank had covered her face with kisses. She would be glad, he predicted, that they would have help on the farm until they had boys of their own.

Kate shifted from her back to her side and stared down at the steel floor. She felt as queasy now as she had that month of her pregnancy, not long after they were married. When she lost the baby, Frank had been so dashed it was almost unbearable, and there had been no sign of another these two years. Maybe her sickness now was not just from the motion of the boat. Perhaps she was with child again.

The ship rose, a high, slow climb, then fell with a shudder. Their large trunk slid across the floor; Frank's shaving mug fell from the sink and shattered.

She thought of that woman lying in blood, and the child beside her, restrained by the maid from throwing himself on his mother's body. God was calling on her to enlarge her soul. She would learn to care for him as if he were one of her own children, and she would help him to forget.

Galena Gazette, June 1, 1895

Plum River, Illinois. There is much commotion and merry-making these days in our community as Lt. Frank Pinkerton (son of Elmer, who died last year) and his wife, Katherine, have settled in at the Pinkerton farm. As if the presence of the refined Mrs. Pinkerton—the daughter of Galena's late missionary pastor, the Reverend Timothy Lewis—were not excitement enough, this Christian couple has brought with them, to rear as nearly their own as possible, a Japanese orphan boy rescued from the lowly society of Nagasaky, Japan. In his sermon Sunday last, Pastor Marshall Pollock called upon his flock to excite in their breasts all the human compassion of which they are capable and to extend every possible kindness and instruction to this heathen child in our midst.

Benji was given new clothes, scratchy pants that ended below his knees and a shirt with a long row of white circles he was supposed to push through holes. There were stiff heavy shoes to wear outside and inside. When he tried to leave them by the door everyone laughed and Blue Eyes made him put them back on.

Papa-san said this was a farm where they grew good things to eat but the food made Benji sick, the big pieces of red meat, the hill of white mush with a thick brown soup running over the top, and the little green things that ran away from the stabber he had to use. Papa-san said he couldn't use the chopsticks he'd found in his trunk.

Outside, everything was too wide and stretched-looking. When he saw the river he understood that he was in the kappa world. He had been bad and the kappas had brought him here. He had never seen a kappa but Suzuki had said they were green with long arms and a shallow dish of water on their heads. Unless you knocked the water out of the dish, they were very strong. Once when he swam in a river in Nagasaki and went down deep to get a rock, Suzuki told him never to do that again. The kappas hid in rivers and they could reach inside your bottom and pull your liver out. Even if you weren't in the river but you were naughty, the kappas could take you there when you were asleep and carry you under the water to their world. Two times he hadn't come when Mama called and once he had kept a frog in his bed to scare her. Then Mama was lying on the floor with her eyes shut and she wouldn't wake up. Suzuki said she would never wake up, that the red on the floor was her life coming out of her breast but he would see her again someday in the Land of Spirits and he should pray for her. Suzuki said it was an accident, but he knew the kappas had killed her because he was bad and then they had brought him to this place. That's why this strange talking sounded like voices through water.

He squatted near the river and looked down at it to see the kappas. The water ran fast and carried sticks and leaves, and once he saw a fish. There was a long-legged bug on top of the water. He poked it with a stick. It could be a kappa in another form. Animals could take other shapes and fool you, Suzuki said, foxes and badgers and birds.

He liked the funny birds here. Chicken. Papa-san read the real word from a big book and then made him say it in kappa language. It was his job to feed the chickens inside their fence. He put corn in the pan and scattered it around him in a circle for them to pick up. They made funny noises, especially the one with the red mushrooms on his head, and he felt sorry for them because of the ugly feet they couldn't help and the loose necks that went back and forth too much. Their feathers were pretty but hard. Papa said someday they would have babies, little soft ones, and he could have one for his own. He always gave the chickens clean water after their food and Papa said he was a good boy to take care of them so well.

Benji's room was near the kitchen and in his room was a bed where he was supposed to stay all night. He was not to pull off the covers and sleep on the floor, but he did, when he could stay awake until the house was quiet. The floor was hard beneath the sheets and thin quilts, but as he fell asleep there, holding the string ball Mama had made for him, it was easier to pretend that he was at home and that when morning came Mama's voice would wake him. Breakfast would be waiting at the low table that looked out on the garden, and there would be miso soup with bits of mushroom he had helped Mama find in the woods, and rice with dried seaweed. This would be in the Land of Spirits, but it would look just like home.

One night when he had a bad dream, he pulled his trunk out from under the bed. It was dark but his hands knew where everything was. The ivory chopsticks with the foxes on the end, the lacquer rice bowl, the kite with the tiger on it. At the bottom was his winter sleeping kimono. He took off the itchy nightshirt and put on the kimono and lay back down. The kimono was soft with thick padding and the silk lining reminded him of Mama. His skin began to feel warm, and when he went to sleep this time he had a good dream. He woke up in the morning before Blue Eyes came in and put everything back into the chest except the kimono, which he folded and slid beneath the mattress where it would be easy to find in the dark.

They went once a week to a place Papa-san said was a temple but it was not quiet and didn't smell like incense. He had to sit on a hard bench with a lot of other people, and the girls in front of him turned and looked quick at him and laughed. On the platform was a big ugly man who talked loud and waved his arms around until his face was red. Papa said this was the priest, who was very interested in Benji. Someday the priest would come to eat with them and Benji should learn many new words so he could talk to him. Benji shook his head because he didn't want to learn kappa language, but Papa frowned and said he must so he could get along in this world.

The day before the priest came to eat, Blue Eyes and the old woman wore long white aprons all day while they cooked. Papa was in the field working, so Blue Eyes told Benji what to do by pointing—at the bucket so he would fill it with water; at the woodpile outside so he would bring more wood for the stove. The house smelled good with pie and cake cooking, and in the afternoon the old woman let him have some warm apple pie with fresh cream on it. Their sweet food was the only kind he liked.

The next morning when Benji was feeding the chickens the old woman came out to the pen. When she reached down to one of the chickens Benji thought she was trying to pet it but she took it by the neck and began to swing it around and around with its body and feet making circles in the air and it made a terrible noise and all the other chickens ran away and tried to fly. Benji shut his eyes and put his hands over his ears and screamed as loud as he could to be heard on the other side of the kappa world and didn't stop until the old woman stuffed her apron in his mouth.

Just his luck, Frank thought, to begin farming in a year of withering drought. By late June, the corn and wheat planted in April had collapsed in the fields. Farmers gathered at Red Olsen's store, talking of rain and rumors of rain, crop insurance, dwindling silage for the cows, bank loans. Bud Case, the burly redheaded farmer whose land adjoined the Pinkertons', said Frank was lucky he'd been late to plant: a smaller investment in money and labor. "Some of that corn won't come back even if we get good rain," Bud said. "But next year will be better." He clapped Frank on the shoulder. "The lean year is usually followed by the fat. The Lord sees to it."

"We'll be fine," Frank's mother said, as they sat at breakfast with Kate, Benji, and the Swede. "As long as the well holds. Frank, you remember what your father used to say."

He sighed. Here came Benjamin Franklin, the great man for whom he'd been named, though his father had said more than once that he wished he could take it back.

"'In time of drought,'" she quoted, raising one finger, "'we know the worth of water.' That's the silver lining."

No one spoke; the forks scraped against the chipped blue plates. The table looked just as it had when he was a boy: the white oilcloth with its raised pattern, the chicken and rooster salt and pepper shakers, the blue milk pitcher. The taciturn, white-haired Swede sat in the same chair he'd occupied when Frank was a child, ever since he'd wandered to the farm—nameless and apparently without a memory—and Frank's father had taken him on.

Frank glanced at Kate, wan and exhausted; there was a streak of flour on her right temple. She gave him a brave smile. She hadn't expected any of this—his mother, the boy who sat mutely staring at his plate of scrambled eggs and corn mush, the grinding work. When they'd visited the farm last April and sat on the porch holding hands, the intoxicating odor of flowering plums drifting across the meadow, they had decided they could be happy here, independent, in their own house. He'd promised Kate a servant girl, but he hadn't reckoned on all the expenses to start up a farm that had lain fallow for two years, since his father took ill.

His mother—as she intimated at every possible opportunity—had saved them by leaving her comfortable situation with Frank's sister's family in Cicero in order to teach Kate how to run a farmhouse.

"These are very good biscuits, Kate," Frank said. "Best I ever had."

"In time of drought," his mother said, "it's the Guernseys will turn a profit. Your father always said as much. Ought to get another one."

"Can't afford it this year." Frank leaned over Benji's plate to show him how to break open a biscuit and butter it.

"Cut back on some fineries, you could." She didn't glance at Kate, but Kate went rigid; she'd just ordered drapery material for the parlor.

"We have to be civilized," Frank murmured, though he agreed with his mother. He and Kate had argued over the draperies; nothing wrong with the old ones, that he could see.

"It was Christian of Bud Case to take care of the Guernseys for us," his mother said, as though Frank had been expecting to return to the farm all along.

"I imagine he made his Christian profit," Kate said, with a tight little smile.

Frank laughed in surprise.

His mother's face turned pink. "No doubt he turned a fine profit," she said. "Thanks to his wife. Olena can churn more before breakfast than some women do in a day."

The women rose simultaneously, bumping elbows, and began to clear the table. "Thanks for the meat," the Swede mumbled, and skedaddled to the barn. Now, there was a Christian man, Frank thought, staying on after his father's death—not that the Swede had the initiative to move on.

As Kate picked up Frank's dishes, she gave him a dark look.

He shrugged and took a sip of coffee, cold now. He'd had words with his mother and had explained his mother's character to Kate. What more could he do?

He looked at Benji's plate, untouched except for one bite of biscuit. "Eat!" he said, pushing at the biscuit.

The boy stared at him, those licorice eyes just like hers.

Frank spooned up some scrambled eggs and held them to the boy's closed mouth. "Eat!"

"Leave him alone," Kate said, turning from the sink.

"He has to eat."

"He does eat," Frank's mother said. "He's partial to my cherry pie—ate half of one yesterday."

"The boy needs some work to build a real appetite." Frank hoisted Benji from his chair, limp as a sack of feed.

There was a chorus from the women: not in the fields, far too hot.

Frank carried Benji out the door and down the steps. Kate came running after him with a straw hat for Benji and a jug of water. The hat fell over the boy's eyes; Frank snatched it off. "That's no good."

"Don't take him—he's too young. He can help me in the garden."

"I was in the fields at five."

Benji gazed back and forth at them impassively.

"What must he be thinking?" Kate said. She laid a hand on his forehead as if to gauge his temperature.

"He'll be fine. *Daijobu, ne?*" Frank said, jiggling Benji.

No reaction, just those eyes boring into him.

They walked along the edge of the pasture where the Guernseys—milked at daybreak—had already found their way to the hill on the other side of Plum Creek. When Frank was a boy with ideas of running away to sea, he had liked to think of that hill as a cresting green wave and the Guernseys as clots of foam. The grass was patchy now, browning in the drought; the cows' cream wouldn't have much butterfat, no better grazing than this.

The Swede was waiting outside the barn with the stone boat—a shallow wooden receptacle with high sides and a seat for the driver—hitched to the Percherons.

"We're getting the rocks out of the field," Frank said to Benji, miming the action. "They push out of the ground in winter; any one of them could break the plow. You'll see how to do it. Easy. Fun." He called up the Japanese word for fun. *"Tanoshii."*

He hoisted Benji to his shoulders and, with the Swede driving the boat, they went down Plum River Road and headed into a cornfield—flattened stubble now. Frank intended to plant winter wheat here later in the season, after the drought had passed; it might bring a good price next spring.

He set Benji on the ground, and they followed the stone boat as it bucked and clattered over the furrows. Frank picked up a rock and threw it into the boat—it landed with a *thwock*—then put a small stone in Benji's hand and helped him pitch it in. "See?" He gave him another stone. Benji hurled it at the boat with such force that it bounced up and out. Benji turned and grinned at him. Frank felt a catch in his throat; his smile was like hers, the same glint of mischief.

"That's *it*. Good boy. *Daijobu.*" He ruffled Benji's thick blond hair, already warm from the sun. "Not so hard, though. Easy now." He demonstrated a slow underhand pitch.

They went on down the row, then another, developing a rhythm. Occasionally there was a large rock that had thrust its way up through the soil; Frank let Benji help him wrestle it out, and they carried it—Frank pretending to stagger—to the boat and set it down.

Benji was a stout little worker. Maybe he'd make a farmer. Stranger things had happened. Frank had never intended to farm, yet here he was. If his brother John—groomed to take over the farm—hadn't died of tetanus not long after their father's passing, Frank would still be struggling to make a go of the import/export business in Galena, and living with Kate at her mother's house. His own mother was a peach in comparison to that woman.

Benji held out a flat rock in his palm.

"Smart fellow," Frank said, looking at it closely. "An arrowhead." He repeated the word; he should have brought his Japanese-English dictionary, though it was cumbersome to manage in the field. He took the arrowhead from Benji's hand. "An Indian used this," Frank said. "A hunter." As they went on, he began to talk about the Indians who used this land before the white man—maybe Benji would begin to absorb some English this way, as Kate kept insisting. He became so caught up in his story about the fierce Blackhawk war that had raged here not so many decades ago that he forgot to look for rocks, and Benji stopped picking them up, walking slowly beside him.

"Papa-san?" Benji said.

Frank knelt beside him. "Benji-san." It was the first time the boy had addressed him directly since that miserable day, when Frank had rocked him to sleep in the hotel room. Benji said something in Japanese he couldn't understand, then stared at him, his face unreadable. Frank gave him a quick embrace. "You're going to be fine. You'll come to like it here. I promise." When they returned to the house, he would look up some words of comfort in his dictionary.

The stone boat was pulling away from them. "Pinkerton?" the Swede called.

As they hurried to catch up, Benji stubbed his toe on a rock and fell; the string ball rolled out of his pocket. Frank watched as he scooped it up and carefully brushed it off. It was like a rainbow, every color of string imaginable. She must have spent hours making it. Benji scrubbed at it with his hand, frantic; there was a stain he couldn't remove. Frank soaked his bandanna in water from the canteen and dabbed at the ball. "See, it's better now. *Daijobu*," he said, though he couldn't tell for sure. "We'll wash it some more when we get home. Water—*mizu*—and soap."

Benji was sniffling, and his hair was plastered to his forehead with sweat. Frank wiped the boy's forehead and neck with the wet bandanna, gave him a drink. "Time to unload," he yelled to the Swede. He hoisted Benji to the seat beside the Swede, and gave him the canteen. The boat dragged around in a wide circle, and they drove back across the field to dump the rocks on the pile already there, then they headed back toward the house.

Frank stared at the ground, still scanning for rocks, but his mind had come untethered. He thought of Butterfly's delicate fingers wrapping the strings around the ball, then laying it out by Benji's futon as a morning surprise—in such a way, she had given him a fan that he now kept in a drawer of his desk. He could see her quiet smile as she anticipated Benji's reaction, then his delight, throwing the ball up and down, the two of them chattering in Japanese. Now he had no one to talk to. If she could have known how her boy would suffer without her, would she have taken her life?

Sharpless seemed to think it was his fault, that she had cared for him more than he knew, was in such despair that she drove the sword into her breast. He shuddered, pushed away the image, went back to a time before that, when they lay on the futon one morning at daybreak, listening to birds in the garden. If he had been true to her, perhaps they would be a family now.

But then he wouldn't have Kate. He wouldn't even have known Kate, but he wouldn't have known that he didn't know her. He concentrated on her face, the iridescent blue eyes, the slightly crooked smile. He thought of her hand in his, the first time they'd danced, the long, serious conversations as they walked the hilly streets of Galena in the rain.

He was deluding himself to imagine that he'd have returned to Butterfly, the man he was in his earlier days. He'd been footloose then, with girls in Cuba, Brazil, California. It had taken Kate to make him want to settle down. She was intelligent without making too much of it, they had interests in common, had both lived in the Orient, and she had an appealing feminine warmth. During their walks, her intimate gaze had invited confidence: He'd told her about his yearning to go to sea ever since he'd read *Two Years Before the Mast* as a young man; about the falling-out with his father and his flight to Hampton Roads; and he confessed his disappointment in the Navy—the inertia of the top brass, the leaking dinosaur of a ship to which he'd been assigned.

He looked at the expanse of land, the island of trees in the distance like a mirage in the shimmer of heat. For a moment it seemed to him that much of his life had been a dream and it was only lately, with the shock of Butterfly's death, that he had wakened to his foolishness, his vanity, and his lust—a no-good, his father had called him—and that now, as if in punishment for his sins, he walked a furrow in the ground behind his father's Percherons, reaping a harvest of stones.

The farmhouse parlor was a lugubrious room, long and narrow, which made rearrangement of the furniture impossible, Kate found. A hideous pump organ favored by Frank's mother dominated the room. There was a love seat of punishing horsehair, a platform rocker with frayed upholstery, and a wicker rocker better suited for the porch. The room faced westward, so that only wan light fell between the dusty brown draperies, and in the summer it was airless and hot. Kate had added to one corner of the room a curio cabinet filled with souvenirs of Frank's travels and of her childhood in China; it would make an interesting focus of conversation when she began to entertain. In the basement she had found a rather handsome bookcase with glass doors. She had Frank carry it upstairs and, after she had dusted and polished it, she placed in it her sets of Dickens and Trollope, her Emerson and Thoreau, and the collected works of Henry Wadsworth Longfellow. Situated between the windows, in lieu of the plant stand with its spindly ferns, the bookcase was a welcome and cultivated addition to the room. Kate planned to replace the wall decorations—a morbid hair wreath; a foxed print titled *The Stag at Eve*—with examples of her own handiwork. Her first sampler, made in childhood—an alphabet with a cross-stitch rendition of Mary and her lamb—now hung above the love seat; she hoped Benji would eventually learn his letters from it.

Benji seemed observant and bright, but he had yet to make progress with English. Of course, it was early for that. He must be frightened in his isolation, and perhaps bored. In the pocket of his overalls he always carried the string ball from Japan. Kate often saw him seated beneath a tree or on the porch, shifting the ball from one hand to the other. The boy needed some new playthings.

On the afternoon that two boxes arrived from Montgomery Ward, Kate sat on the parlor floor with Benji while she opened the larger box. "Toys," she said. "All for you."

She took out a stuffed bear, golden brown with fuzzy ears, and held it out to him. "Bear."

He looked at it, then at her. That stare of his was unnerving. She rocked the bear in her arms, then arranged his arms around it. He looked down at it and set the bear carefully on the floor. Had he never seen a toy animal before? She should have waited until Frank was here with his dictionary to translate, but she wanted Benji to know that the toys had been her idea.

"Here—you'll like this." She took the wooden top out of its box—it was shiny, with red, white, and blue stripes—and set it to spinning in front of him. The colors blurred as the top whirled, then it listed and sped across the floor, knocked against the rocker, and fell over. Benji laughed—you darling, she wanted to say; she had never heard him laugh before—but he made no move to retrieve the top.

She took out a book of Mother Goose rhymes and a silver spoon with his name engraved on the handle, the latter a motivation for him to learn to use table utensils properly. Neither of these items evoked any interest.

He liked the blocks, though, light wood with a high varnish, made in three different sizes. She helped him build a wall, and he began to make stacks of his own. She sat for a few minutes watching him as he carefully placed one block on top of another; he seemed to be counting under his breath.

"I'm glad you like the blocks," she said. He didn't look at her. She hadn't expected a thank-you, but she thought there might have been a glance of understanding, or a smile. Maybe he would never learn to love her, and she might never have a child of her own. The nausea on the journey had been a false alarm, nothing but seasickness, and Frank was disappointed in her once again.

"What's all this?" Frank's mother stood at the parlor door, hands on her hips. Mrs. Pinkerton was a doughy woman, her face a web of wrinkles. Her vanity was her nut-brown hair, which had not a trace of gray in it.

"Benji needs some amusements."

"My children never had any fancy playthings."

"He's lonely," Kate said. Mrs. Pinkerton gazed at the boy without speaking, but Kate knew what she was thinking—that they should have left him where he was. She and Frank had managed to convince her that they had saved an abandoned orphan and intended to make a Christian of him, but Mrs. Pinkerton took a dim view of the enterprise. Soon they would have their own children, she said, and why name the boy Benji? That name should go to her grandchild. Nevertheless, she had a soft spot for the boy and was forever feeding him sweets, ruining his interest in healthful food.

"There's supper to get on the table," Mrs. Pinkerton said.

"I'll be there presently." Kate waited until Mrs. Pinkerton had returned to the kitchen before carrying the other box upstairs to her bedroom. She ripped it open and laid out on the bed a blue flowered print dress that would set off her eyes and an embroidered white nightgown trimmed in eyelet. She would wear the gown tonight with her hair brushed over her shoulders and some of the scent that Frank liked dabbed on her neck.

She took off her apron, changed into the blue dress, and sat at her dressing table, leaning toward the mirror. The color was becoming, and it gave her a pleasant little shock—as always, these days—to see that she looked much the same as ever. A cloud of golden hair, intense blue eyes, a complexion without flaw—in spite of the relentless labor in the house and garden, in spite of Frank's eyes no longer reflecting back what he used to call her luminous beauty.

Ever since their visit to Japan, Frank had lost his appetite for her love. He had suffered a terrible jolt, but so had she. She had thought they could take comfort in each other and, after a few weeks, return to their old habits, albeit with the changes necessitated by Benji's presence. The first two years of their marriage, Frank had been devoted and their love-making passionate; they had taken a secret delight in coupling under her mother's roof, where they had lived until they decided about the farm, stifling their laughter with kisses.

Frank was having a difficult time managing a farm for the first time—she understood that. But as the weeks passed, he receded further from her. He often seemed distracted, silent, looking into the distance. No more embraces or kisses except in the bedroom, where he seemed a stranger, no intimate conversations, no words of love.

He must be consumed with guilt over that woman, his senses dulled by shame. Kate had tried to help him with his burden, encouraged him to talk, but he evaded her. Only reluctantly had he told her the woman's name: Cio-Cio, Butterfly. A name for an exotic beauty, she had thought, but pushed aside the nettles of jealousy. Men sowed their wild oats, and this was in the past, except for Frank's suffering. She would have to be patient and resourceful to bring him back to her. She must try harder, and with God's help, their union would be revived.

"Kate," her mother-in-law called up the stairs. "The men will be in shortly. I've done everything but snap the beans."

She sat on the front porch with the beans, and when she saw Frank coming from the barn, fanning himself with his straw hat, she flew to the road to meet him, seeing herself as he might, the blue skirt belling out, her eyes ablaze with devotion.

He stopped and frowned at her. His nose was sunburned. "What's wrong?" he said.

"Nothing. Why shouldn't a wife come to greet her husband?"

He laughed and shook his head, smacking the hat against his dusty trousers. "Mighty grimy husband," he said.

"Nonetheless handsome," she said. He laughed again.

She went with him to the back porch and after he washed up, handed him the towel.

"To what do I owe this royal treatment?" he said, grinning, one eye shut, as he scrubbed his face dry. "You seen something new in the catalogue?"

"Well . . ." She smiled and looked down at the bodice of her dress, but he was hanging up the towel and even at dinner didn't notice the dress, though her mother-in-law did, her eyes fixing on every button and tuck, as if to measure the cost.

After supper, Frank went upstairs to his study to work on the farm ledger, while Kate sat in the parlor with her needlepoint, Mrs. Pinkerton knitted, and Benji played with his blocks, the marmalade cat purring in his lap.

He was a sweet little boy, but with him in the house it would be impossible for Frank to forget that woman. The mother of his child. The phrase sank into her like lead.

She rethreaded her needle. She must keep in mind that she was partly to blame for this predicament. She should never have insisted on the trip to Japan—a second honeymoon, she pleaded, before they made the move to the farm. The Orient was an interest she and Frank had in common—she'd lived in China as a young child with her missionary parents—and he had some business in Japan, he'd told her, some money he'd invested, a considerable sum. Recovering the money would offset the cost of the trip, she'd pointed out.

He'd not had a chance to look into his financial affairs, for that first morning an urgent note had come, interrupting their lovemaking. The paper had trembled in Frank's hands. "What is it?" she'd asked. "Nothing," he replied, but she'd found out soon enough.

Cio-Cio. Butterfly.

Kate had a glimpse of the woman before Frank shielded her view. Gleaming black hair, skin smeared with something like chalk, painted lips, and, beneath her, a river of blood.

She shivered: a ghost slipping over her grave.

"Time for bed," she said in a bright voice. Benji looked at her. "Cookie?" she asked. That was one word he understood. He followed her to the kitchen, carrying the cat, which he kept in his lap while he ate his cookies at the table. She didn't comment on the untouched glass of milk. The one time she'd insisted, he spat it out. She tucked him into bed, the cat beneath the covers. Mrs. Pinkerton disapproved of animals in the bedroom, but Kate saw no harm in it; the cat was Benji's only comfort except for the ball.

Frank was still in his office, staring out the dark window, the ledger book open before him. She put on her new gown and returned to him. He hadn't moved. "Come sleep, darling," she said. "You're tired."

He followed her to the bedroom, undressed, and got into bed while she sat at the dressing table, brushing her hair. Not so long ago, he would have brushed it himself.

She climbed into bed beside him, moved her pillow close to his. He was lying on his back, his eyes closed. His forehead was sunburned too, she noticed.

"Frank," she said. " I have . . . a wifely concern. That woman . . ." She hadn't meant to begin this way.

"What woman?" he said, opening his eyes to stare at her.

"The poor Japanese woman—Butterfly. I know you're suffering remorse, but you mustn't blame yourself. A normal woman who is set aside will manage to survive, without . . . doing such a thing." She thought of the searing moment in the garden when Richard McCann told her he had proposed to Emily Kettering, in spite of the understanding they'd had.

"Suicide is more acceptable in Japan," Frank said. " A matter of honor."

She studied his profile.

"How long did you live with her?"

He cut his eyes at her. "What does it matter?"

"I'm interested—concerned. How long was it?"

"Not long." He yawned and stretched his arms behind him, knocking against the headboard. "A few months, or weeks . . ."

"Do you think of her often?" Her heart began to pound.

He hesitated, and in that hesitation she knew a lie was forming. "Of course not," he said. "I love only you." He shifted to his side, facing her, and kissed her cheek. "My dear wife," he said. He put his arm around her and closed his eyes and murmured, "You're right, I *am* tired." Within a few moments his breathing began to deepen.

He loved her, then, that woman. Tears stung her eyes. This was more than God could expect her to endure.

It became harder to push herself through the days, hauling water from the pump, wringing the clothes, making conversation at mealtimes. She was bruised deep in her body, where no one could see.

She tried to pray but felt spiritually dry. The pastor at the Plum River church was unlearned, his approach to religion primitive. She could not confide in him, and she had as yet no friend in the community. She was alone in a house with a husband who loved another, and their child. Butterfly's child. Although she continued to attend to Benji, cooking dishes that might appeal to him, trying to teach him words and phrases of English, and although she constantly reminded herself that he had not asked to be born or to suddenly find himself in this alien world, she could not forget that he was the offspring of that woman.

Often in the evenings as she sat with her needlework, an image of Butterfly clicked into her mind, like a colored lantern slide: black hair, elaborately arranged; a startling mask of white face; painted eyebrows and lips; like a mannequin but for the eyes that burned at her. In the next slide the woman was lying on the floor, one arm outstretched, a bloody sword beside her. On the back of her neck were strange white markings covering skin that was muddy brown like Benji's.

She was glad the woman was dead, glad as she punched the needle through the stiff template of her pattern—such a sinful thought that she pricked her finger, then blotted it against the back of the needlepoint. And she wished that Emily Kettering was dead too. To keep back thoughts of Emily dying in childbirth or falling down the stairs of her fancy new home in Galena or wasting away with consumption, her hair growing mousy and thin, Kate pressed the needle into the meat of her thumb. By the time she had finished her first new handiwork and hung it on the wall of the parlor, a constellation of rusty blood spots filled the back of the sampler that read: *Amor Vincit Omnia.*

One Sunday after dinner, a boy named Eli came to play. Benji was helping clear the table but Papa-san said he could leave it and go outside with Eli. Benji had seen him at church, a tall boy with a loud voice and hair the color of sweet potatoes. He had his dog with him, white with black spots and one black ear. Benji squatted down to pet him and the dog licked his face. Both he and Eli laughed and Benji could tell Eli wasn't a kappa because of his laugh that wasn't scary and his nice brown eyes.

Eli said some words Benji couldn't understand. Benji didn't know anything to say but hello; Eli said hello and for a while they made a game out of it, saying hello back and forth and laughing. Then Benji taught him to say *"Konbanwa,"* and they laughed some more. Eli saw Mama's ball in Benji's pocket and pointed to it but Benji shook his head.

For a while they threw sticks for the dog to fetch and then played tug-of-war with the dog, using a long stick. After that they played tug-of-war with each other. Eli was stronger, but Benji held on to the stick so that he was pulled along like the dog. He made growling noises and pretended to bark and Eli laughed so Benji barked louder. The dog began to run around them, barking and jumping for the stick. Benji fell down and Mama's ball rolled out of his pocket. The dog almost got it, but Eli snatched it up first. Since Eli had saved it, Benji let him hold the ball and look at it, but he didn't like it when Eli threw the ball up and down. He held out his hand for Eli to give it back and he did.

They went into the house and Benji showed Eli his blocks and top that were in the parlor and went to put the ball in his room, under the pillow.

When Eli left, Benji went into his room and reached under the mattress for the kimono. If he put the ball inside the kimono no one could find it.

He unfolded the kimono all the way and put the ball in the middle. There was something inside the kimono he hadn't seen before, a square of cloth near the hem. Although the square was the same color as the lining, there were stitches along the edges, and what was underneath the cloth felt stiff.

He tried to loosen the thread and then bit it with his teeth, just like Suzuki used to do. He tugged the thread out of one end of the square and reached inside.

"Okasan!" he whispered. It was a picture of Mama standing by a chair. Papa-san was sitting beside her, holding a watch. Mama's head was turned a little to one side, as if she was listening to him. He held the picture against his face. It was cool and smooth and smelled like tatami.

He heard Blue Eyes and the old woman talking in the kitchen so he put the picture back in the cloth and folded the ball inside it, in a place where it wouldn't hurt the picture, then put the kimono under the mattress. When he left his room and went into the kitchen, everything looked different to him because of his secret. The house was like a picture of a house but he was real, walking around in it. Even if it was a kappa world, nothing was going to hurt him.

That night, when he changed from the scratchy nightshirt to the kimono, he didn't have to sleep on the floor because Mama was next to him. He had a dream about her that he couldn't remember in the morning but it made him happy. When he went out to do chores, he felt Mama still with him, and as he carried in sticks and eased the eggs from beneath the chickens, he told her in his mind what he was doing, and whenever he was by himself, in the pasture with the cows or wading in the creek, he told Mama everything about this place, whispering to her in the language he was supposed to forget.

Life in Plum River would be easier to bear, Kate thought, if they could attend the First Presbyterian Church in the nearby town of Stockton. Reverend Singleton was an intelligent, compassionate man; she might be able to confide in him. And if she was a regular attender of the services in Stockton, she could more easily make the acquaintance of cultivated people; she wanted to organize a women's reading circle and to entertain interesting couples at dinner parties. The farmers and their wives, while by and large kind, were not intellectually congenial. If her marriage was a trial, she at least deserved a satisfactory spiritual and intellectual life.

Since Kate had been raised Presbyterian, Frank was at first persuaded by her desire to continue worshipping in the denomination familiar to her. But Frank's mother put up formidable resistance. The Pinkertons had been pillars of the Plum River congregation since the church was built, Mrs. Pinkerton declared as she and Kate were preparing brisket for dinner, and it would be unthinkable for them to desert Pastor Pollock and the Plum River parish. Her husband and elder son and Frank's grandparents all lay beneath the cedars in the graveyard, and furthermore, her husband had left a sum in his will that had allowed the church to add its fine new steeple and belfry.

Kate had come to dread the sight of Mrs. Pinkerton in the kitchen each morning. No matter how early Kate managed to rise, Frank's mother was always there before her, cracking eggs in a bowl, rolling out biscuits, frying ham, all of her movements brisk and excluding. She wore loose flour sack dresses over her sagging body, heavy black shoes cut out to allow her bunions some ease, and thick glasses that magnified her washed-out blue eyes and the creases around them. Mrs. Pinkerton assigned Kate tasks, and no matter how simple—setting the table, making coffee—Kate felt the old woman watching her with a critical eye.

She treats me as if I were a hired servant, Kate complained to Frank. She means no harm, Frank said, she's been running the house for years. When Kate said that was the problem exactly, and wasn't it time for her to move back to Cicero so she could help Frank's sister Anne, now in confinement with her second child, Frank said she only wanted to help until Kate settled in.

Kate felt already steeped in the lessons of drudgery: the long Monday wash days, Tuesday nights with the flatirons beside the hot stove, the endless preparation of meals, scrubbing floors, cleaning lamp chimneys and woodstoves, pumping the separator each morning, tending the vegetable patch.

Kate wrote to her mother, pouring out the details of her grueling routine and, putting aside her pride, begging for money for a servant girl. I cautioned you, her mother wrote back, you're not suited for such a life. Kate should always remember that she was welcome to come home for a long visit. Her mother did not mention the servant.

Frank said they needed to buy a new harrow before the next season, but he would see if he could adjust the budget to hire a young girl; his mother, however, overruled him. Kate needed to learn how to manage the household in all its particulars before she could give directions to a maid.

"I've learned it all," Kate said, glaring at Frank over the table. "The concepts are quite elementary."

"I don't suppose you've done any canning." Mrs. Pinkerton gave her a sharp glance.

Then you would suppose incorrectly, Kate wanted to retort, but instead said in her sweetest voice, "Why, yes, I've done quite a bit of canning." She'd watched her mother's maid Lavonia put up strawberries; anything she didn't know was available in books.

"I'm glad to hear it," Mrs. Pinkerton said. "We need one hundred jars of canned goods per person each year. There's a heap of beets down cellar—poor Elmer's last crop. It would be a shame if they went to waste." They would can them tomorrow, she said.

"Why do you always take her side?" Kate asked Frank as they were getting into bed.

"I don't. But money is short just now. We'll have a servant next year. Corn and wheat ought to be sky-high after this drought—we might have enough profit for two servants. Though what we need most," he said, putting his arms around her, "is children."

"I hope they'll be born full-grown," she said, "and knowing how to can and plow."

He laughed and pulled her nightgown above her hips.

"Is it just children you want from me?"

"Of course not." He looked at her, shocked. "I adore you, darling," he said, gazing at her with that warm, grave expression that had won her.

She kissed him. "Then take my side."

"I will," he said, pushing into her as she tightened her arms around him. "I do. I take your side."

The next morning, after the men were off to the fields, Mrs. Pinkerton and Kate carried sacks of beets up from the cellar and mounded them on the kitchen table. Kate brought bucketfuls of water from the well, poured it into two dishpans, and she and Mrs. Pinkerton stood at the sink scrubbing the beets. Kate's back ached. She wanted coffee and another biscuit.

Mrs. Pinkerton inspected a beet Kate had finished and gave it a further scrubbing, her heavy underarms jiggling. "We can't have grit," she said.

"No indeed," Kate said under her breath. "No grit of that variety." She put the coffeepot back on the stove to heat and pressed her thumbs into her lower back.

"You may sterilize the jars now," Mrs. Pinkerton said.

"Thank you," Kate said. Her irony was lost on the old woman, still washing the beets.

Kate set the jars into the large copper bath and went outside for water. When she returned, Benji came into the kitchen. Mrs. Pinkerton gave him a cat's head biscuit and he slipped out again.

"Say thank you," Kate called.

The door slammed behind him.

"I'm working on his manners." Kate began pouring water into the bath. "It's very discouraging."

"He's just like Frank as a child," Mrs. Pinkerton said.

Kate stared at her. Water splashed onto the stove top, making it hiss. "Boys will be boys," she managed to say. "All over the world."

"I suppose so," Mrs. Pinkerton said. "The boy problem must be wide-spread." She looked into the copper tub. "Those jars have to be fully covered."

Kate returned to the well, hauling up the bucket with such violence that the rope burned her hand. She gazed down into the water—nothing but darkness—and dropped in a clod of dirt.

After the first batch of beets were scrubbed, boiled, and peeled, the women sat at the kitchen table, layers of newspaper over the oilcloth, pans of beets before them. Mrs. Pinkerton began to quarter a beet and indicated with her eyes that Kate should do the same.

Kate slid her knife through a beet—red, slick, and glossy.

Mrs. Pinkerton began to complain about her lumbago, acting up something fierce today. "Could you manage from this point?" she asked.

"Oh, certainly—please do have a rest." After Mrs. Pinkerton left, Kate pushed the windows open further—a slight breeze, a promise of rain—and sat back down to her task. It was a relief to have the old woman out of the room. Her comment about Benji hadn't meant anything, of course; she would never suspect her precious son of such a thing.

Kate sliced and chopped until her hands were stained purple. A beet slid out from the knife, went skidding across the floor.

She looked at the heap of unwashed beets. Too many for the jars, surely. She piled a good measure of them in a pan and ran to the compost pile at the far end of the garden, where she buried them beneath a layer of leaves and weeds. Elmer's beets. She felt giddy, walking back to the house.

After the jars were filled with the remaining beets, lidded, and rattling in the copper bath, she pulled the rocking chair to the window and began to reread Jane Austen's *Persuasion*. This was the world into which she should have been born: the women poor but genteel, irresistibly witty, eventually marrying wealth. She rested the book in her lap. If she attended church in Stockton, she could become acquainted with Aimee Moore, wife of a prominent lawyer in town. Mrs. Moore was said to be quite intelligent, a graduate of Mount Holyoke Female Seminary; doubtless she'd have read Jane Austen.

She heard Mrs. Pinkerton moving about upstairs and looked at the clock. Almost time for the midday meal; she'd be down soon. Using a heavy cloth, Kate lifted the jars from their bath, poured a bucket of water over them, then set them, as Mrs. Pinkerton had instructed, on the dining room table to cool. The blood-red beets shone in the light like large, dark jewels.

The next day, the jars were ready to go down to the cellar, but Kate was in no hurry to remove evidence of her housewifery, for which Frank and Mrs. Pinkerton had both praised her. Her back was strained, she told her mother-in-law; she would move the beets in the morning.

That night, as Kate lay beside Frank, drifting toward sleep, she heard an odd pinging noise downstairs, then a loud pop, and another, and a shattering sound. There were more pops, faster, like fireworks.

She sat up. "Frank?" and shook his arm.

Mrs. Pinkerton lumbered past their door and down the stairs. There was a scream.

"Frank," Kate said, pulling at him. "Get up." She leapt out of bed and lit a candle.

In the hall she heard another explosion, then the sound of glass raining onto the floor. She flew downstairs.

Mrs. Pinkerton stood at the bottom of the steps, holding a hurricane lamp. Tears were streaming down her face. "Elmer's beets," she said. "The last of his fruit."

In the dim light, Kate could see chunks of beets, shards and splinters of glass on the floor, dark liquid spreading beneath them.

"Oh God," she said, and shouted for Frank.

Another jar detonated, glass pinging against the chandelier, pelting onto the wooden floor. Beets caromed everywhere.

Frank pounded down the steps. "What in hell . . . ?"

"The beets fermented," his mother said, her voice quavering. "Your father's beets are ruined, thanks to her."

"That's not fair," Kate said. "You were giving instructions."

"You said you knew how to can. Everyone knows the jar has to be sealed at the proper temperature."

"Those beets were old—a dead man's beets." She began to sob; Frank put his arms around her.

"Shh," he said. "It's all right. No one was hurt."

"Look at the ceiling," his mother said. "There's no removing the stain of a beet."

"I want to go home," Kate wailed. She thought of her room, the canopy bed, the way the light was in early afternoon.

"You are home," Frank said, holding her tighter. "Go to bed, Mother. I'll clean up in the morning."

Frank helped Kate up the stairs and into bed, then lay with his arms around her.

"This place is a madhouse!" Kate cried. "I can't live with her."

"It would be much harder work for you alone."

"Hire a servant."

"As soon as I can."

She thought of her father, how grieved he would be to see her in this miserable place. She remembered him sitting by her bed when she had the measles, stroking her head, saying a prayer in his soothing baritone.

"I want to go to church in Stockton," Kate said. "And I want you to go with me."

"Yes, darling," he said, kissing her neck. "Whatever you say."

Beginning the next Sunday, Kate and Frank and Benji attended the First Presbyterian Church on Oak Street in Stockton, and Mrs. Pinkerton, for the time being, went with the Case family to the Plum River services.

The veterinarian Horatio Keast was at the Pinkerton farm seeing to one of the Percherons when the Case family came to visit. After he finished his work, he washed his hands at the pump and walked to the house. Pinkerton had invited him to stay for dinner.

The adults were on the front porch, talking about the weather and drinking lemonade. The Case girl was there too, wearing a frilly dress, pouting. Beyond the road, the boys were playing baseball in the pasture. Benji was the smallest of the lot—the runt of the litter, Keast thought—but he was fast, running circles around the other boys.

Keast sat down and exchanged pleasantries. The others returned to complaints about the unseasonably hot autumn and the tornado that had ripped through the town of Elizabeth last week. Two cows had been killed, and a little filly.

The Cases were a good solid family who bore a strong resemblance to one another, redheads every one. Case Senior was a carrottop; his wife was fortunate to have auburn hair, though in Keast's opinion she'd look better without those tight braids around her head. Sometimes Isobel had worn a braid, but it was a loose one down her back, to keep her hair from tangling at night. The Case daughter—she was rocking like a house afire, glaring out at the boys playing without her—had the bad luck to inherit the carrottop and freckles. So had all the children, except for one of the sons.

Suddenly Keast saw Benji come streaking across the road. He ran up the steps and threw himself into Pinkerton's arms. "Papa-san," he said, then let loose a torrent of what must be Japanese.

"Papa," Mrs. Case said. "That's sweet."

"Papa-san is a term of respect boys use for older males in Japan," Kate said. "Normally he calls him Father Pinkerton and myself Mother Pinkerton, to help him feel at home."

"Oh, I see."

Pinkerton said a few words to Benji in Japanese.

"In English, dear," Kate said. The edge in her voice could cut rawhide, Keast thought.

"The boy has lost his ball," Pinkerton said. "The one his mother gave him."

George, Eli, and Sam clambered onto the porch, huffing. "It's George's fault," Eli said. "Benji didn't want to play with it, George made him."

George pushed at Eli. "Did not."

Pinkerton took Benji's hand, led him down the steps and into the pasture. The other children—even the girl—followed. Benji pointed to the river.

Keast and the others watched in silence as Pinkerton and the children walked along the edge of the water, kicking through the tall grass. Keast thought they'd walk down to the road that crossed the river, but they turned back.

They came across the pasture, Benji howling; he sat down in the grass. Pinkerton scooped him up, none too gently, and carried him over his shoulder.

When they got to the porch, Keast said, "Maybe it's on the other side."

"Eli saw it go in the water," Frank said. "It's gone." He carried Benji, still crying, into the house.

"We're so sorry," Mrs. Case said. "We'll bring a new ball." She stood, nodding to her husband to do the same. "We'd better be going. Thank you for the refreshments. And the boys are so sorry, aren't you, boys?"

When she glowered at her sons, they said in unison, "We're sorry."

"Look at that dress," Mrs. Case said to her daughter, yanking at the skirt. "Guess who's going to wash it."

As the Cases took their leave, Keast heard George say to his mother, "It was just a nasty old string thing."

"You hush," his mother said. "The Japanese are different than we are."

Kate and Mrs. Pinkerton put supper on the dining room table—roast pork, vegetables from the garden, yeast rolls Kate had made that morning. There was coffee for the adults, milk for Benji.

After a long day, Kate was looking forward to bed. It was inconsiderate of Frank to have invited Keast, given that she'd lost a baby just a week ago. Dr. McBride and her mother-in-law insisted it was a common occurrence, nothing to be mournful about, so she tried to hold back her grief until nighttime, when she could let her tears seep into her pillow in the dark. Now they'd have to linger in the parlor as Keast went on and on about cows and hogs of his acquaintance.

Benji was still sniffling, staring at his food without touching it. Keast tried to divert him by making a nickel disappear and reappear behind Benji's ear; the boy was having none of it.

Keast pocketed the nickel. "The lad's a long way from home," he said.

"He won't get over being homesick until he learns our language," Kate said. "Frank continues to speak to him in Japanese." What must the Cases have thought of that "Papa-san"? she wondered.

She had thought she'd be able to tell the Cases soon about a child of her own.

"I've just done a little translating," Frank said. "He needs some help."

"It doesn't seem to be working," she said.

"I'm sure he'll learn quickly, either way," Keast said. "He seems to be a smart young lad."

Kate passed the rolls. Everyone was eating but Benji. "Drink your milk," she said, nodding at him.

"Be patient," Frank said. "Oriental children don't drink milk."

"I know that. I lived in the Orient too, as you may recall." I'm the woman you married, she wanted to scream. "But he needs to drink milk, to be tall and strong."

"Drink. Milk," she said in a firm voice, pointing at the glass.

"Papa-san," Benji said, and crawled into Frank's lap.

"No!" Kate jumped up, went to the other side of the table, and detached him from Frank. She held him by the shoulders, facing the table. "Father Pinkerton," she said, pointing at Frank. "And I am Mother Pinkerton." She laid a hand on her breast. "Grandmother Pinkerton," she added, gesturing toward Frank's mother.

"That's too hard for him just now," Frank said.

"He's got to learn. No Papa-san," she said to Benji. She tried to return him to his seat, but he reached for Frank.

"Papa-san," he wailed.

She scooped him up. He kicked and arched his back as she carried him to the kitchen.

"What are you doing, Kate?" Frank called.

She sat him down hard on a stool, held him pinned against the sink, and picked up the bar of lye soap. "No Papa-san," she said. "Why can't you understand?"

He glared at her with fierce black eyes. She pried open his mouth and scrubbed his tongue. "No Papa-san."

He spat at her, clawed his way down, and ran to his room, squalling. Frank went after him.

Keast and Mrs. Pinkerton were silent when Kate returned to the table. She was shaky and perspiring. They began to eat again, listening to the boy sob. Keast avoided her eyes. He left before dessert; there was a mare he had to visit on the way home, he said.

Frank was still in Benji's room. The crying had abated. She stared at the succotash on her plate. She was a terrible mother. Perhaps the miscarriage had been a judgment upon her.

It had been a boy, she was sure of it, even though Dr. McBride said it was too soon to tell.

"I think you are right to discourage the use of Japanese," Mrs. Pinkerton said. "Particularly *Papa-san*."

"Thank you," Kate said, startled.

"It creates a misimpression," Mrs. Pinkerton said.

Kate studied her mother-in-law's profile: the large ears, the nose prominent like Frank's, the firm set of her mouth as she sawed at her meat. She felt a wave of nausea. Mrs. Pinkerton knew. And why wouldn't she? Benji was her grandson, after all.

On Sunday, as was his habit each week, Keast went to visit Isobel's grave, located on a slight rise amid cedars in the cemetery of Plum River All Souls Church. His wife and baby had died in childbirth eight years earlier; his grief was keen and his sense of guilt was not diminished. With his training and experience in birthing all manner of God's creatures, he should have been able to save his beloved Isobel, or at least the child. Horatio Junior, he would have been.

No expense had been spared in the design of her monument. A huge block of green-veined white marble, imported from Italy, had been carved into a Grecian-style temple with Doric columns. The base was etched with leaves of the woodbine plant, which Isobel had loved. Set just below the roofline was the feature of the memorial that drew curious sightseers from other towns: a marbleized photogravure of Isobel. The photograph had been taken in Galena, a year before Isobel and Keast had met; it captured perfectly, he thought, the delicacy of features and fineness of spirit that had in them the quality of the immortal. Isobel's eyes, black as a crow's, looked directly at the viewer. Her face was a perfect oval framed by a cascade of lively dark curls, but nevertheless there was in her face an expression of premonitory melancholy, as if she had divined that one day her eyes would be gazing into those of her mourning husband.

Keast said his prayers kneeling before Isobel's tombstone. Then he stood and in his customary manner began to talk to her, but instead of a recital of the events of his week, he described the part-Japanese boy now living in Plum River, a young lad three years younger than their Horatio would have been. He was bright, with an abundant curiosity and a natural dignity that would serve him well. The boy had a large heart, and loved the animals. Isobel's face seemed to come to life as she listened to him: the dainty pink lobes of her ears, the flush of her skin, the lips slightly parted, as if about to speak.

Isobel would have held nothing against the boy because of his race. She herself was part Sioux. They had attended a performance of *The Mikado* in Chicago and afterward had together looked up Japan in the Book of Knowledge, reading bits of it aloud to each other.

The boy Benji was an orphan, living with a married couple who were well meaning but sometimes insensitive. "Dear Isobel, you would have been heartbroken to see the boy in grief after losing his Japanese plaything and receiving a harsh punishment from his guardian mother. The guardian father, who is fond of the boy, nonetheless later confided to me that he has been a trouble to them. When I asked in what regard, he replied that he often wanders away from the house, causing them much consternation and interruption of work on the farm. I believe the boy means no harm but is searching for whatever comfort he can find in this alien world."

Isobel responded with her whole being, her heart and spirit. Yes, he answered, for little Horatio's sake he would befriend the lad.

Benji and the cat had a language. He named her Kaki, for persimmon, even though she wasn't orange all over, and she followed him like a dog might do, though not in a straight line. She wasn't a kappa, she was a real cat, like Rice Ball.

He showed Kaki the picture of Mama and the writing he had found on the back. He couldn't read it, because he hadn't begun to learn his characters yet, but when he cupped his hands over the writing and Kaki was purring beside him, he could hear Mama saying the message, that he should be as strong as a samurai and that she was proud of him. He carried her message with him every day as he wandered about the farm.

One day the animal doctor was in the barn. His eyebrows were funny, with hairs sticking out. He gave Benji a striped candy stick and showed him what he did to the horses' feet and a sick place on a cow's belly.

Kaki wanted to see, so Benji picked her up.

The man rubbed her head with two fingers until Kaki purred and closed her eyes.

"Kaki," Benji told him.

"Cat," the man said, talking slow. "Kaki, cat," and led him around the barn, telling him the names of the animals in his language. Then they sat on the ground and Benji watched while the man took a piece of wood from his pocket and made Kaki's head come out of it with his knife.

At night Benji whispered to Kaki in cat talk—little words he made up—and she purred back. Sometimes he just thought to her and she understood. When she lay humming on his chest, he liked to close his eyes and think of Rice Ball. He was white all over except the tip of his tail, black like it was dipped in ink. Mama said maybe Rice Ball wrote or made pictures at night when they weren't looking. Rice Ball had gray eyes like a gaijin, a cold pink nose, and stiff white whiskers he didn't like touched. Rice Ball was Papa-san's cat, Mama said, and Benji was a good boy to look after him so well until Papa came back.

One night when Benji had a bad dream about Mama and the blood, he took her picture from its hiding place in the kimono and held it against his chest. He wished Mama had put it there for him but it had been Suzuki because Mama was dead. The dream came back to him. It was too hard to think about.

He pulled Kaki under the covers with him, like he did with Rice Ball in his futon, and thought about Rice Ball helping him fish in the pond, leaning over so far Benji was afraid he'd fall in but he never did, only put a paw in the water and shook it off fast. He remembered his feet in the cool pond, and the orange fish brushing past, and in the fall, leaves that looked like red stars on the water. To go back to sleep, he put himself in the pond, floating with the sun on his face and Rice Ball watching over him.

It fell to Kate to teach the boy English. Frank's efforts, when he made them, continued to involve pidgin Japanese.

She devoted herself to Benji, to win back his trust. She cooked his favorite food—he preferred noodles, with bits of chicken and vegetables—and at bedtime sang nursery rhymes to him, just as she longed to do for her own children. Benji watched her warily, holding the cat. She prayed that God give her renewed patience.

The veterinarian, Keast, had recommended that she consult Miss Lena Ladu, the new schoolteacher who'd just relocated to Morseville, the small town between Plum River and Stockton. Both Keast and Miss Ladu roomed at Mrs. Bosley's boardinghouse, where he had on several occasions conversed with her; she was steady and intelligent, he said, with a good measure of common sense.

Miss Ladu agreed that the boy should be weaned from his native tongue. Since he seemed to be such a bright child, he would in all likelihood pick up English in a natural way, by hearing it spoken in the home. She commended Kate for the approach she was taking. He would probably master nouns first, Miss Ladu predicted; that was the way of American children.

Kate kept the boy with her part of each day as she went about her chores, gesturing, naming: *stove, kettle, bread, broom*. When he stared at her with those eyes, she shifted her gaze away and tried not to think of his origins.

"Land's sakes," Mrs. Pinkerton said one day, when Kate introduced the words *sifter, dough,* and *rolling pin*. "He'll never understand all that."

"Naturally he can't at present," Kate said, trying to sustain a pleasant tone. "But he will, in time."

Mrs. Pinkerton gave the boy a biscuit slathered with blackberry jam; she didn't need to gesture for him to sit at the table. Food he understood. They watched as he devoured the biscuit. "It's a wonder you brought the boy here," Mrs. Pinkerton said, "not knowing a word."

"He's making progress." Kate dumped more flour onto the sticky bread dough and kneaded it savagely. "We saved him, you know. It was God's will."

Mrs. Pinkerton made no comment but to sweep the floor in brisk, dismissive strokes.

Kate's eyes stung. No one appreciated her efforts and her sacrifices, not even Frank. He was indifferent and stubborn in a way he'd never been during the two years of their marriage before the catastrophic trip to Japan. It occurred to her that Frank—though perhaps not aware of it—clung to the Japanese language because of that woman. Kate must give him children of their own; then he would love her as he once did.

One morning Frank came in from the barn, leading Benji by the hand. Both of them were grinning. "He said *cow*," Frank said. "Just as plain as day."

"That's nice," she said. "Good boy, Benji. I've pointed out cows on many occasions," she added. It wasn't fair he'd speak his first new words with Frank, after all the effort she'd made.

Over the next few weeks, there was a flurry of nouns—*foot, bath, dog*—and, before long, verbs—*run, eat, sit*. He had trouble with *l* and *r* sounds, but Miss Ladu thought this would pass in time. By Thanksgiving he was doing so well that he could name several of the pictures in his Sunday school book, but, to Kate's disappointment, not Jesus.

One snowy evening as they were clustered around the parlor stove, he said his first sentence: "Benji want milk."

"Listen to that!" Mrs. Pinkerton said, nodding her approval at Kate.

"Isn't he a smart boy?" Kate said, looking at Frank. Surely he would recognize her hard work with Benji.

"An *American* boy too," he said. "Finally wanting his milk."

In the kitchen, while Kate was waiting for a pot of milk to warm, she opened the door and looked out at the snow slanting down in the dark, a cold, melancholy sight. It hadn't been a baby yet, Dr. McBride had told her; she shouldn't continue to grieve after all these months. There would be another before long.

It was bone cold in the shed, where Frank sat scraping dirt and rust from the point of the turning plow. It was snowing again, but December's ice had sealed the cracks in the walls; he started a fire in the stove and waited, chipping at the bolts with his penknife. It was a relief not to be in the parlor, Kate still morose over losing the baby, even after three months. He had tried to reason with her, to no avail. She snapped at him for the least thing and seemed to have no regard for his own disappointment. It was unnatural.

His mother was patient with Kate; trouble and illness always brought out her best. When he had earaches as a child, his mother would put him to bed, a boiled onion in the throbbing ear, then sit by his side, knitting. His father had complained that she was coddling him. Nothing made the old man angrier than a show of weakness, unless it was disregard for the farm tools and equipment. The used blade is always sharp, he liked to say, quoting Benjamin Franklin. He would be disgusted with Frank, not to have tended to the plow right after planting season.

He opened the stove and tossed in a shank of wood. The log caught quickly, buds of flame along its length. For surviving the winters in Japan, there were kotatsus: an open pit in the house where coal was burned; over the pit were a table and a heavy quilt. He thought of sitting at the kotatsu with Butterfly, heat spreading up through their bodies. They carried the warmth with them to bed.

It was wrong of him to think of Butterfly, disloyal to Kate, but scenes from the early days in Nagasaki rose in him unbidden—her fragrant hair like satin, her legs wrapped around him.

"Damn you." He scraped harder at the rust. She wouldn't leave him in peace; it was her revenge.

The door swung open and the Swede blew in like Jack Frost, his hat and coat muffled in snow. He must have seen the stove's light from the bunkhouse. "Better get up there," he said, gesturing toward the house with his thumb. "Looks like a blizzard."

Frank closed the stove after he left and stepped outside. The house was barely visible through the white curtain of snow; his father used to tie ropes between the house and outbuildings during the winter, so they could find their way during a blizzard. He'd scoff at Frank for having forgotten. Sloth is a fool's virtue, he could hear the old man say.

He bent forward, leaning into the river of wind and snow, the ghostly light from the parlor his guide. When he stood on the porch stamping his boots, his mother peered out at him, her face tight with what looked like anger but he knew to be concern. "Go sit by the stove," she said. "I'll bring cocoa."

He looked into the parlor. "You were so long," Kate said. He hadn't noticed before how pale and thin her face had become.

"Got caught up in work," he said. "Didn't realize how bad it was out."

Benji was squatting by the stove. Frank had never liked that Japanese way of sitting, like doing your business. Even some women sat that way, but not Butterfly.

"Going to get out of these clothes," he said, and went upstairs. After he changed, he went into his study. It was cold as the dickens, with only the heat from the stove below filtering up into the room. He sat at the desk and flipped through one of his father's ledgers—meticulous accountings of outlay and profit. There were occasional brief notes between lines of figures: *Corn done well this year; Grasshoppers wiped us out.* He found the ledger for the year he'd left for sea, 1881 it had been, summer, July; his father had whipped him one too many times. There, July 18, was a notation: *Frank gone.* Nothing more.

Seven years later, Sharpless had introduced him to Butterfly on a warm autumn evening in Nagasaki. A few more years, and here he was, back at the farm with Butterfly's son and an American wife. His father would have plenty to say to all that.

There was a knock at the door and Benji came in, carrying a cup of cocoa; he handed it to Frank without a word and stood staring. His eyes, like hers, accused him.

"What do you want?" he shouted. The boy darted away.

There was a bottle of whiskey in the closet. He found it, took a long draught, and another, then laid his head on the table and slept.

The leaves on the trees were as big as squirrels' ears, Father Pinkerton said, so it was time to plant. This spring he would show Benji how.

Benji sat in Father Pinkerton's lap, both of them holding the traces as the horses pulled the plow back and forth and back and forth across the field, getting rid of last year's crops and making the dirt smooth. Then they started over to make hills in the ground. Benji thought of the hills in Nagasaki; these were nothing but poked-up places in the dirt. Father Pinkerton said what a good job he was doing, making straight rows without any cricks, and that the first time he'd plowed on his own when he was not much older than Benji, his father had said it looked like a drunk had got loose in the field. Father Pinkerton smoothed Benji's hair; it made him feel sleepy, then tired.

The land was so wide it went on and on and the sky came down to it, and there was nothing to look at except the horses' rumps and their shiny tails that sometimes lifted up so the manure could fall out, and nothing changed.

Mama didn't know America was like this.

"Will I always be here?" he asked Father Pinkerton.

Father Pinkerton was quiet and then he said, "People die and leave the earth but they go to heaven."

"Like Mama," Benji said.

"Yes. But you won't go for a long time. Don't you worry about it."

"I want to go to Japan."

Father Pinkerton didn't answer; he was pulling on the left trace to make the horses turn, and they started down the flat space again.

"Why did Mama die?" Benji said.

Father Pinkerton didn't answer, so he asked again.

"We don't know exactly. We found you at a church with a note pinned to your coat. It said to please take you to America."

It was the same lie Mother Pinkerton told. He looked up at Father Pinkerton's face, like the one in the picture. "Mama died," he said, "and you came. You and Suzuki said Mama was dead."

"That must have been the church people who came," Father Pinkerton said. "It's easy to be confused at a time like that."

Mama said Papa-san was coming and then she was dead. "It wasn't church people," Benji yelled.

"Calm down now, and I'll tell you what I know about your mother. She was a geisha, the church people said, which means singer, and she was named Cio-Cio—that means Butterfly in English. She left a note asking for some kind people to take you to America; she signed it herself. They said she was the daughter of a samurai—a brave warrior—and that means you come from good stock. Look, I spy an arrowhead." He stopped the horses. "Want to get it?"

Benji jumped down and started running back to the house, stamping on the hills and spitting on them. Father Pinkerton called after him, but his voice got smaller and then stopped. Benji went through the back of the house where no one would see him and into his room. The women were in the kitchen, so he jammed a chair against his door and took out the picture. The man was Father Pinkerton. He turned the picture over and stared at the writing. It wasn't the church people, the writing said, Papa-san is a liar.

Although Kate had offered to host the first meeting of the women's reading circle, Aimee Moore prevailed. Her house in Stockton was centrally located, she said, and her parlor could comfortably accommodate the dozen women they had chosen to invite. Kate was miffed—the circle had been her idea. In addition to providing intellectual stimulation, reading and talking about books would be a welcome diversion from the disappointment at home. There had not been another pregnancy, in spite of Frank's grim determination.

The circle met on a Sunday in midsummer. There were a dozen fashionably dressed women, all of them from town except Kate. She was glad for her new summer dress, lawn with a sprigged print; it looked as fine as anyone's. Aimee's parlor was pleasantly cool; the open windows, in the shade of large trees, provided relief from the heat. The room was large and expensively decorated, with Turkish carpets, clusters of velvet chairs and love seats, two large stained-glass lamps handmade by Mr. Tiffany of New York—works of art, Aimee informed them—and bouquets of flowers in porcelain vases. There was on one table a framed woodblock Japanese print of two women, which Aimee had displayed in Kate's honor.

She served charlotte russe and tea and passed plates of almond cookies and petits fours. Most of the women had not read the assigned novel, George Eliot's *Middlemarch*, but listened placidly while Kate, Aimee, and Beth Moss, the spinster librarian of Stockton, discussed the themes of the book. Interest picked up when Beth Moss mentioned that George Eliot was a pseudonym; the writer was in fact a woman named Mary Ann Evans.

"Why would she use a man's name?" asked Mrs. Robert Cassidy, an overweight woman whose rings and bracelets cut cruelly into her flesh. She looked around the parlor at the other ladies. "Doesn't that seem a little peculiar?"

"She wanted to be accorded full respect as a writer," Miss Moss said. "She felt that only a man would have been taken seriously."

"If she couldn't enjoy the respect that is associated with being a woman," Mrs. Cassidy said, "I don't know why she'd want to be a novelist."

"Maybe that's why she *was* a novelist," Kate said. "Because she was accorded little respect in the first place."

Aimee called attention to the Japanese print. It had been given to her, she told the group, by a world traveler of considerable means, a classmate of hers at Mount Holyoke Female Seminary. Aimee made reference at every opportunity to having attended Mount Holyoke; the only wonder, Kate thought, was that she had restrained herself so long this afternoon. Aimee gave a short disquisition on the influence of Japanese woodblocks on Western art—Whistler, most notably, she said—then asked Kate if the scene portrayed in the print seemed true to life.

Kate glanced at the picture of two women in kimono seated outside a Japanese house, its sliding doors open to reveal straw mats, a low table, and a large vase.

"As far as I can tell," Kate said, with a nervous laugh. "But I wasn't in Japan long, just a few days. I did live in China, however, as a young girl."

"We're all so interested in your little orphan boy," Mrs. Cassidy said. "You were so brave to take him in."

"We're fortunate to have him with us," Kate said. "He's a wonderful boy."

"How did you find him exactly?" Beth Moss asked.

Kate told the story she and Frank had concocted—Benji being left at the Catholic church, the appeal to their charity, the reason for his name. She said it all calmly, with appropriate animation. She should have been an actress, she thought.

"He's such an unusual-looking child," Mrs. Cassidy said, reaching for a cookie.

Kate's heart fluttered.

"But appealing," Aimee put in. "Really quite appealing."

"If you're referring to his blond hair and his Japanese face," Kate said, "that is unusual to see here, but not in Nagasaki. Nagasaki has a long history of exchange with the West—the Dutch, for instance, have been in residence there since the seventeen hundreds."

A shy woman whom Kate didn't know raised her hand. "Was it a hard choice for you?"

Kate took a deep breath, then told how she'd searched her heart, gone to pray at a church commemorated to Japanese Christian martyrs. "I decided it was the Christian thing to do," she concluded, "and the right thing for a woman to do."

The ladies applauded.

"We don't need to read novels," Mrs. Cassidy said, "when we have such interesting *true* stories to hear."

Before school started, Keast taught Benji his numbers, using marbles and a slate he'd borrowed from Miss Ladu. The boy was a whiz; by September he even understood the concepts of addition and subtraction, though he seemed leery about the prospect of school itself. When Keast suggested to Frank that they let the boy have a look at the schoolhouse, Frank agreed—acting a little huffy, but Keast knew Frank wouldn't have thought of it on his own. Not that he didn't care for the boy, but he lived in a world unto himself.

Halfway between Plum River and Morseville, the school was a small stone building in the middle of a pasture dotted with white and yellow flowers. It had hardly changed since Keast was a boy—the same flagpole out front, the bell over the door, and, along the edge of the pasture, an Osage orange hedgerow that stretched all the way up the slight hill.

Miss Ladu had given Keast the key to the school, but he sat down on the steps to wait for Benji and Frank. They were late. He took out his watch several times, fogged the face with his breath, and rubbed it on his trousers. When they finally appeared, they were walking on opposite sides of the road, Benji kicking a small rock in front of him, Frank frowning, his hands in his pockets. Benji's face had that bee-stung look he got after he'd been crying, and his hair was flat and dirty. His hair had lightened during the summer in the fields so that it was only a few shades darker than Pinkerton's.

Keast rose as they came toward him. Frank took a large book out of his satchel and held it up to show Keast. "A dictionary," he said. "English to Japanese. There will be things he doesn't understand."

Keast said nothing as he turned and went up the steps to unlock the door, but in his opinion Benji knew a lot more than he let on to some people.

The schoolroom was cool inside because of the stone walls. The desks were just as he remembered—the teacher's up front, across from the woodstove, then rows of desks gradually increasing in size to the back of the room. He found the desk where he'd sat his last year; there was an ink stain on it in the shape of a half-moon. Isobel had sat in front of him; he could still see those gleaming black braids. Their Horatio would be in the third grade now.

"Let's find your seat," Keast said to Benji. Frank had located his own last desk—he'd been a student a decade after Keast—and sat down. Benji followed Keast to the front of the room. "This is where you'll probably sit." Keast pointed to the desk at the end of the front row. "Near the teacher. Sit down—see how it feels." Benji slid into the desk, rubbed the top of it with one hand, and put his fingers in the empty inkwell. "Look: There are the letters and words you already know." Keast pointed them out, colorful pictures arranged on three walls of the room.

He went to the chalkboard and wrote an arithmetic problem—7 + 8—and waved Benji forward. Benji wrote the answer quickly.

Frank joined them at the board. "Sharp boy you've got," Keast said.

"Yes," Frank said with an odd smile. "Where did he learn to do that?"

"We've had a lesson or two," Keast said.

"They didn't ease his mind," Frank said. "But you're going to be a scholar, aren't you, buddy?"

Benji nodded.

"Dr. Keast and I were both students here at one time, can you imagine that? Right here in front of the room is where I gave my senior recitation—one hundred lines from Coleridge's *The Rime of the Ancient Mariner*. I still remember it too."

Frank had begun to declaim when the door opened and Miss Ladu came in. A thin woman with a long neck and dun-colored hair, Miss Ladu was considered plain, but Keast liked her sincere smile and the complicated expressions of her face. They'd had several conversations about Benji during mealtimes at the boardinghouse.

"Hello, gentlemen," she said. "So this is my new student. Are you ready for school, Benjamin?"

"Just watch this." Keast wrote some arithmetic problems on the board, then stood back as Benji completed them.

"Perfect," Miss Ladu said. "Benji, I think you're a star pupil already." She bent down to study Benji's somber face. "Don't mind if the big boys tease you," she said. "They always do that."

"He won't mind," Frank said. "He's tough."

"Is that so?" Miss Ladu gave Keast a private smile that said they understood this boy in a way Frank did not; they would be allies on the lad's behalf.

Mother Pinkerton gave him his lunch pail and Benji started off to school, walking slowly down Plum River Road. Maybe if he walked slow enough, it would be over by the time he got there.

In the ditches at the sides of the road were red and blue flowers; butterflies darted and drifted above them. Butterfly, Papa-san had said, Cio-Cio. Mama would be glad he was going to school. Benji is one smart boy, she had taught him to say, his first English. She said he would be a rich man in America but that first he would go to school and learn everything American.

He sat down for a while at the edge of a ditch and played a game with the butterflies. If one lit on his finger, Mama was thinking of him. An orange and black one dipped near him but did not land. That meant she was thinking of him a little bit.

He took the small wooden horse from his pocket. It was dark brown with legs raised like it was running. Dr. Keast had whittled it for him as a present for going to school; it was the best thing he'd ever had except for Mama's ball.

A wagon rattled down the road behind him. It was Mr. Case, on his way to the creamery with his jugs of milk. "Hey, boy." Mr. Case stopped the wagon. "Ain't you going to school?" Benji stood, dusted off his pants. "You'd better get in here." He gestured toward the seat beside him. "You're going to be late. That teacher will tan your hide."

Benji shook his head and started walking again, in the ditch, so Mr. Case could drive on.

After a while he moved back to the road, walking in the dust from the wagon. He walked down the hill, then on the flat part for a long way, and up another hill. His stomach hurt. Maybe he was sick and would have to go home.

Soon he saw the schoolhouse. The walk seemed shorter than yesterday. There were no children outside, so school must have started already. He would have to walk past all the big children on the way to the front.

But he was a strong boy. Mama had said that too. No one would know what he didn't like.

He trudged up the steps and opened the door a crack. There was a mumble of voices. Miss Ladu came over, smiling, and led him down the aisle between the desks. "This is Benji, a very bright boy from Japan. He'll be in the first grade, but you second-graders had better watch out!"

Everyone was too quiet while Miss Ladu showed him his desk, the same one where he'd sat yesterday, and gave him a book. "Your first reader," she said. At the desk beside him was a girl in a red dress and a bow in her hair. She stared at him.

"The third-graders are reciting a poem," Miss Ladu said. "Continue, please." The children lined up near the blackboard started talking again, all together.

After the third-graders went back to their seats, Miss Ladu wrote an arithmetic problem and waved Benji forward. He felt shaky as he walked to the front, like crossing a skinny log over the river.

She put chalk in his hand. It was an easy problem, but the chalk squealed when he wrote the answer.

For the rest of the morning, children who came forward to recite turned to look at him. Benji pretended not to see; he stared at the grain of wood in his desk.

Miss Ladu rang a bell and the other students jumped up, pushing and talking as they headed for the door. "It's time for lunch," Miss Ladu told Benji. "Go on out with the others. You'll have fun."

Outside, Benji looked for Eli but didn't see him. A girl with long brown braids smiled at him, so he sat down on a rock next to her. She didn't have on a fancy dress or shoes like the girl with the bow, and there were freckles under her eyes. "My name is Flora," she said. He couldn't think of anything to say, so he took out his horse to show her.

"It's pretty," she said. He put it on the rock beside him to show how it could stand up even though two legs were raised.

Two big boys came over, grinning down at Benji; one of them snatched the horse.

Benji leapt for it, but the boy dangled it over his head. He had mean little eyes and a missing front tooth. Another boy grabbed Benji between his legs.

"Give it back, Marvin." Eli stepped into the circle and shoved the boy who was holding the horse. Marvin dropped the horse in the dirt for Benji to pick up.

"Let's play Osage ball," Eli said, motioning to Benji.

Benji followed him to the other side of the Osage orange hedge where a group of boys were yanking green, warty-looking balls from the thorny branches. When they divided into teams and Eli chose Benji, some others yelled, "Eww. Don't pick me."

"Shut up," Eli said. "Benji can throw better than any of you."

"They just don't want to be on a Jap's team," Marvin said.

Benji hadn't heard "Jap" before but it sounded bad. "I'm Japanese," he said.

"That's what makes you a Jap," Marvin said. "Jappie Jappie Jappie," he chanted, and others joined in.

Benji shoved Keast's horse in his pocket, grabbed an Osage orange and aimed it at Marvin: The ball splatted on his forehead. Eli and a boy named Jonas cheered.

Marvin ran at Benji and pushed him down. "Say 'Jap.' " He sat on Benji's back and scoured his face into the dirt. "Say 'I'm a Jap.' "

Benji tasted dirt and blood and his nose hurt, but he wasn't going to cry and he wasn't going to say "Jap."

Eli kicked at Marvin, but another boy tackled him. They were all scrabbling on the ground when the school bell rang. Marvin jumped up and ran inside with everyone else, except Benji and Eli.

"Don't tell Miss Ladu," Eli said.

She was waiting at the door. "What happened?" she asked, bending down to look at Benji.

"I fell down."

She frowned. "Was someone picking on you?"

He shook his head.

"Go wash up at the pump then and come to my desk for a writing lesson."

All afternoon Benji sat at his desk writing lines of the *O* Miss Ladu had taught him to make. He filled in one of the *O*'s, making it big and lumpy until it was Marvin's liver, and drew a kappa eating it. Marvin would cry and beg for Benji to make the kappa stop and then he'd die. Benji ground the chalk on his slate until the girl with the bow said stop or she'd tell the teacher. When Miss Ladu said it was rest time for the first-graders, he put his head on his desk and felt in his pocket for Keast's horse. A leg was broken off. He took it out and held the leg in place. Tears came to his eyes, so he rested his head again and put the horse away.

When school was over, Benji walked away fast, then ran down Plum River Road. In the woods beyond the Cases' farm, he ran at a small tree, tearing at the branches and letting his screams out. He kicked up moss and threw chunks of it in the river and hurled rocks at the trees, pounding them into Marvin's face.

He sat on the ground and took out Dr. Keast's horse and looked at it for a while, trying to stick the leg back on. It was ruined. He lay down on the ground, holding the horse, and went to sleep.

When he got home it was almost dark. Father Pinkerton was at the table, and Mother and Grandmother Pinkerton were putting out food.

"Where in Hades have you been?" Father Pinkerton said. "You think just because you're a scholar you can ignore your chores? I did the milking and mucked out the stalls myself."

"Look at him!" Grandmother Pinkerton said. "He's black and blue." She and Mother Pinkerton put down their dishes and came over to him.

Mother Pinkerton pushed back the hair from Benji's forehead. "You're all scraped up. And your nose . . ." She touched it with a finger. "Does that hurt?"

"No," he said, although it did.

"What happened?" she asked.

"I fell down."

Grandmother Pinkerton and Mother Pinkerton looked at each other.

"Mighty hard fall," Grandmother Pinkerton said. "It was some of those sorry town boys, I'd wager. They deserve a good whaling."

"Don't mollycoddle him," Father Pinkerton said. "He has to handle it on his own, just like I did. Come here, boy." Benji went to stand beside him. Father Pinkerton took him by the shoulders and gave him a little shake. "Remember that your mother's people are samurai. That means warrior, fighter."

"He's too small to fight," Mother Pinkerton said. She took his hand and led him into the kitchen. Her eyes were nice while she washed his face and put on some smelly medicine that stung.

At supper, Mother Pinkerton and Grandmother Pinkerton kept telling him to eat, but everything tasted like dirt, even the lemon pie.

The next day, Eli and Jonas, who wore a knit cap pulled down to his ears, walked Benji to school.

"You don't have to worry about Marvin," Jonas told Benji. "He's just a stinking bully. He calls me Wormie." He pulled off his cap to show his head, bald because of ringworm, then put it back on. "I'm gonna put a poison snake in his desk."

"And cow plop," Eli said. Eli and Jonas laughed about how Marvin's face would look when he reached into his desk.

"Then we'll beat him up," Jonas said. "Three against one. We'll smear him into the ground."

Benji's stomachache got worse. He saw an orange butterfly and tried to think about Mama, but she wasn't there.

At school, Miss Ladu had made a big map of Japan and propped it on the blackboard. "We're going to have a special lesson on Japanese geography and culture," she said, "for every grade."

Some boys in the back made shuffling noises with their feet. Miss Ladu stared at them and they stopped. "Any boy who misbehaves will be punished," she said, "and I will visit their parents."

She took up a long stick and pointed at the map. "Japan is comprised of four islands," she said. Benji hadn't known that; he repeated the names of the islands in his mind after Miss Ladu said them: *Ho-kaido, Hon-shoe, Shi-ko-ku, Kew-shoe.* There was a red star at the bottom of *Kew-shoe.* "This is Nagasaki," she said, "where Benji was born. It's the most interesting city in Japan. Many foreigners live there . . ." She turned to look at the class. "In Japan, Americans are foreigners. Many of the Japanese people in Nagasaki are Christians. The notable trades of Nagasaki are shipbuilding and manufacturing." She took down the map and began to write on the board. "And there are several well-known arts:

cloisonné—which is a kind of metalwork—turtle-shell jewelry, kites, and glassware. These words are tomorrow's spelling homework for third-graders and up."

She held up a book about Japan and showed them pictures: farmers in rice fields; a statue she said was famous; and a family—mother, father, and children in kimono—sitting at a low table. "Japanese people are known for their intelligence, hard work, and peacefulness," she said. "What is peacefulness?"

The girl next to Benji raised her hand. "No fighting," she said.

"That is correct. And we will have no fighting in this school."

At lunch Jonas and Eli played jump board while Benji watched. He was too small to play; he couldn't make his side stay down. Benji glanced at Marvin playing marbles, across the school yard, then sat near Flora to eat his lunch.

"Japan is nice," she said.

"So is America," he said, and then couldn't think of anything else.

On the way back inside, Marvin walked close to Benji and whispered, "Why's your hair yellow, Jappie?"

Benji pretended not to hear, but all afternoon he thought of things he wished he'd said: Why does your hair look like cow plop? Why do you smell like manure? Why don't you sit on a nail? He imagined Marvin without any clothes on, sitting on a chair full of sticking-up nails.

After school, when he and Father Pinkerton were milking, Benji asked why his hair was yellow. "Is it because your hair is yellow?"

"Don't talk like that," Father Pinkerton said. "You mention that again and you'll be in big trouble."

Why? Benji wanted to ask, but Father Pinkerton looked too mad.

The season of 1897 looked to be prosperous. By the Fourth of July, when Frank drove his family into Stockton for a holiday celebration at the Moores' house, the corn was flourishing, field after field of green regiments marching to the horizon. If the farm turned a profit this year, he could make up for last season's shortfall and perhaps even afford some of the improvements to the house that Kate was so set on. She was still after him about a servant girl, and she wanted a new buggy, too—essential, she said, if they were to be accepted in local society. By "society" she meant the ladies of Stockton, and particularly that Moore woman, who was causing him no end of expense, as his mother had pointed out. His mother was wearing her usual church costume, but Kate had bought a new dress and hat for the party, and she'd wanted Frank to be measured for a white suit. An extravagance, he'd said; he could wear his white naval dress uniform, though in the outdoor light he could see that it was dingy in spite of Kate's best efforts and had a small, urine-colored stain on the left breast.

Kate had also ordered an impractical white shirt and new knickers for Benji, both already streaked with grime. He had run off just before it was time to leave; Frank found him in the hayloft with that cat and gave him a spanking. Now he was sulking in the backseat of the buggy beside Frank's mother, not responding to her descriptions of firecrackers and sparklers or the promise of ice cream.

Butterfly would judge him too hard on the boy; the Japanese spoiled their children. This is America, he wanted to tell her; he has to learn to behave here. He stared out at the corn, imagining her face tight with disapproval. He'd seen her angry only once—when he told her he had to leave Japan—but afterward they had made love with abandon, her silky hair brushing his chest as she sat astride him. Perhaps Benji had been conceived that day.

"Well?" Kate said.

He glanced at her; she'd said something.

"I'm sorry, dear. What is it?"

"Never mind—a trivial matter. "

He looked at her profile, her regal expression. "Your dress is quite fetching," he said. "Though you look beautiful in anything."

She rewarded him with a smile and he took her hand, cool in spite of the afternoon heat. She was nervous about the party, he realized. "You're lovely as an angel," he said. "There will be no one to rival you."

The Moores' grand white house, which dominated the central block of Maple Street, was studded with stained-glass windows and crowned with a turret. Designed by an architect from Chicago—so Kate had told him several times—it was said to have an indoor privy and a porcelain bathtub with running water, the first such facilities between Chicago and Galena.

In the yard were snowball bushes and a sizable planting of elephant ears. A boy in someone's idea of a sailor suit was sitting astride an iron elk, pretending to whip him with a stick. There were other children in the distance, playing croquet. When they alighted from the buggy, Frank pointed out the children to Benji, but the boy shadowed Frank's mother into the house.

Aimee Moore, a dark-eyed beauty with a generous bosom, greeted them effusively and, before flitting off to her other guests, introduced them to the Stockton pharmacist Louis Hill and his bilious-looking wife.

"Hello, little boy," Mrs. Hill said, bending down to Benji. "I understand that you're from Japan. Look at this." She unfurled a painted silk fan and held it out before him. "From your country. Mr. Hill bought it for me at the Exposition in Chicago five years ago."

"Isn't it pretty, Benji?" Kate said.

"Very pretty," Frank's mother said, to reinforce Benji's nod.

"Those Japanese are darned clever," Hill said, scratching his beard.

"Edna and I went into one of their quaint houses with the sliding doors made out of paper. Quite something. Must be mighty cold in the winter, though."

"And so empty," his wife said. "Hardly a stick of furniture. Is that how they live in the country itself?" she asked, looking at Frank.

"I'm no expert," Frank said. He could feel Kate measuring his answer. "I was stationed there for only a short time."

Kate led Benji off to the croquet game, and Mrs. Pinkerton headed for the dessert table. Frank excused himself and threaded through the crowd, looking for a familiar face.

Aimee Moore materialized. "I've been quite neglecting you," she said, pressing a glass of lemonade into his hands and smiling up at him. She had sloe eyes and her skin was olive and pink. Italian? He glanced at her neck and shoulders. "I hope someday you'll tell me about your adventures," she said. "I'm partial to travel, but my excursions have been quite tame." She touched his arm before moving away. He felt a little spurt of pleasure; he still had a way with the women.

Red Olsen, proprietor of Moresville's general store, was on the porch with a corpulent man sporting a red, white, and blue hatband in honor of the day, the two of them drinking from a flask and discussing the rise in railroad tariffs. Red—still with the mischievous devil-may-care glint in his eye that Frank remembered from their days as school-yard chums—introduced Frank as a naval officer and man of the world, presently a gentleman farmer. The beefy man was Austin Burdett, new president of the Stockton Bank and Trust.

"Ever see any action, Captain?" Burdett asked, offering him the flask.

Frank took a draw of the whiskey: smooth bourbon. "There was a small uprising in Samoa," he said, which wasn't quite true. "The presence of our ships was usually enough to forestall trouble."

"Frank's been all over," Red said. "Spain, Brazil, all those islands, the Orient . . ." He leaned forward with a wink; Frank could smell the whiskey on his breath.

"You the one that brought back that mongrel Jap," Burdett said.

Frank straightened and handed him the flask. "Japan is a superior country, very civilized and mannerly. Yes, my wife and I have taken in an unfortunate orphan. He's a bright boy and already a help on the farm."

There was a stirring inside the house. Kate came out the door, her face vivid with excitement. Frank made introductions while Burdett—none too subtly—assessed Kate's figure. No doubt his own wife resembled a blancmange.

"There's to be a tour of the house," Kate said, taking Frank's arm. "Mrs. Moore is doing the honors."

Frank took his leave with a smile and a slight bow. "You've rescued me from a beast," he whispered as they joined the throng.

She squeezed his arm. "I anticipate the details."

They shuffled along with the crowd as Aimee led them through the frilly parlor, the sunroom, the music room, with its gleaming piano; her husband's library, lined with law books and dominated by the mounted head of a rakish-looking moose, and a large expanse of kitchen, the stove decorated with tile imported from Belgium—"at tiresome expense," Aimee confided.

Upstairs, they peered into fancy bedrooms and had a glimpse of the famous privy—a water closet, Aimee called it, quickly opening and shutting the door. Frank was disappointed; he'd wanted to see how the thing worked. Aimee led the way to the bath.

It was a spacious corner room; the light, filtered through the stained-glass windows, was yellow with streaks of red. The bathtub, gleaming porcelain with a wide lip and bowed legs that tapered to monstrous paws, stood on a rose-patterned carpet. Mrs. Moore demonstrated the miracle to appreciative murmurs, turning the water on and off several times. As she bent forward, a band of ruby-colored light fell across her neck.

Kate was silent as they descended the steps.

"Someday we'll have one of those," Frank whispered. "An even finer one."

His mother was waiting at the foot of the stairs with Benji. There was a red gash across Benji's face, and his clothes were streaked with dirt.

"Goodness, what's happened?" Kate cried.

"He won't tell me. Some trouble with the children, I believe. He wants to go home."

Benji stared at the floor. "Be a little soldier," Frank said, squeezing his shoulder; the small bones beneath his hand, delicate as a bird's, brought him close to tears.

"Captain Pinkerton." Frank turned; he'd forgotten Mrs. Moore behind them. "If you want to take the boy home, my husband and I will see that your wife is safely returned." She gazed at Benji. "Poor little fellow. Did you fall?"

He shook his head.

"I'll come too and get us some supper," his mother said.

Frank's mother sat beside him in the buggy; Benji was curled up on the backseat, his eyes closed. "Hey, bud," Frank said, reaching to shake his foot. "Why don't we stop by the drugstore for a sarsaparilla?" Benji didn't move.

"Let him be," his mother said. "I'm not surprised—that was as snoot-nosed a crowd as I've seen." After a pause she said in a low voice, "I don't know what you were thinking, Frank, bringing him to Plum River." He glanced away and pretended he hadn't heard. "Your wife is a saint," she added.

They passed through town and into the countryside. Dark clouds were gathering and a wind had come up; the air smelled of rain. He'd felt there was no choice but to take the boy, and Sharpless had insisted on it. But maybe Benji would have been better off with his own kind. Frank stared out at the cornstalks stirring in the breeze, his mother a dark weight at his side. She would never understand what he had to contend with—the pitiless life of farming, Kate's delicacy, and the boy, trying to do right by the boy.

He glanced back at Benji. If the boy was going to turn out to be a sissy, he'd never survive here. An image of his father flashed into Frank's mind—the time he'd called Frank a pantywaist because he'd cried at a hog-butchering. I'll give you something to whine about if you don't dry up, he'd said.

At home, he left his mother to tend to Benji, changed to coveralls, and went to the barn. The Swede hadn't mucked out the stalls. Furious, Frank banged on the bunkhouse door, then opened it. Empty. The Swede had gone off on his own Fourth of July toot, probably to the whorehouse near Elizabeth. There was a bottle of white whiskey on the nightstand. He sampled it—corn liquor; it burned like Hades—then returned to the barn, where he looked for the bottle of bourbon he'd hidden in the haymow. Gone, damn that Swede. He gave Daisy a few swipes with the currycomb and, cursing, attacked the Percherons' prodigious heaps of excrement with the pitchfork. The cows came jangling across the road, their udders full. He milked them savagely—what this family needed was another hired hand, not some prissy servant. He carried the milk to the cistern, then

Butterfly's Child • 79

went back to the Swede's place for the bottle. As he walked to the farm-house, a light rain began, raising dust on the road. No fireworks in Stockton this year. "Ha," he said aloud.

In the house, assaulted by the odor of liver and onions, he went up to his office and sat at his desk, gazing out at tree limbs thrashing in the wind. There was a crack of thunder, a bright fork of lightning. It was going to be a hell of a storm. He uncorked the bottle, took a long drink, then another. Likely Kate would spend the night. She'd enjoy that, one of those satiny bedrooms and the bath in the morning. He took another draught from the bottle. He could see her naked, stepping into the tub, then Aimee, the two of them together in the water, breasts floating, Kate's flesh-colored nipples, Aimee's dark ones, her dark thatch like Butterfly's. He'd have them take turns, bent over the edge of the tub. He rose to lock the door and relieved himself in private, as rain hammered against the windows and the dark closed in.

Benji went to his room and took out the kimono. He wanted to talk to Mama in his room, but Grandmother Pinkerton was close by, in the kitchen. "Let's see to that cut," she called. His hands moving so quick that he didn't get to see Mama's face, he took the picture from the kimono and slipped outside. It had started raining, so he put the picture under his shirt.

He ran to the privy and sat down. No one would come until the rain stopped. He took out Mama's picture and covered the other face with his hand so he could look just at her.

"The Sunday-school children are meaner than Marvin," he told her. They were playing a game with long sticks, hitting balls across the grass. One ball came to his feet and he picked it up but they yelled at him so he dropped it. A boy with stuck-out ears made a face, pulling the skin back until his eyes almost disappeared, and said he was a Jap and a Chink.

"I hit him and he hit back," he said. "I butted like a goat and he fell down so hard he cried like a little sissy, even though he's bigger than me. Two other boys threw rocks and dirt but I didn't care."

He leaned closer to the picture. "I'm a samurai. Are you proud of me?"

He wagged the picture to make her say yes, but her face didn't answer. The writing didn't answer. There was only the angry sound of rain.

Kate had felt separated from God ever since the events in Nagasaki. Praying at the mission church there, she had been moved to rescue Benji and to forgive Frank, but that inspiration had faded during the years on the farm. She could have borne the hard work, she thought, she might even have seen it as a trial God set for her, if she had any sense of His presence. One should never allow oneself to fall into the Slough of Despond, she remembered her father saying; "Despair is a shutting out of God." So it was her fault, and not God's, that He had left her.

Her sense of melancholy deepened after the Moores' party that summer and continued into the fall, when Frank's shifts in mood became more pronounced; he was alternately distant and effusive. She no longer believed in his affection, which seemed an effort to cover a growing indifference. He spent many evenings in his office, going over the farm ledgers, he said, but these days he seemed more careless with the farm; even his mother had noted it during haying season, when he left the sheaves in the field to go sour in the rain. They'd had to buy hay for the livestock from Bud Case and other farmers nearby. Once, when Kate had taken some tea to his office, he was looking out the window into the dark.

"What is it, darling?" she asked.

He shook his head as though to clear it. "The railroads," he said. "The tariffs will kill us." But his expression had not to do with railroads.

Sometimes when she went to his office after that, the door was locked, and often he was late coming to bed.

She increased her prayers morning and evening and while she went about the housework, but her words felt as rote as a child's Sunday-school recitation, and her sense of God's absence left her hollow.

In late October, she met with Reverend Singleton in his study at the First Presbyterian Church in Stockton. Though she had often thought of consulting him, shame about her peculiar marital difficulties had held her back.

He sat behind his desk, his hands clasped together as if in readiness for prayer, a well-nourished man with a lap of flesh over his clerical collar and kind gray eyes.

She had intended to begin with her crisis of faith but instead blurted out, "I have some family difficulty . . . my husband . . ."

He cleared his throat and rearranged some pencils on his desk. She couldn't speak her heart; she couldn't mention that woman.

"He is disappointed in me—it seems I can have no children of my own. We . . . have grown apart."

"There are many unfortunate children in the world," he said, looking up at her. "You have brought one into your home already. Perhaps God's intention for you and your husband is to continue this Christian work."

No, she wanted to scream, that's not it, but instead politely excused herself and said she must be going.

One winter afternoon she sat alone in the sanctuary of the church. It was cold and dark, no light filtering through the stained-glass windows above her pew.

"Dear God," she whispered, "help me, give me back my faith. I need You."

She waited. Nothing but the sound of the wind.

She pulled her coat tighter about her and closed her eyes. God had carried her through earlier crises in her life. When her missionary parents sent her home from Harbin at age nine, because they were convinced she could not receive a proper education in China, she had lived with her spinster aunt Nora and attended the schools in Galena. The first months were agony; though Aunt Nora tried hard to be a mother, Kate felt bereft and abandoned. Pastor Williams, an erudite silver-haired man who resembled her father, had prayed with her day after day. Kneeling beside him, the ruby and honey colored light that streamed through the stained-glass windows bathing their hands and arms, she had come to feel God's enfolding presence.

Later, she had undertaken a study of the Bible with Pastor Williams, and he introduced her to secular writers as well, particularly the Transcendalists; they had a number of enlivening discussions about the Oversoul. It was Pastor Williams who had suggested to her aunt that Kate attend college, where she might train to be a teacher as well as further develop what he called the life of the mind.

She had returned from Ellington Women's Institute in Iowa prepared to teach, but during her first week in Galena she met Richard McCann at a dinner party. Richard had recently moved to Galena to take a position in the bank; he was said to have a brilliant future and Kate found him enticing, with his broad shoulders that made her trust him—an impulse that she now saw as childish—and his dark, adoring eyes. He had pursued her ardently, squiring her to dances and to orations at the Desoto Hotel, and they began to speak of marriage.

But then Kate's father died and she went to China for the funeral. When she returned two months later, she found that Richard's attentions had shifted to Emily Kettering, in Galena to visit her cousin.

Emily was a molasses-voiced Southerner, adept at the art of flattery. Kate thought that Richard would eventually reject her as insincere. When Richard came that final afternoon to tell her he had proposed to Emily, Kate disgraced herself by weeping, but Richard was unmoved. He admitted that he was leaving the better woman, but the heart works in illogical ways, he said.

Again she was plunged into despair, through which she was led once more by Pastor Williams. He said it was God's will that she had parted from the ignoble Mr. McCann; she was destined for a finer man. She believed him and gave over the burden of her pain to God.

That finer man had seemed to be Frank—handsome in his naval uniform, on leave to visit his ailing father. They met at a church social to which he had been invited by another woman, but he bought her lunch basket instead and they sat on the lawn, her muslin skirt spread out about her, he leaning back on his elbows, smiling up at her. When he began to call on her, he told her that he was weary of the wayfaring life, and he spoke of the possibility of establishing a branch of his Nagasaki import/export business in Galena. The town had once been a thriving port, but the Mississippi had narrowed there over the years and trade was less brisk than it had been a half century ago. Still, Frank thought there were opportunities in Galena, and his eyes told her that he was speaking not merely of business. Although Kate's first pleasure in Frank's pursuit of her was the dignity of having a suitor, she could feel herself beginning to fall in love with him.

Her mother, soon returned from Harbin, did not share her enthusiasm about Frank. She wondered about his business prospects and his past life as a seaman and thought Kate should marry the pastor, whose wife had died recently; though twenty years her senior, he was a good man, her mother said, and would provide for her. A sailor, accustomed to roaming the world, was not likely to be steady.

She had proved her mother wrong, those first two years; she and Frank had been happy until the tragedy in Nagasaki. The circumstances of Frank's dead mistress and her child were sordid and humiliating, but as she knelt in the Oura Church, praying so hard that she felt her head and heart would burst, she had felt God's presence in the unfamiliar odors of incense and wet stone. Her mind had cleared as she rose, with God leading the way.

Now here she was, doing as God had wished, but somehow she had lost Him. She thought of the farmhouse garden, the wet dirt in her hands, the well with its dark hole. The bed she shared with Frank, a feeling of being chafed and unrecognized. Her fear that the only child in the house would be Butterfly's. She had been near despair for some time, she realized, but she had not called on God.

The time was always ripe, Pastor Williams would say. But what would he know of true despair and spiritual dryness, in the comfort of his rectory, with his new Nordic wife, their brood of blond children?

"Oh, God, you must help me. Please save me. Please give me a child." From elsewhere in the church came a sound, a cough. Had she been speaking aloud?

Mortified, she stood and walked down the aisle, pulled open the heavy door, and stepped out into the frigid air.

There was snow on the ground, and she had brought the cutter with Daisy to pull it. On the way home, it began to snow again. She imagined it snowing harder, the whiteness blurring her vision; Daisy might lose her way in a storm, with the roads and familiar scents obscured.

But they arrived at the farmhouse without incident, a little before supper time. She unhooked Daisy from the cutter and poured oats into her manger.

As Kate walked to the house, she saw the silhouette of Frank in his study, his head bent over his desk. She stood looking up at him through the snow. She wished she could tell him about her loneliness, her sense of failure as a wife. She wished they could discuss their difficulties in a spirit of forgiveness. If only they could talk about Butterfly, she would tell him her theory about his obsession: guilt that he must overcome.

She waved and called, but he did not respond. At one time, not so long ago, he'd have been on the porch looking out for her in this weather. She stared at his motionless figure. She was locked out by Frank as well as by God.

By his third year on the farm, Benji was old enough to be in charge of the milking. It was the chore he liked best, especially on warm mornings with the sun slanting in through the barn door and high windows, and the smell of grass, wet with dew, drifting across the meadow. A samurai wouldn't do this job, but milking had made his arms strong. He wasn't afraid of anyone now, and his samurai grandfather and uncles would be proud.

He rested his forehead against each cow's side as he milked, his hands on the teats gentle and sure; the cows let down easily for him. The Swede had taught him to drink from a teat and to squirt milk in Kaki's mouth; Father Pinkerton said he could get kicked that way but he had never been kicked. Even Bossy, with her bad temper, regarded him with unblinking eyes, and her hide seemed to shudder with pleasure when he drew up his stool beside her.

After the cows were milked, he and the collie Skip led the herd across the road to the meadow, Kaki and the two calves frisking in the high grass. Both calves were heifers, but Father Pinkerton was hoping for a bull from Ivy, because a bull brought a higher price. It was sad to see the calves so high-spirited, because they didn't know that before long they'd be taken away from their mothers. At least they wouldn't be slaughtered like beef cattle; Guernseys were the best milkers money could buy, Father Pinkerton said.

Ivy was a two-year-old heifer in her first breeding. She was near her time, and one morning in late April Father Pinkerton allowed Benji to stay home from Sunday school to keep an eye on her, because she might have difficulty with her first labor. If she started licking her side or switching her tail fast, Benji was to fetch Keast from the Plum River church.

There had been hard rain the past few days and Plum Creek was swollen, carrying on its surface brown leaves and sticks scoured from the edges of the bank. Benji sat with his feet in the water, enjoying his freedom and the sweet odor of plum trees in blossom beside the creek. These plum trees were different from the ones in Japan—they made purple instead of yellow fruit, and their smell was stronger—but Mama would like them anyway. She had gone every day to the fox shrine when the plum trees were flowering there.

Something red bobbed past on the surface of the water. Benji jumped up and ran alongside the creek, dodging around clumps of trees. It could be Mama's ball, or part of it; maybe it had been hit upstream that day and gotten stuck behind a rock and the rain had loosened it.

He glanced back at Ivy, grazing peacefully, and went on.

The current carried the ball faster than he could run, so he jumped into the water. It was deeper than he thought, over his head, and he let himself be carried along with the creek. He kicked his feet to go faster, but his clothes weighed him down, and with his face at the surface of the water he couldn't see the ball. He went past fields of young corn and wheat and empty places. An old man squatting beside the creek grinned at him; it was crazy Ike on the Olsen farm—that meant he'd gone past the Cases' land. It probably hadn't been the ball anyway, just a piece of cloth. He turned to paddle toward the bank, but the muscle of current held him back. He imagined a kappa dragging him down and tried harder, churning his arms. Water filled his throat; he coughed and sputtered, his heart racing. Be a samurai, he told himself. Ahead was a plum branch leaning over the water; he aimed toward it and managed to catch on, then inched along with his hands, squeezing the flower shoots and stickery bark until he was able to leap onto the bank. His legs were weak as a baby calf's. He peeled off his shirt and trousers and lay on his back at the edge of a corn row, the ground a relief beneath him.

The sun was almost directly overhead; they'd be home from church soon. He jumped up and ran along the creek, leaping out of Ike's way when he held out his arm and laughed. Maybe it would be faster to go on the road, but he was in his underwear. He pulled on his shirt, realized he'd left the trousers behind, kept going. The lines of corn flashed past; a low place in the ground set him stumbling, but he recovered and ran on. When he saw the scarecrow wearing Grandmother Pinkerton's old bonnet, he was back on their farm, and then he was in the meadow. From a distance it looked just as he had left it, the cows grazing, Kaki pouncing in the grass. One of the calves was suckling her mother.

Ivy wasn't in the herd. He looked near the river, then ran back toward the barn and saw her high in the meadow, in the shade of a cottonwood tree. She was lying on her side and moaning; he should go for Keast. Then he saw something poking up from her, a big stick; she'd gotten caught on something. But when he reached her side he saw that it was a calf's hind leg. In a breech birth, Keast had taught him, both legs had to come out together.

He dropped beside her and tried to push the leg back in, but blood gushed out and Ivy bawled louder, her eyes rolled back in her head.

He sat on her back, as he had once when helping Keast, and felt the calf through her hide. It wasn't moving. But that was all right, he told himself, it wouldn't breathe until it had some air. He had to get the leg back in. He knelt on the ground again and pushed harder. Ivy made terrible sounds and blood poured out of her so he stopped, holding the calf's hoof in his hands, staring down at the muck of blood and manure, the spears of red grass.

"What the hell?" Father Pinkerton was there; Benji hadn't heard him come. "Where's Keast?"

Benji tried to say there wasn't time, but Father Pinkerton yanked him up by the collar. "You think you can birth a calf? Where are your trousers?"

Benji pointed down the stream.

"You just lost me twenty dollars, maybe more, on this calf, and the mother looks like a goner too. Why in Hades were you swimming when you were supposed to be watching?"

"*Okasan . . .*"

"Your mother's gone." Father Pinkerton gave him a shove. "She's as dead as these cows. Go get Keast and the Swede. I'll deal with you later."

Benji took off across the field, pressing his feet down hard on small rocks and anything else that hurt.

The Swede and Keast were in the house. Benji burst into the dining room and yelled at them. They didn't move. Everyone stared. Grand-mother Pinkerton was holding the gravy spoon in the air.

"Speak English, Benji," Mother Pinkerton said. "What's happened?"

He looked at his arm, smeared with blood. "Mama," he said, and everything went black.

Keast and Pinkerton and the Swede carried the dead cow and calf behind the barn. The Swede went to fetch shovels.

Pinkerton took a long pull on a flask of corn whiskey. "God damn that boy," he said.

"There was nothing I could have done," Keast said again.

"If he'd been watching you would have had the chance to try."

Keast shook his head. There was no use talking to Frank Pinkerton when he didn't care to listen.

They started digging. The sound of shovels doing this work was always the hardest part of it. He'd dug Isobel's grave himself.

When the hole was big enough, they laid in the cow and her unbirthed calf.

"There goes a fortune," Pinkerton said, as they started covering them with dirt.

"I'm sure the boy was doing his best," Keast said. "He loves the animals."

Pinkerton snorted. "Not enough to keep him from skylarking in the creek. He's caused us nothing but trouble." He held his shovel under one arm to take another slug from the flask.

Keast wanted to ask if he regretted bringing the boy with him from Japan. Instead, he said, "Would you have any objection, Pinkerton, if I occasionally took the boy with me on my late-afternoon rounds from time to time? Following the completion of his chores, of course."

"What in tarnation for?"

"He might learn some things useful to you here on the farm."

"If you're trying to spare him a licking, Keast, you're wasting your breath."

"It wasn't his fault." Keast dropped his shovel and began walking to the house. "You bred her to too large a bull."

Benji was sitting at the kitchen table, pale as a haint. There was an untouched stack of hotcakes before him. Old Mrs. Pinkerton was trying to persuade him to eat; Kate was busy at the stove.

"How you doing, fellow?" Keast asked as he sat down.

Benji said nothing.

"That calf was too big to come out," Keast said. "I couldn't have saved it or the mama."

Kate set a plate of hotcakes before him. Keast had no appetite, but he dug in, to encourage the boy.

"I killed them," Benji said in a small voice.

"You did not," Keast said. "Let us make this clear. The calf—"

Frank stumbled in through the door. He had a peeled switch in his hand and he reeked of whiskey. "Time to get this over with," he said, grabbing Benji's arm.

"No!" the women cried.

"The bull was too large," Keast said, rising from the table. "Wait . . . It wasn't . . ." but Pinkerton ignored him.

"You're lucky it's not a whip," Keast heard him say as he pulled Benji out the door. "If it were my father, you'd have a whip."

The next morning Keast came to collect Benji for a ride. "I felt in need of a companion," Keast said when they started down the road in his buggy. "I hope you don't object." He gave him a striped jawbreaker; Benji thanked him and put it in his pocket.

"What would you say to being my helper with the animals?" Keast asked. "After school and your chores, that is. I could pay you a little."

"Why?" Benji said.

"I don't have an assistant and I could use one."

"Okay," Benji said.

"What will you do with the money?"

"Buy a cow."

"Ho, now. You don't need to buy anyone a cow any more than I do. No human can save a hog from cholera or a horse from glanders or a heifer carrying an outsize calf."

"Okay." Benji was staring out at the cornfields, blinking—trying not to cry, Keast could tell.

They rode on a ways without speaking. Keast turned in to the cemetery of the Plum River church and stopped the buggy. Benji followed him through the grass, past the gravestones and cedar trees to the monument.

"This is where my beloved wife, Isobel, rests," Keast said. He showed Benji the picture near the top of the stone. "Our son lies here too," Keast said. "They perished in childbirth on June nineteenth, 1887." He took a handkerchief from his pocket and gently dusted the picture. "For years I scalded myself on account of their deaths, but this was only vanity. Sometimes there is nothing a human body can do on behalf of another creature, human or animal. Whether or not it is God's will, or only Nature's whim, it is a fact of existence."

"My mother died," Benji said.

"That's a hard thing for a young fellow." Keast put his arm around his shoulder.

"I have her picture."

"That's good. A picture can be a comfort."

"Don't tell anyone."

"I won't mention it. You can count on me."

Benji edged closer to Keast. "Was it an accident with Ivy?"

"Yes, it was Mother Nature's accident. Nothing about it was your fault."

Kate gave birth to a boy one morning in April 1900. At last she was a normal fecund woman who could please her husband.

"Darling," Frank said, kissing her and the baby—his name was Franklin—and thanked her again and again.

"He's beautiful, isn't he?" she said, even though he was no such thing—red-faced, with little bandy legs—but he would be.

Frank went to town to spread the news of his boy, and his mother arranged the pillows so Kate could sit up to nurse the baby.

The labor had been arduous—twenty-eight hours—and she was weary. The baby sucked hard at her breast, but the milk would not come. "Only because I'm tired," she said.

"Just relax, dear," Mrs. Pinkerton said, patting her arm, "and the milk will come."

Mrs. Pinkerton appeared often, with blancmange and aspics; sometimes Benji carried the tray. He liked to watch the baby and touch his tiny fingers, but Benji's presence made Kate nervous. She needed solitude to make the milk come.

Kate thought of the cows, how easily they let down, morning and night. She began to worry that her milk would never come. By the end of the second day, the baby was limp from hunger and crying. She felt the house in suspension, waiting. She imagined the long parlor below her an empty teat, and the kitchen a dark mouth.

Dr. McBride advised compresses for her breasts and said that if the milk did not come soon, the baby would need a wet nurse.

She began to cry. She cried and cried and then, at last, the milk let down. The baby sucked peacefully, making her breasts tingle, and when he was away from her, in his bassinet, her milk spilled out, wetting the front of her gown.

He was a sweet baby, healthy, with navy-blue eyes that wobbled in an effort to focus on her. She should be joyous, thanking God, but a heaviness settled into her. She didn't want to get up and lingered in bed, even though she needed to help her mother-in-law with the diapers and the other washing, the cooking, the cleaning. The thought of another layer of chores, the years of motherhood stretching before her, was enervating.

After his day in the fields, Frank rushed up the stairs to hold the baby. It wouldn't be long, he said, before Franklin was helping on the farm. The next child would be a boy too; should they name him Timothy, after Kate's father? Fine, Kate said; she was too exhausted to think about it.

The first night after Kate's convalescence, Frank eased into bed, extinguished the lamp, and lay close to her, caressing her arm, then touching her waist, her thigh. "We should start another one," he said.

"Not yet," she said, turning away from him. "I'm so tired."

The boys at school said people mated the same way animals did; they talked about it in the outhouse and compared their wieners. Jonas and Sam laughed at Benji's wiener, but Eli said that was because he was short and he'd do fine with a short girl. Eli, Jonas, and Sam let Benji watch in the woods while they rubbed themselves to see who could make jism the fastest. Benji couldn't do it, but Eli said that was okay, he was too young.

Benji spied on Mother Pinkerton behind the screen on bath night. In bed he thought about Father Pinkerton putting his wiener into her before Franklin was born and then he thought about Mama. Father Pinkerton had done that to her too.

And it was Father Pinkerton's fault that Mama was dead. She had said Papa-san didn't know about him yet and when he did he would be happy, but then he came to Nagasaki with Mother Pinkerton. It wasn't an accident with the sword. He had killed her himself because he was married to Mother Pinkerton.

After that it was hard to look at Father Pinkerton or talk to him. In the fields, when Benji walked behind him, he imagined sticking a pitchfork into his rear and knocking off his head with a baseball bat, smashing it like an Osage orange. The thoughts made his teeth hurt.

No one knew exactly when Benji's birthday was, but they celebrated it at the end of April. The year after Franklin was born, Father Pinkerton said he was going to take Benji to Galena on his eleventh birthday for a big surprise.

On the train they sat opposite each other. Benji stared out the window, ignoring Father Pinkerton's badgering him to guess what the surprise might be. It was probably nothing special. He thought about his real birthday. It could be any month, and all these years he'd lived through the day without knowing. He looked at Father Pinkerton's reflection in the window, his large ears, the nose that was like his. Maybe his birthday really was in April and Father Pinkerton didn't want to admit how he knew. Benji could ask him what month he'd left Nagasaki and then add nine months, but if he asked, Father Pinkerton would say, what did that have to do with the price of onions? And if he told him what, he'd get a whipping later.

Benji turned and looked at Father Pinkerton jouncing up and down in his seat. They stared at each other; Father Pinkerton looked away and looked back again.

"What's got into you?" he said. "I took a day from the fields to give you a good time, and you look about as pleased as a mule eating briars. Shall we get on back home?"

"No," Benji said. "I'm just thinking about something at school."

"You have a girl already?" Father Pinkerton grinned. "When I was your age I had a girl."

Benji looked back out the window and imagined asking him how many girls he'd had in Japan. If he said none, Benji would kick him in the stomach.

"I hope you're looking forward to your surprise," Father Pinkerton said.

"Yes," Benji said. "Thank you."

In Galena, they walked with a crowd of other people from the train station down a road that led along the river into the country.

Ahead, Benji saw a tent—maybe one of those religious tents, he thought, but then he heard the jaunty music. "A circus," he said. The circus he'd seen once in Stockton had smelled bad, and the freak show was fake.

"Not just any circus," Frank said. "It's Japanese."

"Japanese?" Benji felt a jolt of excitement.

"Yes, sir, all the way from Nippon."

"The people are Japanese?"

Frank laughed. "I knew you'd like it," he said.

Benji ran toward the tent, his heart thudding. The man taking tickets wasn't Japanese, but there was a billboard that said SATO AND SONS' JAPANESE CIRCUS. Benji tried to look inside the tent, but the ticket seller pushed him back.

When Frank got there, they went inside, into the odor of mildew and popcorn. The tent didn't have a top; there was an irregular circle of blue sky instead.

The front seats were taken, so they sat halfway up a rickety tier of benches. A bald man in a kimono was sweeping the ring with a large broom. A Japanese man. Benji could hardly stay in his seat.

The ringmaster was an American in spangled clothes and a tall hat. Benji didn't listen to him, because right then a line of horses trotted out, a man standing balanced on each one. They were all Japanese, with dark hair and black eyes, just like he wanted to look. His heart was going so fast he could hardly breathe. As the horses went around the ring, the men did somersaults on the horses' backs, then leapt off and back up again. Benji imagined doing that on one of the horses at home. If he practiced in the pasture, it wouldn't hurt so much to fall off.

There were jugglers and contortionists next, then the trapeze artists. "Ladies and gentlemen," the ringmaster bellowed. "Welcome the Elixir of the East, the Orangutans of the Orient, Soonayo and Sachi. For this performance only—I repeat, for this performance only—these daredevils of the ether will perform without a net." There was loud drumming as the man and woman scaled the rope to the high wire. They stepped onto it and bowed in a way that Benji remembered, first in one direction, then the other. As they went across the wire together, the man skipped like a child and pretended to fall, making the audience gasp, but Benji knew he wouldn't fall. He was strong; he was Japanese. The woman had long, gleaming black hair, the prettiest woman Benji had ever seen. He read her name in the program—Sachiko; the man was Tsuneo. Soonayo, he remembered the man saying. He whispered it to himself, looking at how the name was spelled.

They climbed higher up. Tsuneo swung out on a trapeze, then Sachiko leapt into the air and caught his legs. The crowd's cheers faded as Benji watched them swing like a pendulum, their shadow moving back and forth on the surface of the ring.

There were clowns—one with a blond wig who made the audience laugh. Benji hated them for thinking a blond Japanese was funny. Next was a lion tamer, then a snake handler, but Benji kept thinking about

Tsuneo and Sachi. At the end, all the performers came out and began to walk around the ring, bowing. Benji ran down the steps and wedged himself in front of a crowd of tall men, where Frank couldn't find him.

Tsuneo appeared before him. Up close, he looked older than Benji had imagined, with lines at the corners of his eyes. "I'm from Japan," Benji said, pointing to himself. "Nippon."

Tsuneo shook his head. "No English," he said.

"Nagasaki?" Benji said, but he had moved on.

Sachiko was next. "Nagasaki?" he said to her, and she shook her head but said something in Japanese that sounded like music. She bowed and was gone.

Going home, the train was more crowded. Benji looked out at the fields and thought about Tsuneo. He wished Tsuneo was his father.

"Did you like it?" Father Pinkerton said. "The tickets were expensive, and I took a day off planting."

Benji stared at him. Father Pinkerton came and went in his vision. "Why did you adopt me when you're already my father?" he said.

Father Pinkerton's face got red, and he gripped his seat as if he were about to fall off. "I was not already your father."

"I used to call you Papa-san."

"That was to make you feel at home."

"Why do I look like you?"

"Be quiet," he hissed, glancing across the aisle. A man who had been watching them retreated behind his newspaper; a woman in a feather hat continued to gaze at them through an eyeglass on a stick.

"I could prove it," Benji said.

"What are you talking about?"

Benji looked back out the window and closed his ears against Father Pinkerton's angry whispers. They passed a herd of cattle, a barn, a woman in a sunbonnet chopping weeds. He couldn't show him the picture, because he would tear it up.

"You killed her," Benji said, his heart racing like the train. The landscape became a blur.

Father Pinkerton jerked him up and pulled him to the end of the train car. They stood between the cars on metal plates that bucked and scraped against each other. "Now, you listen here." He took Benji by the shoulders. "I didn't want to tell you, but this is the truth: She killed herself. Hara-kiri, they call it. It's considered noble in Japan."

"No!" Benji shook his head until he was dizzy. "She wouldn't do that, she wouldn't leave me."

"She left so you could have a better life in America."

"I hate you," Benji yelled. "I hate America."

Father Pinkerton raised his hand, dropped it. "Ungrateful little bastard," he said, and went back into the train car.

Benji burned Father Pinkerton from his mind. He would never think of him as his father again. He would call him Father Pinkerton, but he wouldn't mean it. He stood balancing on the platform without holding on, like the Japanese on their horses. Maybe he would fall and maybe he wouldn't.

For three days after the circus there was heavy rain. Frank was late planting—as his mother had reminded him several times—so he set out to the fields the first fair morning and guided the Percherons through thick mud with the plow. Given his luck, there would be a dry spell after he dropped the seeds. Farming was like being at sea: So much depended on the fickle weather.

Once the chill of early morning lifted, the sun was warm. The fields would dry out in a day or two; maybe he should wait, he thought, but pushed on, struggling to keep the plow at the proper angle. After he finished one row, he paused to take a breath and turned the Percherons in the opposite direction. As he went on, pulled by the powerful horses, his mind wandered to Sachiko, her glowing face and muscular legs, the way she arched her back when she let go of the trapeze and reached for her partner. Tsuneo was surely her partner in all ways.

Butterfly was smaller than Sachiko, more delicate. She would have a filmy multicolored costume, to suggest a butterfly. He could see her floating through the air toward him. Later, in the circus wagon, they would lie together, he slipping into her quietly so the others wouldn't hear.

"Butterfly is dead, you fool," he cried aloud. All around him stretched the empty fields and the merciless sky.

The plow was listing to one side. He stopped the horses and jumped down to adjust the trace chains on the off-side Percheron, then slapped its flank. The horses began to move before he got behind the plow, before he could think, and the point of the plow ran over his foot, cutting through the boot and his flesh.

"Whoa!" he screamed. The horses stopped and waited. He looked down at the boot, already leaking blood. Not fit to be a farmer, his father had always said. The pain was searing, but he climbed back on the seat and worked the ground to the end of the row, then turned the horses back toward the barn. He put the horses in their stalls and went hobbling to the house, calling for Kate.

It was a deep, nasty wound, with black dirt embedded in the flesh. Dr. McBride was summoned; he cleaned and bandaged the cut, ordered Frank to keep his foot elevated. Kate was to bathe the wound every few hours, to guard against infection. No one mentioned lockjaw, but the possibility hung in the air.

For days, Frank lay on their bed, his swollen foot throbbing. Perhaps he would lose the foot; perhaps it was God's punishment. Sharpless had said he was callous with Butterfly, that her death was his fault. Now here he was with her son, but, like a Judas, he'd denied him. He shifted in the bed, closed his eyes, and tried to pray. He was in a thicket of sin and consequence.

One afternoon, when Kate came in with bouillon and toast and felt his forehead, Frank said, "You're an angel. I don't deserve you." He clutched her hand. "Don't ever leave me."

"Don't be silly." She bent down, kissed his forehead. She smelled of roses.

When Dr. McBride came later that week to change the bandage, Frank imagined telling him the whole story, the reasons for his injury, his history beginning with the day he'd met Butterfly, but he said nothing as the doctor took ointment and gauze from his bag and wrapped his foot again. "You're going to be fine, Frank," he said.

But he was not fine.

Not long after the circus, Benji dreamed that he looked at the picture and it was blank. He woke up, his heart thudding, lit the candle, and took the picture from the kimono pocket. She was still there gazing at him. He thought of the blood, her closed eyes. "Why did you do it?" he shouted. "What about me?"

He shoved the picture back in the kimono pocket and put it on the floor of the closet. He would never look at it again.

But the next day at school, he worried that Mother Pinkerton would find the picture and show it to Father Pinkerton, who would throw it in the kitchen stove.

He told Miss Ladu he was sick and ran home to put the kimono back under his mattress. The following day at school he worried that they might turn the mattress for spring cleaning and the kimono would fall out and the picture too, because he'd never sewed back the top of the pocket.

That night he took a needle and thread from Mother Pinkerton's sewing room and fixed the pocket, but he couldn't stop thinking about other things that could happen when he was gone. The house could catch fire like the Olsens' barn and he would never see her face again. Or a tornado could carry her away.

He remembered that four was a bad number in Japanese, the same word as for death; if he saw four of anything—four cows standing together, four birds in a tree, four pieces of bread on the table—he had to take out the kimono and look at the picture. He came home sick from school so often that they had Dr. McBride take a look at him, but the doctor said he was as sound as an American dollar.

It was a Sunday afternoon in June. Though the air was sunny, a soft rain rustled the leaves outside Keast's window. If Isobel were here, they would go for a drive and look for a rainbow, but somehow he couldn't stir from his chair. He was content enough—church was over, and an afternoon of leisure lay before him. He was whittling aimlessly, waiting to see what form would emerge from the block of cherry he was working. A fawn, perhaps. Maybe he would give it to Miss Ladu, though he didn't know what Isobel would think about that.

There was a knock on the door. Benji. "Now, here's a welcome surprise," Keast said. "On your way home from church?"

Benji shook his head.

Keast asked if he'd like to go for a drive, but the boy shook his head again. They went out to the back balcony of the boardinghouse and sat down in rocking chairs.

Benji looked skittish, glancing at old Mr. Green at the end of the porch. Clearly something was troubling the boy. Keast took up his whittling again, to give him time. Benji had grown into a fine specimen of a boy—still short for his age, but that was natural given his race. He looked pure Japanese when he wore a cap, as today, with his light hair pushed out of sight. Miss Ladu said he was a wonder in school, already on the third reader, and he'd written a remarkable report on slavery and abolition. The only trouble was, he was shy and made few friends. Keast had found that, if not pressed, he would occasionally open up and talk a mile a minute. Sometimes on their drives to visit the animals, Benji would tell him about school, a girl named Flora, and his ambition to go to Japan.

The boy sat still in his rocker. Mr. Green got up and limped inside.

"Something on your mind?" Keast asked him.

Benji reached into his pocket, pulled out a photograph, and handed it to Keast quick, as if it were on fire. "It's a secret," he said.

Keast put on his reading glasses to look at the picture. "By golly," he couldn't help saying. There was Pinkerton, sitting next to a Japanese woman in her native dress; she was standing, looking straight into the camera. The photograph was scored with vertical creases and a small nib was missing in one corner.

"Your mother?" Keast said.

"Yes."

"And your father." He looked at Benji; the boy nodded.

Keast refrained from saying he'd thought as much.

"No one at my house can see it," Benji said.

"I understand," Keast said, nodding.

"My mother killed herself."

The block of wood Keast was holding between his knees fell onto the floor. He stared at the boy. Benji was gazing out at the garden as calmly as if he'd just made a comment about the weather. His hands were in fists, though.

"I saw her," Benji added, and turned to look at him. They sat in silence for a moment; Keast could feel the confiding and the receiving settle in.

"You're some boy," Keast said, "to have come through all that." He looked at the picture: She was a pretty woman with something sad about her face. He wanted to ask about the circumstances, but perhaps Benji had said all he could. Isobel would have known how to comfort him.

"There's writing on the back," Benji said.

Keast turned it over. Lines of chicken tracks.

"I wish I could read it," the boy said.

"Probably their names and a date."

The boy sat somberly looking at the writing, then his face brightened. "With her whole name, maybe I can find her family someday."

"I bet you can."

"Where can I keep it?"

Keast thought a minute. "The store and the bank are closed. Let me see what I can rustle up."

Keast went into his room and from the bottom drawer of his dresser took out a blue tin box filled with mementos of Isobel: some photographs, an onyx ring, two handkerchiefs, a lace collar, and, in an envelope, a lock of her beautiful black hair. He took the things out of the box and put them back in the drawer, carefully wrapped in a sweater. Tomorrow he would buy a new box. The key was in a dish at the top of the dresser. He went back to the porch, laid the box in Benji's lap, and put the key in his hand.

"This should do," he said.

"Thank you." Benji carefully laid the picture in the box and stared at it.

"Looks kind of lonesome in there, doesn't it?" Keast said. He went inside to his desk and brought back an empty soap tin that had belonged to Isobel. A picture of flowers—lilies of the valley—adorned the cover. Benji laid the picture in the tin and put it in the box, then took from his other pocket a small leather pouch. "Money," he said. "I saved it from my allowance. Someday I'll go to Japan and put her picture on her gravestone."

"Well," Keast said. "That's a noble thing. It's a long way, but I'm sure you can make it." He watched as Benji laid the pouch into the box with the picture and locked it.

They talked about where to keep the box. It could be found at his house, Benji said, and he didn't want to bury it in the ground. If he put it in the bank, someone might mention it to his father. Keast said he'd be honored to keep it if Benji would trust him. They put the box in the bottom drawer of the desk, and Benji kept the key.

As Keast drove Benji home, he kept glancing at the boy, thinking of all the sorrow he had endured. Too much sorrow could deform the spirit.

After he dropped Benji off at the farm, Keast started toward the cemetery for his weekly visit to Isobel, but at the fork he turned his horse and headed back to the boardinghouse. It was almost dinnertime, and Miss Ladu would be there, pretty as a sunflower in her seat across the table.

It was the end of the day, almost evening, when Keast went to the Pinkerton farm a few days later. Tied to the back of his buggy, trotting along at a fine gait, was a black colt with a white blaze on his nose—four years old and broke to the saddle, though he hadn't been ridden much yet.

Keast spotted Frank and the Swede and Benji at the pump, washing up for supper. Frank turned to look, scratched his head, said something Keast couldn't hear.

Keast was nervous. He should have asked Frank first but had been afraid he'd say no. He hadn't been honorable in that. He did know there was an empty stall and plenty of hay and oats for another animal. Frank couldn't object on those grounds.

Benji came running toward him.

"Look behind me," Keast said. "He's yours."

Benji let out such a yell that Keast was surprised the roof didn't lift off the house. The horses shied to the left.

"Can I ride him?" Benji said. But he was already on his back.

"Be careful." Keast got out of the buggy, adjusted the stirrups, and untied the reins. "He's not experienced."

The pony bucked a couple of times, then tore off down the road. Benji stayed on as if he were glued there, reared back like an Injun.

Frank had come over to the buggy. He stared down the road. "What in thunder is that?"

"A friend of mine had a colt he wanted to get rid of," Keast said. "He's healthy—I don't expect he'll be much trouble." No more than your "orphan" has been, Keast wanted to add, but held his tongue.

He named the colt Kuro, which meant black, one of the few Japanese words he remembered. He liked to ride bareback, Kuro's muscles flexing beneath him, their sweat mixed together. He was Tsuneo, and Kuro was a Japanese horse, his mane and tail flying as they galloped down the roads.

Sometimes he pretended he was riding all the way to Japan, where he would find the house he had lived in and his mother's family, and sometimes he rode into the past, before she died, when she'd say, "Wake up, Benji," but it didn't matter which as he soared past the blur of golden fields, his mind floating, riding into the life that was coming to meet him.

One year passed, then two, and there were no more children, not even a false start. Kate blamed herself, for resenting Franklin at first; this was God's judgment upon her. It wouldn't have mattered to her; Franklin was enough—such a beautiful, affectionate child—but Frank needed more boys for the farm.

And he was unhappy. Ever since she'd known him, Frank had enjoyed the occasional drink—a sup, he called it, of bourbon or rum, a habit from his days at sea. His mother didn't approve, but Kate had found the smell of whiskey manly, and at first it had made him expansive and more affectionate. But lately he often came to bed reeking of liquor and—she couldn't help it—she turned away from him.

One fall evening he came from the threshing red-eyed and unsteady. During supper he snapped at Franklin and Benji for playing at the table; he threatened to whip them both.

Kate sent the children outside with their dessert. "This is too much, Frank. You can't work in an inebriated condition. You might lose a foot next time."

His mother agreed; she suggested prayer and more regular attendance at church.

He rose abruptly and climbed the stairs to his office. A few minutes later, Kate followed him.

She found him at his desk, staring out at the fields. He hates farming, she thought, and he wishes he had never married me. She felt a spike of tenderness as she touched his face, his creased neck. He took her hand.

"I'm not the right wife for you," she said. "I'm sorry."

He stood and embraced her, enveloping her in the odor of whiskey. "You're the perfect wife," he said. "I adore you."

"Please stop drinking so much," she said.

He murmured something that sounded like assent.

That night he entered her and, to their astonishment, she became pregnant, a pregnancy that held. She gave birth, though with much difficulty, on a rainy June evening in 1904, to a seven-pound girl named Mary Virginia, after Frank's mother. Frank celebrated with a magnum of champagne—a gift from the Moores—toasting his daughter, Kate, Franklin, Benji, his mother, the Swede, the Moores, the Cases, the cows, the Percherons, Daisy, Kuro, and the next child, who would most certainly be a boy.

Eli and Jonas often came home with Benji, the three of them sitting at the kitchen table near the stove while Benji helped them with long division and fractions. Benji wished Grandmother Pinkerton would leave so they could keep talking about girls—Eli was sweet on Helen, and Benji wanted to ask if they thought Flora favored him—but she stayed in the kitchen cooking and washing pans that didn't need washing and watching them work. "My, my," she sometimes said, looking down at Benji's paper full of figures. "We didn't know so much in my day."

After his friends left, Benji brought in coal for the stoves, did the milking, and fed and curried the horses. After supper, he told Franklin a story, an ongoing saga he'd made up for his brother about two samurai boys, one Japanese, one American, then went to his room to study. It was the best time of the day, at the desk beside his stove, Kaki in his lap or curled at his feet, studying books that carried him away from the farm. By the time he was fourteen, he was ahead of everyone else in arithmetic and reading and knew the history books almost by heart. He liked American history, especially the Indians and the Gold Rush, but was more drawn to other civilizations—the pharaohs and pyramids of Egypt, the Spartans of Greece, the Roman Empire.

There was nothing about Japan in the school history text, so Miss Ladu ordered a book on the history of Japan and he learned about the lords and samurai who used to rule Japan, and about Commodore Perry, who sailed his black ships into the bay of Tokyo and made Japan trade with America. When Japan began a war against Russia that September, he kept up with it in the newspapers—excited that his small country was fighting the Russian bullies. Miss Ladu had him present a report on the war, which he illustrated with a map showing Port Arthur, where the surprise attack had been, and the sites of the other battles.

"I liked your report," Flora said at recess. "I think you're very intelligent." She looked straight into his eyes and smiled. She had a chicken pox scar at one side of her mouth, but on her it was pretty.

When class started again, he couldn't pay attention but sat looking at Flora two rows ahead of him: her thick braids, the slightly crooked part in her hair, and the little bones in her neck when she bent over her work. She was left-handed and wrote with her left arm curved around the top of the desk; all her letters slanted backward. Miss Ladu had tried to make her use her right hand, but it was hard and she made a lot of blots. Sometimes, when she was supposed to be writing, she put her pen on her desk and sat with her head bowed. Today, though, she was writing, very slowly.

After school Benji caught up with Flora as she was walking down the road to Morseville. She was wearing orange button shoes and a coat that was too big for her. "I have to go to the store for my grandmother," he said.

"That's nice." She smiled at him. "You're a considerate boy."

He felt like skipping. "You're considerate too. I'm sorry you're left-handed."

She looked at him, startled.

"Because it's more trouble for you, I mean."

She didn't say anything. He kicked a rock. Now she wouldn't think he was smart.

"Do you like long division?" he asked. Her class had just started on it.

"No," she said.

"I could help you with it. Mathematics is my best subject, after history."

"Thank you," she said. There was a silence, just the sound of their feet on the road. He couldn't think what to say.

"Is it nice in Japan?" she asked.

"Yes, but the girls aren't as pretty."

She looked down at the road, but she was smiling.

He jammed his hands in his pockets and, to keep from grinning too much, began to whistle.

When they got to the corner a block from her house, she said, "I'll see you tomorrow." She didn't say, "at school," so maybe that meant he could walk her home again.

But the next day, when they were talking at recess, Marvin came up behind them and started making kissing noises, and after school they went their separate ways.

Sometimes on the weekends he went into Morseville and walked past her house, hoping she'd come out. It was a gaunt house, painted yellow, with a shed out back where her father made coffins. Her father was a sour-looking man with a glass eye, and because he looked a little peculiar and because he made coffins, the boys at school made up mean stories about him—how he sometimes measured the coffins wrong and had to cut off the dead person's feet. Marvin swore that he'd seen blood leaking out of a coffin at a funeral. Benji wondered if Flora had guessed about the stories; if he heard Marvin tell another one, he'd beat him up.

In the spring Miss Ladu had a few students stay after school one day to recite their pieces for the end of the year. After Benji practiced his memorized report on Japan—expanded to include Confucianism and the primitive Ainu people of Hokkaido—he sat and waited for Flora to say her lines from *Hiawatha*. They left together and, since there was no one else around, he walked with her to Morseville.

She asked how long he'd lived in Japan.

"Until I was five," he said. "My mother died, but I'm not an orphan. It's a secret—don't tell anyone."

"I'd never tell." She looked at him solemnly. "I hate my stepmother," she said.

"I hate mine too," he said, even though it wasn't quite true.

Again they said goodbye a block away from her house; she didn't say, but he guessed her parents would disapprove of her walking with a boy, especially a Japanese. After supper, he drew a picture of her and put it in the bottom drawer of his desk, beneath his arithmetic papers, where no one would find it.

At elocution day, Benji gave his report to a crowd of parents and townspeople. He was nervous, so he pretended to be talking just to Flora, who looked at him intently, nodding. She had on a soft-looking brown dress, and her hair was loose from the braids.

When the program was over, Benji wandered through the crowd, looking everywhere, but he couldn't find her; her father must have taken her home. He tried to look as if he didn't care.

The family and Keast came to congratulate him. Franklin pulled at Benji's shirt; Benji picked him up. "You were the best," Franklin said.

"Excellent," Mother Pinkerton said. "We were amazed."

"I wasn't," Grandmother Pinkerton said. "I always knew he was smart."

Father Pinkerton shook his hand, slipping a silver dollar into Benji's palm. Benji stared at it, the most money he'd ever had at once. "You're a scholar now, aren't you? Don't get too biggety."

"A scholar indeed," Miss Ladu said, joining them. "He could be a teacher in a few years if he wanted to, or go to a university." She and Keast exchanged glances; Benji could tell they'd talked about it.

"A university," Benji said.

"Yes—you could study anything you wanted to. A Japanese boy graduated first in his class at Yale a few years ago."

"Sounds expensive," Father Pinkerton said.

"There are other schools," Miss Ladu said, "right here in Illinois. You might win a scholarship."

At home, Benji lay on his bed, pretending Flora had heard the conversation. She would think him all the more intelligent if he went to a university, and maybe her father would let him marry her then. Maybe she'd like to go with him to Japan. He'd get rich and they could have houses in both places.

The next Saturday, when Keast took Benji on his rounds, Keast asked what he might like to study.

"I don't know. Mathematics, maybe. I want to get rich and go to Japan. Do you think I can get rich before I go to Japan?"

"Not with mathematics—as a businessman, maybe. But I believe you can do anything you set your mind to."

"Could I marry an American girl?"

Keast smiled. "You've got a sweetheart?"

"No—I was just wondering."

Keast was silent for a while before he said, "Some people might disagree, but I don't see why not. Isobel was part Injun, and my mother never minded."

Benji looked at Keast's rough face, the stains on his coat. He hadn't thought of Keast having a mother.

"I bet your mother was nice."

"A noble woman," he said. "After my father died, my mother raised us three children on her own." He looked at Benji. "We all have our fortune and misfortune," he said. "When you come up against fortune, don't let it pass you by. It might not come again."

For Benji's fifteenth birthday, Keast gave him a globe on a stand like the one in the schoolroom: the seas white, the continents and islands various shades of brown, the mountain ranges slightly raised. Benji put the globe beside his desk and traced his path across America and the Pacific Ocean over and over. Nagasaki was on the far side of Kyushu, at the tip of the carp's head.

He asked Father Pinkerton for the Japanese–English dictionary he'd taken to school when they went to visit that first day. Father Pinkerton claimed not to know where it was, but one morning when he'd gone to buy some farm equipment, Benji looked for it in his study. He found it in the cupboard, beneath a stack of ship's logs, old seed catalogues, and a musty tartan blanket. It was a large black book with thin pages that smelled slightly of spice. As he flipped through the pages, a butterfly wing fell out, blue and black with patterns that looked like eyes. He picked it up with care, but it was old and fragile and came apart in his fingers. Maybe Father Pinkerton had been with his mother when he found it. Damn him. He sliced cuts in the tartan blanket with his penknife. If Father Pinkerton asked, he'd say it must have been moths.

Keast let him keep the dictionary at the boardinghouse. On weekend afternoons, after he'd finished his chores, Benji took a notebook and sat on the balcony outside Keast's room, writing Japanese words and their definitions in English. It was disappointing that there were no Japanese characters in the book for him to compare with the writing on the picture. The dictionary—with the words spelled out in Roman letters—was obviously for tourists. But if he studied the words in the notebook every day, he would be able to make himself understood in Japan. When a few words came back to him—*neko* for cat, *gohan* for rice—he began to feel Japanese.

It was his country that was winning the war against Russia, and people in Plum River and Stockton respected him for it. After Benji began—at Keast's recommendation—working part-time in Red Olsen's store, some of the customers, even grown men, talked to him about the fight in the Far East. They said if Japan didn't keep Korea open, it would be bad for American exports, including agriculture. One day, when Father Pinkerton came by the store, he joined in the conversation at the butcher counter, bragging about the import/export business he'd had in Nagasaki, suggesting that the Japanese ships wouldn't be winning if it wasn't for training by the American and British navies. He'd been an instructor himself, he said, when he was in Nagasaki.

Later that evening, when they were walking up from the barn, Benji asked Father Pinkerton to tell him more about the naval training, but he shook his head and said that the details were secret.

"When you were doing the training—was that why you lived in Nagasaki with my mother?"

Father Pinkerton stared at him. "I don't know what you're talking about," he said.

The cleared space around the Pinkerton farmhouse, though large, had for vegetation only trees—including the oaks, apples, and a stately walnut Frank's grandfather had planted—and a thin circle of daisies and sweet william around a neglected birdbath.

When Kate had difficulty falling asleep after an exhausting day of housework and tending to Mary Virginia and Franklin, she'd summon up images of her mother's garden in Galena: in summertime, a sea of flowers on which the house seemed to float. In the backyard was a bed of white flowering plants, designed to show to best advantage in the moonlight from the bedrooms and the sleeping porch at the back of the house. She remembered being put to bed at dusk as a child, in the years before they went to China, how the delicate fragrances wafting up to her room became entwined in her sleep. It would bring her peace, she had decided that spring, to make a garden here.

With the help of a colored boy who worked as a handyman in Galena, Kate transplanted from her mother's house a variety of flowers. By that summer, white lilacs, peonies, fragrant flowering stock, and snowball bushes formed the white garden in back of the house. Coneflowers, larkspur, hollyhocks, and snapdragons flourished along the iron picket fence and near the two-seated glider beside the well. In fall, a variety of asters made a meadow of the yard, along with the goldenrod Kate had planted in spite of her mother-in-law's insistence that goldenrod was a common weed and made her nose itch.

Kate's garden attracted an alarming number of butterflies: black swal-

lowtails with yellow markings that flitted from flower to flower, tortoise-
shells, and an occasional dazzling blue Diana.

Frank was in his office on the Sunday afternoon in early autumn when
the great river of monarch butterflies poured down around the house. He
glanced out the west window, where only minutes before there had been
nothing but the familiar limbs of the bur oak. The branches were covered
with orange butterflies—perched on the surfaces of leaves, hanging from
the smallest twigs. The wings were veined and rimmed with black, with a
pattern of white dots about the edges; those that caught the light were
iridescent and silken as a kimono. The tree was alive with their movement. He thought of Cio-Cio's bent legs opening and closing and opening, inviting him in. His heart began to race.

He edged past his desk to stand by the window. The ground was as
thick with orange butterflies as if they had been painted there. They lined
the iron fence and clung to the milkweed in the ditches; on the dirt road,
clumps of butterflies flickered in puddles from last night's rain. The air
congealed; he could hardly breathe. He pushed up the window and
leaned forward to shake the closest branch of the tree. Butterflies swirled
upward, resettled. One lit on his arm. He shook it off, slammed the window down, and, holding on to the desk, returned to his chair, where he
sat slumped, head in his hands.

A butterfly was in the room. It swooped before him, inches from his face,
then flitted to the ceiling and down to the filing cabinet. He turned, watching it, feeling he would faint. When the butterfly returned to him and sat
pulsing on the ledger, he swiped at it, hardly noticing as ink spilled across
the page and the edge of the desk, soaking into the leg of his trousers.

Benji was returning from Keast's place when he noticed butterflies floating around him, dipping, dropping onto fences and the leaves of trees.
He held out his arm; an orange-and-black butterfly perched on his
wrist—a slight tickle. His skin aflame, he reined in Kuro. Butterflies filled
the air as far as he could see, like weather in a dream.

* * *

At supper, Grandmother Pinkerton said the butterflies were monarchs migrating south. "I haven't seen them since the year Elmer broke his leg. Usually they pass through east of here."

"I hate them," Kate said.

When Frank came late to the table, smelling of whiskey, Kate rose, saying she had a headache, and went upstairs. Frank ate quickly, ignoring Franklin and Mary Virginia's bickering. He asked Benji if he'd done the milking; when Benji said no, he was going to do it soon, Frank said never mind, jammed on a straw hat, and went to the barn.

That night in bed, as Kate slept beside him, Frank cursed the butterflies coating the roof of the house, the ground, the trees. His chest felt odd, as though thousands of tiny wings were fluttering beneath his skin.

He pushed back the covers and went downstairs, out the front door. At first, in the light of the rising moon, he could see nothing but the bulk of the house and the dark trees. He touched a clematis vine on the fence; butterflies rushed up at him. He walked down the road toward the barn, sensing them around him, in the ditches and the meadow grass. They seemed to give off a faint perfume in the night, a dusty sweetness. It was Cio-Cio's revenge; she was haunting him still.

In the barn he leaned against a stall door, opened another bottle of corn whiskey, and drank until the sensation in his chest was gone.

In bed again, he fumbled for Kate.

"No," she said. "You're thinking of her."

He yanked up her nightgown.

"Stop." She pushed at him.

He straddled her, pinning down her arms, and forced himself inside.

When he lay spent, he heard her weeping. He reached for her. "What's wrong? I didn't—" but she flung his hand away. "I'm your husband," he said.

As he fell into sleep, he felt the mattress shift and then heard, faint, as if from a great distance, a door click shut.

Benji woke from a dream he could not remember. It was nearly dawn, the sky beginning to go gray. He went outside, to the back garden where dark triangles of butterflies slept in the flowers, and knelt among them. His mother hadn't wanted to leave him, but she had wanted him to come to America. She had put the picture in the kimono so he would know that. When he closed his eyes he could hear her singing—*"Sakura, sakura,"* a song about cherry blossoms, he remembered—and he remembered walking hand in hand with her along the edge of the bay as she sang, her voice as pure and clear as water.

Keast's room was stifling, with no cross breeze through the windows on the warm Indian summer night, and he lay sleepless and sweating in a bed made uncomfortable by his restlessness. He hadn't had a spell of insomnia since the year after the deaths of Isobel and Horatio. This time the cause was desire rather than grief, but the two states were not dissimilar, Keast thought, as he pitched from side to side, battling his mattress. Longing was a torturous affair, no matter what the cause.

A few evenings ago after supper, as he and Lena sat on the porch looking out at butterflies in the garden, she had touched his bare wrist. He couldn't recall what she'd been saying, but his skin still held the memory of her light touch. Could be it was a message, though likely not. She had taken his arm several times, when alighting from the buggy. And she was a woman who had the general impulse to touch, he had noticed that, smoothing her skirt or her hair, running her hand over a page she was about to read. Still, he should have been man enough to cover her hand with his, lift it to his lips.

He was a coward, and a fool, to entertain the slightest notion that a woman twenty-five years younger than himself might find him suitable as a mate. Even for a woman closer to his age, he would be no prize, with his belly that would press into her, his lumpish, lined face, his tendencies to catarrh and boils, his sour breath. He snored, and his feet were unsightly, with bulging yellow nails and bunions that had to be soaked in vinegar water each night. But he had over the years put aside a tidy sum; he could provide her a comfortable home and respite from her work. Though she might want to continue teaching; she had a passion for it, one of her finest traits. Her devotion to young Benjamin was touching to witness.

She likely had a passion for life too—he had often thought so—with her strong young body, the firm breasts that it hurt him to think of. Smaller breasts than Isobel's, upturned, he imagined, and milky flanks. He touched himself, removed his hand, and gripped the brass bedstead. It would only increase his longing, and afterward he always felt a twinge regarding Isobel, even though he knew she would bear him no grudge.

Since Lena had touched his hand, he had evaded her, staying out on his rounds long past the usual hour and reading the newspaper at breakfast. He had likely missed his opportunity, not taking her hand, not speaking for all this time. If she had meant what he hoped, she would think him disinterested or timid. Tomorrow she was going to Joliet to visit her mother, not to return for a week, he had heard her telling Mrs. Bosley in the hall. Her voice had sounded so cheerful and full of music that he wondered if a young man waited along with her mother. On several occasions she had alluded to a friend in Joliet.

In the distance was the long throaty call of a horned owl, a sound lonely as a train whistle, and, farther off, a faint response. There would be love somewhere this night in Morseville.

He thrashed out of bed and went to look out the front window. Across the street, the saloon was closed; a drunk Injun lay on the board sidewalk. Otherwise the town was empty, the rutted street and closed shops a desolate scene in the sharp light of the moon, deep shadows in the alley beside the dry-goods store. If she should leave this place, he could not bear it.

He struck his hand against the window sash. He should ask to drive her to the train station. By golly, he would. She would have made other arrangements, but should she be willing to alter them, that would be a sign. He swallowed down his queasiness and sat at his desk, now afraid to sleep, lest he should miss her departure.

She wore a dress that favored her green eyes, and she smelled of lemon soap. Mrs. Bosley had planned to take her to the train station, but Lena seemed pleased by the new arrangement. He wished he had thought to wear his new shirt. At least the buggy was presentable.

The ride to Stockton was short, just under three miles, but he lengthened it, taking the back road. They were mostly silent. She mentioned a book she was reading. Her profile was lovely in the dappled light as they rode beneath the trees.

He had loaded three valises into the back of the buggy, surely more than necessary for a week.

"Will you see your friend, then?" he said.

"I have many friends in Joliet," she said. "It's my birthplace."

"They're fortunate to know you." What a thing to say.

"You look weary, Horatio. I hope you'll take care of yourself."

He glanced at her hands, folded in her lap, and pulled the horse to a halt. His heart was going like a bellows at Christmas. There were purple asters in the ditch. He sprang out and picked a handful, stood by her, and presented them with a bow.

She looked astonished. It was hopeless. But he had begun.

"Lena—would you consider an old man for a suitor?"

She met his eyes steadily. "I don't think of you as old, Horatio."

Sweat rolled into his left eye. He took out his handkerchief—none too clean—and wiped his face.

"Do you mean," he said, "a possibility?"

"Yes." She smiled and swung her legs over the side of the buggy. He lifted her down and kissed her.

He was in a daze for the remainder of the ride, holding her hand until they came into Stockton, seeing her onto the train, a proud man, a new man, blowing a kiss to her at the window, watching the handsome train recede. As he rode back toward Morseville by the same road that had altered his life, the world seemed newly alive and he was part of it. He skirted the town and, before starting on his rounds, drove out to the cemetery to tell Isobel.

"You always were impulsive, Kate," her mother said, embracing her. "But of course I'm delighted. I hope you're planning a long stay. What about the children?"

"They'll manage," Kate said. "Frank's mother will be glad to have free rein."

They sat in the parlor with tea and cookies. The room hadn't changed over the years, each piece of dark furniture in the same place where it had first been planted: the brown velvet love seat on which her mother perched, crocheting a doily, chairs of punishing horsehair, end tables cluttered with memorabilia from China. A photograph of her father in his clerical collar looked benignly upon them from the mantel. In one corner of the room was the spinet piano where Kate had practiced Bach airs and inventions, the sheet music still on the stand, as if she had left home yesterday instead of twelve years ago.

Her mother sipped at her tea, cast a glance in Kate's direction. "What's wrong, dear?"

"My life is unbearable," Kate burst out. Tears sprang to her eyes. "Frank . . ."

Her mother went still; she set down her crocheting and stared at her, blinking. "What is it?"

"He . . ." Kate thought of him grunting, shoving into her. "My husband . . . in an intimate moment . . ." Her face went hot.

"Of course he isn't a gentleman." Her mother took up the doily again, her mouth set in a grim line. "You should have married Pastor Williams."

The clock on the mantelpiece chimed, straining with the effort. Four o'clock; soon Frank would be coming in from the fields. She'd left before dawn. All day he would have thought of her note on the kitchen table. At supper, her empty chair would accuse him.

"I advise you to keep to yourself as often as possible," her mother said, "though I do not speak from personal experience. Your father was always a gentleman."

Kate's teacup rattled in her hand. She set it on the table and watched her mother crochet with a new ferocity. Her face was closed; she wanted to hear nothing further.

"I'm going for a walk," Kate said. She rose, crossed the room, and paused at the door, yearning for her mother to call her back.

"You'll be back for supper?" her mother asked.

"Yes." She waited, but there was nothing more.

She went quickly down the front steps, thinking of her father, of sitting in his lap when she was a child. But she wouldn't have been able to tell him either; he would be horrified. How could she tell anyone—even her old friend Marianne—that her husband was in love with a dead woman, for whom she was only a substitute, or that she was raising their child, a secret from the world.

She walked past the shops on Main Street, looking in the windows to avoid the eyes of others. She should have gone the back way to cross the river. Too late now. How dreadful if she should encounter Emily Kettering—Mrs. McCann now, perfectly turned out, a lady of leisure, a triumphant little smile to accompany her gushing salutation. Kate hurried past shoes and boots, confections, feathered hats, a man being shaved by a barber, the razor gliding through the foam.

She went on, walking faster, toward the river. Frank unpinning her hair, slipping off her gown; beautiful as an angel, he said. In bed he used to be tender, considerate, and their pleasure had been mutual. That Butterfly woman had made him a savage. Her vision blurred with tears as she started across the bridge. She glanced down at the water, the swift current.

She went on—block after block of houses, husbands returning from their work, children in the yards, the smells of supper—and headed into the countryside, so hot and thirsty she felt she might faint; that would be a relief. She walked and walked until she wore her thoughts away and there was nothing left of her but motion.

When she returned to the house, she found a tin of butter cookies in the kitchen and took them upstairs. She got into bed, ate all the cookies, and went to sleep. In the morning her mother brought tea and a coddled egg on toast. Kate sipped at the tea, put the tray aside, and returned to her pillow.

"You're not well," her mother said. "We should call the doctor."

"I'm only tired," Kate said. "Let me rest in peace." She slept through lunch and supper, again and again plunging into the liquidity of sleep, the haven of it.

Her mother brought her a Bible, soft foods, tonics. A letter from Frank arrived. *We miss you sorely, dearest one, please hurry home. The children are distraught.*

No apology, of course. Kate tore the letter in half and shoved it beneath the mattress. She thought of Franklin in the yard, his face somber, looking down the road for her. Mary Virginia would cling to her grandmother, her eyes puffy from crying. She should have left them a separate letter, she should write to them now. But she closed her eyes and they faded away.

There were more letters from Frank; she put them beneath the mattress and swam back into sleep.

One afternoon her mother came to tell her that Frank was in the parlor.

"I'm not well enough to see him."

"He's your husband. You've been away from him for two weeks."

Kate shook her head.

"Don't be absurd, Kate."

When she didn't move, her mother went away and reappeared shortly with a box of chocolates and a vase of pink roses. "He says he has more gifts for you at home. He wants you to come with him."

Kate pulled the pillow over her head and drifted away.

A week later she awoke in the middle of the night and could not sleep again, even with the tonic.

She lit a lamp and sat at the dressing table, staring at her reflection. Her hair was tangled but her face was the same, as if she were the same woman.

She couldn't stay here. Her mother wouldn't want her indefinitely—she had made that clear—and there would be the humiliation of it, people talking. And there were the children. She thought of Mary Virginia's sweaty little hands patting her face, of Franklin looking gravely at her, his eyes delphinium blue, like hers. It had been terrible of her to leave them; even worse, she had barely thought of them. What kind of mother was she?

She would keep herself from Frank, as her mother had advised, until he came to his senses, and devote herself to Franklin and Mary Virginia. They needed her; even Benji needed her. She would make Franklin's favorite lemon pie, a new dress for Mary Virginia; every night in the parlor she would conduct devotionals, with particular attention to Benji. She had failed him in that regard; she had never managed to bring him to God. She must try harder. At bedtime she would say prayers with each child, and every morning and evening she would spend an hour in private prayer.

And she would continue to develop her intellectual interests and social circle. The suffragist Charlotte Cross was coming to Stockton soon, to give a presentation at the town hall. She would persuade Aimee Moore to let her host the pre-lecture dinner. Although Aimee—who had known Miss Cross at Mount Holyoke—had invited her, Kate's house would be particularly suitable for the event, given that Miss Cross had a strong interest in the Orient. Miss Cross would enjoy talking to Benji and Frank, and it would give Kate pleasure to show Frank that she thought nothing of his misdeeds, that she could even speak of Japan herself in the most casual manner possible, that he was irrelevant to her.

She would make trips to the Art Institute and the opera in Chicago—Aimee and her husband had invited her more than once—and take up piano again. Her Galena teacher had considered her something of a prodigy, and she had given two successful recitals when she was a young woman. Frank knew she wanted a piano; perhaps that was the surprise.

In the morning she wrote to Aimee and prepared for her return.

The day that Kate had departed, Frank woke late, with a violent headache. He vomited into the chamber pot and pulled on his clothes. Downstairs, his mother set coffee before him and handed him Kate's note.

"It's surprising she didn't tell us aforehand," she said, and turned back to the stove. She was cooking eggs; the greasy odor made his gorge rise again.

The paper shook in his grip. Her sentence sloped down the page, not her usual fine penmanship. She hadn't signed it.

Last night's dream came to him: butterflies feeding on his skin. He looked out the window.

"They're gone," he said.

"She went alone," his mother said. "All the children are here. I told them that their grandmother is ill, that word came in the night."

She shook scrambled eggs onto a plate and put it before him. He inched it away, tried a sip of coffee. "She took the new buggy," his mother said.

"Buggy," he said aloud, then repeated the word in his mind.

"Bud Case came by. Benji and the Swede went with him."

"Christ," he said. Today they were threshing at the Miller farm.

"You'd better call on our Lord in all sincerity," his mother said. "Your uncle Edward lost everything on account of the bottle. It's the devil's poison."

"That's not it." He stood, pushing back the chair. It fell; he righted it and headed to the door.

"You never had this trouble before you deserted the Plum River church," his mother said. "Go to Pastor Pollock, Frank, I beg you. Ask him to pray with you."

He shook his head. "I'm sorry, Mother," he said, under his breath. "I'm sorry for every bad thing I ever did."

Outdoors, he spied a butterfly in the lilac bush, another skimming along the fence. A butterfly lit on his shoulder; he slapped it and stared at the smear of orange on his palm. He rubbed his hand on his trousers.

"God," he whispered, "Jesus Christ our Lord and Savior." There was no answer; there never had been. He walked unsteadily to the barn.

The men had taken the Percherons, and Daisy's stall was empty. He'd lost her. His Kate. Katie.

He started mucking out the stalls. Goddamn butterflies. They were a plague as sure as the crickets his father had called Idaho devils, as sure as the grasshoppers that stripped the fields, the chinch bugs, the corn black with them.

Butterfly devils, feeding at his soul.

He'd been a good enough man at one time, a man of discipline aboard ship: first mate, then lieutenant, everything in order, the medical kits, spare clothing for the men, the chamber pots emptied on schedule. Teaching new hands to haul the lead, to navigate, respected for doing more than his share. Night watch, the smell of the open sea, the shudder of the ship beneath him like a large animal, the slosh and slap of waves against the hull—it had been intoxication enough. He'd traded the world of water for the world of dirt, and he was the dirtiest thing in it.

The next evening, after a day of threshing, he went to see Keast at his boardinghouse. He was still out on his rounds. Frank waited in the parlor, Mrs. Bosley passing through occasionally, giving him coy smiles. He'd kissed her once when they were young; she was Nellie Green then.

He went outside to wait and, when he saw Keast coming up the street in his buggy, fell in step beside him. Keast greeted him heartily, said he'd be glad for a smoke before supper.

In his room, Keast offered Frank some whiskey.

"I've given it up," Frank said.

"Wise of you," Keast said, pouring himself a slug.

Keast sat down in a hard-back chair, motioned Frank toward the upholstered one. He looked pretty goddamn cheerful for a horse doctor, smiling, holding out the box of cigars as if he were a gentleman in a drawing room.

Frank took a cigar and lit it. He couldn't think how to begin. "I believe I'll take you up on that drink," he said. "Just a snort."

Keast handed him a glass of bourbon and he drank it down. "I've lost Kate," he said.

"Ah. Surely not."

"She's gone to her mother."

"Women go to their mothers sometimes."

"She's not coming back."

"Go to her, then."

"It's not like that. It's desperate. Beyond anything you can imagine." He looked down at his hands, grime under the nails, the knuckles that would never scrub clean. "I haven't always been honorable," he said. "In Japan . . ."

Keast was regarding him steadily; Frank met his eyes.

"No one of us is perfect," Keast said. "Man or woman."

"I must win her back," Frank said. "What can I do?"

"You could write to her—a love letter."

"That won't be enough."

Keast sighed, took another drink.

"You're leaning on a slender reed," he said. "But, in my experience, women appreciate gifts."

When Kate returned three weeks later, Frank led her into the parlor.

"Surprise!" he said.

Kate stared at the new bay window.

"It's not quite finished," he said. "But I thought you'd be pleased—you admired the one in the Moores' parlor. Do you like it?"

"Yes," she said in a faint voice. "I'd thought . . . maybe a piano."

"I worked like Jehoshaphat on the window," he said. "And here's another little gift. Look at your pretty bird." He picked up a wicker cage from a table by the window. "A lovebird," he said.

"Oh," she said.

"You could teach it to sit on your finger." He started to open the cage.

"Don't," she said. "It will spoil the carpet."

That night he slid into bed, careful not to touch her. "I was thinking," he said. "Maybe we could take a holiday, to Lake Geneva in Wisconsin, just the two of us. What would you say to that?"

"That would be fine," she said in a dull voice.

"What do you want from me, Kate? I'm giving up drink—I'm trying for all I'm worth."

"I want you to forget that woman," she said.

"She's nothing to me. You're the only woman I've ever loved."

She was silent—weighing his words, he thought.

"We shouldn't have brought Benji here," she said. "He's a constant re-minder. Not that I don't care for him. He's a good boy. But it was a mistake—the whole thing was a mistake."

"What whole thing?" His hands went cold.

She didn't answer.

"Kate, I'll do anything . . ."

"Give me a while," she said, and touched his arm. It was a beginning.

Kate had a note from Aimee: How sublimely generous of her to be willing to host the dinner for Miss Cross, but she had long since begun preparations, invitations written, delicacies ordered. However, if Kate would like to offer a tea party, in spite of the late notice . . .

Kate tossed the letter aside. It was just as well. She had begun to suspect she was pregnant.

It had been a month and a half since the incident with Frank. It would be as if that woman was the mother and she merely carrying the seed.

She prayed to miscarry, took scalding baths, rode Daisy hard over stubbled fields, consumed large quantities of castor oil. She thought of forcing a stick inside, but it could break and then there would be the unthinkable humiliation of Dr. McBride's extracting it.

Several times a day she looked for spots of blood in her underthings: That was how the earlier troubles had announced themselves. Perhaps it wouldn't hold.

If it did, she wouldn't meet Charlotte Cross, wouldn't be going to Chautauqua, art museums, or the opera. For at least two years, she would be chained to this baby.

One morning she vomited into the chamber pot. "Oh, no," she said, and began to cry.

Frank put his arm around her. "Kate, are you—"

"It isn't mine," she said, and jerked away from him.

* * *

Aimee took time out from her preparations to pay a visit, once she learned of Kate's confinement. "It's too bad about the timing," she said. "Miss Cross will be dashed not to meet you. But for such a delightful reason—I'm happy for you."

Kate stared at Aimee in her fussy bows and poplin. "Thank you so much, dear," she said in a deliberately saccharine voice. "You are too kind. Now, if you'll forgive me, it's time for my nap."

In preparation for Charlotte Cross's visit, Miss Ladu taught a lesson on the suffragists. They were brave women, she declared, her cheeks flushed as she talked over mutterings from some of the boys, and they had already won some victories: The states of Wyoming, Idaho, Colorado, and Utah allowed women to vote in their elections. Why shouldn't all women vote? she asked. Wasn't everyone equal?

Benji, in the back row—he was in the most advanced class now—glanced at Flora two rows ahead, then raised his hand and stood. "In my opinion," he said, "everyone is equal, including females and people of all races." Flora turned her face slightly, letting him see her proud smile. He sat down, his heart hammering.

There were a few boos, but Miss Ladu said he'd made an excellent point; Negro men had long since been enfranchised, as were all male citizens of the United States.

"No wonder she's an old maid," Marvin said at recess, and the next day he and several other students were absent. A few who attended said their parents hadn't approved of the lesson.

"Are you going to the lecture tonight?" Benji asked Flora as they walked in the direction of Morseville. It had become their habit that he walked her partway home every Friday, under the guise of his having an errand to do in town.

"My father probably won't allow it. You'll have to give me a full report." Her face had changed over the summer: It was fuller yet more angular, and there was something new about her eyes; she was prettier than ever. She also had breasts now that would just fit in his hand; he tried not to look at them. "I think you should be a teacher," she said.

I'd like that, he thought of saying, if we could teach at the same school. But her father would never let her be with a Japanese. "You know I'm going to Japan," he said. "It's my destiny."

She nodded. They'd talked about Japan one day last summer, when they went for a walk on the other side of Plum Creek. It had been so hot that day he could smell the warmth of her hair, and ever since he'd carried the image of her wistful look when she asked if he was ever coming back from Japan. Maybe she would become a suffragist and do anything she wanted to; maybe she would defy her father.

They'd come to their parting place, beside a walnut tree at the edge of Morseville. His fingers brushed against hers as he handed over her books.

"I wish you could come to the lecture," he said. "Miss Cross is going to show pictures of Japan."

"I'll try," she said, smiling straight into his eyes. She'd grown taller over the summer too; it would be bad if she grew any more, though Grandmother Pinkerton said she didn't think he'd attained his full height yet.

He went on toward Morseville, whistling, hoping Flora was watching, though she couldn't watch too long, because of her father. When he glanced back, she had disappeared.

He had a real excuse to go into town today, to get the photograph of his mother from Keast. Since Miss Cross had traveled in Japan, she might be able to read what was written on the back of the picture.

Keast wasn't at home, but the door was unlocked as usual. Benji opened the bottom right drawer of the desk, took the picture from its box and gazed at it a moment. He was fifteen now, which meant the photograph had been taken about twenty years ago. Frank no longer had a mustache and his hair was thinner, but that pickle of a nose hadn't changed. His mother had been beautiful, with a delicate face and soft eyes. One of her feet in its high clog was turned at almost a right angle to the camera; along the hem of her kimono was a pattern of butterflies. He felt a flare of rage at Frank; he'd tear him out of the picture, but that would destroy the writing. Even though the picture was creased, the writing was still clear, written in dark ink. With a rush of excitement, he slipped the picture into his pocket. At last, he might learn something that would lead him to his real family.

* * *

Benji and Frank had been invited to the pre-lecture dinner at the Moores' house. Father Pinkerton complained about going to hear some ignorant spinster blather about the fair sex—what could she know?—but Mother Pinkerton said he had to attend, for politeness's sake. He groused throughout the drive to Stockton, but when they entered the Moores' house, he was all smiles and bows.

At dinner, Mrs. Moore introduced Benji to Miss Cross as the "part-Japanese young man" who had been adopted by Lieutenant and Mrs. Pinkerton.

That damn lie. When Miss Cross said, "How good of you," to Father Pinkerton and smiled at Benji, he could hardly smile back.

Father Pinkerton said most of the credit was due his virtuous wife. "She much regrets her absence," he said in a practiced-sounding voice, "but looks forward to your visit tomorrow."

They were seated directly opposite Miss Cross. Benji decided she resembled her name—eyebrows grown almost together, tight little lips. But he began to like her better when, during the soup course, some of the men talked about how the Japs were getting swelled heads now that they'd beaten the Russians, and she gave him several sympathetic glances. He noticed she had big breasts.

Mrs. Moore shifted the talk to Miss Cross, who talked about the urgency of voting rights for women. When there was no response except from Mrs. Moore—Miss Cross could count on the support of herself and her husband, she said, though Mr. Moore made a sour face—Miss Cross outlined the itinerary of her travels in the past year, over much of the globe. "I traveled most extensively in Asia," she said. "Japan was my favorite country—so picturesque."

She leaned toward Benji. "From which part of Japan do you hail, young man?"

When he told her and she said she'd been there—such a gorgeous city, the bay like a Norwegian fjord!—Benji was so elated he could hardly eat.

As Frank yammered on about the Nagasaki kite contests and his import/export business—showing off as usual—Benji debated the best way to approach Miss Cross for a private conversation later. Right after dinner might be the best time to ask, but as soon as dessert had been consumed, Aimee Moore took Miss Cross away so she could prepare for the lecture.

"Damn suffragist," Frank muttered as they got in the buggy. Benji didn't say he thought she was nice; it would only cause a spat. He was relieved when Father Pinkerton stopped the buggy at the saloon and said he'd be along in a while, he had to talk to Bud Case about next year's seed corn. Frank would probably be there all night, so Benji wouldn't have to worry about showing Miss Cross the picture. He would speak to her after the lecture; maybe he could pass her a note beforehand.

The hall was crowded and noisy, filled with the smells of tobacco, muddy boots, and perfume. Benji looked around for Flora, bracing himself for her absence. Of course she wasn't there. In front were two rows of reserved seats, where the party guests had been instructed to sit, but Benji found a place beside Keast and Miss Ladu midway back. Keast was beaming, Miss Ladu glowingly serene; it was rumored that they had an understanding.

"What do you think of these suffragists?" Keast asked Benji, with a wink at Miss Ladu.

"They're all right," he said. "I think they're fine."

"You're in the minority," Miss Ladu said. "I'm glad to be seated beside two allies."

During the wait, Benji touched the tin in his pocket several times. Miss Cross had said Japan was her favorite country; that was more than he'd hoped for. She could surely read at least some of the writing.

At last the Moores and Miss Cross appeared. Mr. Moore and Miss Cross sat in the front row, while Mrs. Moore and a younger woman fussed over a vase of flowers on the podium, moving it here and there and finally setting it on the floor.

Mrs. Moore introduced Miss Cross at length, going on and on about their college days and treasured friendship and Miss Cross's stalwart efforts for the public weal. Benji glanced around at the crowd: mostly angry faces, except for a few of the women. Frank hadn't appeared.

When Miss Cross took her place at the lectern, she cleared her throat, peered around the hall, and announced that she was going to educate her listeners about the conditions for women in several red-light districts of the world.

There was a collective gasp. "Prostitutes, she means," Keast whispered to Benji.

"I know." Sometimes Keast treated him like a baby.

Miss Cross had a collection of lantern slides, which she projected against a curtain after the lights were dimmed: landscapes and temples in Bali, Siam, Korea, and Japan, along with women engaged in what she called the water trade.

She spent the longest time on Japan, since she'd lived there nearly a year. In Japan, she told them, it was often the custom to display prostitutes on a row of separate small stages, and when the women were chosen they went behind a screen with their customers. When she showed a row of prostitutes in kimono kneeling on their stages, Benji felt his ears redden; people might say his mother had been a prostitute. He was glad now that Flora hadn't come.

"You may wonder why I have done this survey," Miss Cross said, "and why I am presenting it to you."

"Yes," one man yelled. "We wonder. There are ladies present."

"We must not shy away from the circumstances of women worldwide. There are prostitutes in every city—not only in Shanghai but in Chicago." George Case had said there were prostitutes in Elizabeth and Galena; George and some of the other boys were always talking about "taking a little trip to Elizabeth," but Benji knew they hadn't, not yet. They'd all gone to spy on Belinda Apple, who lived in a shack outside Morseville and didn't pull the curtains when she undressed at night; he was partly sorry he'd done that. When the room came back into focus, Miss Cross was talking about how women should have the vote. His thoughts rose and dipped throughout that part of the speech; Miss Ladu had been much more interesting about it.

At the end of the talk there were some boos along with scattered applause. Most of the crowd fled as if the building were on fire, but a small knot of people gathered around Miss Cross.

Benji moved closer to the front and sat waiting during the long conversations. He felt conspicuous sitting alone, but he had no choice. He had brought a message from Mother Pinkerton, he would tell anyone who asked.

Finally most of the group dispersed. Miss Cross and Mrs. Moore began to gather their things, and Mr. Moore went outside to get their buggy. As Mrs. Moore was carrying away the flowers, Benji darted up to Miss Cross and asked if he could speak to her privately about a confidential matter.

She looked amused but said yes, and when Mrs. Moore returned, Miss Cross told her she would join them outside directly. Mrs. Moore gave

Benji a bright, curious look, her head cocked in a way that made him think of Mother Pinkerton's bird.

"I believe in women's suffrage," he blurted out.

Both women laughed and Mrs. Moore said, "Excellent, we'll press you into our cause."

Mrs. Moore went out to join her husband, glancing back at them several times.

Miss Cross and Benji sat down in the front row, Miss Cross's dress rustling. "So you were persuaded?" she said. "I'm so pleased. A number of males do support us, quite openly. It's nothing to be ashamed of."

Benji looked around the hall—only a man in the back, sweeping. He turned away from Miss Cross, took the tin from his pocket, and removed the picture, careful to arrange it writing side up.

"Can you read this?" he asked.

She peered down at it.

"It's important," he said.

"I'm so sorry," she said, "but I know only a few scraps of Japanese, and that in conversation. Is it a photograph?"

Before he could think, she took the picture and turned it over.

She stared at it, then at him.

"She's my mother," he said. "She was a geisha, not a prostitute."

"That's evident. She's quite lovely." Miss Cross frowned. "And this is . . ."

She touched the picture of Frank, then looked up at him.

"You mustn't tell anyone." His throat felt thick. "The only reason I showed you was . . . the writing. . . . I'm going to Nagasaki."

"To find your mother," she said.

"No. She killed herself."

Miss Cross drew in a noisy breath. "You poor lad." She took his hand and squeezed it. "This is the kind of tragic circumstance I've been investigating."

Mr. Moore reappeared and began walking toward them, adjusting his hat. Take back the picture, Benji told himself, but his hand wouldn't move.

Mr. Moore's feet thundered on the floor. "What do we have here?" he said, glancing over Miss Cross's shoulder at the photograph. Benji snatched it from her and put it in his pocket.

"Oh." Miss Cross turned to Mr. Moore. "We've been discussing the rights of women and so on. Such a fine young man."

"Yes, indeed." Mr. Moore cleared his throat. "I know the family well." He would not look at Benji. "My wife has sent me to escort you," he said, with a slight bow to Miss Cross.

Miss Cross rummaged in her valise, took out a folded fan, and gave it to Benji. "It's Japanese," she said. "For good luck. I hope you will travel to Nagasaki. And this may interest you . . ." She pulled out a small paper book; on the front, printed in black letters, was *Women's Suffrage: A Brief History*. "I wrote it myself."

She shook his hand and said goodbye. As she and Mr. Moore walked out together, talking in low voices, Benji felt a spike of glee.

Outside, the crowd had dispersed. Benji looked down the street at the saloon. Frank's buggy was still there.

He started running down the street toward home. But that would look suspicious, he thought. He slowed to a walk. The moon illuminated the fronts of houses, cast deep shadows between them. He shivered and, at the edge of town, began to run again.

It wasn't his fault; he hadn't meant any harm. He'd only wanted her to translate the writing. Anyone would understand that. Miss Cross understood. She wouldn't tell, and Mr. Moore probably hadn't been able to really see the photograph. He'd take the picture back to Keast's tomorrow, and no one would know.

In the morning, Kate prepared finger sandwiches and apple tarts, then took a rest so she would be fresh when Aimee Moore and Miss Cross arrived for tea. She had just dressed in her loosest frock, not yet tight about the waist, and gone down to find the children when the Moores' colored manservant arrived with a note.

There had been some confusion about the train timetable, Aimee wrote, and Miss Cross deeply regretted that she would be unable to call. Aimee would be taking her to the station, so—alas!—she would have to suspend her own visit until a later day.

Kate stared at Aimee's pretentious handwriting, the way the end letters looped back across the words. Now Aimee would be able to claim full proprietorship of Miss Cross, dropping allusions to their intimacy at every meeting of the women's circle from now until eternity.

It was just as well; she was tired. She ate two of the tarts and took herself back to bed.

On Monday morning, Kate and her mother-in-law were struggling with the week's wash, Kate perspiring and her hair undone. As she was wringing out one of Frank's union suits, she was dismayed to see, through the front window of the kitchen, Aimee Moore descend from her buggy.

She ran upstairs to repair her coiffure. Such uncivilized timing. Aimee knew she didn't have a servant girl for wash day.

By the time Kate returned, Mrs. Pinkerton had shown Aimee into the parlor, where she sat perched on the davenport in a voile dress and feathered hat, looking around at the furnishings. At least the room had been tidied in anticipation of Miss Cross's visit.

"How are you, dear?" Aimee said, rising and looking into Kate's eyes with an expression of exaggerated concern, as if her condition were a terminal illness.

They sat down, Aimee apologizing for the impetuous timing of her visit; she politely refused tea.

"I'll come straight to the matter." Aimee took one of Kate's hands in hers. She was wearing lace gloves, soft as a second skin, but her grip was firm. "Although I hesitated," she said, "given that you are—" She broke off and looked once more around the room.

"Has someone died?" Kate said. She thought of her mother, a telegram.

"Nothing so simple as that, I'm afraid." Aimee turned her gaze back to Kate; her expression of sorrow had deepened.

"What is it?"

"I wouldn't mention it at all, but if word somehow . . ."

"Word of what?" Kate's mouth went dry.

"Miss Cross is a highly principled woman, as I'm sure you understand, but quite passionate in her convictions and not one to restrain her views."

Kate stared at the feather curling down over Aimee's forehead, not quite grazing her skin. Frank must have committed some indiscretion at the party, perhaps even an attempt with Miss Cross.

"I have to confess that Charlotte is a bit outspoken for my taste and lacks certain nuances of judgment. That is why I feared . . ." Another squeeze of the hand.

Kate's heart began to flutter. "Feared what?"

"That you would hear of this eventually." She took a deep breath. "Charlotte has spoken to me of Benjamin's parentage. The boy meant no harm, I suppose."

"He's lying," Kate burst out.

"No doubt, though he did show Miss Cross a photograph of your husband and a Japanese woman—"

"What photograph?" Kate cried.

"I gather it's about so. . . ." Aimee released Kate's hand and arranged her fingers to describe a small rectangle. "Your husband was younger, though still quite recognizable, Charlotte says, and she thinks the woman is probably a geisha. Benjamin said that the woman is his mother."

"He's an orphan. We don't know who his parents were."

"The photograph might be quite beside the point—a souvenir that gave Benjamin a misimpression. On the other hand, Miss Cross is so persuasive." A little smile played at one corner of her mouth. "Not that I agree with her, necessarily. But my husband saw the photograph as well."

Kate jumped up. "Please leave," she said.

Aimee's hand went to her throat. "I was only . . . I'm your friend," she said.

"I hate you," Kate said. "Get out."

Kate fled from the room and up the stairs, flung herself on the bed, biting the pillow to keep from screaming. When the sound of the buggy wheels receded into the distance, she flew back downstairs, through the kitchen—Mrs. Pinkerton was outside hanging clothes—and into Benji's room.

The little traitor. She yanked open the top drawer of his desk: pencils, erasers, protractor, a butterscotch candy covered with lint, a small drawing of that girl, the undertaker's daughter. A Japanese fan. She opened it, threw it on the floor, and ground her heel against it. Heathen. She dumped the contents of the side drawer on the bed and searched through the papers, her hands shaking badly. Schoolwork, articles from some veterinary journal, folded notes written in a childish hand. She went through the papers again, felt around the edges of the drawers, bent down to look for an envelope pasted to the underside of the desk. She began to go through the shelf of books, flipping through each one, upending and shaking them. A few pressed flowers fell out, and a canceled stamp. *Women's Suffrage: A Brief History,* by Miss Charlotte Cross. She ripped off the cover, tore it into bits, fanned through the pages, shook it upside down, and spat on it.

In the closet, she turned out all the pockets and felt inside the shoes. There was a box on the floor. She pulled it out: the top she'd given him, the bear, a turtle shell, a whittling knife. She stabbed the bear with the knife, then grabbed the pillow from the bed, ripped it open, and pounded it on the bed. Feathers flew into the air.

"Kate!"

She spun around. Mrs. Pinkerton stood gaping in the doorway, laundry spilling from her basket.

"He's ruined us," Kate said, squeezing the knife against her palm until she felt nothing at all.

Benji walked home from school alone, avoiding the Cases and even Flora. The other boys had talked about Miss Cross's prostitute pictures at recess in high, excited whispers, and Marvin said Benji's mother was probably a prostitute. They'd gotten in a fight, and Benji held Marvin's face against the dirt until he said she wasn't. Somebody had told Miss Ladu and now he had extra homework for tomorrow. He picked up an Osage orange from the road and aimed it at an old shed; it splatted against the tin. He was sorry Miss Cross had come. She didn't even know Japanese.

If Marvin could see the picture of Mama, he'd know she was a geisha; even an idiot like him could tell the difference.

The Guernseys were crossing the road to the house. They came earlier now that it was late fall and there was less grass in the meadow. The sky was heavy with clouds too; it smelled like rain. Bossy, the lead cow, didn't like to get wet; Benji stopped to rub her head and tell her he'd be back soon. He'd eat whatever Grandmother Pinkerton had laid out for him before he did the milking.

Frank was leaning against the door of the barn. "Get in here," he said, gesturing with his whip. His face was blotched. Drunk again. Benji hurried on past.

Frank ran after him and caught his arm.

"Where's that picture?" he said.

Benji's mind slid into a smooth hard place. "What picture?"

"You know damn well what picture, you bastard. That Moore woman was here, and Mother Pinkerton is in a hell of a state. The doctor had to come." Frank raised the whip.

"You can't whip it out of me," Benji said. "I'd die first." He turned, pivoted around Frank, and ran toward the barn.

Benji moved fast, throwing the saddle on Kuro, tightening the girth, slipping on the bridle.

"Where the hell you think you're going?" Frank shouted, stumbling toward him.

"To get the picture of your bastard's parents. If you follow me, I'll tell everyone in town."

He took off down the road, urging Kuro into a gallop. His heart was hammering but his mind was clear. He took a mental inventory: twenty cents, and, in his saddlebag, an apple from lunch. He glanced back: The road was empty. Frank would be fumbling with Admiral's tack. Benji could outrun him easily if he didn't have to stop by Keast's.

He took a back way to Morseville, pushing Kuro hard down a rutted lane and through a pasture, then a patch of woods. He tied Kuro to a post around the corner from Keast's boardinghouse.

There were only a few people in the street—women looking in the dry-goods-store window and a colored man leading a horse toward the livery stable. One of the women glanced at him briefly; later she'd say she saw him, the Pinkerton orphan on the run.

When she turned away, he hurried inside the boardinghouse and up to Keast's room, yanked open the desk drawer, and took out the tin with the picture in it and the leather pouch full of money.

Back down the stairs—Mrs. Bosley's voice, the smell of supper cooking—but no one saw him as he went out the door and down the street.

He took the back road west toward Galena, Kuro's legs pumping beneath him as a plan began to gather in his mind. He'd make his way across the country, working on farms; they always needed help making barns snug for the winter, repairing tools. Then he could get a job on a merchant vessel going to Japan. He hadn't meant to go to Japan so soon, but nothing ever happened the way you planned it. He wished he could have told Flora and Keast, but he couldn't think about that now.

Ahead, two walls of corn stalks made a long rattling tunnel and the sky bore down on him. He touched the right pocket of his trousers where the picture was. Once he was in California, he'd have someone read the writing and then he could find his family in Nagasaki. He could make it, he and Kuro. What would he do with Kuro? They might not take him on the ship. He'd think about that later too.

It was a long way, six thousand miles. He saw himself on Kuro, a small speck moving slowly across the globe, and the reins went slippery in his hands.

A breeze had come up, moving through the corn, a hollow sound. The stalks above his head made him dizzy. He'd been lost in a cornfield once, every direction he went the wrong one, walking, then running, his feet slipping in the mud, his mind confused about the sun. He could have died; even grown men died in the corn. It had happened to Jed Stevens last year. He rubbed his face hard with both hands. He was thinking crazy.

He let Kuro slow to a trot as they passed out of the fields and into pastureland, a cattle farm. Herefords mostly. Frank had always talked big about raising cattle. "You couldn't cut it," Benji said aloud, "you goddamn sousehead, you stinking piece of dung." He thought of Frank coming toward him with the whip and put his heels to Kuro's sides again. The road behind was still empty.

When Kuro tired, Benji let him walk and concentrated on the remnants of prairie at the edges of the road. The grasses in their fall colors and the bobolinks swooping above made him think of Flora. She said the bobolink's song made her happy even when nothing else could. The bobolinks were migrating; what would cheer her up now? He swiped away tears. He couldn't be a sissy; he had to concentrate on his plan.

The road passed a small stream, where Kuro drank, the rings on his halter clinking. They followed the stream across the railroad tracks into a cluster of trees beside the water. He would spend the night here, sheltered in the woods, and just in time too; it was getting dark. He removed Kuro's saddle and tack, brushed him down, and tied him to a sapling. Upstream, he found a skirt of hickory nuts beneath a tree. He ate the nuts and shared his apple with Kuro. He'd have to stop in Galena for food and other supplies. He wished he had his knife with him, and his slingshot for killing jackrabbits. There was a lot to wish for. He had to stop that kind of thinking. Using the saddle for a pillow, he settled down for the night at the base of a large pine.

Images raced through his mind: Flora's pretty feet in the water when they sat beside the creek last summer; the family at the table tonight, Franklin crying when he heard his big brother had left, Frank with the whip. Miss Cross looking at the picture. She must have told. Damn suffragist, cross-eyed bitch. Not that Frank didn't deserve it, the lying bastard. Then he thought of Franklin; he would never hear the end of it at school, and Benji wouldn't be there to protect him.

The ground was knobby beneath the pine needles and he was shivering with cold; he'd buy a poncho and blanket, a bedroll. He turned again and again, thinking he would never sleep, but then it was morning and a light rain was falling.

He was nervous on the road to Galena. If Frank had started off early to find him, he might catch up this morning. He could probably guess what direction he'd gone. Frank wouldn't want him except to whip the stuffing out of him and to get the picture. He pushed the tin deeper into his pocket. Would any of the family want him now?

He passed a farmer driving an empty cart, then a buggy headed the other direction, in it a man wearing a bowler hat. The man's eyes were distracted; he didn't see Benji. Closer to town there was more traffic; he kept his head down as he guided Kuro along the edge of the road.

In Galena he ducked into a dry-goods store, bought beef jerky and a hunk of cheese, a slingshot, a slicker, a horse blanket and a blanket for himself, a bottle of mineral oil in case Kuro developed colic. His money bag was considerably lighter; no sleeping bag until he found work.

Kuro could graze on wild grasses, but he also had to have oats. In the feed store across the street, a suspicious-looking man with a boil on his neck sold Benji a small sack of grain. "Where you off to, boy?"

"To see my grandfather." It was a good answer; Keast would say he had his mind on straight. As he packed the saddlebag, he felt a burst of good spirits.

He pulled on the slicker and set out on the north road toward East Dubuque. He'd cross the Mississippi there and then he'd be in Iowa, his first state.

It was raining harder. Kuro's hooves made sucking sounds in the mud. Don't throw a shoe, he prayed. Benji had to let him walk now and conserve his strength.

He passed several houses on the edge of town, then it was farmland again. Up ahead he saw a wagon filled with bare-limbed shrubs and evergreens—a tree salesman. Late in the year for a tree salesman. He hoped this was no one he knew. The driver was sitting in the wagon in a straight-back chair beneath a rigged-up canopy to keep off the rain. As he went by, Benji glanced at the man—a jovial face pursed around a cigar—relieved not to have seen him before.

The man removed the cigar. "Peach of a day, ain't it?" he said, then popped the cigar back in his mouth.

It was late afternoon, and raining harder, when he passed through East Dubuque to the bridge. Kuro shied at the bridge, but Benji urged him gently with his heels and they started across. The bridge creaked and swayed in the gusts of wind. Kuro shied again, knocking against the wooden rail. Benji looked through the veil of rain down at the river, at whitecaps in the boiling current. "Come on, boy." He snapped the reins and Kuro reared, nearly unseating him. He jumped off and tried to lead him forward, but Kuro threw back his head and reared again.

The rain was drumming down so hard now it stung Benji's face; he could feel water seeping beneath the neck of his slicker. "Come on, damn you." He tugged harder at the reins; Kuro danced from one side of the bridge to the other. There was a sudden blast of wind, and a sheet of rain hit them like a wave. Kuro flung his hindquarters to one side, smacking the rail so hard it made a cracking sound, then started to gallop. "Whoa!" Benji ran beside him, holding the reins; then they slipped from his hand, but he kept running, trying to stay even with Kuro. The boards were slick; if Kuro fell, he'd break a leg and have to be shot. But Kuro ran steadily, his hooves hammering against the bridge. Benji pushed himself faster, breathing hard, his chest burning. He caught one rein, jerking Kuro against him, then lost his grip and Kuro pulled ahead. If he lost his horse, he couldn't make it. Then, through the rain, he could see a street in the distance, brick buildings; thank God, they were almost there.

Kuro clattered down the curve at the end of the bridge and onto the street. He wouldn't go far. Benji found him around a corner, his ears flat against his head, rain streaming down his face like tears. "I knew you could do it, boy," he said, putting his arm around Kuro's neck and rubbing his forelock. Whistling, he led Kuro down the street to find a livery stable where they could both stay the night. He was a samurai, on his way home.

Part Two

Butterfly:
My little god! My dearest, dearest love,
flower of lilies and roses.
May you never know that for you,
for your innocent eyes, Butterfly died!
So that you may go away over the sea,

and when you are older, may feel no pain
at your mother's renunciation.
My son, sent from the throne of Paradise,
look carefully at your mother's face,

so that a trace of it will remain with you,
look carefully! My love, farewell!
Farewell, my little love! Go, play, play!

Pinkerton:
Yes, all at once
I see my mistake
and I feel that I shall never be free
from this torment.
I shall never be free.

Keast had crisscrossed Jo Daviess County that day—a horse with glanders in Elizabeth; a report of hog cholera near Galena—and supper was already in progress when he returned to Morseville. He washed up outside the boardinghouse, went into the dining room, and took his place across from Lena. Smiling, she served his plate; he watched her beautiful hands, imagining her across their own dinner table next spring. She was set on marrying when the lilacs were in bloom, though he was impatient at the delay, an old man like himself. The wedding date had provoked their only arguments.

After supper, he and Lena took a brief constitutional, wrapped up against the chill. "It would be a fine season for matrimony," he said, imagining them warm together beneath a pile of quilts. She laughed, as if he was joking. She had work to do for the next day's classes, so they squeezed hands good night outside the door of her room and—after he glanced around; no one in sight—he gave her a kiss. Her lips were willing, and her arms tight around him. It was hard to fathom why she'd want to wait.

In his room, he poured a glass of brandy and, with a sigh, sank into his chair with the latest issue of *Hoard's Dairyman*. There had been several cases of foot-and-mouth in Ohio; God forbid that it should spread here. He'd witnessed a plague in Wisconsin when he was a boy; there had been massive slaughter.

He put down the paper. This was no subject for the evening hour. He should be watching Lena in the firelight as she sat reading or sewing; he could distract her with a kiss on the neck and lead her to the bedroom.

Lena wanted children, as he did; it was high time for her too, at twenty-seven years old. Maybe she was harboring some doubts. He finished off the brandy.

As he crossed the room to refill his glass, he noticed that the bottom drawer of his desk was open. He pushed it shut with his foot, then turned to look. He hadn't opened it. He squatted beside the drawer.

The tin that contained Benji's photograph was missing and the box had been left unlocked. That wasn't surprising—he'd taken it a couple of other times, just to look at her face, he'd said—but it wasn't like him not to lock the box and close the drawer. He was careful that way. He felt in the back of the box for the boy's pouch of money; nothing but a blank space. He jerked the drawer all the way open. Keast's mesh bag of silver dollars was still there, so this wasn't a case of theft.

He walked to the window. It was full dark now, eight o'clock according to his watch, which had been losing time. Late for a visit to the Pinkertons; perhaps he should wait until tomorrow. He sat back down and stared at the drawer, an uneasiness starting in his belly. He could say he'd come to warn Frank about the foot-and-mouth disease, given that he'd been talking lately of investing in beef cattle. Not a moment to waste, he'd say, and that was the truth; Frank was prone to impulsive purchases.

He went to the stable for Ulysses and headed for the farm. On the way, a sprinkling rain began. A circle of light from his lantern bobbed along the road and illuminated the weeds in the ditches. He'd give Frank the intelligence about the cattle, then casually ask if he could speak to Benjamin, who was likely studying in his room, nothing amiss. Perhaps he was planning to buy a birthday gift or some such for his sweetheart and, not knowing the cost, had taken the whole pouch of money.

Lights were burning in the Pinkerton kitchen and an upstairs bedroom. Old Mrs. Pinkerton was cleaning the stove, scrubbing the surface as if her life depended on it. She nodded at the coffeepot and he poured himself a cup, even though it smelled burned.

"I suppose the children are in bed," he said.

She bent over the stove, gripping the edges; the vertebrae of her spine looked painful beneath the cloth of her dress.

"What is it?" he said.

"Benji's gone." She began to weep, pressing the back of one hand against her mouth.

He led her to a chair at the table. She needed whiskey—so did he—but Frank probably kept it elsewhere.

"Where?" He lowered himself to a chair, his legs unsteady. "Do you know where?"

She shook her head. Her eyes were swollen; she'd been crying for some time. "Benji showed around a picture of Frank and his Japanese mother. There's talk of it in town. Kate . . ." She bit her lip, tears streaming down her face.

"He wouldn't do that," Keast said. "That photograph . . ."

She looked up, stared at him.

"What happened?" Keast said.

"Frank ran him off."

Keast pushed back from the table and hurried outside. He led Ulysses to the barn. Just as he had expected, Kuro was gone.

He stood listening to the sound of rain on the tin roofs of the barn and shed. Out in this weather, no shelter. Why hadn't the boy come to him?

He rode Ulysses hard toward town, then took the road west. He might have been fool enough to strike out for California on twenty-two dollars. The business with the photograph made no sense. He tried to place the problem in the center of his mind, but it kept sliding away.

Ulysses stumbled. "Ho, boy," Keast said, and gently pulled him to a halt. A horse could fracture a leg on this pitted, gully-washed road. He'd have to set out in the morning, with a reasonable plan. Though the boy could be anywhere.

He turned Ulysses back toward town. If only he'd come back on time today, Benjamin might have been waiting for him. He thought of Mrs. Pinkerton's tears, envying them. His chest was painfully full.

At the boardinghouse, he went to Lena's room, grateful for the stripe of light beneath the door. He tapped lightly and she came, in her dressing gown, reading his face. "Benji's gone," he said. "God knows where." She drew him inside and took off his wet jacket and trousers and shoes while he explained, and they lay together on her bed, the comfort of body against body.

The next day was sunny, with a current of cold in the air after the storm. On the way out of Dubuque, Benji stopped to buy a compass for sixty-five cents, which left him just over fifteen dollars. He'd have to find work before long, and a place for the winter. They could die, caught in a blizzard.

He and Kuro headed west on the main road out of Dubuque, Benji whistling to tamp down his fear, until he realized that the tune was "The Ash Grove," Flora's favorite song. She would know by now that he was gone. He could see her bent head as she walked away from the hollow tree where they sometimes left notes for each other. He'd write to her soon and explain. He thought of her pink lips, her hand in the grass close to his when they sat by the river last summer. He should have kissed her that day.

He pressed Kuro into a canter. He couldn't be mooning on this journey.

They passed houses that grew smaller with the distance from town, and then they were in farm country. The harvest was finished here, except for a few late threshers working the wheat. He paused at the edge of one farm, considering whether or not to ask if he could join in the threshing, but there seemed to be plenty of hands and the work would be completed soon. Maybe by the time he got to the other side of Iowa or to Nebraska he could find a job helping in a dry-goods store and live above it.

Several wagons loaded with pumpkins and sacks of coal rattled past. The men tipped their hats, though some looked at him curiously—

a stranger in a hurry; a Chink, he would look to them, with his light hair hidden beneath his cap.

What would they be saying about him in Plum River? He could see the men gathered around the stove at Red Olsen's store. *I always knew that little Jap was sneaky,* Austin Burdett would say. Red might take up for him, and Bud Case for sure, and Keast. Keast would know he hadn't meant any harm. His eyes stung; he pushed the image of Keast's rough, craggy face from his mind.

He put his heels to Kuro's side and they galloped past a farmhouse and a woman at the well, up a long hill.

He paused at the top of a rise. Below him was a wagon slumped partway into a ditch. A short fat man was standing in the road, yanking at the reins of his swaybacked pinto, but the horse didn't budge. When Benji got closer, he saw that it was the tree salesman he'd passed yesterday on the other side of the river. "Fool horse don't have the brains God gave a whore," he said as Benji came even with him. "Shied for no reason atall and look what a pickle she's put me in, me already a day late—shoot, two or three days late—to deliver some prime apples."

Benji dismounted and went to look at the wheel mired in the ditch. "My horse can pull that out," he said, "if you can push from the rear."

They substituted Kuro for the nag in the wagon traces; Benji urged him forward while the man swore at the wheel: Kuro pulled hard, the cords of his neck muscles standing out. "I don't want to injure my horse," Benji said, but just then the wagon broke free.

"I knew that hoss could do it." The little man walked toward him, his feet turned outward almost at right angles. He was bald, with an untrimmed reddish beard. "Mighty obliged to you," he said, holding out a pudgy hand. "Moffett's the name, Digby Moffett, purveyor of fine trees and ornamentals since 'ninety-two. Who might you be? If you're a Chinaman, you must be a rich'un to ride such a horse as that."

"I'm an American," Benji said, jerking back his hand, "though there is some royal Japanese blood in my veins."

"Hey, now, I's just fooling with you. I knew you was a good man the moment I laid eyes on you. Let me pay you something for your trouble." He dug around in his pocket and extracted a quarter. "Where you headed, boy?" he asked as they exchanged horses.

Benji explained that he was making a cross-country journey with the eventual goal of visiting some wealthy relatives in Nagasaki, Japan.

Moffett whistled. "Holy cats. All the way on your steed?"

"We can make it. I just need to find some work along the way to sup-plement my capital and a place to winter over."

"Yes, sir. You've got to settle down before the blizzards hit." Moffett studied him. "Why don't you ride along with me for a spell? I might be able to help you. I know these parts real well."

Benji shrugged. "Okay," he said. He didn't have any other offers.

They started moving slowly down the road, the swaybacked horse plodding along with her load.

Moffett lit a cigar and, gesturing with it, began to talk: about trees—there were your trash trees, maples, and your aristocrats, elm and oak; about his life story—born on a tobacco plantation in North Carolina, mi-grated early to greener pastures; and about business deals in which he had been wronged.

This man was nothing but a blabbermouth. "Maybe I'd better be get-ting on," Benji said. "I've got to find work right away."

Moffett scratched his forehead delicately with one finger. "Let me make you a proposition. I could use an assistant, late in the year as it is. You know how to plant a tree?"

"Yes," Benji said, looking at the scraggly collection in the wagon.

"I'll pay you fifty cents for each tree you put in the ground."

"Planting's hard work," he dared to say, "especially this time of year."

"Fifty-five cents, then, plus room and board. I know this route like the palm of my hand. Now, you ain't going to find a better deal than that. Plus which, I'll find you a situation for the winter. And to top it all off"—he gave Benji a wink—"I'll show you some fun along the way."

For the next few days, Benji and Digby, as he said he should be ad-dressed now that they were partners, made their way south and west through the gently rolling countryside of Iowa. From the crests of hills, Benji could see for miles, the squares of farmland a huge rippling quilt of gold and light-brown stubble and black earth. The only trees were clus-tered around farmhouses; Digby claimed to have planted most of them himself.

Progress was slow, and sales were scant, in spite of Digby's long con-versations with the farm wives, his talk often sweetened with a ribbon or some sparkly thing from what he called his opportunity box. Digby grumbled that some other tree man had beaten his time, and the truth of it was that most people in the Midwest didn't know to appreciate a good tree when they saw one. By the end of the first week, Benji had pocketed only three dollars and seventy-five cents and again said perhaps he'd best be moving on, but Digby said, "Now, hold on, at the next stop I got a surprise you won't want to miss."

"What is it?"

"You'll see. Some friends of mine. We'll have a square meal and a fine roof over our heads, for starters." They had been sleeping in barns and haystacks, and the farm wives who fed them gave handouts at the back door, as if they were tramps.

Benji cantered ahead to give Kuro some exercise and to escape Digby's blather. They were miles from the main road; this had been a mistake. The sky was low and gray, the fields bleak beneath it. Longing for home swept over him: Franklin—Benji had just been teaching him to ride his new pony—Grandmother Pinkerton's chicken and dumplings, the warm parlor stove, his bed with the kimono—he'd never see that kimono again—Flora. He thought of her dark eyes, the curves of her breasts beneath her brown checked blouse. She'd started to put up her hair this year, like a young woman. She'd think of him less and less and then forget.

He charged back to Digby. "I've got to get to a town with a post office," he said.

"You read my mind. Town is precisely where we're headed. I have some friends in Fairfield—we'll find us some mighty comfortable circumstances," he said with a wink.

At the end of the afternoon, after a failed attempt to sell some scrawny lilacs, nothing more than sticks now, that Digby insisted had been preordered, they came to a hamlet, just a few stores and houses at a crossroads. Benji scanned the stores—feed, dry goods, a harness shop. There was a saloon but no post office that he could see. On the far edge of the settlement they stopped in front of a small, unpainted frame house. There was a sign in the window: SEWING, PLAIN AND FANCY.

Digby rapped on the door, and a tired-looking woman peered out. "Digby," she said, in a voice that implied, You again.

"Lovely Arabella," Digby said with a bow. "Can you accommodate two wayfaring strangers for bed and board? I've brought you some lilacs."

"It's early in the day," she said, looking from one to the other. Benji felt her taking in his foreign appearance.

"Who's that one?" she said.

"An Oriental potentate," Digby said. He took out his money pouch. "This is on me, son," he said to Benji. "You've earned it."

"A dollar for you," the woman said. "Including supper. A dollar fifty for the Chinaman."

Benji stared at the bills as Digby counted them out. It wasn't fair they charged more for him. "I'm not Chinese," he said.

"Indeed not," Digby said. "This gentleman is a direct descendant of President Grant's valet, a man of Japanese nobility whom the president found in Jay-pan."

Arabella gave him a skeptical look.

"And he's very clean," Digby said.

"He'd better be. Come on in, then."

There were two women in the kitchen, busy at the stove. The younger one had reddish-blond hair and a face that just missed being pretty. She gave Benji a smile as he and Digby sat at the table.

"You like that one?" Digby said. "You pick any one you want."

Benji felt a tingling in his groin. "Is this a whorehouse?" he whispered.

Digby grinned. "You bet," he said.

The younger woman began cooking onions. The smell was arousing. Benji watched her skirt, imagining the buttocks beneath.

When supper was ready, the three women sat at the table. There were introductions: the younger one, Francette, sat across from Benji. Lucinda, the dark-haired one, was across from Digby. Arabella, at the head of the table, passed around beef hash, poached eggs, corn mush. It was like eating anywhere, Benji thought. He kept stealing glances at Francette. Her eyes were nice, light brown, with a tolerant expression.

The women talked about the weather. Digby told a long story about a tornado he'd survived. Benji's stomach felt so excited he could hardly eat, and when the meal was over, he waited until everyone else had stood and turned away before he got up, because his excitement was showing in his pants.

Digby consulted with Arabella, and then he and Benji went out to the side yard to plant the lilacs, Benji digging while Digby smoked his cigar and supervised.

"Your first whorehouse, eh?" Digby said with a chuckle.

"No," Benji lied. It didn't look like the whorehouses boys at school claimed to know about—women in fancy underwear, red carpets, a player piano. "It's just not like the ones I'm familiar with."

"The product is pretty much the same everywhere." He ground out his cigar in the dirt. "Stamp down those bushes real good. Arabella went out of her way to give us some grub too. She always been partial to me."

Arabella met them at the door; the other women had disappeared.

"Room two for him," Arabella said to Digby. "The usual for you."

Digby led the way upstairs. Benji's heart was pounding.

"Here's your spot." Digby opened one of the bedroom doors. There was an iron bed with a blue-and-white quilt, a braided rug on the floor. It looked like an ordinary room. Benji sat on the bed and waited, clasping and unclasping his hands. Should he lie down? What if he couldn't do it? Maybe he should tell her it was his first time.

It grew dark. He should have thought to ask for a candle. They must have meant for him to lie down in the dark. He took off his shoes and eased onto his back. He hoped Digby had arranged for Francette to come.

Finally the door opened. It was Francette, carrying a kerosene lamp. The lamp cast shadows on her face and showed wrinkles on her neck. In the kitchen, she had looked younger. She was wearing a silky white robe with fur down the edges.

"Here I am." She set the lamp on the table and lay down beside him. "How are you, then?" Her lips and cheeks were red, and she smelled too sweet. She ran her hand down his body and cupped it between his legs. "Oh, my," she said.

She stood and dropped the robe to the floor. Her underwear was plain, nothing like he'd seen in pictures.

"What do you want?" she said.

"I don't know. Whatever you usually do."

She smiled as she unlaced her corset. "We'll figure something out," she said. "Don't worry." She put the corset on a chair behind her. Her breasts were smaller than he'd hoped, and her ribs showed. When she stepped out of her bloomers, he began to pull off his clothes.

She sat on top of him and he knew what to do. But it was over too quickly, an explosion of pleasure. "I'm sorry," he said.

She swung her body off him as if he were a horse.

"It's all right," she said. "You're no different from any other man, even if you are from China." She got up and put on her clothes. "You sleep here," she said. "Digby has paid for that."

After she left, he went through it all again; this time it lasted longer. He rolled away from the wet spots he'd made on the sheets. As he went to sleep, he thought of Flora, her pretty brown eyes, the little scar beside her mouth. Now he could never write to her; he had lost her forever.

Frank took a drink, just a small one, and swung up onto Admiral. Someone had to go to the store. His mother refused—she'd have left Plum River by now, she said, if poor Kate didn't need her so badly—and they couldn't keep sending Franklin and the Swede. Last time Franklin had come home crying and wouldn't talk about what happened, though Frank had a pretty good idea.

Away from the windbreak of trees on Plum River Road, the wind was biting cold. Overnight they'd had a light snow, a salting of it on the fields. A jackrabbit flashed across the road. If Benji made a slingshot, he could get his meat that way. He'd likely freeze to death, but he had himself to thank, not giving a turnip's thought to those who'd raised him.

Keast. There was another Benedict Arnold. Knew about the photograph all along, his mother said. Not surprising. Thick as thieves, the two of them, from the start.

He took another nip as he turned onto the main road to Morseville. Lard, flour, vanilla, a rasher of bacon, a bottle of tonic for Kate. She refused to see Dr. McBride. No point trying to convince her; she'd always been headstrong. If she hadn't begged so hard, he never would have taken her to Japan, and they wouldn't be in this predicament.

In Morseville, Frank paused at the store. That Norwegian whose name he never could remember was going in, gave him a sly grin over his shoulder. Son of a bitch.

He'd go pay a visit to Keast first, give him a piece of his mind. Maybe two pieces. He'd be in now, Saturday morning, snoring like a hog.

He hitched Admiral in front of the boardinghouse and went around back, out of sight of Nellie Bosley. She'd already be spreading tales from here to kingdom come. Nothing like a spurned woman to trade on your bad fortune. On the stairs he uncapped the flask and took a long draught, then another when he reached the upstairs balcony.

He pounded on Keast's door. There was a clatter, something rolling across the floor. Then silence. He rapped again. "Keast?"

"Pinkerton?" Keast said from the other side of the door. "Any word of Benji?"

"Come out and I'll tell you."

Keast cracked open the door. He was still in his nightshirt.

"Why didn't you tell me about that goddamn picture?"

"The boy took me into his confidence. I'm sure he meant no harm."

"Harm?" Frank could hear his voice, high and sissy. "Tell my wife that," he said in a lower voice. "I hold you responsible, Keast."

"I didn't sire the boy."

Frank shoved him, knocking him into the room, and gave him a jab in the gut.

A woman screamed. Over Keast's head, he could see a form wriggling deeper into the bedclothes, a rabbit gone to ground.

"I'll be damned," Frank said, grinning.

Keast yanked his arm, pulled him outside, shut the door behind him. His hair was sticking up all over and he smelled of sex. Frank took a swing. Keast shoved him, grunting, and Frank fell against the porch railing. There was a cracking sound. He looked behind him—a long way down.

"Go sleep it off, Frank." The door slammed.

He took another drink, finishing off the bottle, and started down the stairs. Holier-than-thou horse doctor. He wasn't one for whores. Must be the teacher. He laughed and spat into Nellie Bosley's holly bushes.

In the yard, a colored boy had a bonfire going, bits of smoldering leaves rising in the air. As Frank stood watching, Butterfly seized him— her warm skin in the morning, the satin blanket of her hair. His legs trembled. Gripping the rail, he made his way to the bottom of the porch stairs and at the well splashed a dipperful of water on his face. Sharpless would say he'd had it coming. He nestled the empty bottle behind a bush.

The store was humming with Saturday-morning customers. He held back at the door. He ought to come when the crowd had thinned out, but his mother would blow blue thunder if he didn't hurry back with her things. And Katie needed her medicine.

When he stepped inside, a few heads turned in his direction. A woman smoothing out fabric stared. He tipped his cap to her—Mrs. Burdett, the banker's lard-assed wife. Bud Case was nowhere in sight. Bud was usually here on a Saturday. Hello, Frank, he'd have said, and slapped him on the back.

Silence fell as he walked to the counter. Red Olsen was toting up purchases for that librarian woman—Moss her name was—who Kate used to be so cozy with. A stringy girl he'd never seen before was putting things in sacks.

Miss Moss gave him a sharp glance as she left. Mean little eyes and buck teeth; no wonder she slept alone.

"Frank," Red said, not quite meeting his eyes. "Think we're in for more weather?"

"Not betting against it." Frank gave Red his list and stood looking through a seed catalogue. The place was quieter than a funeral. Just a tourist picture, he wanted to yell at them, none of your goddamn business.

"Flour, lard, vanilla." Red set the items on the counter. "Bacon." The tonic he slipped into a small sack without comment.

Frank pocketed his change, glanced around the store at people pretending not to look. He turned back to Red. "Don't expect Keast in here this morning," he said. "Bedded down with a woman." Red stared. The girl beside him snickered. "Don't ask me who. I've got . . . I've got . . ." He couldn't think what he was going to say. He picked up his packages.

There was murmuring as he made his way to the door. Someone— a woman—laughed.

He pulled himself onto Admiral and started down the street. He hadn't seen the photograph, that he could recall, but he vaguely remembered it being made: a little man shrouded behind a black cloth, his feet in tight-looking shoes. It had probably been her idea, her keepsake while he was gone. Of course she'd give it to her boy, his keepsake of her.

Tears came to his eyes, making a blur of the houses and trees and a man crossing the street in the distance. He felt suddenly homesick for his father.

When he was outside of town, it began to snow. There was a wind behind it, blowing sparks of cold against his face. He closed his eyes. Admiral would carry him to the farm.

By mid-November it was freezing even in the daytime, and nights were miserable. Digby invited Benji to bed down with him in the hayloft, when they were lucky enough to be put up in a barn, but Benji preferred to sleep beside Kuro in the stall, the horse's warm breath on his neck.

Food was scarce. They must look like tramps by now, Benji thought; housewives had become more reluctant to feed them. Some days they lived on nothing but apples and hickory nuts. The emptiness in Benji's stomach became a gnawing fear. He had a bit more money now, even after buying a jacket lined with sheep's wool—Digby had raised his rates for digging in nearly frozen ground—but no place for the winter. Digby said he was determined to find him a sinecure; that's why he kept traveling west instead of turning back like a more sensible man would have done. He claimed to have numerous connections, but after each of his private consultations on Benji's behalf, he came back shaking his head. There was one sure place, though, not far ahead, and he would see him settled in it. He owed him that much for hauling him out of the ditch and being such a loyal partner. "I've gotten right partial to you," he said, "and that's the Lord's truth. You've got a fearsome journey, but you're a determined little cuss. I believe you'll make it."

"What is this sure place?"

"A surprise." Digby lit a cigar and cackled. "I de-dog guarantee you'll like it."

For the next few days, as they rode through the flat gray Iowa landscape, not a tree in sight, Benji tried to ignore his doubts and concentrate on his final destination. He let the word *Nagasaki* roll through his mind,

summoning up the photograph he'd seen in a book of the bay there—
a deep inlet of water, with mountains all around, a glimpse of upturned
tiled roofs.

In the evenings, while it was still light, he found a private spot and
took his mother's picture from the tin box. Covering Frank's figure with
his thumb, he rested his eyes on his mother's serene face. And in the dark,
before sleep, he brought his mother's image to his mind. He didn't believe in heaven, but maybe somehow she would be able to sense his returning home to his own people, to Japanese soil.

One morning when Benji woke, there was snow on the ground, and
the sky was low and white. He slid lower in his bedroll and closed his eyes.
Kuro was stamping at the ground, neighing. He needed to shake the
snow from Kuro's blanket, give him some oats. By golly, he imagined
Keast saying, it's time to get going.

He kicked out of the blankets, fed Kuro, and tried to comb the snow
and ice from his mane with his fingers. There was no wood for a fire. He
pushed at Digby, who was snoring in the bed of the wagon, wrapped in
quilts he'd stolen from a wash line. "All right, dammit," Benji said.
"Where is this so-called sure thing? You've been wasting my time."

Digby reared up, rubbing his eyes. "Let's not get scrambled up here. I
ain't about to leave you at the mercy of the snows." He reached into his
bedding, pulled out a cigar stub, and lit it. "I can tell you about the
widow woman now that we're about to hit into her place. Those last
trees"—he jerked his head toward a dry pair of conifers—"are for her."

"They were for that farmer who turned them down yesterday."

"They're for the widow woman now, a condolence gift."

"She'd better help me," Benji muttered, "or the condolences will be for
you."

They set out down the road, he and Digby gnawing at icy knobs of
bread from yesterday's handout.

The widow woman lived just ahead, Digby said, outside Ottumwa,
and ran a dairy farm on her own. Her husband had died last spring, and
when Digby asked about her plans she said she had no plan but to stay
there; no bank or lawyer was going to run her off. "She needs the help
bad," he said. "She's got three head of chaps, but they're either too young
or too no-count to carry any weight. You'd be doing her a favor, with all
you know about animals, and you'll be getting yourself a soft deal. Cows
pretty much take care of themselves."

"She would have help by now."

"I'm reckoning not. She wouldn't be a real popular boss lady. But you'd get on with her okay—you get along with everybody, I've noticed that about you."

"What's wrong with her?"

"She's got a temper hotter than a potbellied stove at Christmas. Though to tell the truth, I don't mind a little fire in my women." He gave Benji a sidewise grin. "She's part Injun. She can't help her temper, and she don't really mean it. And since she's racial, she won't hold your race against you, like some might. This is by God a sure thing, and I know you won't be sorry."

Benji looked up at the sky and sighed. "How far?"

"We should make our arrival this afternoon."

By noon it had begun to snow again, a large-flaked, steady snow that meant business. Kuro frisked along, but Digby's horse plodded more slowly than ever. "See what a pickle I got myself into?" Digby said.

"Your pickle? What about mine?"

"You're going to be set up, but I've got all the way back to Missouri to consider."

They stopped in Ottumwa to buy some tooth powder, to freshen up for the widow, and a bottle of brandy as a gift. "She likes her whiskey, I don't mind telling you," Digby said. Benji noticed a cigar factory and a large dry-goods store; if things didn't work out at the widow's, he'd come back here and beg for a job.

It was nearly dusk when they turned down her road. Ahead, through the swirling snow, Benji saw a farmhouse in need of paint, a large barn, several smaller outbuildings.

At the front steps, Digby climbed from his wagon, brushed snow off his coat, and said, "You wait here. I'll handle the preliminaries."

He was gone a long while. Benji trotted Kuro up and down the road on his lead, trying to keep warm; his feet and nose were numb.

Finally Digby burst out the door and down the steps. His face was red and his hat was at a cockeyed angle. "He ain't dead yet," he said. "Last year he was as good as dead." He looked indignant, as though the man hadn't kept a promise.

"I knew it." Benji kicked at the snow.

"Hold on now, hold on. The negotiations are proceeding. He's still sick in the bed—I know she needs help. She's invited us for supper."

Benji took the horses to the barn and rubbed them down. There were four milk cows, a quarter horse, a Percheron, and three empty stalls. Not much of a dairy operation; the others must have been sold off. He put their horses into two of the stalls, fed and watered them. There was plenty of hay in the loft; someone had been looking after her. Farmers always looked after others in need, especially a woman. Either she already had a hired hand or didn't need one. He'd been crazy to stick with Digby. A fool and his money are soon parted, he could hear Frank saying. He imagined grabbing the whip out of Frank's hand, lashing him across the face. This was Frank's doing. If Benji hadn't had to leave so fast, he could have planned this trip in some reasonable way.

At the house, he knocked at the door; no one appeared, so he let himself in.

A white iron bed stood in the parlor, a bald man lying in it, his eyes closed. His face was gray; he did look almost dead. A small white dog sat on the bed near the man's feet, watching like a sentinel. Benji walked quietly toward the voices in the kitchen.

Digby was at the table, sopping corn bread in buttermilk. A woman was leaning against the stove, her arms crossed over her chest. She was tall, with a spadelike face and black eyes. She flicked her eyes toward Benji; she had said no.

"He's a trained veterinarian," Digby was saying. "I've seen evidence of it. When my nag got a stone bruise, he knew just what to do. And he knows how to get wind out of a colicky horse."

"So do I," she said.

Digby turned and put a hand on Benji's shoulder. "He's on his way home to find his mother's people, all the way to the Orient. You got to help him, just on a temporary basis."

She sighed. "I can't afford another mouth."

"He eats like a lovesick sparrow," Digby said, "and he don't take up much space. You'd be mighty glad to have him."

She looked at Benji, not unkindly. "Sit down, boy," she said, "and help yourself to some food. You can stay the night, Digby, both of you, but that's all I can manage."

"Now what?" Benji said, when she'd left.

"We'll think of something," Digby said.

The children came in for supper: Otto, a husky boy of fourteen; Hans, younger but strong-looking; and a little girl, not much more than a baby, with black eyes like her mother's. The woman followed; her name was Mrs. Weber.

She ladled out a thin soup and sat down with them.

"You need you some more help," Digby said. "You wouldn't have to pay him."

She looked at him; Benji sat up straighter and tried to look helpful. He wished Digby hadn't said that about the pay.

"In the winter he could stay in the barn—he don't mind that at all. He loves the animals. Days your boys couldn't get out for the snow you'd be glad for that."

She shook her head.

Down the hall her husband cried out, a feeble yelp of pain; she jumped up and hurried to him.

Digby leaned close to Benji and whispered, "Canker on the brain. Blinded, can't speak. You can see she needs the help."

They went to the barn for the night, Digby carrying a lantern the woman had loaned them. He lay down on a cot in the corner, his ankles crossed, his hands behind his head. "This must be where the hired man stayed," he said. "Once upon a time, you'd have been appreciated."

Benji swore under his breath and walked toward Kuro's stall.

"Come here, got something for you." Digby sat up and rummaged in his bag. He held up the bottle of brandy. "She don't deserve it, and you got a man's problems now."

Benji walked back toward Digby. "You were wrong about another thing too," he said. "That woman's not an Indian—she just has dark hair." He took a long pull from the bottle Digby handed him. "Tomorrow I'm going to town," he said, "and I want my bonus. I'll be needing it."

Digby's head bobbed up and down. "You'll get it," he said. "I've got to do some figuring, though. I've had extra expenses, coming this far."

"It was your idea about this so-called widow."

"I done the best I could. I always done the best I could, can't no man say otherwise." He stood up. "You can have the cot for the night and keep the brandy. I'll bed down in the hayloft, and tomorrow I'll see what more I can do about the situation."

"Ha," Benji said. He sat on the cot and drank as Digby teetered up the ladder to the hayloft. Fat idiot. Maybe he'd fall and break his neck.

He took another drink. At this rate, he'd never get to Japan. A month of traveling and only in Iowa, stuck here for the winter, nowhere to go.

He and Kuro couldn't keep on in the snow. They had to take him at the cigar factory or a store, though they'd be suspicious of him, a vagabond, a mongrel Jap.

It had gotten dark, but his hands were too cold to light the lantern. He kept drinking to blot out his thoughts and finally went to sleep.

He woke at first light. The cows were lowing; maybe he should start the milking. She might pay him a little for that. He sat up, dizzy and sick, his head pounding. Just like Frank, he thought.

On the floor beside the cot was an envelope. He ripped it open: Digby's watch fell out. There was a note: *Contrary to your assertion,* it read, *I came this distance to help you out. You may keep this watch, which belonged to my father, who fought valiantly at the battle of Bull Run, or you can sell it for a handsome bonus. Good luck on your journey. Yours truly, Digby Moffett, Esq.* There was a postscript: *I had no choice than to do what I done, since I came this far so late in the year and have to get back quick before the blizzards, but I had your benefit in mind as well. I think you will find I have improved your situation considerably.*

Benji stared at the note, reread the postscript. *No choice . . . get back quick.* He jumped up and ran to Kuro's stall. It was empty, just trampled straw and an overturned water bucket. "No," he yelled. "No, no!"

Digby's nag was in her stall. He kicked her door hard and ran outside. The wagon was outside the barn, poles resting on the ground, the box of trinkets on the front seat.

Kuro. He opened and closed his hands. Kuro. He walked in a circle, held to a fence post, pounded it to keep from crying. His loyal buddy. He thought of the day Keast had brought Kuro to the farm; they'd understood each other from the start.

He ran back inside and saddled the other quarter horse—he'd explain later—and galloped down the driveway to the road. The cold air numbed his face. Without Kuro, he had nothing. Alone, his journey over. He couldn't even get to town.

He pressed the horse faster, galloping east, retracing the route they'd followed. He looked for Kuro's tracks in the snow, but it was impossible; the road was blurred with hoof prints. He met several people, farmers, a man in a buggy; none of them had seen a fat man on a black quarter horse, but Digby had set out before light. Benji kept riding straight east, though Digby could have taken a crossroad and hidden God knew where. "Horse thief," he shouted, his voice ringing across the fields. He'd kill him, string him up in one of his trees. He'd better not have harmed Kuro.

He rode hard until noon, when his borrowed horse was streaked with sweat. He turned back, letting the horse walk, tears streaming down his face. There was a searing pain in his chest. What now? He'd walk to Ottumwa before he'd ride Digby's nag.

A horse came rushing toward him; the rider had a rifle under his arm. Then he saw it was Mrs. Weber, in a heavy coat and man's hat. She pulled her horse up beside him and raised the rifle. "You're going to jail."

"No," he said, "Wait. I'm looking for Moffett—he stole *my* horse. I was bringing yours back." He took Digby's note from his pocket and handed it to her. "He left during the night on Kuro. Now I'm done for."

She stared at the note, turned it over, read it again. "You better be telling the truth. Why didn't you ask before taking my horse?"

"I was in a hurry to catch him."

"How long you known Digby Moffett?"

"I just met him on the road a few weeks ago."

"That was a misfortunate piece of luck." She tucked the rifle back under her arm and studied him. "Where are you from?"

"My father and stepmother live in Illinois. I'm on my way to Japan, where I was born—Digby was telling the truth about that. And Kuro—my . . ." He clenched his jaw.

"You know how to read?"

His face went hot. "Just because I'm Japanese doesn't mean I can't read. I've been to school—I'm in the top grade."

"Christian?"

"I have three gold stars for Sunday-school attendance."

"All right," she said. "You can stay with us for a while, until we find your horse and the worm that's on his back."

Kate was ill with mother's sickness, vomiting every morning into the chamber pot beside the bed. As soon as this phase passed, she would leave; she had to leave this place, the gossip, the humiliation, Aimee and her tribe relishing the exposure of the elaborate lies she had told about Benji's origins. She could see them in Aimee's parlor, gathered for the women's circle meeting, their tea growing cold, their eyes glittering as they leaned forward, devouring morsels of fact and rumor. Mrs. Cassidy would declare she had never been so shocked. I always suspected it, Aimee would say, setting off a clamor of excited agreement: Her Christian duty, indeed!

They would whisper at church, and Reverend Singleton and his wife would discuss the scandal at their dinner table. If only she had confided in Reverend Singleton, he might be able to help her now, but it was too late. There was no help.

She kept to her room, sleeping much of the day with the aid of the tonics Frank had brought her.

One day she dreamed about Benji, that she had given birth to him herself. He was bleeding from his mouth, and she was covered with his blood. She jerked awake, pulled down the covers, and looked—nothing—then fell back onto the bed. She could hear Mrs. Pinkerton downstairs, cleaning, scraping chairs about. Kate got out of bed, put on her robe, and went to stand by the window, putting her forehead against the cold pane. There was a freezing drizzle, the ice beginning to coat the trees, the limbs shining in the cold light of late afternoon. The garden had buckled, the coneflowers, the black-eyed Susans, the lettuces shriveled. She thought of

Benji huddled against the door of a shop in some strange town. He might die of exposure in this weather; he might already be dead. She felt a wave of vertigo; it was too much to think about. She went back to her tonic and to sleep.

Sometimes Mary Virginia tiptoed into the room and wriggled into bed with her. "All right," Kate said, "if you be quiet and go to sleep." Mary Virginia would lie still, her hot sweet little breath on Kate's face, and stare at her. "Is Mama sick?" she said one day.

"No. Mama is just waiting for the stork."

"Why?"

Kate closed her eyes, saw the air thick with orange butterflies.

"Why, Mama?"

"The stork is going to bring us a baby."

"I'm the baby." Mary Virginia thrashed and kicked. "I'm the baby."

"Go on, now." Kate gave her a nudge. "Go help your grandmother. Mama needs to sleep."

One evening she woke to see Franklin at the door. He was on his way to bed, holding a candle. His shirttail was out and his trousers were too short. He'd grown without her noticing.

"When is Benji coming back?" he said.

"I don't know."

"Will he come back?"

"No," she said, in a sharper voice than she'd intended, and Franklin slid away. "I don't know. How could I possibly know?" she called after him. "Franklin?" When he didn't return, she took out the tonic and drank herself back to unconsciousness.

At night she was wakeful, after her long spells of sleep during the day, but lay turned away from Frank, feigning sleep. When he whispered "Kate?" and touched her shoulder, she deepened her breathing. He disgusted her, the stale smell of his nightshirt, the alcohol on his breath. Often he rose and went to his office or down the stairs. He was miserable too, but she could not help him.

One afternoon Mrs. Pinkerton woke her to say she was worried about Franklin. "He never came back from the milking," she said. "I've looked for him everywhere."

Mrs. Pinkerton's eyes and head seemed too large, as if Kate were looking at her through water. She forced herself up; the room was spinning. "He's at school," she said.

"He doesn't go to school anymore," Mrs. Pinkerton said. "We can't get him to go. His pony is gone—Frank thinks he's trying to find Benji."

Kate thought of him at her door in his outgrown clothes, his eyes wide and anxious. It was her fault, her darling boy. "I can't lose him," she whispered.

"Frank will find him."

Kate followed Mrs. Pinkerton down the stairs, holding tight to the railing.

They looked out the windows of the dining room and parlor. It was a perfectly still day, the branches of the trees not stirring, as if the world were holding its breath. The house was silent.

"Mary Virginia," Kate cried, looking around.

"Playing with her dolls," Mrs. Pinkerton said.

They sat in the parlor, Mrs. Pinkerton knitting a white baby blanket that fell over her knees. It was long enough to be a small shroud.

"I've killed him," Kate whispered. "I told him Benji wouldn't be back."

"Hush. It's bad luck to talk that way. And it's none of your fault." She flicked her gaze up from the needles.

Mary Virginia ran into the room and shoved something at Kate. "Baby," she said. It was the ugly rag doll that Mrs. Pinkerton had made from a sock.

"They'll be hungry when they get back," Mrs. Pinkerton said, rising.

"Hungry," Mary Virginia said. "Me and the baby are hungry."

Kate put Mary Virginia in her high chair and laid the table, her hands trembling. Mrs. Pinkerton brought corn bread and a pitcher of milk, poured milk for the three of them, then sat with Kate at the table.

Mary Virginia held her cup to the doll's mouth. Milk splashed onto the doll and the high chair.

"Stop that," Kate said, snatching away the doll. "Eat. Be a big girl."

Mary Virginia drummed her feet against the chair. "Baby!" she cried, then "Frankie!"

"Shh," Kate said. "Franklin and Papa have gone to a meeting."

Mrs. Pinkerton gave her a look. The wrong thing to say. But what could she say?

Her mother-in-law lifted Mary Virginia from the high chair. "Bedtime for the big girl," she said, and carried her upstairs.

Kate took a swallow of milk. It tasted off. She went to the parlor and picked up her needlework, but her fingers would not move; she was sick with fear.

Finally Frank was at the door. She flew to greet him.

He shook his head.

"Someone must have seen him," Kate yelled. "Go back. Keep looking."

"A group of us will go out tomorrow at first light," Frank said.

Kate let out a sob. Frank reached for her but she pushed him away, ran, stumbling, up the stairs. Maybe she would trip and this would all be over.

The next morning Kate went downstairs when she heard men's voices: Bud Case and his son Eli, Red Olsen, Keast. The men kept their eyes averted from her; she shouldn't have come down in her nightgown, and she with child. What was she thinking?

"We'll find him, Kate," Keast said, but his face lacked conviction. There were pouches under his eyes; he'd been awake all night too.

Mrs. Pinkerton gave them sacks of food, and they left in a racket of boots and door slammings and horses. Then, silence again.

Kate dressed and walked down the road, then crossed the meadow and followed the edge of the little river. She was light-headed, her first time out in weeks. The water was moving swiftly, foaming around the rocks. Franklin had loved playing here. She thought of the time he'd come into the house shouting and waving a fish Benji had helped him catch.

She'd been fine then, a normal mother. She remembered frying the fish, the oil sputtering in the pan. She held to a plum branch and hung over her reflection in a still pool of water at the edge of the river. Kate. Kate Lewis Pinkerton.

She went back to the house, to her room, and fell into a deep sleep. When she awoke in the afternoon and descended the stairs, there were cakes and pies on the dining room and kitchen tables.

"Is he dead?" she cried.

"No, dear, there's no word yet."

"Then they shouldn't bring food." Now they'd be talking about her again; what kind of mother lost two boys? "Has Aimee Moore been here?"

"She brought that pie." Mrs. Pinkerton nodded toward it. "Raisin."

Kate crushed the lattice crust with the heel of her hand and threw the pie in the slop bucket.

"Dear, you need to go upstairs. You're going to harm the baby, being so upset."

Kate laughed. "Good," she said. "I hope so."

"Hush, Mary Virginia will hear. Why don't you have some more of your syrup?"

Kate went up to Franklin's room, remade the bed with fresh sheets, dusted his table and desk. Lined up on the desk were small carvings Benji had made for him: an owl, a skunk, a horse, a cat. She should have known Franklin would go after him. She picked up the cat and gouged the sharp tip of an ear against her arm until the spot burned with pain.

It was three days before the men returned. They'd gone all the way to the Mississippi, inquiring at each town along the way, and crossed into Iowa. One woman in Galena thought she had seen him, while she was sweeping her porch, but couldn't be sure.

Kate fainted that night after supper and Dr. McBride was called, against her wishes. She turned her face away from him as he examined her and did not answer his questions. He ordered her to remain in bed for the remainder of the pregnancy.

Hour after hour she lay listening for the sounds of a horse on the road, the silence pulsing in her ears. She could remember Franklin's voice exactly, the way he said *Mama?* with a lilt at the end. Hours and days inched by. She tried to pray.

It was almost Thanksgiving, in the afternoon, when there was a commotion downstairs. Mrs. Pinkerton ran up to tell her. "Praise God, he's been found."

Kate fell, rushing down the stairs, and slid partway, thumping hard against the edge of the steps.

"Darling." Frank was bending over her. "The baby . . ." He touched her belly.

She reached for Franklin, kissed his cheeks, his forehead, his head. His hair was filthy. She smoothed it back with both hands.

"I couldn't find him, Mama." He began to cry.

"But you tried. I was so frightened—don't you ever, ever . . ." Before she realized it, she was shaking him.

"Kate." Frank helped her stand. "Here are the kind people we have to thank—Mr. and Mrs. Schultz. They've brought him all the way from East Dubuque. He was sleeping in their shed."

Mr. Schultz gave a slight bow. "We saw the notice in the paper." His face was broad and grave. His wife, a slight woman buried in a fur coat, stepped forward and took Kate's hands. Kate felt how cold her hands were in the woman's grasp.

"I know you've been in anguish," the woman said. "I couldn't bear it if my children ran away."

Kate's face went hot. "Thank you," she managed to say.

"I see you're expecting another," the woman whispered, then said in a louder voice, "Such a brave little boy you have. It's too bad about his brother." She pressed her thumbs into Kate's hands. "I pray you'll find him too."

December the 14th, 1905

Dear Benjamin,

I have made many a go at this letter and seem to get bollixed up each time, so I have decided to take the steer by the horns and write to you straight out, just as if we were talking.

First off, I know you are grieved by the loathsome theft of Kuro, but you must not mortify yourself on this account. This villainy was in no way your fault. A horse thief is not going to advertise himself as such. Though I believe most human beings to be sound at the core, there are some putrefied ones, and more than a few of these have a slick outer surface through which it may be impossible to penetrate. I will do everything in my power to apprehend this swine and recover Kuro. You have made an excellent start yourself, in alerting the sheriffs in Ottumwa and Dubuque and, as you say, it is likely that someone in Iowa will have seen the varmint. If this odious Mr. Moffett imagines that he will be able to hide himself and a handsome quarter horse under a bush, he is as much a fool as he is a devil. If you could provide even a rough drawing of the wretch, I will see that it is posted across the plains and into the southern regions, where you think he might have returned.

In the meantime, remember that Kuro is a spunky, smart fellow. I think of him as a quadruped version of you, and I believe that he will endure come what may.

I was heartened and indeed overjoyed to know that you are well and that you have found a sinecure for the winter months. The German woman sounds sensible and fair-minded, and I am surmising that it is a great comfort to her that you are reading aloud to her sightless husband.

As for your family, I can report that they are doing well enough. In accord with your request, I have not informed them of your whereabouts, but all were relieved to hear of your safety and general good health.

Your stepmother will give birth in the spring and has been much confined to the house. Franklin is becoming a little man, and your sister is sprouting up like a sunflower and is the charm of Plum River. Your grandmother is as hardy as ever, though she misses you sorely, as we all do, but you must not let thoughts of that stand in the way of your journey.

Now for some glad tidings:

Lena and I were married on December 1st in Plum River Church, and a giddier production you have never seen, but all the frills and furbelows were well worth the happiness that I now enjoy. I never expected such again in my lifetime. The only shadow over the day of ritual was your absence. Lena and I both have remarked several times that if you'd been here I'd have had you standing by me to keep me from quaking in my boots, for—this may come as a surprise to you, young friend—I have ever found you a steadying influence, even when you were a sad little chap who had just lost his mama.

All in all, I stoutly believe that you will make a success of your life, of which this journey comprises a significant segment. You are traveling alone through perilous chasms and dark thickets, but it is such experience that can make a great man.

Enclosed is a monetary contribution to your progress. Lena and I hope this will help see you on your way. By my calculation, it should be enough to carry you by train to California and to establish yourself there awhile as you are making ready for your passage to Japan.

Yours truly,
Horatio C. Keast

Dressed in a new suit, bowler hat, and fine black shoes—parting gifts from Mrs. Weber—Benji leaned against a train window, watching Iowa recede. The sounds of the locomotive's whistle and the wheels clattering on the rails were urgent and thrilling. He was on his way at last.

It had been a long winter of snow and gray skies, but now in mid-April the ground was thawed and the farmers were at their plowing. Through the open window he could smell spring—the odors of the rich, turned earth, the thickets of wild plum along the streams, already in blossom. The fragrance of plums would always remind him of Flora, their walks along Plum River in the spring.

He had tried several times at the Webers' house to write to her but had sat paralyzed at the kitchen table before the sheet of paper, images of Digby, Kuro, the bridge in the rain, Frank's whip, tumbling through his mind. There was too much to say. Maybe, like Keast, he should begin as if speaking to her in person, as if she, and not that old man snoring in the seat across from him, were here.

What would she think of him in the bowler hat and suit? And what of his black hair, colored with shoe polish at Mrs. Weber's suggestion, so he would fit in with the other Japanese in San Francisco? Flora might laugh. Looking at his reflection in the dim mirror of the Webers' hallway, he had been startled to see a young man, but he hadn't decided if it was a distinguished or ridiculous-looking one. Mrs. Weber said he looked very handsome, but Otto laughed and said he was a dressed-up monkey.

There was stationery on the little table between the seats. *Chicago, Burlington, and Quincy Railroad, All Aboard,* it said across the top; beneath was a picture of a long train with smoke streaming from the engine. Flora would like this paper, and if he wrote to her on it, it would be the closest thing to having her here.

He searched in his shiny new valise for a pencil. *Dear Flora,* he wrote, *I have thought of you every day, in circumstances that would surprise and even shock you. I spent the winter at the house of a dying man. It was terrible to watch him suffer. When I read to him, I thought of how you and I used to read Longfellow and Shelley to each other beside the river.* He stared out the window. He'd also thought of Flora when he rubbed the old man's forehead and arms with the pine oil that seemed to soothe him, imagining that if Flora could see him she would know he'd make a good, kind husband. *I made the coffin,* he continued, *nothing as fine as your father's work, of course, and I dug the hole myself, to spare his children. His wife said after we laid him in the ground that he had always been such a considerate man; she thought he waited to die until the ground was no longer frozen.*

This was no letter to send to a girl. He crumpled the page, stuffed it in his pocket, and began again. *Dear Flora, How are you? How is school? I hope you are very well, and your family too.*

I have had many adventures. Maybe someday I can tell you about them, though it would be better if I could see you. I don't know when, though.

I am on a train just like the one shown above, on the way to San Francisco. The train is going too fast for me to write straight, so I hope you don't think I'm drunk. He erased *drunk* and substituted *don't think I've forgotten Miss Ladu's—Mrs. Keast's, rather!—penmanship lessons.*

So I'd better say good-bye for now. I will write to you again, though. Say hello to the plum trees for me. Your friend, Benji.

P.S.—How is your little gray kitten? Maybe a cat by now.

He put the letter in an envelope and wrote decisively, *To Miss Flora Rosser, Plum River, Illinois,* then laid his hand on the envelope. Her fingers would touch where his had been. Maybe she would think of that, though probably not.

Mrs. Weber had packed food for the journey—corned beef sandwiches, hard-boiled eggs, corn bread, coconut cake. While he was eating, the man across from him woke with a snort, rubbed his small, bloodshot eyes, then stared at Benji as if he were the continuation of a dream.

Benji smiled and introduced himself; then, since he felt a rude question coming on, he added, "I am Japanese by heritage, but I have lived in America for many years, so I am also an American."

"You see all kinds, riding the rails." He was Homer Skakle, he said, a farm-equipment salesman from Omaha, on his way home after three months, but it had been worth the outlay of time and money. Farmers were lulu over the new McCormick thresher. He began eyeing Benji's food. "I'll give you ten cents for one of those eggs."

"I might be needing it," Benji said. "It's a long way to Denver." Mrs. Weber had advised him to take a hotel in Denver, to get at least one good night's sleep.

"You can get anything you want in Omaha. Train stops there for an hour. Chicken pie, venison."

"I can't buy chicken pie for ten cents."

Skakle reached in his coat pocket, jingled his change. "All right. I'll give you thirty cents for the egg and some cake. Haven't eaten since before Dubuque."

"Fifty," Benji said.

"You Japs drive a hard bargain. That's how you beat those Russkies, I guess."

"Japanese," Benji said. "Russian." Ignoramus. He quickly repacked his food into the lunch box and moved to another car. He leaned against the seat with his eyes closed, imagining shoving a whole egg into Skakle's mouth. It was the kind of thing he used to tell Kuro. His eyes stung, thinking of Kuro, but he'd be damned if he would cry.

In Omaha he changed to a faster train equipped with Pullman cars. Though he could afford only coach, he walked through the train after it got under way to see the sleeping cars and the fancy parlor he'd heard about. The parlor was decorated with flowered carpets, painted ceilings, and chandeliers that swayed side to side with the movement of the train. There was a group of men at a table playing cards; their cigar smoke filled the room. One of them gave him a hard look; he turned and headed back to his seat.

In the next car he was startled to see a Japanese man sitting alone, smoking a cigarette and gazing out the window. He was a thin, balding gentleman in expensive-looking clothes.

Benji walked slowly past him, hoping the man would glance his way, but he continued to look out the window. There was an open book in his lap, the pages written in what must be Japanese. At the end of the car, Benji pushed open the door and stood for a few minutes on the platform between the cars, enveloped by the exciting turmoil of the train's sounds and smells. This was no time to hang back; he hadn't met a Japanese person except Tsuneo in all these years. Quickly, before he could change his mind, he went back into the car, stood beside the man's seat, and said, "Excuse me, are you from Japan?"

The man looked up at him, not speaking for a moment. "I am Japanese," he said, "with my home in San Francisco."

"That's where I'm going!" Benji said. "San Francisco, then Japan. May I talk to you?"

The man nodded at the empty seat across from him. "*Dozo*," he said.

Benji removed his hat and sat down. His heart was hammering.

The man handed him a card: *Yasunari Matsumoto, Purveyor of Fine Tea and Silk, 1633 Dupont Street, San Francisco, California.*

"I have not seen Japanese east of Denver," Mr. Matsumoto said. "You are not pure Japanese, of course."

Benji looked at his reflection in the window, his shoe-polish-blackened hair, streaked in some places he hadn't noticed with the hat on, his eyes like his mother's, and his nose, pickle shaped, like Frank's. He felt a burst of anger at Frank.

"My mother was from a samurai family," Benji said. "She's no longer living, but I'm going to Japan to find my relatives."

"Ah." Mr. Matsumoto smiled and put aside his book, so Benji continued, telling him he'd grown up on his American father's farm and had just left to go to San Francisco. As soon as he made his fortune, he was going to Japan.

Mr. Matsumoto folded his hands beneath his chin. "How shall you make your fortune?" he said with a little smile.

Benji glanced down at Mr. Matsumoto's card.

"I'd thought about the import/export business," he said. "My father did some of that in Japan."

"But already you know farming. Many Japanese in California are successful in this. Too successful for some," he added. "The white farmers are very angry that Japanese do so well. But you can do this also, make good profit growing strawberries, lettuce, or sugar beet."

Benji had decided he would never plow another row. Instead, he said, "That would take too long."

"You think to make fortune in one month?" Mr. Matsumoto laughed, covering his mouth.

"No, but . . . I need to get to Japan as soon as possible."

"You must have patience. I can introduce you in California. I know many people, including Hakumi, the biggest grower of strawberries."

"Thank you very much," Benji said. "I'm experienced in business too."

"How can this be, on a farm?"

Benji told him about working as cashier and bookkeeper for Red Olsen.

"*Ah so?* But this is difficult way to make a fortune. I think you had better work hard on a strawberry farm, then become manager and owner. That way you can make your money."

Benji looked down at his hands, the coat sleeves that were too long in spite of Mrs. Weber's alterations. He felt foolish; he should go back to his seat.

"You haven't told me your name," Mr. Matsumoto said.

"I don't know my family name yet. My first name is Tsuneo." If he showed Mr. Matsumoto his mother's picture, he could read the back of it for him. Then at least he would have his samurai name.

"You are Tsuneo in farmland?"

"No, Benjamin Pinkerton. Benji."

"I think you had better adopt some temporary Japanese last name. Sato, maybe. Easy for Americans to say."

Benji reached in his pocket to take out the picture, glanced across the aisle at the family there, the woman and one of her daughters watching them curiously.

"I'd like to talk to you about something later," Benji said. "In private. Maybe at the Denver station? I think the train stops there for an hour."

"I disembark in Denver, I'm afraid, and will be on the way to my hotel."

"I'm getting off there too. Could we meet?" Benji took a deep breath; he'd never been so bold as this.

"I will be very busy, meeting with matrons interested in my silk. But . . ." He took a small notebook from his pocket. "Perhaps tomorrow afternoon we can meet for tea at Brown Palace Hotel. This where I stay; anyone can direct you. Shall we say four o'clock?"

"I'll be gone by then."

"In that case, please come visit me in San Francisco. I shall be there in a week or so." When Benji did not move, he bowed slightly.

"Thank you," Benji said, imitating Mr. Matsumoto's bow. "I will see you there." He returned to his seat and stared out at the endless sea of prairie grass. He thought of going back with the picture, but Mr. Matsumoto had dismissed him coldly. Maybe they wouldn't like him in Japan either, for not being pure Japanese. But he was Japanese in his heart; he would show them.

They arrived in Denver early the next afternoon. The train jolted to a stop, shuddering and creaking. Newsboys raced up and down the platform, yelling, waving newspapers. A man reached out the window, grabbed a paper. He and the people around him began to talk loudly. One woman broke into sobs. Benji heard "San Francisco" and "earthquake." He scrambled off the train and bought a newspaper.

FLAMES RAGE UNCHECKED. SAN FRANCISCO HEAP OF EMBERS.

He stared down at the headline, the drawing of the city on fire. His destination.

San Francisco, California, April 18, 1906. An earthquake at 5:16 o'clock Wednesday morning immediately followed by fire destroyed the business portion of San Francisco and a big part of Santa Rosa. . . . Wild rumors have been circulated that 3,000 are dead, but we believe this will be no more than 1,000 persons, and 200 are probably Chinese.

People were shouting, shoving past him. A woman with thin gray hair sat on a suitcase, her head in her hands.

All the district between Market Street and the bay, including Chinatown, is in flames, he read. *The beautiful Stanford University is in ruins. President Roosevelt and Congress . . .*

He tried to read further, but his eyes wouldn't work. He let himself be swept along by the crowd.

The mass of people parted ahead of him, flowing in two directions. He saw a few people clustered around a man who had fallen. "Jap," one of them said.

Mr. Matsumoto. Benji forced his way through the crush, using his valise as a shield. A man was bent over him, holding his wrist.

"Is he dead?" Benji cried.

"No, but his heart is going double time."

Benji squatted beside him. "Mr. Matsumoto, it's me, Benji. From the train."

Mr. Matsumoto's eyelids fluttered. He said something in Japanese.

Benji picked him up and carried him toward the station. "Coming through," he shouted. "Emergency, coming through." In the station house, he shouted for a doctor.

"No doctor," Mr. Matsumoto said. He opened his eyes and looked at Benji. "Take me to Waraji. Wazee Street."

Benji found a porter—a colored man in uniform, guiding people into hansoms—and asked if he could direct them to Waraji's on Wazee Street.

"That's in Hop Alley," the porter said. "China and Jap town. Take the number-two trolley." He pointed to a small train car, clicking along the street on rails. "Only two blocks from the last street, on Sixteenth Street."

"We need a hansom—this man is sick."

"White folks gets all the hansoms," he said, shaking his head.

Benji reached into his pocket for a five-dollar bill. "Please, sir?"

The porter looked at the money, grinned, and whistled to an old colored man in a cart. "Hop Alley," he said. "Mighty quick."

Benji held Mr. Matsumoto upright as they drove past the tall buildings of downtown Denver. He was startled when he looked straight ahead: the Rocky Mountains, snow-covered and wrinkled, just as they looked in the pictures, but much larger than he'd imagined. They filled the whole sky.

They came to Wazee, a muddy street lined with small shops, cloths hanging over the doors, and larger buildings that looked like warehouses. A few men were in the street, gathered around a cart with a broken wheel.

"Waraji," Benji shouted to them. "Where is Waraji?"

A man with a kerchief around his head pointed down the street, talking rapidly in what must be Japanese. He had never dreamed there were Japanese in Denver. He felt a flood of affection for the old man, now leaning against him, who had brought him here.

They stopped in front of a plain wooden building. The driver helped Benji take Mr. Matsumoto inside. The hallway was dark, lit by a single gas lamp; at the end of the hall was a room filled with long wooden tables. Two men sat eating at one of the tables; they looked up and one shouted, "Eeh! Matsumoto-san." He called to someone in the kitchen, and a ruddy-faced man appeared. Mr. Matsumoto took his hand. "Shin-san," he whispered. All the men followed as Shin-san helped Mr. Matsumoto to a smaller room and laid him on a bed there.

Tears slid down Mr. Matsumoto's face, and he said something in a reedy voice. Benji heard "San Francisco."

"Wah!" the men said. One grabbed at his hair and ran out of the room.

"Doctor for Matsumoto-san?" Benji said.

"No doctor," Shin-san said. "We take care of him."

A wet cloth was brought, and smelling salts, a blanket, some whiskey. Mr. Matsumoto opened his eyes; he must have just fainted from the shock, Benji thought.

The men, talking nonstop in Japanese, helped Mr. Matsumoto stand and led him to the dining room, where they brought him food and more whiskey. Mr. Matsumoto continued to cry, gesturing as he talked. Shin-san translated for Benji: He was worried about his friends and thought his shop must have burned.

"You save Matsumoto-san," Shin-san said with a bow. *"Domo arigato."*

More people arrived and crowded onto the seats at the tables. Some looked at Benji curiously, but after Shin-san explained in Japanese, they gave deep, enthusiastic bows. He was given whiskey, some familiar-tasting soup and noodles. Soba, he remembered. His mother had made noodles like this.

Soon he was sleepy; he wanted to put his head on the table. Their valises were at the station, he realized; he should go get them, but he couldn't stir. Someone led him to the other room, to a bed, and put a cover over him. He fell asleep with the sound of Japanese in his ears.

The day after the earthquake, Benji took Mr. Matsumoto to the office of *The Denver Post* to learn what they could about survivors. They jounced along in Shin-san's cart, which had a listing wheel, the motion shifting them back and forth against one another. Mr. Matsumoto counted on his fingers the names they'd be looking for: Hiko Ueda, his helper, and several friends who had shops near his in Chinatown.

"You have no wife?" Benji asked.

"Once I had a wife, but she died of a fever. Better than to die in the fire, I think."

There was a rambunctious crowd outside the newspaper building—men and women of all ages elbowing for room to look at a list posted on the window. A woman in a lavender hat and veil fainted and had to be carried away. Mr. Matsumoto remained in the cart while Benji wriggled through the crush and read the names: *Annie Whelan, killed while asleep in her bed, 2782 Sacramento Street; Myrtle Minze, Langdon Street, killed under cav-*

ing wall; unknown white men, Front and Vallejo Streets . . . There were no Japanese listed.

A man with a cigar clenched between his teeth came to post more names. "No Chinks," he said, glancing at Benji. "Read the newspaper."

Benji bought a paper from a newsboy, scanned the front page, and read aloud to Mr. Matsumoto: *"An eyewitness reports that the Chinamen are streaming out of Chinatown, which is in cinders. The Chinamen are not reporting their dead, nor are the Italians and Greeks."*

"No one is asking them," Mr. Matsumoto said. "And no one mentions the Japanese, who also live in Chinatown."

They picked up their suitcases at the train station, then started back to Waraji's.

In the distance, the white line of mountains gleamed in the light. "Too many mountains in America," Mr. Matsumoto said, with a dismissive wave. "Mount Fuji is better, standing alone." He closed his eyes and folded in on himself; they rode the rest of the way in silence.

At dinner, Mr. Matsumoto made a speech to the crowd gathered in the restaurant. Benji heard his name: Shin-san told him that Matsumoto had praised him for treating him as a son would do. Afterward, there were toasts to Mr. Matsumoto, who was leaving the next day, and to Benji.

As they were getting ready for bed, Benji said, "Matsumoto-san, I'd like to ask you a favor."

"Anything," he said, with a bow. "You have saved me."

Benji found the tin deep in his pants pocket and took out his picture.

"This is my mother," he said, kneeling beside Matsumoto's cot.

"Ah so." He held it up to the light. "And your father. Now I understand your face."

"Could you please translate what's written on the back?" Benji held his breath while Mr. Matsumoto took a small pair of glasses from his pocket and arranged them on his nose.

"It says *Officer* . . . some name I cannot pronounce."

"Pinkerton."

"And Cio-Cio—this means Butterfly—*June thirteenth, 1888."*

"And her last name?"

Mr. Matsumoto studied the picture. "I believe she was a geisha. Geisha do not have last names. These are given only to persons of upper classes in Japan. Many Japanese living in Denver have no last name."

"But she was from a samurai family." He choked back tears.

"Perhaps so. But she would erase her name, I think."

Benji turned off the lamp and lay staring up into the dark, his eyes burning. At least she could have left him a name. Now all he had was Tsu-neo, borrowed from a stranger in a circus.

The next morning, Benji and Shin-san took Matsumoto-san to the station. "Please come to me after some time for recovery," he said to Benji, then gave a quick bow and hurried up the steps of the train.

It was mid-June, and poor Katie was past her time. Her color was poor, and her hands and face were as swollen as yeast dough. The doctor told Frank she'd be fine, but he looked concerned and came to check on her every day. She was moodier than ever, some days not speaking, other days begging him to sit beside her on the bed and listen to things he didn't want to hear—nightmares, giving birth to a black snake that turned into a pool of oil when it dropped out of her, or to a human baby with two heads and eyes like a goat's. No, no, he'd say, stroking her arm; she was going to have a fine baby, a strapping boy. It must be a boy—Kate was so large. He'd been a big newborn himself, gave his mother a hard time.

He was worried about money too. His mother was right, he probably should have held off on the indoor bath, but Katie needed the comfort and his mother shouldn't be emptying chamber pots at her age. There had been the cost of enlarging and refurbishing Benji's room for his mother so her room upstairs could be transformed into a nursery, and there were now more wages to pay, to a retired farmer who'd be taking Benji's place in the fields. The cost of seed had gone up, along with the railroad tariffs. He couldn't make it through the season without a loan.

Frank met with Austin Burdett, president of the Stockton Bank and Trust, on a warm Thursday afternoon. Burdett sat behind his oversize desk, smiling unpleasantly. It would be Frank's third loan in as many years, he said, as if Frank weren't aware of the fact, and money was tight everywhere due to Roosevelt's excessive spending. The interest rate was the best he could do, Burdett said. For collateral, there was of course the farm.

He held out a box of cigars. "Cuban. Help yourself." Frank shook his head. Burdett cut and lit a cigar for himself, taking his time. Frank looked at the plump fingers, the nails neat as a woman's. Rich boy from Chicago; he'd never touched a plow or an ax handle in his life.

Frank glanced around the room—fancy chairs and tables, a marble hearth. On the mantel were an ebony clock and a bust of a man who appeared to be Burdett himself. Katie would laugh to hear that, if she were feeling well.

"Now, Frank." Burdett leaned forward, a show of concern on his face. "What is your plan for repayment? I'd hate to see you in trouble."

"There will be no trouble. It's going to be a profitable year."

"Let's hope so," Burdett said. "Is that newfangled thresher living up to expectations?"

"Yes, indeed," he said, though in fact the gears of the thresher had seized up and it now sat in the fields like a large rust-colored insect. He and Bud Case had gone in together on the thresher, and Frank still owed him money. Bud was prospering—he had plenty of boys—but he didn't like to let a loan cool off.

"Well," Frank said. "I guess that's about it, then."

He started to rise, but Burdett tapped his fingers on the desk.

"How do you plan to spend this sum?"

None of your beeswax, Frank wanted to say. He stared at Burdett; with his double chin and dewlaps and hard little eyes, he looked like a hog with its head just lifted from the trough. "General expenses," he said. "I've fallen behind—we all have."

Burdett sat silent, waiting for more.

"Itinerant labor, mostly."

"Soon you'll have a new little addition, I understand," Burdett said with a wink. "Before you know it you'll have a—what—ten percent increase in your labor force."

Frank's face went hot. "Not for long. If it's a boy, we plan to send him to a university. Brains run in the family, on my wife's side. Franklin's a genius, his teacher says. He can go anywhere. Yale, Harvard."

"I guess that will be hard on the farm," Burdett said, rising.

"The farm will be self-sufficient by then. I'm planning to invest in livestock—Guernseys and hogs." Frank stood. "How's *your* wife?" he asked, smiling at the thought of her huge rump and belly, Burdett mounting her.

Burdett frowned. "Just fine. Enjoying spending my money." He stood and rounded the desk, clapped a hand on Frank's shoulder.

They walked out of Burdett's office and to the front door of the bank in silence. Frank burned to punch him.

"The transfer will be made this afternoon. Good luck." Burdett held out a white paw; Frank squeezed hard, enjoying Burdett's wince.

"Good luck yourself," he said.

He went down the steps and swung up onto Admiral. He thought of going by the post office. Keast had heard from Benji, and Frank hoped for a letter himself, but there wouldn't be one. He ought to get back to Kate anyway.

He headed out of town, taking a road that skirted Morseville and Plum River.

Benji had always preferred Keast, ever since he gave him that horse—now stolen out from under him—but it hadn't been Keast who'd saved him from a life in the gutters of Nagasaki, who'd fed and clothed him. No one seemed to appreciate—least of all Benji—how much Frank had done for the boy, what it had cost him.

He'd treated the boy badly—a thousand times he'd wished he could take it back—but, damm it, seven months was a long time for Benji to hold such a grudge that he wouldn't even write to his grandma.

It was a hard thing about Kuro, though; he knew the boy was suffering over that.

He took a short detour to the east forty, to check the most recent planting of corn. It was up six inches and looking frisky. If they had some decent rain this year, he might turn a profit from the corn and the barley. He'd planted the back forty entirely in barley, more resistant to drought; last year Bud Case had done well with it.

He turned onto the road that led home. At the Case farm, Franklin and Mary Virginia were in the front yard with a passel of those redheads. "Papa!" Franklin yelled, and ran out to him. "Mama's having the baby!"

Frank dug his heels into Admiral and they flew toward the house. He shouldn't have dallied in the fields.

Several hundred yards from the house, he heard her screaming. "Kate," he called, "Kate, Katie," and charged toward her.

He left Admiral at the gate, ran indoors. He'd never heard such screaming, hardly a pause for breath. He pounded up the stairs.

His mother stepped outside the bedroom, closed the door behind her, holding the knob.

"Let me in," Frank said. "I have to see her."

"Not now, dear. You wait downstairs. Or go on to the fields. It'll be a while."

There was a long bellow, ending in an "Oh, God, no." He heard the doctor's voice, a low murmur.

"What's wrong? Why is she screaming like that?"

"She's just stalled." His mother squeezed his arm. She looked exhausted, dark hollows under her eyes. "You run on now. She'll be fine."

He paced through the house, picking things up, putting them down. She wasn't going to be fine. Nothing was going to be fine. He was losing everything. There was a pile of green spring onions by the sink. He ate one—gritty; it hadn't been washed. In the parlor he tried to read the newspaper, a story about the farmers' effort to unionize, but Kate's screams drove into him like long, hot nails. "Dear God," he whispered, "don't let her die."

His head began to itch. He took off his cap and scratched hard, digging in with his fingernails until his scalp was on fire. If only she'd stop screaming.

He needed a drink. Kate wouldn't mind, in these circumstances. He went out to the barn, climbed to the hayloft, reached to the top of the beam that was his hiding place. The bottle was almost empty; he drained it.

The Swede had a bottle somewhere. In the bunkhouse, he looked in a closet, in the chest of drawers, under the bed. Finally he found it, in plain sight, by the washbasin. White whiskey of some kind; it scalded going down, then it soothed him.

He went out, stood in the road. The screaming seemed fainter. Maybe it was just the distance. The cows came toward him from the pasture, bells clanking. Animals knew what to do. He followed them to the barn and milked them, then carried the pail of milk to the cistern near the house.

There was silence in the house now. He ran inside and up the stairs. The door was locked. He jiggled the knob. "Mother," he whispered.

Dr. McBride opened the door partway; Frank couldn't see in. "She's resting," he whispered.

"Is she . . ."

"She's all right. A breech birth, but she should be all right. Please make some coffee—just leave it on the stove. Then take yourself for a walk." He closed the door.

Frank started the coffee, spilling grounds on the table, the stove, tried to sweep them up with his hands. There was a scream; he jumped, dropping the grounds on the floor. The screaming continued, pulsing in his ears.

He found the bottle of cooking sherry in the pantry, sat down at the table with it, waited for the coffee to boil. He took a long drink, put his hands over his ears.

The Swede came in, expecting supper. "She sounds in a bad way," he said.

"No, she's not, she's fine. What would you know?"

Frank pushed up from the table, took a dollar from his wallet, and handed it to the Swede. "Go get yourself something to eat in town." He went past the Swede, out to the barn, up to the loft. He mounded some hay—not much left, they'd just made it through the winter—and lay down. The horses were munching their oats; the Swede had fed them. He should have thought of it himself. But he was so tired.

He closed his eyes, dozed for a moment. The sound of the Swede saddling his horse woke him.

The coffee. He sat up. He'd forgotten. He ran up the hill, breathing hard, and burst in through the front door. The whole place smelled of burnt coffee; the pot's contents were bubbling on the surface of the stove. He snatched up the pot and set it outside on the kitchen steps, cleaned the stove, then started over.

Kate was moaning now, a normal sound, like animals giving birth. After the coffee had boiled, he took a cup of it to the doctor and went to sit on the porch. Dusk had fallen; a bobwhite was calling from the edge of the field. He put his head on the back of the rocker. He was a little dizzy. "Please," he whispered. Then he was asleep.

It was dark. Someone was tapping his shoulder. "Frank." It was Dr. McBride; his hair was wild and his shirttail loose, but he was smiling.

"Congratulations, Frank," he said, pumping his hand. "You have two healthy new babies. And Mother is doing fine."

Frank blinked. "Two? Are you sure?"

The doctor laughed. "Yes. Twins."

"Twins," Frank said. The word was strange in his mouth. "Boys?"

"A boy and a girl."

A boy. And she was fine. He grabbed the doctor, kissed his rough cheek, and ran up to Kate. His luck had finally turned.

Shin hired Benji as a dishwasher at Waraji's; he liked the work, surrounded by the newly familiar smells of Japanese food, and soon was able to carry on simple conversations with the other men in the kitchen and the customers. There were occasional white customers, loggers and farm workers mostly, and Benji was in charge of waiting on them and ringing up their meals at the cash register.

Willa Overstreet, a white waitress, had recently begun working in the restaurant. She spoke no Japanese, which caused some grumbling among the customers, even though they knew Shin didn't have a choice; there was a shortage of Japanese women in the community. The owner of the Beef and Noodle, a Japanese restaurant near the Platte River that catered to workingmen of all races, had hired a white woman and a mulatto as waitresses in the past year.

Benji was enlisted to teach Willa some simple phrases and the names of Japanese dishes, so she could communicate with the customers and the cook; they quickly became friends.

Willa was a slender woman with sandy-brown hair, older than Benji—about twenty-five, he guessed. Her eyes were small and her face was a little too long, but there was something in her manner that reminded him of Flora—her erect posture, a way of holding her head. Though poorly educated, she was clever and learned the Japanese phrases quickly. Their tutoring sessions gradually lengthened, and they often sat talking in a corner of the restaurant until well after closing. Benji was relieved to have long, easy conversations in English again, and he felt a kinship with Willa, both of them homeless.

Willa's mother, a seamstress, had died nine years ago—she had never known her father—and she dropped out of school to work as a maid. She liked it better at Waraji's than at her rich employer's house, she said, even though the pay was less, because she didn't have to put up with any guff from hoity-toities.

She had been engaged twice, most recently to a man who worked for the railroad and left her for a woman he met at a stopover in Kansas City; earlier, she had an understanding—or so she thought, she said—with a boy she had known at school.

"I knew a girl at school," Benji said. "Someone I liked—but I never could have married her."

"Why not?"

"Look at me. A mongrel Japanese."

"That doesn't bother me."

He told her about his parents, how his mother killed herself and he was taken away from Japan to live in Ilinois. When he showed her the picture of his mother and Frank, she reached to take his hand. "You poor kid," she said, "you've had it rough."

That night he walked her to her trolley; on the way, they stopped in an alley, where he kissed her and she let him touch her breasts.

Benji asked Fumio, the owner of the dry-goods store, if he and Willa could occasionally meet in the attic above the store, after closing.

Fumio agreed. "It's hard to be without a woman, *ne*? I'm lucky to have a wife." But he warned Benji not to cause him any trouble with "the white man."

Benji promised to be careful; they would enter and leave separately, and only when the street was deserted.

They met two or three times a week, making love and talking. Once they fell asleep in the attic; when they woke there was light at the small window. Benji looked out; already there were people on the street. He went down to the shop and borrowed a furoshiki cloth for Willa to wear as a scarf. A few white laborers worked in the area. "Don't let anyone see you," Benji said.

"Nobody's business but ours." But she looked frightened; her lips and her hands were cold. He watched from the window as she appeared on the street and, head bent, walked quickly out of sight. Damn the white men, he thought; hypocrites, as if none of them visited the Negro prostitutes or the Japanese women at the bathhouse. It was time for him to go home, to Japan.

He'd been saving a portion of his wages in Shin's safe. By next spring, he calculated, he would have enough to get there. Not as a rich man, but maybe he could get rich in Japan, in the import/export business as Matsumoto's partner.

He wrote to Matsumoto, who had reestablished himself in a new building outside San Francisco's Chinatown, and asked if he could stop in on his way to Japan. The man who had saved his life was welcome at any time, Matsumoto wrote back. He had a new enterprise, he said, in which Benji could be useful.

Benji couldn't bring himself to tell Willa about his plans; the time never seemed right. She brought him gifts—a scarf she'd knitted for next winter and a flannel shirt that fit perfectly. "You did it without measuring me," he said, astonished.

"Oh, I've taken your measure," she said, running her hands down his body. "I know your measure exactly."

One morning when Benji was having breakfast, Shin laid a folded newspaper in front of him. There was a letter to the editor: A Japanese laborer and a white waitress from the Beef and Noodle had been seen spooning on the bank of the river. *What have we come to that this should be tolerated in the Queen City?* the writer asked.

"You have to stay away from Willa," Shin said.

There were more letters published in the paper; the city council looked into the matter. A delegation came to Waraji's—three men in business suits and bowler hats, which they didn't remove. Benji was cleaning the tables; he kept his face turned away. Shin offered them beer, some excellent Japanese tempura, but they remained standing.

"Where's that white waitress?" one of them said.

"She's not here," Shin said. "She comes at dinner."

"Not anymore she doesn't," one of the men said. "There's a new law—no white women in Jap or Chink joints."

When they left, Shin and Benji looked at each other. One of Shin's eyelids was twitching.

"No one ever saw us," Benji said.

"It's not your fault." Shin dropped to a chair, rubbed his face and head with both hands until his hair was sticking up in clumps.

Willa and Benji said goodbye that night in the kitchen, after she'd been given her final wages. "I'll pray for you," she said, her eyes watering, "if you'll pray for me." They shook hands, and she was gone.

That night, before he could be mournful, he packed his things and the next morning, Shin and Fumio and their wives saw him off at the station. On the platform they pressed gifts into his hands—envelopes of money, charms for good luck. Fumio gave him a carefully wrapped package: a kimono and haori jacket to wear in Nagasaki.

As the train pulled away, Benji leaned out the window to wave at them. He sat down hard and balled up his hands, digging the nails into his palms. He was always leaving; his whole life he had been leaving.

But as the train began its ascent, following a long curve that hugged the side of a mountain, he felt a surge of elation. Ever since he had seen the range of Rocky Mountains in his schoolbook, he had thought of it as a wall between him and Japan. Now he was crossing that wall.

They went through a series of tunnels in rapid succession—dark, light, dark, light, like days and nights sped up, hurtling through time.

The train slowed as it climbed higher. Although most of the car was full, there was no one in the seat opposite Benji, so he took off his shoes and stretched his legs straight out. He glanced across the aisle at a middle-aged couple watching the scenery from their window. The woman wore glasses like Grandmother Pinkerton's; he wondered what she would think of this trip—she'd never been out of Jo Daviess County in her life.

He imagined writing to Frank, informing him that he was going to find the family of the woman he'd killed as surely as if he'd shot her with his rifle. He thought of Frank with his belt after the cow and calf died, the first of several whippings. When he found his Japanese family, he would tell them everything; he pictured them sitting around a low table like the ones he'd seen in books, his grandparents perhaps, an aunt or uncle, cousins. Maybe they would have heard of him, had even seen him after he was born, or he might be a complete surprise. He'd better wait to make the memorial stone for his mother until he had shown her picture to the family, as proof he was her son.

Shin's wife and Fumio's wife had each packed him boxes of food. In the lunch box was rice topped with fish, and dried seaweed, which he ate with chopsticks. The couple across the way dined from a basket of fried chicken, biscuits, cherry pie. When she saw him eyeing it, the woman offered him a slice of pie. He thanked her and she passed it to him on a napkin. He devoured it—delicious, as good as Grandmother Pinkerton's. He was going to miss American food. And Grandmother Pinkerton, Franklin, Mary Virginia. Keast. He felt a tightening in his throat as he thought of Flora, probably engaged by now or married. He'd better not start feeling sorry for himself. No point in it, as Keast said; you only get sorrier.

The woman asked about his origin and destination; she had a kind, open face, so he confided that he was headed to Japan, to find his mother's people. "It must be real interesting there," she said. "We saw the Japanese exhibit at the Chicago World's Fair, and they had such quaint little buildings. Didn't they, Horace?"

Horace looked directly at Benji for the first time. "Yep," he said. "How do they make those tile roofs curve up like that?"

"I don't know," Benji said, and Horace turned back to the window.

"Come sit with us for a spell," the woman said. "Horace knows all the sights." There was no polite way to refuse; Benji left his bag on his seat and moved across the aisle to sit beside the woman. She smelled like starch.

They were the Stones, from Winnetka, Illinois, and had made this trip twice before to visit their daughter in San Diego. Mr. Stone said they'd soon be coming to the Continental Divide, but it turned out that most of the places he knew about had to do with calamities: a runaway freight car full of corn syrup, which rolled off the tracks and into a fancy house in Tolland; the collision in '04 between a freighter and a passenger train racing for the same siding. "Fifty killed," he said, nodding with grim satisfaction.

"And it wasn't far from here"—he tapped Benji's knee—"a young couple got off the train at a depot and wandered into the woods for a little smooching and she got eaten by a grizzly. They never found the remains."

"At one time I was planning to cross the mountains on a horse," Benji said.

"Oh, you'd never have made it."

"The pioneers did. And the forty-niners."

"Not all of them. Some got caught in the snow and ate—"

"Horace, that's enough," his wife said.

"Well, it's a fact. And there was a Japanese fellow . . ." Mr. Stone paused for emphasis, his eyes glittering at Benji. "A cook for the men who were building the railroad—this happened on the other side of the mountains, near Glenwood Springs—who was killed for his stash of money."

"That was a long time ago," Mrs. Stone said, frowning and shaking her head at her husband. "It wouldn't happen now."

"Maybe not, but people still go prospecting for that money. The conductor told me, our last trip."

Benji glanced around the car. There were no other empty seats, so he moved back across the aisle and stared out the window, picturing Mr. Stone being devoured by a grizzly.

Mrs. Stone leaned across the aisle. "He didn't mean anything by it," she said in a low voice. "Would you like some more pie?"

Benji shook his head and turned back toward the window, trying to ignore the Stones' tense, whispered conversation. They were going through high mountains now, along a ridge, glistening snow-covered peaks as far as he could see. He touched his waist, the wide cloth money belt beneath his shirt that Fumio's wife had made for him. It had secret pockets that held most of his money—five fifty-dollar bills. It was as safe a way as there was to carry money, Fumio said, and once he got to Japan he wouldn't have to worry, because there wasn't any theft there.

Digby Moffett had made a lot of his being Japanese; he probably thought that gave him more of a right to steal Kuro. What was a Jap doing with such a fine horse?

Most people in Plum River hadn't cared that he was Japanese, after they got used to him. Except Flora's father.

He looked down at his hands, thinking of the honeysuckle rings he and Flora had made for each other. They had been children then, naïve; of course Flora's father wouldn't have let him marry her. He wouldn't have been able to marry any white woman in America, even Willa.

He stared back out the window. In general, Japanese women were better, he decided, prettier and more refined. He thought of Fumio's wife, the gleaming rosy skin of her face, the way she bowed, the slender hips beneath the kimono. He closed his eyes and thought about her, letting himself rock with the train, and went to sleep.

When he woke, he could see below them a wide, winding river, from this distance like a flattened snake; it must be the Colorado. The river straightened as it cut through a gorge. The train rattled over a shaky bridge, then began to descend, jerking and bucking, the brakes squealing. Benji thought of the runaway syrup car—Stone wouldn't live to tell about the catastrophe if they derailed here—but soon they were moving beside the river, green and beautiful and wild, no people, just deer grazing beside it, an elk, and a red fox running along the bank.

The train moved away from the river and then, in late afternoon, joined it once again. Benji opened his bag and took out the box of food Fumio's wife had packed: onigiri rice balls, bean cake, and an orange. As the train moved through a landscape of steep red canyons that glowed in the fading light, sculpted rocks standing alone like chimneys without houses, Benji ate slowly, storing up images of America to describe for his family in Japan.

Lena came with gifts for the babies: silver rattles, a complete set of the Book of Knowledge, and a large jigsaw puzzle of the United States. "My husband thinks ahead," Lena said with a laugh. "Already he's visualizing them at their studies."

Kate and Lena sat in the parlor with tea, on opposite sides of the small table. Marriage had made Lena prettier; her face was softer and her eyes more expressive, shining, taking everything in.

Kate closed her eyes. There was something terribly wrong with her that she had no interest in marriage or her babies and that even Franklin and Mary Virginia seemed distant to her. Frank had hired a servant girl, Sylvie—the only condition under which his mother would stay—but, still, the least thing exhausted her. Soon she could excuse herself and go back to bed.

"How are you, Kate?" Lena asked.

"Not quite well." Yesterday Frank had taken her for a ride in the buggy to give her a change of scene, but she didn't want to go to town, where people would see her, and the sight of the fields made her eyes go out of focus. She was in the wrong place. Somewhere in life she had taken the wrong turn and had not entered the portal into the world where she was meant to be.

"I think you need stimulation." Lena turned to look at the bookcase. "Are you reading?"

"No."

"I'll bring you the new Edith Wharton. We're discussing it at the next women's circle meeting—they recently asked me to join. I'd be so pleased if you'd go with me."

Kate's face burned. "And have them gloat?"

Lena studied her. "People have a much higher opinion of you than you might imagine."

Kate looked at her hands, arranged politely in her lap. No one knew what she imagined. Giving tonic to the babies until they slept and never woke up.

"Why don't we take a little excursion," Lena said, "once the babies are old enough to be without you for a day? We could ride the train to Chicago, just the two of us. Wouldn't it be delightful?"

Kate nodded. She thought of the train plunging forward, devouring the miles, carrying her away from here.

Mrs. Pinkerton and Sylvie brought the babies in for Lena to admire. Lena held them up one after the other, proclaimed them perfect rosebuds, and handed them back to Sylvie. "How they've grown!" she said.

"They still have no names, I'm afraid," Mrs. Pinkerton said, with a glance at Kate. "We haven't even been able to send birth announcements."

"Names are difficult, aren't they?" Lena said, smiling at Kate. "There's so much to consider."

"They do have names," Kate said. "The girl is Rose and the boy is Wharton."

Mrs. Pinkerton stared at Kate. "The next boy's name was to be Elmer. Surely Frank doesn't agree."

"Of course he does." Kate dropped a lump of sugar in her tea and stirred it briskly. "He's my husband, you know."

Lena murmured something and took a cookie from the tray.

"Oh, I like Rose," Sylvie said. "What do you think, Rosie-posy?" She kissed her nose.

The Swede had found Sylvie somewhere. She was fifteen, with braids the color of pale wood wrapped around her head, wide-set brown eyes, and pimples on her forehead. She was a terrible cook—corn mush that turned Kate's stomach, and eggs scrambled too long, and muffins hard as rocks. But she knew how to turn a carpet, Mrs. Pinkerton said, and she was good with the babies. Kate hated the sight of her.

When Mrs. Pinkerton and Sylvie left with the babies, Lena came to sit beside Kate on the davenport.

"What a pretty watch," she said, looking at the oval pinned to Kate's shirtwaist.

Kate glanced down at it: the ornate gold bow at the top, a sprinkling of daisies on the face. "It was Frank's gift to me for the babies," she said. "I can't read it, but anyone who looks at me can tell what time it is."

There was a silence. Kate stared at the crusted sugar in the bowl.

"Forgive my directness," Lena said, "but you must set the incident of the photograph aside. You've nothing to be ashamed of. You've been a stalwart wife and raised Benji under the most difficult of circumstances."

"I tried." Tears spurted from her eyes.

Lena placed a handkerchief in Kate's lap. "You can't let a few gossips ruin your life. This is your time, Kate." Lena's expression was fierce. "Your life."

Kate held the handkerchief to her face, then placed it on her skirt, folded and refolded it. Embroidered kittens. Her tears stopped abruptly.

When Lena began to talk again, Kate saw them from a distance, two women on a sofa, one leaning forward, like a painting, and later she could not remember what more was said.

After several delays, the christening date was set for a Sunday morning in mid-September 1906, when Kate had agreed to the names Elmer and Margaret Rose.

It was a lovely day for the ceremony, Mrs. Pinkerton said when Kate came down for breakfast, and didn't big brother and sister look fine? "Stand up," she said to Franklin and Mary Virginia. "Let Mother see."

Franklin was wearing new knickers and a starched white shirt; Mary Virginia, a pink dress with flounces at the hem.

"Very pretty," Kate murmured. The room was spinning and her legs felt flimsy. She gripped the back of a chair.

"Someone will have to stand in for me at the ceremony, I'm afraid," she said. "I'm not well."

"You only need to eat," Mrs. Pinkerton said. "She hasn't been eating," she said, looking around the table.

Frank helped her sit down. "You're my princess," he whispered. He was wearing his naval dress uniform, now too tight around the middle.

He looked absurd, and the uniform would only inflame people's thoughts of his past.

It was all absurd, the five of them at the round table as though everything was quite as it should be. The thought of the roundness of the table made her dizzier.

"No," she said, "I won't be able to manage."

Mrs. Pinkerton gave her a stern look. "Doesn't she look lovely, Frank? Such a lovely mother."

"A madonna," he said, buttering a biscuit for her and coating it with crab-apple jelly.

Kate shook her head. She was no mother any longer; they would be better off without her. She glanced at Franklin; his eyes avoided hers. Mrs. Pinkerton had told her that the Swede had taught him to shoot and that not long ago he had brought home his first pheasant. If she was still his mother, she would not allow it; at seven he was too young, it could be dangerous.

The ride to Stockton was brutally hot; the drought had persevered into autumn and the pastures were withered. By the time they arrived at the church, Kate's dress was filmed with dust.

The sanctuary was already full, people talking and fanning themselves. The crowd went silent when the family was ushered inside and started up the aisle. Kate stared straight ahead.

This was a drama, a play, and she was an actress—noble mother, devout wife, libeled by some but a true Christian who had done all she could for Butterfly's child as well as for her own children.

In the front pew, turning to smile, were the godparents, Lena and Horatio Keast, and she made her way toward them gracefully, with poise alighting beside Lena, and after the Epistle and the Gospel readings and "Amazing Grace," which she sang in alto counterpoint, they were all going forward to the baptismal font, Frank carrying Elmer as was appropriate and she, Rose. Rose was damp and smelled like ammonia.

The font was by the side door, which was open for ventilation. Prisms of light fell through the stained glass above the altar and threw blades of red and yellow across the font and the babies and her arm.

Now the baptismal prayers, the charges to parents and godparents, the water, the obligatory crying of babies, the appropriate amused murmuring from the audience.

It was over. She was not quite fainting. Just a sip of air, she whispered to Lena, and handed her the baby. Quickly she stepped out the door, glided down the steps, and began to run.

Clinic Notes

Dr. Roland Schlensky,
Willowbranch Sanitorium for the Insane

Katherine Pinkerton, 39, white female, farm wife, four children brought to term. Abandoned newborns at church door. Assay rest cure, baths, laudanum, occupational therapy; employ restraints as necessary. Diagnosis: insane by childbirth and possible cessation of menses. Observe for indications of dementia praecox. Outlook: poor.

Interlude

Pinkerton:
Evening is coming

Butterfly:
And darkness and peace.

Pinkerton:
And you are here alone

Butterfly:
Yes, yes, we are alone,
and outside the world.

Keast sank into his chair at the dinner table and inhaled the lusty odor of the lamb stew Lena placed before him. When she returned to the kitchen, he listened to her moving about, his darling wife, visualizing her breasts shift beneath her blouse as she reached to the cupboard. He looked around the dining room, which was modest but attractively furnished, the curtains she had made stirring in the light breeze. The cottage suited them exactly for now; once the family grew, he aimed to build a larger house just outside town. It was almost dark, a fine spring evening, the sound of birds pipping as they prepared to roost. After dinner, he and Lena would have a bath, then bed. He tucked in his napkin, spread it over his belly, and took a deep breath. His good fortune was God's own miracle.

She returned with rolls and his glass of beer. A little smile for him but no kiss on the forehead. He caught her hand, touched his lips to the silk of her inner wrist, but she gently pulled away and took her seat. It was hard to read her face exactly in the dimming light, but there seemed a small crease in her forehead, the beginning of a frown.

"What's wrong, sweetheart?"

"Nothing really." She passed the butter. "Just something a little odd."

He waited.

"I'll tell you after supper," she said.

"The baby?" He felt a shiver of anxiety. She had been with child for six weeks according to his calculations.

"The baby's fine." She glanced at his stew. "Don't let it cool. I know you must be ravenous. Where did you go today?"

She was as stubborn a woman as he'd known, when she chose to be, so he began to eat, chunks of tender, moist lamb limned with fat, rutabaga, carrot, and to talk about his rounds—leaving out as many dull details as possible—the melanosis that was overtaking the Cases' horse Rebecca, the phrenitis he suspected in a coach horse. It had probably been struck about the head; no need to tell her that. "Then there was . . ."

She glanced several times at the sideboard. He looked; nothing out of the ordinary that he could see, a vase of flowers, her sewing basket.

"What in thunder is it?"

She shook her head. "A bizarre coincidence. Are you ready for coffee?"

"I'm ready for the coincidence," he said.

"All right." She rolled her napkin and slid it into its ring. "Today at the women's circle meeting, Aimee Moore—"

He snorted. "Don't let that woman rile you," he said.

She stood and went to the sideboard, brought back a pamphlet, and laid it before him.

He held it up to the light of the gas chandelier. A program of some kind, apparently. He squinted to make out the letters.

"It's an opera," she said. "*Madama Butterfly* is the title. Aimee and her husband recently attended a performance in Chicago."

He looked up at her. Her face was stern, a little schoolmarmish.

"Are you hankering to go?" he said.

"No. Look inside. Here." She opened the program to the first page, smoothed it out. "The name of this character—an American Navy lieutenant, Benjamin Franklin Pinkerton."

"Hmm." He scratched his head, dirty and itching. All afternoon he'd had thoughts of her washing it, she leaning over him in the tub.

"The opera takes place in Japan," she said. "Lieutenant Pinkerton and a geisha have a child—a *blond* child—but he marries an American woman named"—she tapped her finger against the page—"Kate. *Kate.* The geisha kills herself and the Pinkerton family takes the boy away."

"Well." He held the program up to the gas chandelier, looked at the names. "That's something."

"Odd, isn't it?"

"Yes. Very odd. But in nature there are many—"

"This isn't nature. It's an opera."

"In Chicago."

"Yes, and all over the world, apparently. It's by Puccini, one of the finest living composers."

He flipped through the program—a biography of the great man, notes about the singers, an advertisement for the Palmer House, then back to the beginning. *Act I: Nagasaki.* Benji was from Nagasaki. The back of his neck prickled. "Just a bizarre coincidence, as you said."

"But a coincidence that will cause talk. Thank goodness Kate isn't here to know about this. Horatio, I want you to go warn Frank."

"I doubt Frank will hear about it." Poor bastard had the devil's share of luck. "This will blow over," he said.

"It's the children I worry about," Lena said. "They'll hear about it. You can count on children to talk and be mean."

He sighed, closed the program, and aligned it with the edge of the table. On the front cover was a Japanese woman with chopsticks in her hair. He thought of Benji's photograph. "Mrs. Pinkerton will need to know," he said.

"Yes. You'd better take some smelling salts." She covered her face with her hands. "Maybe I should go too. Oh, it would be the end of Kate."

He rose from the table and put his arms around her. She had a soft cottony smell. He wondered if she had remembered the bathwater. "Don't worry, sweetheart, we'll figure it out. I'll go to the farm tomorrow."

Frank sat in his office in the noon light, his head bent over the ledger. He couldn't remember why, last month, he'd written down *Hogs, $1.50 per lb. on the hoof,* when he didn't have any cash hogs or plans for acquiring any.

He looked out the window at the black fields, where in a few months there would be waves of corn. Bud Case had already prepared his ground; Frank would have at it this week.

He turned back to the line of figures. He desperately needed a good year, to keep Kate in the private asylum. He'd visited the public hospital, filled with epileptics, screamers, and biters; it stank of urine and worse. If he let the hired girl go . . . but then his mother would leave. It would be a good year; he was sure of it. He took a long drink of whiskey from the flask, set it carefully beside the miniature ship in the bottle that he sometimes told people he'd made himself, although he'd bought it from an innkeeper in Liverpool. The bottle was covered with dust. Since Sylvie had taken over, things had gone to hell. Kate was the only one who'd taken any care with his things. He thought of her pretty hands, her wrists that looked fragile as porcelain, the dullness in her eyes now. He sipped the whiskey, held it in his mouth before he let it run down his gullet. She would chide him for drinking, but what did she expect, leaving him to raise the children on his own. His mother had been right: She was too delicate for farm life.

Someone was coming up the steps. Probably the Swede, wanting his lunch. Frank had forgotten to tell him his mother was having her Sunday meal at the Cases'.

"Frank?" Keast poked his head inside the door. His hair was freshly trimmed and he reeked of pomade. "Mind if I come in? I've brought some salve for Admiral's hocks."

"On a Sunday?" Keast was dressed in his church suit and cravat. A bowler hat was under his arm.

"Just thought I'd drop by while I was thinking about it." He put the jar of salve on the small table by the door and stood looking out the front window at the pasture. "Fine view," he said, jingling the change in his pocket. "Your grandpa picked out a good home site." He turned toward Frank. "Reckoning, eh?" he said, nodding toward the desk.

"Afraid so." Keast wanted something. Frank couldn't remember when he'd last paid him.

Keast drew up a chair to the desk and sat down heavily, his buttons straining. "How is everyone? Kate?"

Frank shook his head, and they exchanged a long glance. There was nothing but sympathy in Keast's face; he'd forgiven him for that time at the boardinghouse.

Keast looked down at the floor, picked up a scrap of paper, and put it on the desk. "Frank, there's something strange I need to apprise you of. Perhaps it's of minor consequence in the larger view, but Lena and I thought . . ." He cleared his throat. "Because of the children."

Frank stared at him. Someone must have seen him at the whorehouse in Elizabeth.

"There seems to be an opera—" Keast said.

"A what?"

"Opera. Those highbrow plays with music." Keast gave a dismissive wave. "The women seem to like them."

Keast usually got to the point. "What's this about the children?" Frank said.

Keast took a noisy breath. "It seems that Aimee Moore attended an opera in Chicago not long ago . . . and—this is the damnedest thing— Benjamin Franklin Pinkerton and Kate Pinkerton are two of the major figures. Lena is going to appeal to the women's better instincts, but . . ." He took something out of his pocket and laid it on the desk. "We thought you'd better know."

It was a program, with a picture of a Japanese woman on the front. *Madama Butterfly*. The words blazed up at him.

"And you'll see . . ." Keast opened the program. "Here are the names of people in the drama: American Navy Lieutenant Benjamin Franklin Pinkerton . . ." He ran his hand down the list. "Kate Pinkerton. And there's a child at the end, a blond Japanese."

Frank blinked. "Is this something they got up at school?"

Keast shook his head. "It's in Chicago on the stage and all over—New York, Lena said, Italy. Italy is where it started, apparently."

"I've never been to Italy."

"It's hard to figure," Keast said.

Frank stared at the list of characters: Sharpless. Suzuki. Butterfly. His mind wouldn't move forward.

"If the opera took place in Italy, it would be one thing," Keast said, "but with the setting in Japan . . . since people know your ties there . . ." Keast shook his head. "Maybe Lena can forestall gossip for now, but the children, when they hear of it—and it seems inevitable—the children will be confused and upset. Teased."

Frank tried to turn the page, licked his finger, tried again. *Act I: A hill outside Nagasaki. Cho-Cho-san is waiting for her American lover, Lt. Benjamin Franklin Pinkerton . . .*

"This isn't real," Frank said.

"No," Keast said. "Just an opera."

Frank rubbed his face hard. He was the one who ought to be in the loony place. Keast must be making this up. "It's a coincidence," he said, "a hoax."

"That's what I thought at first," Keast said. After a pause he asked, "Where's your mother?"

"Out. Good Lord, don't tell her."

Keast shifted in the chair. "We have to have a plan for the children."

Frank took another long drink.

Keast put a hand on his shoulder. "Take it easy, friend." He glanced at the whiskey. "Can I get you some coffee?"

Frank pulled away and stood, looking for a moment at his desk—the scattered papers, the ship in the bottle, the ledger with its doodles in it. He snatched up the program, slid the flask into his back pocket, and shoved past Keast. Keast followed him downstairs, but he waved him off.

Outdoors, Frank crossed the road and climbed through the pasture to the copse of trees where the cows took shelter from the hot sun in summertime. It had always been the place where he could think. He'd made his decision to go to sea sitting beneath this bur oak.

He sat on an outcrop, looking away from the house. The downward tilt of the meadow in front of him made him think of the sea, the ship at the base of a wave.

He opened the program and made himself read through the summary of the first act of the opera. It hadn't been like that, this wasn't true. There had been no wedding, no relatives, no talk of conversion to Christianity. He felt a splinter of relief.

But Suzuki. Sharpless. That was uncanny. And Butterfly, for God's sake.

Someone had stolen his life. He was being persecuted. What had he done to deserve this? As if the photograph wasn't enough.

He thought of Benji escaping on his horse. Benji had known his mother's name—he'd told him in a weak moment—and he remembered Suzuki. When he was young he had often spoken of her. Likely he remembered Sharpless. That must be it. When Benji showed that photograph to the suffragist, he must have told her everything he knew. Then the suffragist—God damn her hide—had passed on the story. Maybe in Italy. She had bragged about her world travels, all the snoots she knew.

Rage boiled up in him. He imagined lashing Benji with a cat-o'-nine-tails, wrapping it around his neck, and tearing off that suffragist's clothes and making her march through town naked. In the saloon, the men would take turns with her. Aimee Moore too—she was in on this.

He was suddenly very tired, as though he'd been knocked in the skull by a jib coming around too fast. He closed his eyes and pitched forward, facedown in the grass.

Part Three

Butterfly:
One fine day we'll see
a wisp of smoke rising
from the distant horizon of the sea.
And then the ship will appear.
Then the white ship
will enter the harbor
thundering out its signal.
You see? He's come!

San Francisco was a cacophony of hammers, saws, and the smash of wrecking balls against concrete. There were few street signs, so Mr. Matsumoto's map was little help as Benji made his way in heavy fog from the train station toward what a large X on the crumpled paper designated as *Japantown in the Western Settlement.* Miracles had been accomplished in rebuilding the city, a porter on the train had told him, but there were still hulking skeletons of buildings, materializing eerily in the mist, and heaps of rubble in the side streets.

He passed a house pitched halfway onto a sidewalk, then went into a café with bright flowers in a window box. "No Japs!" a skinny blond waitress said, and a man pushed him out the door. He bit his tongue as he stumbled, cursing, down the steps. The taste of iron. His face burned; he shouldn't have colored his hair with shoe polish. But Mr. Matsumoto had said that San Francisco was becoming prosperous for Japanese.

He kept walking toward what seemed to be west. People shook their heads or pointed in different directions when he asked for the western settlement. He kept going, his feet hurting in his cheap new shoes. Finally a young woman with sweet brown eyes led him several blocks and told him to walk about a mile until he came to a tree lying across a road, turn left, then right at a church, and he would be there.

Suddenly the streets were full of Japanese men, laborers working on buildings and holes in the streets. There were shops with signs in Japanese. He asked an elderly woman at a vegetable stand if she knew Yasunari Matsumoto. "Ah, Matsumoto-sama," she said with a deep bow, and led him through a park and down a leafy street.

Mr. Matsumoto lived in a large clapboard house in need of paint. He was writing at a table in the kitchen; he leapt up and bowed when Benji entered, full of apologies for not having met him at the station. "I am doing urgent work," he said, gesturing toward the table. "Just now I am composing letters to President Roosevelt and officials in Japan. The mayor wants to put Japanese children in separate schools. We cannot allow this!"

Mr. Matsumoto's mission had enlivened him. He look tanned and healthy, moving spryly through the house and up the stairs, showing Benji rooms crammed with pallets and cots for Japanese refuges who had lost their homes during the earthquake. Most were out doing construction work in their new neighborhood, he said. "Although we have lost everything in the fire, Japanese gained in one way—we have swelled in this part of the city called Japantown."

His own room was sparsely furnished: two mattresses on the floor, a small battered chest, a desk heaped with papers. "Even I lost my ancestor shrine," he said. "If my assistant Ueda-san had lived, I believe he would have rescued it for me, along with my little dog."

He turned to Benji. "I have prepared this place for you." He gestured toward one of the mattresses. "You please be my assistant now."

Benji stared at the mattress. "Thank you," he said. Mr. Matsumoto must not remember that he was on his way to Japan.

"Someday we will return to import/export business," Mr. Matsumoto said. "But now we must help our fellow Japanese. Most of them speak no English. You can help them with nighttime lessons and, during the day, there are many, many things to be accomplished. Please excuse me now, and make yourself at home in this humble place."

Benji lit a cigarette and went to stand by the window. The fog had lifted. In the yard were rows of lettuce and a maple tree. He remembered the maple tree in the yard of the house in Nagasaki, the red leaves floating on the pond in autumn. He was going to find that tree and that pond. How could Mr. Matsumoto have forgotten?

They went to the public bath together, where Benji met the refugees staying at the house. Mr. Matsumoto showed him the Japanese way of bathing, washing off first with soap and water from a bucket, then stepping into a hot pool of water.

"You look a strong man," Mr. Matsumoto said.

Benji laughed. "Growing up on a farm will do that," he said.

"You can assist us well, I think."

"For a while, before I go to Japan," Benji said, but Mr. Matsumoto, leaning back in the water, seemed not to hear.

At dinner that night, the men sat crowded around the table, eating noodle soup and drinking sake, their faces flushed from the bath. Mr. Matsumoto told Benji that anti-Japanese sentiment, which had increased since the end of the Russo–Japanese war, had grown more intense since the earthquake. "Now there is more building work, labor unions and the newspapers say more feverishly that Japanese continue to take the white man's job. There are riots against Japanese. This is why you must assist me," he said, pouring more sake into Benji's cup. "You supervise the men while I continue my work helping Japanese obtain American birth certificates. Since all their possessions are destroyed in the fire, no one can say they have no certificates. So we obtain new ones, and the men can become citizens and own property of their own. This is only fair in the great democracy of America, *ne?*"

Benji shifted uncomfortably in his chair. It was selfish of him to be thinking of leaving. "Yes," he said. "Your work is very important."

For the next few days, Benji tried to supervise the construction of the new Japanese YMCA, but communication was difficult. The men showed him what to do as they raised the wall and roof. Benji had helped at several barn raisings, so the work was familiar and much more gratifying, to be laboring with his fellow countrymen. In the evenings, he gave English lessons to the men after dinner, but they were all too tired to make much progress.

And he kept thinking of Japan. One afternoon he walked to the Embarcadero on the bay, to see the ships at dock. An ocean liner, the SS *Minnesota,* was preparing for departure to Japan. Maybe they would take him on to swab decks or help in the kitchen. He could be in Nagasaki in three weeks.

That night, as he and Mr. Matsumoto lay in their beds in the dark, Benji's words tumbled out before he lost his courage. "I'm sorry, but I must go to Japan soon. All my life I've been yearning for it. From Nagasaki I'll help you however I can—and I'll send things for the shop when the time comes."

There was a silence, no sound but that of the rain against the window.

"San Francisco is not your home," Mr. Matsumoto said at last. "And if you had not helped me, I would not be here to help others. Therefore, I cannot refuse you."

"Thank you—I'm very grateful."

Mr. Matsumoto turned on his side, away from him. There was another long silence, then Mr. Matsumoto said in a cool voice, "A gentleman should have a passport, and for a passport you need a birth certificate. I will help you."

Benji thanked him again, but there was no answer.

A few days later, Mr. Matsumoto took him downtown to the records office. A ferret-faced man in glasses—Mr. Purcell, according to the nameplate—was at the window marked *Vital Records*.

When the man looked up, Mr. Matsumoto said, "We have come to see Mr. Smithson, if you please."

"Mr. Smithson has been reassigned. I am in charge of this division now." He arranged his glasses higher on his nose. "May I assist you?"

"I am Yasunari Matsumoto, a leader in the Japanese community. We have come to acquire a birth certificate for this young man, whose records perished in the fire."

Mr. Purcell shook his head. "Too many new birth certificates have been issued. There will be no more without proof."

Mr. Matsumoto laid his hat upon the counter. "Perhaps you do not understand, as you are a novice to this position. The entire Chinatown burned, so all papers were lost."

"My orders are to issue no further birth certificates without proof. And you have no proof."

"No proof was required previously."

"Now proof is required," Mr. Purcell said, looking through some papers on his desk. "It's the new law."

"I am his proof." Mr. Matsumoto cleared his throat and straightened. "I am his father. He was born here, on Delancey Street, above my shop, Matsumoto Finest Wares, well known over San Francisco and beyond."

Benji didn't dare look at Mr. Matsumoto. He felt his face growing red as Mr. Purcell looked back and forth between them.

"Can your wife vouch for this as well?" Mr. Purcell asked with a little smile.

"Ah, my poor wife died in the flames." Mr. Matsumoto looked down at his hands. "Now my only consolation will be that our son, born on American soil, has his rights restored as an American. My son, Benjamin Matsumoto." He put his hand on Benji's shoulder.

Mr. Purcell rose and left the room. While he was gone, Benji and Mr. Matsumoto stood without looking at each other. Mr. Purcell returned with a form. "This is the last one, Matsumoto," he said, and disappeared into another room.

Mr. Matsumoto filled out the sheet in his spiky script—*Benjamin Matsumoto, born 819 Delancey Street, August 19, 1890; Yasunari Matsumoto, father, born Kyoto, Japan, 1846; mother Fumiko Matsumoto, born Kyoto, 1853.*

"In Japan," Mr. Matsumoto told Benji, "I am Matsumoto Yasunari and you will be Matsumoto Benjamin, with the honorable family name primary. This is my first lesson for you."

After Mr. Purcell collected the form, Mr. Matsumoto and Benji walked in silence down two flights of stairs and out the door. The sidewalk was buckled in places; they had to walk in the street. All around them were the sounds of sledgehammers and pikes.

"Is that my name now, then?" Benji said, shouting to be heard above the noise.

"If you like."

"Do you have other sons this way?"

"You are the only one. You saved my life, so you are the son of my heart."

Benji couldn't think what to say. He studied the cracked sidewalk.

"Don't be doleful," Mr. Matsumoto said. "You have gained American citizenship and extra father in one swoop. To tell you the truth, you may not need passport, but I need a son."

"A son." Benji thought of Frank across from him on the train: I am not your father. His eyes watered.

"Matsumoto and Son." Mr. Matsumoto waved his arm. "Can you see the sign above the shop? Yes, you will be the junior partner, sending me goods from Japan. In the meantime, you will work for our mission, *ne*?"

While waiting for his documents to arrive, Benji taught English, rounded up dogs and cats that were homeless after the earthquake, and accompanied men to possible places of permanent work on farms in Watsonville and Sacramento. When Mr. Matsumoto put Benji in charge of the construction of a new house on a nearby street, Benji protested. "I know nothing about building."

"In this way you will learn. You must be skilled at enterprises beyond farming."

One foggy morning in November, Mr. Matsumoto brought a pot of tea to the construction site. He and Benji sat on the just-completed steps; Mr. Matsumoto poured tea and looked up through the mist at the rafters. "I see you are progressing. Very good." He patted Benji's knee. "I have come to tell you of a prospect. We Japanese intend to bring wives from Japan. All our young men must have women, *ne*? And they can bear children on American soil and there can be no dispute about their citizenship. You are citizen, but you have no wife. What will you say to a wife?"

"A wife? Here?"

"Perhaps you might be wise to stay, Benji-san, and take a wife in America. It may be difficult for you in Japan—forgive me for saying so—not being pure Japanese."

"But I am Japanese, dammit," Benji exploded.

"With an American father."

"Now I have a Japanese one."

"This is true in our hearts, but some biology is involved, I'm afraid."

"I'm not going to Japan to find a wife, anyway."

Mr. Matsumoto looked into the distance. "You are fixed on Japan," he said.

"Yes. I'm sorry. You've done so much for me . . . but I must find my family."

"*Daijobu.*" He waved his arm and, after a silence, cleared his throat and turned to Benji, smiling. "What about myself? Do you think I shall have a wife?" He pretended to preen, smoothing back his hair, as before a mirror. "Am I too old for a woman to admire me?"

"Women will fight over you," Benji said with a laugh.

Mr. Matsumoto's smile faded. "Maybe a sweet wife can take away my sorrow." He shook a finger at Benji. "But she must be a good cook! No more noodle soup." He stood and gestured for Benji to rise. "Now. I must give you a lesson. Since you will go to Japan, you must be as Japanese as possible. Number one, no swearing. Very polite, please."

"Yes. I'm sorry."

"Bow from the center of your body for an important person, such as your father." He demonstrated; Benji made a deep bow. "Yes. And you must be disciplined and work hard."

"I've worked hard all my life," Benji said, trying to keep his voice even. "I'm working hard now."

"Please continue to do so. And respect your elders."

"Yes, sir," Benji said with another bow.

Mr. Matsumoto looked at Benji's hair. "There is also your appearance to consider. I am hatching a plan."

The next night, after dinner and the washing up, Mr. Matsumoto asked Benji and Murata, the cook, to remain in the kitchen. He rummaged in his brown satchel, took out a bottle, and, with a flourish, handed it to Benji. *Grierson's Hair Dye,* the label read; *Permanent coloration for the sophisticated gentleman. Results 100% guaranteed. Color: black.*

"Much better than shoe polish," Benji said.

"Yes, it's a good timing for you, this invention. Maybe I will use some myself, when I take a picture for my bride."

Mr. Matsumoto spoke to Murata and then to Benji in Japanese. "Did you understand me?"

"A little. Mostly. You were giving directions for the dyeing."

"Not good enough. From now on we speak only in Japanese."

Benji leaned over the sink and Murata poured some dye onto his head, then scrubbed it into his scalp, with Mr. Matsumoto talking in Japanese—exclamations and corrections, as far as Benji could tell. Mr. Matsumoto was right: He knew the cadence of Japanese from his childhood and had regained some of the basic vocabulary in Denver, but there were many words he didn't know.

Murata wrapped Benji's head in a towel, dried and combed his hair, then Mr. Matsumoto held up a mirror. "Transformed," he said. "*Kurata.* There's a word for you to learn." Benji stared at himself; the dye was an improvement, but there was nothing to be done about the nose.

When the passport arrived in the spring, Mr. Matsumoto reserved a second-class berth for Benji on the *Toyo Kisen Kaisha,* bound for Nagasaki with calls at Hawaii and Yokohama en route.

He left on May 15, seen off by Mr. Matsumoto and Murata. Mr. Matsumoto gave him a packet of money and a bag filled with bottles of hair dye. "Some men depart with whiskey bottles," he said in Japanese, "but you with dye—this shows you are unique." Then he added in English, "But you are unique in many ways."

When the ship was under way, Benji went on deck and watched the coast of California until the details blurred and it was a viridescent stripe, then a line of gray, then gone. He was severed from America.

The next day he sat on deck, gazing out at the water. He thought of the voyage to America: a nauseating terror, and Mama's ball, holding Mama's ball.

He had watched her make that ball, winding and winding the colored threads and then rolling it toward him, smiling.

He saw her lying on the tatami, her eyes closed, her face chalk white. A grasshopper jumped along her bloody sleeve. His body jerked; the book fell from his knees. He bolted up and began to walk the deck, holding on to the rail as the ship rose and fell, then went to the bar and drank beer after beer until the image of her face was gone.

That night he lay turning from side to side in his bunk, a man named Kazu snoring above him.

He got up and went to the deck. There was no moon, just streaks of light from the ship on the dark ocean. He imagined jumping. It made him shudder, the thought of plummeting down, water filling his lungs, trying to claw back to the surface, too late. He lit a cigarette, his hands shaking, glad for the warmth of his feet in his shoes.

In the morning, lying in his bunk, he took out his mother's picture and looked at her beautiful, sad face. She had wanted him to remember her, he reminded himself; she had carefully stitched the picture into the kimono.

Kazu looked in and Benji showed him the picture. "Ah, your mother. She will be glad to see you, I think."

At breakfast Benji told Kazu the story of his mother's death. Kazu shook his head. "Very tragic," he said. "Why did your father come with his wife? This is cruel, *ne*? It caused your mother a terrible shock in the heart."

"Yes," Benji said.

"But she behaved in unusual way. I think often if a Japanese mother must kill herself, she will take her child too. So she must have some special hope for you."

Benji stared down at his bowl of rice. He could have been lying on the tatami too. He thought of his mother's soft eyes. She could not have brought herself to do it. And perhaps what Frank had said was true, that she thought he would become a successful businessman in America.

The ship docked in Hawaii for a day, to refuel. Benji walked along the beach, looking at the breakers without seeing them, impatient to be going.

The night after they left Hawaii, they encountered a violent storm. For two days the ship pitched; waves crashed onto the deck, and water trickled through windows in the lower cabins of second class. Benji, nauseated and dizzy, gripped the edge of his bunk as Kazu prayed above him in Japanese.

After the storm passed, the ocean was calm again for more than a week, then there was a quieter turbulence—dishes sliding off tables, men walking like drunks. It was *kuroshiwo*, the black current, Kazu said, that ran out from Japan; they were getting close.

Benji stood on the foredeck, looking into the distance, his eyes blurred by the wind, thinking of the times he'd ridden Kuro, pretending he was flying to Japan. Kuro galloping so fast, as if he understood, had given him hope that he'd get here, and Keast had helped by giving him Kuro, and in so many other ways. Kate had helped too, he realized with a start. It must have been hard for her, taking him in. She hadn't always been kind, but mostly she had tried. Once, she'd told him she knew what it was like to suddenly be wrenched from home; she'd felt abandoned, sent away from her parents in China.

He felt a surge of gratitude for her and for Grandmother Pinkerton, and for Keast—both of the Keasts. For the kind people in Iowa, and Shin, Fumio, Willa; Mr. Matsumoto, his father now—they all had helped him survive. Without them, he would not be on this voyage. He wished Eli could see him leaning over the railing, looking out at the Pacific Ocean.

He didn't go ashore in Yokohama; he wanted Nagasaki to be the first place he walked in Japan. They sailed along the coast, the land in and out of sight, for two days. Much of the time, he stayed on deck, unable to sleep or eat.

When the ship arrived in Nagasaki Bay, it was raining and the hills around the water were shrouded in fog. The water beside the wharf was too shallow for the ship to dock there, so Benji and the other passengers climbed down rope ladders in the rain to small boats that ferried them ashore. Benji stepped out of the boat, his legs shaking. He had an impulse to kneel, to touch the ground with his forehead; instead, he looked up the hill at the tile roofs in the mist. He was home.

Books were not allowed, the doctor told Kate; reading agitated the mind. She must rest and benefit from the salubrious treatments.

Several times a day a nurse brought brown drops to her room and a tincture that tasted of licorice, making her sleepy but not sleepy enough, so she pretended to be deranged in order to have more medicine, in occupational therapy insisting that she would crochet a book, at meals quoting in a loud voice passages from "The Over-Soul" in response to any question, and the medicine was increased, along with the duration of the baths, where she lay with her eyes closed, her mind floating away from everything around her—the faint stench of urine, the loony in the next tub—and from the circumstances that had brought her here.

Some women fought the baths, but Kate liked them. Even when the water had gone tepid and her skin was wrinkling, her mind drifted to a town in California where she had stopped with her parents on the way to China, and she lived there now with her father, in a small sunlit house tended by servants, a lady's maid, a cook, and a gardener, and although the gardener labored at the digging and pruning, each day before dinner she went with Father into the yard and gathered lemons, oranges, and a basket of sweet-smelling lavender and roses for the table and before going inside sat in a chair in the golden light, holding the flowers, her eyes closed, the sun bathing her face: paradise.

One day she fell asleep in the bath and slipped beneath the water. When she woke, retching, slung over the edge of the tub, someone was pounding her back, and for a time the baths were discontinued.

Kazu had suggested that Benji stay at the Seamen's Home, an inexpensive boardinghouse operated by missionaries, until he could find permanent lodging. He recognized it by the signs above the door and on the porch: CHRISTIAN ENDEAVOR HOME FOR SEAMAN; HOT TEA COFFEE AND COCOA ALL HOURS; ICE CREAM SUNDAES MADE TO ORDER. On the hill overlooking the bay, the home was a two-story white clapboard house like those in Illinois. He'd expected to begin his time in Nagasaki in a Japanese house with tatami floors; at the noisy dining table where beef stew and potatoes and watery cabbage were served, it was as if he hadn't left America.

He was disappointed to find that most of the houses on the two hills overlooking the bay were owned by Westerners, and the street beside the water—where he walked the first morning after his arrival—was lined with expensive Western-style hotels and shops with signs in English.

But the street itself, and the view of the water, seemed familiar: He must have been here with his mother, watching for Frank's ship. He looked down at the packed earthen street, damp from last night's rain; his footsteps could be touching hers.

People flowed past him in both directions: Japanese men with bare legs pulling jinrickshas, foreigners in most of them; a man balancing two buckets on a long pole; two self-important-looking Western men speaking a language he'd never heard. A Japanese woman approached, a baby on her back. Her kimono was dark blue, with thin white stripes, her face rosy and delicate. "A beautiful baby," he said in Japanese; she gave a bow without looking at him, but when he turned to watch her after she'd passed, she gave him a curious backward glance. His mother would have been about that age when she carried him on her back. Waiting for Papa-san. How could Frank have come here with Kate? If they hadn't come, his mother would still be alive, and he'd have lived in Japan all his life.

Wandering through the other streets at the base of the hill, he found more fancy hotels and shops that catered to tourists and consulates of several countries, including America. He went inside the office of a news-paper, the *Nagasaki Express,* and placed an advertisement: *Bilingual gentle-man seeks employment in import/export concern; experience in bookkeeping and all aspects of office work. Please contact, in person or by letter, Matsumoto Ben-jamin, residing at the Seamen's Home, 26 Oura, Nagasaki.*

He walked away from the water and up a steep hill, then down. The flagstone street led through a hilly, crowded neighborhood of dark wooden houses, all Japanese houses, he saw with exhilaration, their paper sliding doors open to the light. The morning was already warm and per-fumed by the flowers that spilled here and there over the stone walls. A pretty young woman in kimono dumping a pail of water in the street smiled up at him, and he felt a surge of happiness; this was the beginning of his real life.

At the foot of the hill was a cluster of shops with cloth curtains hang-ing at the open doors, Japanese characters written on the cloth. He peered in—two women examining bolts of material in one, barrels of sake in another. There was a tofu shop—he recognized the gleaming slab of custard from a similar store in Denver. Tangy odors drifted out the doors of restaurants; he chose one, noisy and crowded, and took a seat at a low table.

It was a soba shop. Everyone was eating thin brown noodles, dipping them in bowls of sauce. His mother had fixed cold soba in the summer; he could remember the table, the sound of her kimono as she knelt, the door open to the garden, a brilliantly colored dragonfly.

The woman who came to take his order had strange eyes, gray, almost blue. He had an impulse to take her hand.

He had an order of soba and sake, then another, listening to the voices that surrounded him. As Mr. Matsumoto had said, the Nagasaki dialect was somewhat different from his own Kansai speech, but, except for a few phrases here and there, Benji could understand. It was his mother's language, after all.

* * *

That evening he asked one of his dorm mates—an American sailor named Oliver—if he knew where the geisha lived.

"In the red-light district. Some of us fellows are going tonight—want to come along?" He looked up from tying a shoe.

"Geisha aren't prostitutes," Benji said, his face going hot. "They're artists."

"What's a matter, your sister a gee-sha?"

"It's *geisha*." Benji jumped up from his bed. "They're trained in dance, singing, and Japanese musical instruments like the shamisen."

"Gee, okay, Mr. Intellectual. All I know is, they're not for the likes of you and me." He gave Benji a wink. "Some good whores over there, though. You'd better come along."

It was almost dark when the group of men—Oliver, another American sailor, Henry, and a Scotsman named Alex—headed for the district that Alex said was called Maruyama. He was a university student on holiday, obviously more intelligent than the others. Benji walked beside him as they descended the hill where he'd been earlier in the day—called the Hollander Slope, Alex said, because geisha and courtesans used to come up the hill from Maruyama to visit the Dutchmen in their enclave.

They climbed another hill to a quiet, elegant street lined with two-story dark-wood buildings. "Your gee-sha," Oliver said, with a wave of his hand. Benji's heart sped up. He saw no women, only men walking quietly along the street, Japanese and a few well-dressed foreigners. The doors of most buildings were closed, but a few small places—a bar, a confectioner's—were open, light spilling onto the flagstones. Benji heard snatches of French and some language he didn't recognize. At the end of one block was what seemed to be a restaurant, with an elaborate garden in front; from beyond the heavy closed doors, Benji could make out the muffled sounds of a woman singing and the eerie melody of a plucked instrument, perhaps a shamisen. "Let's go in," he said. His mother might have performed in this very place.

"Too rich for the likes of us," Oliver said. "Come on."

They turned left, walked through a maze of streets, paused in a bar to fortify themselves, and Oliver led them to what he called the best house in town.

It was a long, low building where young women knelt in cubicles open to the street; in each, an older woman beckoned and called out to passing men. Benji glanced down the row of women in their bright kimonos and garish mouths, some sitting with their heads bowed, some staring straight ahead, expressionless.

It looked like one of the pictures Miss Cross had shown that night. Maybe she had brought her camera here. He thought of the hall in Stockton, the boos for the suffragist, his photograph. It had done him no good to show her the picture. He felt a twist of guilt. But it had probably all blown over by now, the incident forgotten.

"I fancy that one." Alex pointed to a small woman—a girl, really; she looked no more than fourteen—in a red kimono.

Oliver and Henry both made choices, and the three stepped up to the cubicles.

"What about you?" Oliver called to Benji. "Don't you like girls?"

Benji turned away from them, heading in the direction of the geisha quarters. Shameless, all three, even Alex; he should have known better than to come with them. The crowds were larger now, and he didn't recognize any of the shops or streets. He went faster, moving through alleys that smelled of urine and rotten vegetables. He slipped on something, almost fell. Someone laughed: a boy sitting alone on a curb. Please take me to the geisha quarter, Benji tried to say in Japanese, then "Geisha-san," in English, holding out a coin. The boy snatched the coin, hitched up his pants, and started trotting down the street. He was skinny, his legs like sticks, but he moved so quickly that Benji could hardly keep up. Nothing looked familiar as they ran past back entrances, barrels of garbage. Two drunk workmen were slapping each other on the back, laughing. Maybe the boy hadn't understood, or maybe he was misleading him deliberately, for more money. But they jogged into a quieter area, passing a tearoom, a kimono store closed for the night, then burst onto the wide main street. "Geisha-sans," the boy crowed, pointing at a restaurant. Benji gave him another coin.

It was the same restaurant they'd passed before. One door was open; he had a glimpse of golden tatami, just as he'd seen in photographs. Several women were singing now, their voices high-pitched and urgent. There was a burst of raucous male laughter, then a woman's voice alone, half talking, half singing, ending in a squeal. More laughter, then a drum along with the shamisen.

He moved closer, bending to peer in. Nothing but more tatami.

When a man appeared at the door, Benji took out his wallet and removed some money. The man slapped it. *"Ie, ie,"* he said, with a shooing motion.

Benji backed away, his face burning. A gauche American, no better than Oliver. He took off down the hill, running hard.

He passed a woman gliding along the street: a gleaming kimono, elaborate hair, the profile of a face, painted white. A geisha. He slowed, holding his breath. He wanted to speak, to take her arm, but of course it was impossible, so he went on, his heart pounding. When he turned at the bottom of the hill and looked back, he could make out nothing but a white mask floating on the darkness.

In the morning at breakfast, Benji found a response to his advertisement: *Dear Sir, I am Tsuji, owner of Japan Shop. Speak English. You come soon to me in Funadaiku-machi.*

With directions from the missionary's wife, he started once more down Hollander Slope. When he found the area of shops, he turned left and soon was there, walking between long rows of stores that flew American as well as Japanese flags from the eaves. Although it was early, there were a few tourists in jinrickshas, peering in through the open doors of the shops at kimono, woodblock prints, Noh masks, jewelry. There were signs in Japanese and a few in English: PHEASANT SKIN OF POREAT; OLD JAPANESE SWORD AND GUARD AND KNIFE HANDLE; YOUR FINE BUTTON SHOP; and, at the end of the block, THE JAPAN SHOP. Attached to the roofline was a huge sign: SOUVENIR OF ALL KIND.

Inside, two American sailors were buying cigarettes from a gray-haired man in kimono. Benji looked around at the trays of postcards set out on counters, tortoiseshell necklaces—Mr. Matsumoto would like those—silver cigarette cases engraved with scenes of Nagasaki Bay. In a bamboo birdcage, a pair of twig-colored birds chirped and hopped back and forth between perches.

The sailors left and Benji introduced himself, using phrases of English and Japanese to show he was bilingual. The man bowed solemnly and said in English, "I am Tsuji, owner of Japan Shop." Then, without a pause, he asked, "You have seasick?"

"No," Benji said, startled. "I'm fine now."

"Good. You start now? New ship is in harbor."

Birdcage in hand, Mr. Tsuji led the way to an alley where he had a cart full of his wares. He wedged the birdcage between two small chests and they started out, pulling the cart up the long hill Benji had just descended. He wanted to ask about the wage and the duties, but it was all he could do to keep pace with Mr. Tsuji. They clattered down the long flights of stone steps that led to the wharf, and Mr. Tsuji pointed toward a ship anchored offshore. "Arrival today," he said. Without further explanation, he loaded two nets of his wares into a small, wobbly boat, gave Benji the birds to put between his feet, and they paddled out toward the ship.

Already some tourists were being ferried to shore in similar boats, Americans by the look of them, mostly men, but a few with their wives, including one stern-looking couple Benji imagined might be more missionaries. Tsuji snatched the birdcage from Benji and held it up as they steered past one of the incoming boats. "Nightingale! Best Japanese bird." When there was no response, he held up a gleaming tortoiseshell necklace. "Every kind of thing you want—postcard, necklace, doll." He glanced at Benji, who called out, "The Japan Shop has the finest wares in Nagasaki." No one looked their way as the Americans were rowed past; maybe Mr. Tsuji wouldn't hire him, if they made no sales.

Small boats were clustered all along the edge of the ocean liner, like barnacles. There were a few other boats loaded with souvenirs, but most of the small craft were empty, waiting for the remaining passengers. Near the bow of the ship were several coal-loading barges; men scurried up and down rope ladders to feed buckets of coal into the ship's furnace. Shouldering one of the net bags, Mr. Tsuji scampered up a rope ladder dangling over the side of the ship; Benji followed, clutching the birds.

About a dozen passengers—all of them Westerners—were still lined up on deck, as uniformed men went down the row with official papers and information about hotels. Benji noticed a middle-aged woman defiantly alone, in an oversize hat; he thought again of Miss Cross.

Bowing and still holding up the tortoiseshell necklace, Tsuji went along the line hawking his wares; Benji followed, feeling foolish as he held the birds aloft. Who would buy a souvenir before visiting the town, he thought, but to his surprise there were several sales of postcards and a painting of Nagasaki Bay.

"Next time you come early, we do better," Tsuji said as they stepped back into the wobbly boat. Apparently it was settled; he had a job.

Frank's mother said they couldn't stay in Plum River; the scandal about the opera would be too hard on the children. Just yesterday, in the general store, Mrs. Cassidy and another woman whispered behind their hands when they saw her; Mary Virginia and Franklin would endure far worse.

She was right; they would have to move.

It took some time to settle his affairs. The Cases bought the land—though the bank took most of the profit, because of his loans—and Keast and Lena were to move into the farmhouse, in exchange for their taking on the twins for a time. They'd wanted to pay him, but he refused; what they were doing to help him with Elmer and Rose was of incalculable worth, and it wouldn't do to have his father's house fall into disrepair. A farmhouse without land would be hard to sell, as he pointed out to Keast, so they were doing him a favor in that way too.

He planned to send for the twins once he established himself in the farm-machinery business and could buy a house of his own in Cicero. His sister's house would be full to bursting as it was, with his mother taking over the only spare room, and Franklin and Mary Virginia moving in with their cousins. His sister said there was no room for him except in the shed, but it was solidly built and could be weatherproofed and heated with a stove in winter. That suited him fine: He'd be glad for the privacy, and he would be on the road for Wilkes Brothers' Farm Equipment most of the time anyway.

They set out for Cicero at daybreak on a Monday morning in early September, Frank in the buggy that carried his mother, Franklin, and

Mary Virginia; the Swede drove the cart loaded with their belongings. Frank took the long road around Plum River and Morseville and the heart of Stockton, so they could avoid the stares of busybodies.

They passed the fields he and the Swede had planted in wheat this year. Case and his threshers had already been at work there, the sheaves shining golden in the first light. The farm that his grandfather and father hacked from sod and rock. How many times had he heard that story? His father would be enraged but not surprised. Would spit on the ground. A fool and his farm are soon parted. He would never understand how Frank had tried, all the labor, some good years, some bad luck. Least of all would he understand about the opera, or moving on account of it. Darn-foolery, he'd call it.

Frank glanced back at his mother, holding Mary Virginia; she was staring straight ahead, her eyes red from crying. It was hard on her, but it was hard on him too, something no one seemed to understand.

After all, he'd been born here, in the Plum River farmhouse, and had grown up in these fields and woods. His first memories were of sitting in his father's lap, holding the reins of the plow, and the smells of fresh-turned earth and damp corn. Eventually he'd itched to get away and never should have come back, shouldn't have brought Kate here, not with Benji, but there had been some pleasure in these twelve years, even in the hard labor of farming. And Kate—lying with her at night, her firm breasts beneath his hand, her lovely thighs. The laughter that sometimes seized her, bringing tears to her eyes.

He'd been the one to go through Katie's things. The sewing machine and mannequin he'd left for Lena to use for the time being; maybe some-day Kate would be able to use them again. Most of her possessions he'd packed and stored in the attic, but some things he couldn't leave behind. In his trunk were the locket engraved with their entwined initials, the silver brush and mirror set—only a simple comb was allowed at the asylum—her atomizer of lavender toilet water, her pillow, a feathered hat she'd been wearing the first time he met her, the alphabet sampler she'd made as a child, the first needlework she'd done at the farm and had hung proudly on the parlor wall: *Amor Vincit Omnia.* Darling Katie.

Franklin sat beside him on the front seat, silent as stone. With his up-turned nose and eyelashes that were almost too long for a boy, he bore a startling resemblance to his mother. He was tough, though: Frank had seen to that.

"Want to take the reins?" Frank asked him.

Franklin shook his head.

"Gum?"

Franklin looked at him. "How will Benji find us?"

Benji. Frank stared straight ahead, took a breath to steady himself.

"I don't think Benji will be back, son." He put a hand on Franklin's knee. Franklin jerked away and looked the other direction, into the woods.

"I wasn't the one to go flouting a photograph," Frank said.

"Frank," his mother said.

"Well, I wasn't." His ears went hot. And he hadn't been the one to go sending dirty laundry to some opera writer in Italy. He had written to the man—Puccini was his name, in Milan; Lena had found the address—but hadn't received an answer to his request for an explanation about the theft of his life.

In his new work he would be Tom Pinkerton—that's how he'd introduced himself at Wilkes Brothers' central office in Chicago. He'd have to remain Frank in Cicero, his home base, with the family there, but no one in Cicero knew an opera from an owl hoot.

Frank touched the whip to Admiral's back and jolted him into a canter. Mary Virginia woke up and began to cry. "Shh," his mother said. "It's all right."

"I want Blondie," Mary Virginia wailed.

"There will be cats at your cousins' house," his mother said. "I'm sure you can have one as your own."

"I want Blondie. I didn't even get to tell her goodbye."

Frank thought of the whiskey packed with his shaving things in the small suitcase. When they stopped for lunch, he could get the bottle out while rearranging things in the cart. The Swede would probably be glad of some fortification too.

"Slow down, Frank," his mother said. "You're jiggling us to bits, and the cart can't keep up."

Frank pulled Admiral to a sharp halt, leapt out of the buggy, and walked back to the cart. "Let's change places," he said to the Swede. The Swede shrugged and stepped down; he didn't ask for an explanation—he never did. They set off again.

That night they stayed at a hotel in Sycamore, and after a slow start the next morning because of his mother's dyspepsia, and two hours lost to a broken axle in the afternoon, they arrived late at his sister's house.

"The children have gone to bed," his sister whispered, "but we've saved some supper for you." She looked disapproving, her forehead etched with wrinkles. She was a younger version of his mother: brown-haired, heavyset, though without the kind heart. His brother-in-law, Morris, in the background with his pipe, was a weak-chinned man who owned the local feed store and was active in church affairs. He wouldn't think to offer a drop of whiskey.

Frank looked at the gleaming brass umbrella stand, a rubber plant with leaves so shiny it looked waxed. His sister's famous housekeeping.

He declined supper, left his mother to settle the children, and went out to the shed. A lamp was burning there and the place was warm, the coal stove already installed. There was a narrow bed, a tall oak dresser, a hat rack for his hanging clothes, a braided rug. No desk, as he'd expressly requested for his work. Probably thought he wouldn't reimburse them. Tomorrow he'd buy a grand desk with plenty of drawers. He was going to be a success—a natural salesman, they'd said in Chicago—and he knew the ropes, with his experience; he'd introduce labor-saving equipment to farmers all over Illinois. A big rolltop desk. He'd put it by the back window, facing the orchard.

He stripped off his outer clothes, got into bed, and downed the rest of his whiskey. Enough to burn his innards but not enough to knock him out.

It was just as well he'd sold the farm. Maybe that Italian had done him a favor. He was a traveling man at heart, not a farmer, and at last he'd make a decent living, enough for a pretty cottage where there would be room for all the children, his mother too if she liked.

The mattress was thin and hard. For what seemed like hours he hung at the edge of sleep, a jumble of his father's maxims coursing through his mind—glass houses, stitch in time, small leak great ship, well done twice done, sticks and stones.

He got up, took Kate's pillow from the trunk, and lay in bed holding it, a soft goose-down pillow that still retained some of her scent. The truth is, Katie, he told her, I'd have lost the farm eventually.

He woke to the noise of stones pounding the roof, but when he looked out the window saw only a windfall of apples dropping from the trees.

Benji's salary included living quarters above the Japan Shop, in a small apartment shared with Mr. and Mrs. Tsuji; he occupied their son Haruki's former room. Haruki, a tall, thin, bespectacled man who was a houseboy for an American missionary couple in the Oura district overlooking Nagasaki Bay, came for dinner the first Sunday.

"My parents are curious about your background," he said in English, as he sat down at the table. "I have offered to translate."

Benji thanked him but said he would like to try to manage in Japanese, since this was now his home. Haruki looked disappointed. "Ah," he said. "I understand."

For dinner, Mrs. Tsuji served champon, a thick Chinese soup that was a specialty of Nagasaki, she said. When Benji pulled a tentacled sea creature from the soup and quickly nestled it beneath the noodles, Haruki laughed. *"Ika,"* he said. "Squid." Benji described his first encounters with American food, the peas he'd chased with a fork, the slabs of beef.

Mr. Tsuji asked about his history in America. Benji told them about growing up on the farm, the long return journey to Japan to find his mother's family. "And has your mother died?" Mrs. Tsuji wanted to know. They all looked so interested that he poured out the story: his geisha mother and American father, Frank's desertion and return with an American wife, his mother's suicide.

Mrs. Tsuji gasped and covered her mouth. The men stared at him.

"I have heard of something like this," Haruki said.

"When? From whom?"

"I overheard some foreigners chattering about it at my former employer's house, a few years ago."

"What did they say?"

"Just as you described. I remember that at the time it struck me as perhaps a romantic foreigners' tale."

"But it happened; I was there when she killed herself."

"*Ah so?*" Mrs. Tsuji said. "How old were you?"

When he told her, she said, "Poor boy," and patted his hand. "This is truly a tragedy, *ne*?" She gave Haruki a stern glance.

Benji took out the tin containing the picture. "These are my parents," he said. There was silence as they passed the photograph around the table.

"Could I talk to your employer?" Benji asked Haruki.

"I am sorry to say that she no longer lives in Nagasaki."

"But I must find my mother's family. Maybe someone else will remember."

"Your search is best made in Maruyama, I think," Haruki said. "I will be happy to guide you, but I must caution you that the geisha world is secretive."

"And my son does not know the geisha," Mr. Tsuji said with a laugh. "You must be a rich man to be acquainted with the geisha."

"I can manage to guide him quite well," Haruki said stiffly.

On Haruki's next day off, he and Benji climbed the hill to Maruyama in the early afternoon. June's rainy season had begun, a hard rain pelting against their umbrellas. "We won't see so many people in the street on such a day," Haruki said. "But at least we can begin our inquiries."

Benji wanted to take in every detail—the pattern of flagstones on the street, the glimpse of startlingly green moss through a slatted gate, the entrance to a shrine that seemed familiar—but Haruki strode ahead through the narrow, twisting streets. He didn't have much time, he'd said; "Mrs. Foreigner" required him back early, to serve at a musical evening.

He finally slowed his pace on a quiet back street where there were several handsome wooden buildings, each two stories high. Geisha residences, Haruki said. Along the upper balconies hung red and white lanterns, each with a geisha's name written in black. "When she goes out to her parties at night, she carries her own lantern," he said. "Yoshi," he read aloud, "Suwa, Tsuru, Shige."

The gates to all three houses were locked; they rang and pounded, but no one came. At one house a woman's face appeared at an upstairs window and was quickly gone, a pale blur.

"We will visit the shops frequented by geisha," Haruki said. "This is my next idea."

They went into a kimono shop where a stooped woman with missing teeth was waiting on another elderly woman, smoothing out a length of brown silk patterned with golden and dark brown bats. "Perhaps she is an *okasan*," Haruki said in a low voice, nodding at the customer. "A geisha mother." When Benji whispered back for him to ask, Haruki shook his head. "It would not be polite to inquire directly," he said.

When the customer left, Haruki told the woman about their search and Benji showed her his mother's picture. She shook her head. "There are many hundred geisha in Maruyama," she said.

They visited a tabi shop that sold the white socks worn with kimono; a geta shop, where a man and his son made wooden clogs of all heights, including the high ones favored by geisha; and a store that specialized in long clay pipes like those Benji had seen in woodblock prints of geisha and courtesans, but no one recognized his mother's face.

Discouraged, they went into a bar for some warm sake. The bartender, after hearing of their quest, said they must go to the tea shop around the corner, owned by Chiye-san, a former geisha renowned for her discretion.

Chiye-san was a silver-haired woman with erect posture, dressed in a black silk kimono. Benji guessed she was in her fifties, but she had a mysterious beauty, a long oval face, a wise expression. She brought them tea, poured it with graceful precision.

"Excuse me, Chiye-san," Haruki said with a bow. "We are looking for information about a former geisha, the mother of this young man . . ." He nodded at Benji; she bowed in his direction. "Her name was Cio-Cio-san, and she lived in Maruyama in the eighteen-eighties and 'nineties but died tragically by her own hand—when this man's father"—he nodded at Benji again—"returned to Nagasaki with an American wife."

Benji laid the picture on the table. Chiye-san lifted it, holding it in both hands, then carefully set it down again. "I am sorry," she said, with a bow. "It could be that I have seen her, but I do not recall. My memory is beginning to fail me, I'm afraid."

"But I have to find someone who knows her," Benji said, trying to keep his voice level. "What do you suggest?"

She looked out the open door into the rain, then turned back to them.

"Please forgive me for saying that Cio-Cio is perhaps not a geisha name in itself. We are all associated with the butterfly. Many have a butterfly crest on their kimono." She gestured, palm up, to the small butterfly embroidered on the sleeve of her kimono. "We usually have a professional name, but perhaps there has been no Cio-Cio in Maruyama."

"But . . . look . . ." Benji turned the photograph over to show Chiye-san the writing on the back of the picture. "Doesn't that say Cio-Cio-san?"

"Yes," she said. "Pardon me. I must be mistaken." She bowed again, her hands on her thighs. "I wish you good fortune in your search," she said, and retreated to the rear of the shop.

They started down the hill, following a narrow street of stone steps. Benji thought of the day he'd learned his mother's name, sitting on Frank's lap on the plow, and of that fall, when the butterflies in the garden had seemed a visitation. Mr. Matsumoto hadn't mentioned anything odd about his mother's name.

"Chiye-san is wrong," he said. "All my life I've heard of Cio-Cio-san."

"Perhaps a pet name given by a foreigner who cannot pronounce Japanese," Haruki said.

"My father knew a little Japanese—he was here for a while."

They passed a stone torii; Benji knew from the book he'd read in Plum River that a torii marked the entrance to a shrine. He looked in—there was a garden, blue hydrangeas heavy with rain, a small shrine set at the back. Haruki pointed out another geisha house just below the shrine.

"The shrine seems familiar," Benji said. "Maybe I lived in that house."

"No one but geisha and their apprentices live in a geisha house."

"Are you certain?" Benji said, looking back at it. "Not even children?"

"Perhaps some girls in training, but no boys, I am certain. I know about geisha because I am Japanese."

"I'm Japanese too. My mother was a geisha."

"But your father is American."

The implication was clear. It was just as Mr. Matsumoto had warned. In Japan he was not pure Japanese. In America he was not an American. He was a mongrel, belonging nowhere.

"My mother came from a samurai family," he said. "I'm going to find them."

Haruki was silent, then said, "Please forgive my rudeness. I am certain that you will," and they continued in silence through the heavy rain.

* * *

A few days later, when there was a break in the weather, Benji returned to Maruyama by himself and went to the shrine he'd noticed before. Looking at the paths that twined through the garden, the masses of hydrangeas, the open shrine sheltered by a roof, he felt a quiver of memory. A woman in a flowered summer kimono was praying before the shrine; he stared at the back of her neck, a graceful stem beneath her elaborately arranged hair. She might be a geisha.

When she moved away, her face turned from him, he stepped to the front of the shrine and looked into its dark interior, at the wooden and bronze objects there. He had no idea what any of it might signify. He pulled the long braided straw rope to ring the bell for the god's attention and clapped twice; somehow he remembered that. He closed his eyes and waited.

Nothing. He stepped back, a tight feeling in his chest. The woman emerged from the back of the shrine, her head bowed. He watched her go, then followed the path around the shrine. There was a smaller shrine set farther back, among a cluster of evergreens; as he walked toward it, he saw a stone fox to the left of the entrance.

He hurried toward it, holding his breath, and stood before the fox. It was crudely made, of soft stone that had weathered badly; part of his snout was missing. He touched its head, mottled with black spots, ran his fingers over the ears. It was the fox that had frightened him as a child. They must have lived close by.

That night he asked the Tsujis where a geisha might have lived with an American. In Juzenji, Mr. Tsuji said without hesitation, the neighborhood on both sides of the Hollander Slope, not far from Maruyama.

"Hollander Slope!" He'd walked there many times now, perhaps close to his home without being aware of it.

"Juzenji is the mixed neighborhood of Nagasaki," Mrs. Tsuji added. "Often a foreign man lives in this place with a geisha or courtesan, and some descendants of such unions live there too."

"Is that the only place they could have lived?"

Mrs. Tsuji said that some Japanese men married geisha or courtesans and lived elsewhere, and that a few wealthy foreigners might take their geishas to live in the Oura district overlooking the bay, but most stayed in Juzenji.

* * *

Juzenji was a maze of houses, small gardens, and alleyways. For several weeks, on his days off, Benji walked through the narrow alleys of the neighborhood. He encountered some foreign men: a Frenchman with a limp, several sailors in European uniforms, an American sailor who made him think of Frank. He was exhilarated to see people with light eyes or hair that was not pure black: people like himself.

Behind the rows of houses at one perimeter of the neighborhood was a huge stone wall that seemed familiar—the way it cast a deep shadow over the adjoining houses and gardens—and there was a gate here and there, the way a door was set adjacent to the yard, that made him think one or the other of the houses could have been theirs, but he was not certain. Although everything seemed smaller than he remembered, the area and the quality of light stirred him, and he was positive that he had walked with his mother on the flagstone steps of Hollander Slope, going down the hill to the shops, up the hill to look at the ships in the harbor.

He was reluctant to go from door to door to ask about his mother—Mrs. Tsuji had warned him that people might be wary of talking to a stranger—but he always carried the picture in his pocket.

One day a plump gray-haired woman carrying a string bag of groceries stopped him in an alleyway. "You come here often," she said. Her creased face was kind, so he told her he might have been born in the neighborhood and showed her the picture of his mother and Frank. "Do you recognize either of them?"

She squinted at the picture. "Possibly I have seen the woman—I cannot say with certainty. The man looks like many Americans. He is your father?"

Benji told her about Frank's betrayal, his mother's suicide. Had she heard of it?

"There are many sad partings here in Juzenji," she said. "The foreigner comes, the foreigner goes; that is usually the way of it. Sometimes," she added, looking at him, "he leaves behind his souvenir."

"Do you know of a place for rent here?" he heard himself say. "A room or a small apartment?"

"Perhaps," she said, looking at him closely. "Please come." He followed her farther down the alley, where she slid open a gate made of wooden slats and led him into the house. She invited him to sit at a small table in an untidy room and brought tea, grunting as she sat down to join him. She was Fukuda Taki, she said, whose husband, a carpenter, had died recently; their one child had died quite young. She asked about his employment, how long he had been in Japan, his future plans. After he told her everything, including the years in America, the long trip here, she studied him gravely.

"I will need to speak with your employer," she said, "but I believe a place can be arranged for you here, to our mutual benefit."

The Tsujis said they would miss him, but the move seemed appropriate. Mr. Tsuji gave him a raise so that he could afford his new quarters.

Benji settled into a small tatami room upstairs in Mrs. Fukuda's house, overlooking the front garden. In addition to his modest rent, he helped Mrs. Fukuda with chores in the house and contributed groceries for the breakfasts and dinners she cooked for him. She was glad to have him, she said; she had been lonely.

In the shop, Benji learned to use the abacus and to make change in Japanese currency. He made an addition to the inventory—Western-sized shoes and socks for men, sent by Mr. Matsumoto—that proved to be popular with tourists and businessmen from the Oura district. With the money Mr. Matsumoto sent him, Benji shipped objects made of tortoiseshell—eyeglasses, hair ornaments, jewelry—to San Francisco. His career in import/export had begun.

He returned often to the fox shrine, where he showed the photograph to anyone who seemed approachable: a man who worked on the grounds, a woman—beautiful, possibly a geisha—who gave him a slight smile as she was leaving. He went deeper into the pleasure district, going farther down small alleyways and lanes, to shops and teahouses and bars. A few people said her face might be familiar, but no one could recall her name. No one remembered Cio-Cio-san.

Keast settled Ulysses in what he still thought of as Pinkerton's barn, gave him a good brushing and an extra measure of oats. It had been a hard day. On the way to the house, he looked out at the late-afternoon sunlight on the greening meadow, the plums in flower along the river, thinking of the day Benji lost his ball. It had been a warm day in autumn, Indian summer.

"You're late, Horatio." Lena met him at the door. "I was worried."

He consulted his watch. "It's the usual time."

"You said you'd be home early."

"I'm sorry, darling." He kissed her and brushed a smear of flour from her cheek. "We had to go from one end of the county to the other. And I stopped by the post office." He drew the envelope from his coat pocket to show her, but she was already headed toward the kitchen. The twins were in their high chairs at the dining-room table, Elmer throwing crumbs to the cat, Rose sucking her thumb.

"Hello, sugar lumps." He gave each one a kiss on the head. "Where's Charlotte?" he called. He'd looked forward to holding her.

"Already in her bassinet. She wore herself out crawling all day."

He returned the letter to his pocket and sat down. The table was set with Lena's best china, and wineglasses stood at their places.

It wasn't their anniversary, and she'd already told him she was pregnant again.

Lena came in smiling, bearing a huge platter of pork roast surrounded by crusty potatoes. Sylvie followed with a bowl of peas fresh from the garden, baked apples, yeast rolls. His mouth watered.

"Pour the wine, Horatio, it's on the side table."

He reached for it—an excellent burgundy they'd been saving for a special occasion.

"What's this all about?" he said.

"Your birthday! Why do you always forget?"

"Because I want to," he said, too quickly, then saw the shadow cross her face. "But this is wonderful, sweetheart, thank you so much." He poured their wine, lifted his glass. "How could a man be happier, with such a wife, such a family?"

They began to eat; he was ravenous. He'd tell her about Benji later. The children were fussy and had to be put to bed in the middle of the meal, he carrying Elmer, Lena with Rose.

"Quite a family we're accumulating," he said as they closed the nursery door. He embraced her and patted her stomach.

"I want to have more," she said.

"More?"

"Four or five total, including the twins."

"Oh, my." He followed her down the stairs.

"You don't want me to teach—I might as well have a class at home."

They sat down at the table. He picked up his knife and fork, put them down. "I'm an old man, Lena, fifty-five. I can't leave you with a house full of children."

"You're as healthy as a horse. And you certainly don't act like an old man," she said with a sly look.

"You're an inspiration," he said. "But it's something we have to talk about."

"Later," she said. "Let's enjoy the evening."

She brought in a cake, fresh coconut, and two wrapped gifts—onyx cuff links and a fine shirt she'd made for him. He took off his work shirt, put on the new one, and she helped him with the cuff links. "There," she said. "More handsome than any young blade."

"Ha," he said, and kissed her. He hoped their child would be a male, to help Lena in her old age. Not that he didn't have something set by, but she'd need a man.

After cake and coffee, they went to sit in the porch swing. It was the loveliest time of day, the gloaming, with its dusky, mysterious light. The air was perfumed with the lilacs he'd planted for Lena when they moved here.

"I'm sorry you missed your lilac wedding," he said.

"This is just as good. Better. And we made an early start on our family."

He sighed.

"What's wrong?"

"Benji's gone to Japan and didn't bother to tell me." He showed the envelope. "My letter was returned from San Francisco. Look at this: *Return to sender. B. departed for Japan, will advise, Y. Matsumoto.* Benji hasn't written to me since that postcard."

"He's on an adventure. And he's young. You'll hear from him."

He took her hand and looked out at the pasture, the light almost gone, the oak tree a dark indistinct shape. It was true: The young didn't understand time, how it rushed by, fast as that little river.

Just before New Year's it began to snow, blowing in first from the bay, then fanning out over the city, large flakes drifting down with a heaviness and ease that suggested something long stored had finally been released. When Benji walked from Mrs. Fukuda's house toward the shop early the next morning, it had stopped snowing, but few people were out. In the silence, with all the houses blanketed by snow, time seemed erased. It could have been a hundred years ago; it could have been twenty years ago, when he was a boy, and his mother was alive. At the bottom of the hill, he turned and looked up Hollander Slope. The children of the wealthy foreigners had owned sleds, he remembered, and he'd watched enviously as they zoomed past him, screaming with delight. His mother had given him a large metal cooking pan to use as a sled, but it hadn't worked on the hills, so she tied a rope to the handles and pulled him back and forth across a flat patch of snow.

He started to turn left, toward Funadaiku-machi. The tourists wouldn't be coming today, he realized—there was no real need to go to the shop—so he went to the right, up the slope toward Maruyama.

An old man was dragging a bag of coal down the main street of the pleasure district, leaving a gray trough behind him in the snow, and a group of boys, red faced and poorly dressed—urchins, Grandmother Pinkerton would have called them—were shouting insults as they lobbed snowballs at one another. A snowball stung his ear; he turned and grinned, tempted to join the game, but he wanted to get to the shrine while he might have it to himself.

The stone torii at the entrance and the branches of trees around the perimeter were rimmed with white. He was glad to see that the snow covering the path and garden was pristine; his were the first footprints. When he pulled the rope to make his prayer, snow fell onto his head and down the neck of his coat. He shook out the collar, put his hands together, and closed his eyes. His mind jumped about; he needed to learn some prayers in Japanese.

He heard footsteps, barely discernible, as though the sound was part of his imagining. But then there was a woman's voice—"Excuse me"—and he stepped aside to let her pull the rope. Irritated, he moved without glancing at her to the fox shrine at the back of the grounds, pulled the rope, and closed his eyes again. But his solitude had been disrupted. He looked at the fox, his old friend, his broken snout filled in with snow, his eyes erased by it, and brushed the snow from the top of his head.

"Excuse me," he heard again. He turned; the woman's head and the lower part of her face were swathed in a blue cloth. She looked up at him mischievously. "I was hoping to see you today," she said.

"Oh?" She didn't look familiar, though it was difficult to tell with her wrapped up like that.

"I've seen you from the window," she said. Her mouth moving beneath the cloth was enticing.

"What window?"

She turned and nodded toward the geisha house below them.

"You're a geisha?"

"Do you think so?" she said, still with that flirtatious expression. "Thank you."

He looked at the fox to hide his confusion.

"You like our fox," she said. "Is he carrying prayers for you?"

"You're very inquisitive," he said, adopting her tone. "But you haven't answered my question. Are you a geisha?"

She pulled back her scarf, revealing a prominent nose and a pointed chin. "What do you think?" she said.

"Well . . . maybe so," he said.

She laughed. "We may as well be truthful. I am a maid who cleans the geishas' floor. You and I are similar, Mr. Foreigner, both of us mongrels. I think your mother is a Japanese and your father a Westerner. Am I correct?"

"Yes."

"There are many of us in Maruyama. But you have not been living in Japan."

"How do you know?"

"Your speech confirms it. And I've seen you here often—a stranger, with urgent prayers."

"I'm praying to find information about my mother, who was a geisha."

"Ah?" Her face was interesting, the way its expression changed so quickly.

"I know my mother brought me to this shrine, so I think she might have lived in the house where you work."

"People come to Umezono Shrine from all over Maruyama," she said. "So this is not a good clue, I'm sorry to say."

The picture of his mother was beneath his heavy coat and shirt today, in the money belt to protect it from the snow; he couldn't take it out here.

"Could we meet tomorrow?" he said. "There's something I'd like to show you."

"It is not so easy for me to leave my work. But perhaps on Saturday at this time I can meet." She covered her face with the scarf, gave a bow, and walked quickly away.

"Wait," he called, "tell me your name," and started after her, but she scurried across the snow, down the incline, and disappeared into a side door of the house.

By Saturday, the snow had begun to melt, dripping from the tips of branches and the roofs; rivulets of water coursed down the sides of the street as he climbed the hill to Maruyama. In the main shrine, patches of moss and rocks were visible in the snow, but it was colder beside the smaller shrine, where there was still a heavy white crust on the roof. He greeted the fox—the stone icy beneath his hand—pulled the rope, and prayed that she would come. After a few minutes, he turned to look at the entrance, then at his watch. She wasn't coming. It was pointless anyway, he told himself. She couldn't help him, she was only a maid.

"Good day!" he heard behind him.

He whirled around. She was smiling, petals of snow on her scarf looking as if they'd been arranged there.

"Where did you come from?"

"I was behind the shrine. I like to observe you."

"You're very mysterious," he said, laughing. "Are you a fox?"

"Yes," she said. "I knew you were intelligent. Let's find a congenial place for our talk."

She led him through the back streets of the pleasure district to a small bar, where they sat at a table and ordered warm sake. Her name was Rinn, she said, which meant independent spirit; she had chosen it for herself. Her mother was a prostitute who gave her to the geisha house when she was a baby; the nationality of her father was unknown. "He left me his curly hair," she said, taking off her scarf. "Therefore some unkindly call me a Jew."

Though her hair was pulled back tightly from her head, Benji could see that it was wavy and glossy black. "I think it's nice hair," he said. "Very nice." He wanted to touch it.

She put the scarf back on.

"No, leave it off," he said, but she tied a firm knot beneath her chin.

"Do you always wear it?" he asked.

"Maybe not always. What have you brought to show me?"

He took out the tin, carefully unwrapped the picture, swathed now in several layers of rice paper.

"This is my mother," he said, "and father."

She studied the picture. "Much as I thought," she said.

"You're too young to have known her, of course," he said. "But I was hoping perhaps you could introduce me to an older geisha who might remember her face."

"As a lowly maid, I cannot make an introduction. You must be a wealthy man to meet a geisha."

With a sigh, he put away the picture.

"Perhaps I could take the photograph," she said, "and show it to someone myself."

"Oh, no—I couldn't part with it."

"You don't trust me?" she said with a false pout.

"I don't know you at all," he said, "but even if I did . . . Maybe you could ask your *okasan* if she knows of a geisha called Cio-Cio-san by her patron—she killed herself when he betrayed her."

"Oh." Her face went still. She made a movement toward him.

"I witnessed it," he added.

She touched his hand.

"I was taken to a farm in America—so different from here I thought I was in the kappa world. It was . . ." He coughed; his throat had closed up. "All my life . . . But now that I'm here—" He broke off. "All I find is mystery."

"Ah." She was looking at him closely; her expression was steadying.

"I'll do my best to help you," she said. "There is a kind geisha at my house, Megumi-san; I will ask her advice."

"Thank you so much." He felt shaky, suddenly on the edge of tears.

"Don't go," he said, when she rose.

"I must return to my slave work," she said. "But one week from today, will you come again to the shrine? Perhaps then I can have some news for you."

The next week, and the next, they met at the shrine and went to a bar or restaurant. Megumi-san had not heard of such a story exactly, Rinn said, but she was willing to make discreet inquiries. "Of course, the suicide must have taken place not in Maruyama but elsewhere—in the house where you lived—so the geisha may not have heard of it."

"Wouldn't they wonder what happened to her?"

"Many people disappear in Maruyama," she said.

"Don't you disappear," he said.

She blushed, her cheeks a vivid pink.

"Will you visit me in Juzenji?" he asked.

She ducked her head. "I will tell you at our next meeting."

The next week the plum trees were in bloom around the perimeter of the grounds, a miracle of delicate white blossoms in winter. He stood beside one of the trees, breathing in the subtle fragrance.

"Do you like our trees?" she said, appearing beside him. Her head was uncovered and her face glowed in the reflected light of the flowers. "The plum tree is sacred to the geisha and others in Maruyama—the shrine is named for plum trees—Umezono. We make prayers with plum seeds—all of us, not only geisha." She showed him a stone vat he hadn't noticed before, filled with small dry seeds. There were thousands of seeds; he picked one up and rolled it gently between his fingers.

"I guess my mother made prayers with these seeds," he said, "for my father to come back." He dropped the seed back into the vat. "A waste," he said.

"And as a lonely child perhaps sold to the geisha house, she would pray to see her family. I can understand her."

He looked at her. "Do you ever see your mother?"

She shook her head. "She may live here in Maruyama, but I am as an orphan."

"You don't look for her."

"She is dead to me."

"Because she left you," he said, "she gave you up."

They stood silently looking at the flowers. "I can come to your house the next week," she said in a low voice, almost a whisper. "Megumi-san has very kindly said she will arrange the time for me."

"That's wonderful," he said, his heart speeding up. "Please give her my thanks. I'd like to meet her someday," he added.

"It is impossible," she said. "She is a geisha, as I told you." She tied her scarf back on her head. "I wonder if you would be unhappy to know a woman who is not a geisha."

"I would like to know you," he said.

Walking home, he began to feel nervous; his invitation to Rinn had been impulsive, without considering how he could arrange it. Mrs. Fukuda was usually at home, and it would be impossible to take Rinn upstairs without her noticing. But at dinner that night, when he stammered his request to bring a female visitor, Mrs. Fukuda seemed pleased. "I will prepare refreshments for you," she said with a smile, "and go to visit my niece."

Rinn arrived late; it seemed to be her habit. He could hardly speak as she came in; he gestured awkwardly toward the table and said, *"Dozo."*

"Do you like my kimono?" she said. "Do you notice the pattern of plum blossom and pine? Chosen just for you."

"Very nice," he said. His hand shook as he poured the tea.

They sat in silence drinking tea until Mrs. Fukuda's cat jumped on the table.

"Naughty boy!" Rinn picked up the cat and held it against her chest; it began to purr loudly.

"He likes you too, I see," Benji said.

"This means you like me as well?" she said, tipping her head to one side.

"I suppose I do," he said.

"I am very honored," she said, with a little bow; was she mocking him or not?

"Are you real?" he blurted out.

She stared at him, then laughed. "I hope so," she said. "Otherwise I've suffered a great deal for no purpose."

He looked at her as he poured more tea; it overflowed her cup, spilling across the table.

She leapt up. "Megumi-san's kimono!" she cried.

He ran for a towel and handed it to her. "I'm so stupid, always clumsy."

"Don't worry—it's blotting out." She dropped the towel, stepped forward, and kissed him.

"Ah—Rinn-san." He put his arms around her: They stood kissing, with the cat twining around their legs, then he led her upstairs.

"This is my room," he said. He glanced toward the closet where the futon was stored. He couldn't think how to proceed.

"I'd better take off this damp kimono. Aren't your clothes quite damp?"

"Oh, yes, quite damp."

He undressed and watched her remove layer after layer, then she stood looking at him, her skin luminous in the light of late afternoon.

"You're beautiful," he said.

"No man has ever said so before. I think you must be wrong."

"You've known the wrong men," he said, kissing her. He fumbled with her hairpins and she stepped back to remove them, letting her hair fall. Long and wavy, it reached her waist. He embraced her from behind, to bury his face in her hair, then together they took out the futon.

Each week that winter and spring she came to the house late on Saturday afternoon; their times together lengthened, as they lay talking into the night. Benji told her about his spasms of anger at his mother for leaving him. He felt guilty, he said, because she must have been in great pain.

"I understand you," she said. "You can never know what were your mother's thoughts—perhaps she felt she had no choice. I think this was true for my mother, though sometimes I feel great anger, as if I am a piece of trash she has discarded. But how can she make her living with children to care for, and how can she perform her job without the risk of children? So she must give them away. At least she found a good geisha house for us, instead of a brothel."

Megumi-san was her sister, Rinn said. Both of them had been sold to the geisha house in hopes that each would become a geisha, but in addition to her unconventional appearance, which soon revealed itself, the *okasan* said that Rinn was too impudent to be trained as a geisha. "Am I too impudent for you?" she said, turning toward him with a smile.

"If you weren't impudent, I'd never have met you."

"I think you're very brave," she said. "I knew your temperament, from watching you. Therefore I made myself brave to meet you."

They lay looking at each other.

"Together we will find your mother," she said.

"Even if I never find her," he said, "I have found you."

Frank came to visit. He looked older, the lines so deep in his forehead they might have been made with a knife. They sat in the curdled light of the parlor, with its smell of dusty lace curtains, he clasping and unclasping his hands. The house was fine, he said, the children were well. He did not call them by name.

An image of a crying baby stabbed at her. Franklin, wailing with a stomachache, breathless, inconsolable. Mrs. Pinkerton gave him paregoric in his milk and he slept.

She thought of paraffin, the way it lay thick on a jar of preserves, and she stared hard at Frank's face until it was barely familiar.

That afternoon during her nap, she dreamed that she was on trial for a great crime but no one would tell her what it was. Her father drilled a hole in her side to measure the depth of the problem. She woke up screaming.

Hands pulled a tight sleeve over the middle of her body; her arms were pinned to her sides. In the distance she could hear someone playing a piano, badly, a Bach air that had been her first recital piece.

She sang the air as it should be, but the woman in the next room shouted, "Stop that racket!" and when the nurse came she said Kate had better be a good girl or she'd be moved to a different ward.

"It is possible that I have a surprise for you," Mrs. Fukuda said as she and Benji were finishing breakfast.

"What?" He looked around the room.

"Come for a walk and you will see." Her smile was enigmatic. "Bring the picture of your mother, please."

His heart leapt. "Why?"

"Because I am not certain. We shall see."

Mrs. Fukuda washed the dishes with maddening slowness, took off her apron, and led him out the door. They started up Hollander Slope.

"Where are we going?" he asked.

"I do not want to disappoint you too much," she said.

Benji could hardly contain his energy. Something to do with his mother. The sound of the cicadas vibrated in his body.

Halfway up the hill they turned in to a small flagstone alleyway and walked past houses of brown wood, tile roofs. A red cloth flapped on a clothesline; two boys, one with skinned knees, jumped off and onto the curb, pushing and laughing in their game. At the end of the alley was the massive stone wall that marked the neighborhood's boundary.

They stopped at a house shadowed by the wall; a frail woman leaning on a cane greeted them. Mrs. Fukuda made introductions; the woman's name was Mrs. Kondo, and her husband awaited them inside.

Mrs. Kondo led them into a musty room where her husband was setting glasses of cold barley tea on the table. "Please sit down," she said, and they settled themselves at the table. There was silence while Mr. and

Mrs. Kondo studied Benji. He looked at Mrs. Fukuda; she was gazing elsewhere.

"Forgive me," Mr. Kondo said, "but the son I remember was light-haired."

What son? Benji felt like shouting. There was much to be said for American directness. Thinking of Mr. Matsumoto's lessons, he bowed and said, "I am blond." He touched his dyed hair. "My effort to look more Japanese."

"Ah so desu ka," Mr. and Mrs. Kondo said in unison. They looked at Mrs. Fukuda, who nodded and smiled.

"Benji-san, show them the picture," she said.

His hands trembling, Benji took out the rice-paper box Mrs. Fukuda had given him, unwrapped layers of tissue, and laid his mother's picture on the table. Mrs. Kondo held it close to her face. "This is the woman I remember."

"At last," he burst out. "Someone who knew my mother. You're certain?"

Mr. Kondo looked at the photograph. "Yes, we have known her," he said. He and his wife gazed at each other. There was another silence. Benji made himself wait.

"She lived just across the way," Mrs. Kondo said.

"With you," Mr. Kondo added. "The son."

He leapt up. "Can we go?"

"Indeed," Mrs. Kondo said. "Presently we will go."

He sighed and sat down.

No one moved. There was to be discussion.

"You can't imagine my feeling," Benji said. "Did you know her well?"

"Only slightly, I regret to tell you," Mrs. Kondo said. "She was quite aloof—you and a maid were her only companions. Sometimes she would leave for the day or the evening, going to Maruyama, we supposed. Occasionally a gentleman came to call, perhaps once a month."

"The man in the picture? My father?"

She shook her head. "I do not recall this man. He was not the visitor."

"Who was the visitor?"

"An American—a businessman perhaps, rather distinguished-looking. He usually wore a tall hat."

"I remember this man," Mr. Kondo said, tapping a finger on Frank's picture. "One day he came to borrow a rake—his Japanese was very poor.

We didn't see him often. After he departed, I thought your mother would return to Maruyama—we both wondered how she managed on her own, especially after you were born."

With a bow, Mrs. Kondo returned the picture to Benji.

"What was her name?" he asked.

"Midori," she said. "Suitable for her—it means beautiful girl. She was quite beautiful, *ne*?"

Midori. Benji stared at the picture, attaching the name to her face.

Mr. Kondo suddenly began to talk. He had been in the garden pruning a rosebush on the tragic day, he said. It was late afternoon when he saw some Americans coming down the alleyway—a woman carrying a white lace parasol and two men. "One of them was the man in your picture, another the gentleman who sometimes visited. The woman I had never seen before. They went into the house." He leaned toward Benji, his eyes wide, enjoying his story. "I remember . . . I had a feeling . . ." He looked at his wife.

"He did," she said. "He had a premonition."

"They were inside only a short while before I heard a cry," Mr. Kondo went on. "Later I thought that must be you, the son. Soon the Americans left, carrying you, crying, wailing. We were perplexed what to do."

"I thought we should go to the authorities," his wife said. "We had some argument about it."

"I regret I did not go into the house," he said. "Perhaps I could have saved her."

His wife shook her head. "Very much blood. She must have died immediately."

"Did you . . . see the place?" Benji made himself ask. He was relieved when she said no.

"The authorities described the tragic scene to us," she said.

"Before the authorities came," Mr. Kondo continued, "some men carried her away. The little maid must have fetched them. Her body was wrapped in a dark cloth and placed in a cart." He bowed toward Benji. "I am very sorry to tell you this," he said.

Benji looked down at the picture, trying to turn his thoughts away from the shrouded body, the cart. "Did she ever mention any relatives? Or where she was born?"

"I am sorry to say that I did not inquire," Mrs. Kondo said, "but she seemed to desire her privacy. I remember she liked to sing and to play the shamisen."

"You liked to frolic with your cat," Mr. Kondo said. "Always you were chasing it. Once you climbed that tree in front of your house to fetch it."

"Yes," Benji said, with a laugh. "Rice Ball." He had a sudden memory of the cat purring beside him on the futon, the warm body against his. "Could we possibly go see the house now?"

"We regret . . ." Mr. Kondo said with a bow. "The original house has been torn down. Another has taken its place."

"Oh, no."

"Perhaps you would like to go into the yard," Mrs. Fukuda said.

Benji couldn't speak. So much searching, then hope, then nothing.

"Could you introduce us?" she asked Mrs. Kondo.

"There's no need—the owners are away at present. We will accompany you."

They left the Kondos' house and went across the alley. Mr. Kondo opened the gate and Benji stepped into the yard, the others behind him. He looked around at the patchy grass; a stone lantern, slightly askew. A maple tree but no pond. "I thought there was a pond," he said, "with lotus and frogs."

"I believe it was filled in," Mrs. Kondo said. "We have trouble with mosquitoes here."

He gazed at the tall, dark house where his had once stood, erased by this one. He could remember only a sliding paper door at the front and pink flowers by the entrance. There were no flowers by this house, and the windows were square and ugly. In his room there had been a round window—the moon window, his mother called it.

He turned from the house to the tree, looking up at the smooth stippled trunk, the large crotch of limbs. He had sat there; it *was* his tree. That seat must have been lower when he had climbed up; maybe his mother had boosted him. He ran his hands along the trunk, held a leafy branch against his cheek.

The others remained by the gate, talking in low voices while he walked the perimeter of the property. His yard. His mother's yard. He gathered a handful of dirt and put it in his pocket, along with a pebble from the ground. Before he left, he took a leaf from the maple tree and placed it in the box with his mother's picture.

* * *

When Rinn came the next Saturday, Benji told her about the visit as they lay entwined on the futon.

"Midori," she said. "A bit unusual—perhaps that may help us trace her, though we cannot know for certain if this was her geisha name or true name."

"Two names! We'll never find out about her."

"Don't be so gloomy. A geisha mother might have known Midori, I believe, whether it was her performance name or personal one." If they could find the geisha mother, Rinn thought, perhaps they could learn where she came from, the name and location of her family, since most of the geisha houses kept records. Megumi was quite willing to make inquires all over the district when she could, and Rinn promised to come the moment there was news.

For several weeks Benji was in a state of agitated excitement, glancing up each time a customer entered the shop, in the evenings listening for Rinn's voice at the entrance of the house. Sometimes at twilight he walked through the streets of Maruyama, carrying his mother's name in his mind as he looked at the geisha houses and stood beside the fox in the Umezono shrine. He found a withered plum beneath one of the trees there and added it, along with his prayer, to the vat of sacred plum seeds.

Summer turned to fall and Megumi learned nothing. It could be that his mother's geisha house was no longer in existence, Rinn said; there was a fire in Maruyama a few years ago, she told him, that had destroyed several of the houses. "But it's more likely," she said, "that any geisha who might remember her has chosen to remain silent. The geisha world is a closed one, as you know, and Megumi is perhaps too young to penetrate it. They might not want to speak of a suicide performed under ignominious circumstances."

Benji and Rinn sometimes wandered through the temple graveyards near Maruyama, looking for his mother's grave. Although they found two stones with the butterfly crest of a geisha etched into the base of the monuments, the names were Tsuru and Hana. There was no Midori.

One evening, he returned alone to the graveyard at a temple where he'd met a sympathetic priest, climbed the steep steps past row after row of gravestones, and stood at the top of the hill, looking out at the water shining in the last light and the dark shapes of the mountains that surrounded the bay. It was a commanding view. He would have a monument made for her and put it here.

He arranged with the priest to buy a space beneath a sheltering camphor tree; the priest also agreed to find an appropriate stone marker. Benji took the picture of his mother and Frank from the box and carefully cut out her image, then tossed Frank's picture into his desk drawer; later he would decide how to dispose of it. Mr. Tsuji introduced Benji to a maker of Arita ware, who was able to set his mother's portrait in porcelain, like the one of Keast's wife, and fix it to the stone.

On a Sunday afternoon in mid-October, Benji and Rinn stood at the memorial with the priest for a ceremony of blessing. It was a fine but melancholy day, the sky deep blue, the trees ablaze with their final color, in the air an undercurrent of cold that intensified the fragrance of the camphor tree beside the monument. The priest recited a sutra. Benji and Rinn put chrysanthemums in the vases on either side of the stone, and he stood looking at the picture, thinking of the day he had found it sewn into his kimono, the tin box he had carried it in, traveling with it all the way to this moment. His mother's eyes gazed back at him, cool and mysterious, revealing nothing. He turned and led the way out of the graveyard, and after bidding goodbye to the priest, he and Rinn went to a restaurant that overlooked the bay. They sat, their knees touching beneath the table, talking and drinking sake while it grew dark and lights came on in the ships at anchor and in the houses across the water.

She could not remember her face. There were no mirrors in the asylum, the nurses said, because someone might cut herself. It had happened before, they said. Kate looked for her face in every surface that might give it back to her: the steel icebox in the kitchen, the glass door of the cupboard. At night, in the lighted parlor, a window with the dark behind it reflected her shadowy image.

She cupped her hands over her forehead, nose, mouth, and tried to recollect herself, but could not. She was fading.

She asked Norma Brinkley, a new patient who occupied the next bed in the ward, to describe her face. "Sweet," she said. "Tired."

"Are my eyes blue?"

Norma peered at one eye, then the other. "I believe so," she said.

Norma was a large woman with an opulence of flesh beneath her chin. Her eyes, dark and quick, took in everything. She had no doubts about her solidity. There was nothing wrong with her, she said, except she no longer bled and her husband didn't want her any longer.

Kate needed to bask in the sun, Norma said, and her face would freshen up. If she would go to occupational therapy instead of lying on her bed all day, they might let her go outside, on parole. Maybe they could go together. Norma would be granted parole soon, she was certain.

Kate was assigned to work in the kitchen. Her first day, she scrubbed potatoes until her back ached. The next day she did laundry, with a washboard just like the one at home, the same boiling and rinsing and wringing. She thought of the kitchen in Plum River, the oilcloth on the table, the milk pitcher with a rooster on it, Mrs. Pinkerton's shoes misshapen by bunions. She saw Mary Virginia's little blond head as she stood beside her, cutting out biscuits with a thimble, and began to cry, a quiet sluice of tears sliding into the water, but no one noticed; the other laundress was wiping her face too, wet from perspiration.

The next day she was the cook's assistant, gutting a rabbit, peeling potatoes and rutabagas. An attendant came to watch. "You're making progress," she said, and a few days later Kate was granted parole.

She went out with Norma and several other women and a man who worked on the wards. The sun bathed her arms and face, and she drank in the fragrance of fresh clover. At the back of the property, Kate found a litter of kittens beside a fence. She took one without asking and put it beneath her shawl on the sore place in her side.

Beyond the fence was a hill that cut steeply down into woods; past the trees, on a rise, were fields of corn. They marched back along the edge of the property and looked at the asylum farm, the barnyard beside the fence. She stared at the unpainted barn, the hay spilling out of the mow, a well with a pump handle, the overhead roof of the well rotted away. There was a chicken on a mule's back, piled sacks of grain, a wooden chair lying on its side.

It was a mirror of the life she'd left, cruel in its accuracy.

She thought of the children, the dirt beneath their toes, Franklin and Mary Virginia running after fireflies. The babies.

They would have missed her at first but not now. What would Frank have told them? Perhaps that she was dead, thinking it the kindest thing. She squeezed the kitten so hard that it clawed her arm and dropped to the ground.

Franklin was old enough to know. They should all know. She felt a splinter of excitement, looking at the barnyard. They should all know she loved them.

Later in the evening she slipped out alone. It was almost dark. Invisible in her brown dress, a kerchief over her hair, she moved across the lawn. She walked along the fence to find a gate that would open to the farm, a stile perhaps, like those in nursery rhymes she had read to them, but there was none. She lay down near the barnyard, pressed against the fence. When morning came she was still there, the nurse striding across the wet grass to capture her.

Mr. Tsuji had several woodblock prints in his shop—a few landscapes and one of a woman combing her hair. When Benji asked if she was a geisha, Mr. Tsuji said no, with her colorful costume she was sure to be a courtesan; a geisha's kimono would be more subdued.

Benji asked where he could find prints of geisha. "Inexpensive prints like these, you can find on the street by the wharf," Mr. Tsuji said. "For better quality you must go to a shop that specializes in ukiyo-e, paintings and books as well as prints." He drew a map of a shop several blocks away, and on his next afternoon off, Benji set off to find it.

When he reached the street, he had difficulty locating the shop, since he couldn't read the writing on the noren hanging in front of the doors; an elderly man looked at the name written on the map and led him to a small shop, pulled back the curtain, and called, "Wakama-san."

There was nothing on view in the store, only a bare counter and a low table on the tatami. The place smelled of fine wood and, faintly, of incense. An elegant man in glasses and a dark summer kimono appeared from behind a curtain, knelt on the platform, and bowed. Benji explained that he was looking for a print of a geisha, preferably from Nagasaki, but he would like to look at a number of prints in his collection.

"Often the location is ambiguous," Wakama said. "I will need more guidance as to your preferences, since there are geisha by many artists—Utamaro, Eishi, and so on, who depicted denizens of the flower and willow world."

"I apologize for my ignorance," Benji said with a bow, "but I'm willing to learn. If you could choose just a few prints from your collection for me to look at, I'd be grateful."

Wakama-san gave a stiff bow and disappeared into the back of the shop. He was gone a long while. A gray-haired woman appeared, set out tea and cakes on the table, and gestured for Benji to sit down, then departed. He ate and drank in silence. There was no sound, except from the street.

Finally Wakama-san reappeared carrying a folder of prints, which he placed on the counter. "Forgive me for being so long," he said. "It was hard to choose from my favorites." He allowed himself a little smile.

Benji stood beside him as the man laid the prints on the counter, then held up one of them. "This quite modest portrait I believe is from Nagasaki. It is not particularly valuable, as the artist is of modern times."

The geisha's face was natural, not stylized in the manner of the other prints. She looked small and sad, holding a fan before her in an artificial pose. She wasn't beautiful like his mother, but she had the charm of realism.

He propped the Nagasaki geisha on a makeshift tokonoma in his room and, in the mornings as he lay looking at her, thought of the other prints, boldly vivid and elegant, laid out on Wakama-san's counter. He could have a collection too, in his own shop, for discriminating tourists who couldn't find their way to Nagasaki's interior; he would specialize in ukiyo-e. He wrote to Matsumoto to ask about a joint venture with prints and received an enthusiastic reply, along with money for a large purchase. For every twelve prints Benji acquired for him, he was to keep one for himself for his trouble. *I am proud of my son, who shows much initiative,* Mr. Matsumoto wrote. *If you have discipline, you can succeed. Perhaps you can learn much about ukiyo-e prints and paintings from Wakama-san. Have you begun to master the written language? You will need this for your accounts and so on.*

Mrs. Fukuda introduced him to a retired teacher in the neighborhood, a man with steel-gray hair and small glasses who didn't want to charge him for the Japanese lessons, as he had nothing to do these days, he said, except tend to his bonsai and be a bother to his wife.

Every night after dinner, Benji sat at his desk and practiced, over and over, the hiragana characters in the simplest alphabet. It reminded him of writing *O*'s on his slate in Miss Ladu's classroom. He thought of Flora, on her pretty wrist a charm bracelet he'd given her with money he'd earned at Red Olsen's store. He had thought of the bracelet as a declaration, though they'd never spoken of it. A naïve dream. He could hardly recall her face.

He saw Rinn less often now. "When shall I come again?" she asked one morning as she was leaving. She stood before the mirror on his tansu, pinning up her hair.

"I'm not sure. I'll call for you."

She turned to look at him. "Don't you care for me any longer?"

"Of course. I'm just very occupied trying to start my business."

"If you spend too much time on business, business is all you will have."

"You don't understand." He began to fold up the futon.

"Yes, I'm a pampered, ignorant woman who knows nothing of the affairs of men and money." She pulled on her haori jacket. "I was just a convenience for you to help you find out about your mother."

"How can you say such a thing?"

"It is easy. I think, then I open my mouth and speak."

He watched from the window as she went down the street. Her gait was uneven, one hip rising slightly with each step. He felt a pang of guilt that he'd never asked what caused her problem. If it was a birth defect, it could be passed on to children. He looked down at his hands, shocked to have had such a thought. He sat at his desk to practice his writing before going to the shop, trying to block out the image of her rising and falling hip, the thought of it somehow arousing. She could become pregnant, he thought with a cold spot of fear in his stomach.

For weeks he occupied himself with work, visiting other shops that specialized in woodblock prints, and beginning his study of kanji. Often he worked so late into the night that Mrs. Fukuda had to wake him when it was time for work.

One morning at breakfast she said, "I don't believe I've seen Rinn-san in quite a while."

"Mmm." Benji kept his gaze focused on the newspaper. He was making progress; he could read the headlines now and often got the gist of stories.

She removed his soup bowl and put rice and fish before him.

"Every day we all get a little older," she said.

He began to eat his fish and turned the page to the shipping news.

"You will regret missing the opportunity to marry such a sincere woman who loves you."

"What?" He stared at her intense eyes, the cluster of small moles on her forehead.

She laughed. "Shall you as an American require a go-between?"

"No," he said, "when the time comes I will not." He gulped the rest of his tea and headed for the door.

"She may find another man," Mrs. Fukuda called after him. "I think you would regret it."

Busybody, Grandmother Pinkerton would call her.

In early December he had dinner at the Tsujis' house. Mr. and Mrs. Tsuji and he and Haruki sat with their legs dangling over the warm coal kotatsu as they ate shabu-shabu—sizzling chicken and vegetables served from one pot. The men were drinking beer; Mrs. Tsuji, tea. Haruki dominated the conversation, complaining about Mrs. Foreigner. Benji asked why he hadn't stayed to work in the shop. "It doesn't suit my temperament," Haruki said.

Benji noticed Mr. and Mrs. Tsuji exchange a quick glance; beneath that glance he sensed a long history of interchange and understanding. He asked how long they'd been married. "Too long," Mr. Tsuji said with a laugh; his wife gave him a playful slap on the arm and said, "Forty-two years as of next April." When Benji asked if it had been an arranged marriage, she said, "Oh, yes, very few Japanese marry for love, but love can be learned, as I keep telling my son."

Scowling, Haruki rose from the table and gestured for Benji to follow. They had agreed to go drinking after dinner. When Benji bowed and thanked the Tsujis for their hospitality, Mrs. Tsuji said, "Please come anytime. You are our second son."

He and Haruki went to a bar nearby and sat at a counter drinking warm sake.

"Are you opposed to marriage?" Benji asked him.

"Too much trouble," Haruki said with a wave of his hand. "Once I liked a woman, and my father hired a go-between to approach her. She kept me in suspense for weeks before saying no."

"You have to keep trying," Benji said. "You'll find someone."

"Too much trouble," Haruki said again.

After they parted, Benji found himself walking up the hill to Maruyama. He knocked on the back door of the house where Rinn lived. An elderly woman with a scarf tied around her head peered out at him.

His heart was racing. "Please ask Rinn to come out," he said. "It's urgent."

"Rinn-chan is away, I believe."

"Away where?"

"A small holiday, perhaps, I cannot say for sure."

"When will she return?"

"*Sumimasen,*" she said with a bow. "I have no information."

"Please ask her to contact me—Matsumoto Benji," he said, just as she was closing the door.

Filled with dread, he began to visit shops and restaurants in the Maruyama area. Most people said they did not know a woman of Rinn's description; those who did claimed ignorance about where she might be. It was like looking for his mother again.

One day just after the New Year he saw her coming out of a shop with a package and ran to greet her. Her cheeks were red, her eyes gleaming; she looked frighteningly happy.

He ran to her. "Where have you been?"

She flicked her eyes at him. "I am surprised by your sudden concern."

His throat went thick. "I missed you. Please come back."

"Now he misses me," she said to the sky. "So the slave must hurry to his palace."

"I was worried," he said. "Please come just once."

"I am rather busy," she said, but she was smiling.

They agreed that she would come for dinner on Sunday. When he told Mrs. Fukuda, she clapped her hands in delight. "We'll have a feast."

"There's nothing special about this occasion," Benji said. "She's only coming for dinner."

Late Sunday afternoon it began to snow. He thought of meeting her in the shrine when it was snowing; he felt a flicker of anger, as if Rinn were controlling the weather too.

She wore a long coat over her kimono; on her umbrella was a thin layer of snow. With the white flakes swirling behind her, she could have been the subject of a ukiyo-e print by Hiroshige. You're beautiful, he longed to say.

Mrs. Fukuda came to greet her and, with a great amount of exclamation, accepted Rinn's gifts of dried bonito and a box of sweets. Mrs. Fukuda said she was about to finish up with dinner; would Rinn like to help?

The two women disappeared into the kitchen, behind a jangling bead curtain, talking and laughing as hot oil sizzled in the pan.

He hadn't imagined the evening like this. He paced the room, picked up a book of haiku, put it down.

Finally the women came in with the food. They sat down to eat: a delicate soup, sashimi, chawan mushi, a variety of pickled foods, including plums from the Umezono Shrine, and tempura.

"I've never cooked tempura before," Rinn said, with an uncharacteristically shy expression. "I hope you can bear it."

"Very good," he said, though the sweet potato was greasy and the batter fell off the shrimp.

Rinn went to the kitchen for fresh tea. Mrs. Fukuda leaned forward and whispered, "You could live here, with myself as the honorary mother-in-law."

He shook his head, laughed, and lit a cigarette.

Mrs. Fukuda retired early; Benji and Rinn climbed the stairs. His hands trembling, he removed Rinn's layers of kimono, kissed her breasts, and led her to the futon, but after several minutes was aware that he wouldn't be able to make love. "I'm sorry," he said.

"Let's just sleep together like two contented bears," she said, and drew him to her warm bosom.

When he had difficulty sleeping, he disentangled himself from her and went to look out the window. There was a quarter moon; the snow on rooftops gleamed eerily in the dark. What did it mean, his sudden inability? He'd never had this difficulty with a woman before. He turned to look at her indistinct shape in the dark room. She had left him without a word, without a warning.

In the morning he awoke to her caressing him, and he turned to her, his body alive. "Darling woman," he said in English, looking down at her; he knew no equivalent in Japanese.

"You see. I am good for you." She pulled him tighter against her.

As they lay together in the sweet sad aftermath of love, she said, "We should be together, *ne*?"

He rolled onto his back and stared up at the ceiling. "Where were you?"

"What does it matter? I have returned." She sat up abruptly. "What do you wish for us?"

"That we go on as before. But no leaving without explanation."

"I see." She rose and began to dress.

"You're going?"

"Yes, why not? I'm a very busy woman."

Benji jumped up and began pulling on his trousers and shirt. "Why can't you explain where you were all that time?"

She shrugged. "Because this is all that matters to you."

"It's I who have been the slave." He rushed down the steps; she wasn't leaving before he did.

Mrs. Fukuda had opened the door to air out the first floor, where the odors of last night's dinner still hung in the air. She was in the kitchen, preparing breakfast. He looked out at the snow, the footprints of some animal there. If Rinn left now, she wouldn't return.

He started back up the stairs. She was just coming down. They froze, staring at each other.

"Do we need a go-between?" he blurted out.

"There has been no one between us," she said.

He took her arm. "What if we don't get along?"

"This is the risk of life."

"Shall we try?" he said. He heard Mrs. Fukuda go still in the kitchen.

She stepped down and embraced him. "I think we will do better than try."

"No more leaving," he said.

"If you don't leave . . ." She put a hand flat against his chest, then against hers. "Neither will I."

They turned and walked to the bottom of the stairs, where Mrs. Fukuda was waiting with her congratulations.

The doctor warned him that she had changed in the past months, but at first he did not recognize the woman who was led into the parlor by a coarse-looking nurse. "Sit down, Mrs. Pinkerton," the nurse said, guiding her, none too gently, into the chair opposite his.

She was shockingly thin, her dress hanging wilted on her frame, and the eyes that he had loved, sapphire and full of life, were dull. Her face was gaunt, almost skeletal.

"Hello, darling," he said, and reached to take her hands. He had planned to say, Happy anniversary. "You're not wearing your wedding ring," he said.

"They wouldn't glue it on," she said in a flat voice. Was it humor or madness?

"I've brought you some presents." He laid a large wrapped box on her lap. Her fingers plucked at the bow; he unwrapped it himself. "From Montgomery Ward," he said, standing to hold up a silky blue dress.

She touched it as if she didn't know what a dress was. He felt a wrench of guilt, thinking of how he'd scolded her when she'd bought dresses on her own, trying so hard to please him.

He opened the next box, in it a blue shawl that he arranged around her shoulders. She seemed to like that, at least; she drew it close around her.

"Lemon crisps!" He held out an opened tin of cookies. "Mother made them. She remembered they're your favorite sweet." She made no move to take one.

"You need to eat, darling." He shook the tin. "Have you not been eating?"

He should take her home to Cicero; his mother and sister would see that she ate. She wasn't violent, the doctor said. But it would be hard on Mary Virginia and Franklin to see her like this, and he was hardly at home now, on the road for days at a time.

He wanted her back; he wanted to be able to tell her everything. He took her hands again. "Katie," he said, "I miss you."

She stared at the floor.

"Do you know me, Katie? I'm Frank, your husband."

"Frank," she said, with something like a smile.

"That's right. Look, sweetheart, I almost forgot, I brought you a book of poems—maybe you could hide it under your mattress," he said in a mock whisper.

The Kate he knew would have laughed.

"Where are the babies?" she whispered.

"With Mother." Thank God she didn't know that the twins were living with the Keasts in the farmhouse. "Everyone is fine," he said. "The children are fine."

Her face went blank. It must be the medicine. Last time the nurse said she was taking new medicines.

He led her to the sofa and put his arm around her, hoping that she would lean against him, lay her head on his shoulder. But she was rigid; he could not move her. She'd always had a will of iron, he thought with a flash of anger.

"Goodbye then," he said, but did not move. He looked around the parlor, nicely furnished. She had no idea of the sacrifices made to keep her out of the state asylum. She might be glad he'd sold the farm—she'd always hated it—but she'd be humiliated to know the Cases had bought it, humiliated to know that the Moores were making contributions toward her upkeep. Aimee Moore's penance, he thought bitterly; if not for her, Kate probably wouldn't be here.

He reached into the tin of cookies, ate one, then another—too sweet, but he kept eating.

The nurse reappeared. He stood, brushed the crumbs from his shirt into his hand, and put them in his pocket.

The nurse lifted Kate; she seemed limp as a doll.

"What's wrong with her?" Frank cried. "She's worse."

"She tried to run away on two occasions. We've had to confine her."

The nurse's eyes were large and moist. She was kinder than she had first appeared.

He did not look back as he left the room and went outside. He mounted Admiral and pressed him into a canter, managing to hold back his tears until they were well away from the asylum.

Ed McAuley's farm wasn't far, outside DeKalb. Last year he'd bought a fancy combine. He could use a second plow, all the land he had. Frank couldn't bear the thought of going home to his empty bed, the picture of Katie on the dresser.

He spied McAuley and his men in the middle of a vast cornfield. On the way out to them he broke off an ear of corn and inspected it: much meatier than any he'd ever grown. Must be a different variety. His years of farming gave him an advantage over other salesmen, who came at it from a business point of view.

McAuley didn't need anything, he said, but directed him to the neighboring farm, a fruitless call. The old geezer said he hadn't recovered from the panic of '07 and anyhow the old farm equipment was best; he was still using his father's plow and harrow and didn't intend to change. No point in arguing.

It was a late-summer afternoon that under other circumstances would have been beautiful, hot but with a nice breeze, the kind of day when Kate and his mother had made strawberry ice cream and they all sat out on the porch eating it, looking out at the sunset. The little quarrels of those days seemed inconsequential now. Those ridiculous beets.

In DeKalb he could stop in at the whorehouse. He felt filthy to think of it after seeing Kate, but a man had to survive somehow. He pressed Admiral harder, but he couldn't canter for long. Getting to be an old man like himself.

But once he reached town, the thought of the whorehouse sickened him. He stopped by the saloon for a bottle of whiskey and a sandwich, then went to the White Rose Hotel and drank himself to sleep.

Benji and Rinn were married in the spring, at the shrine where they had met in Maruyama. A slight breeze stirred the leaves of the plum trees and lifted a wavy strand of Rinn's hair that had escaped her Shinto headdress. Mr. and Mrs. Tsuji and Haruki stood with them, and Megumi and Mrs. Fukuda, all in their best kimono. Benji looked at Rinn and his improvised family; at the shrine, decorated with long strips of folded white paper for the wedding; at the flowers coming into bloom; and up at the sky, the blue less intense than an American sky. Everything was shot through with beauty. He had never dreamed of such happiness.

Keast would be glad for him. He felt a sting of guilt; he must write to Keast.

Benji and Rinn settled in at Mrs. Fukuda's house; she insisted that they take as much space as they needed and appointed herself honorary mother-in-law. She taught Rinn to shop and cook, at first with limited success. The rice was sometimes scorched and the tempura soggy or greasy.

Privately, Rinn said Mrs. Fukuda made her nervous—all that hovering. "And the time of your arrival is unpredictable, so planning the meal precisely is impossible."

"I'm building our future," Benji replied.

With Mr. Matsumoto's handsome gift of money for their marriage, Benji began to collect antiques for a shop of his own. Some days he walked throughout the city and into the countryside to buy from small shops and street vendors, carrying home lacquer chests, suits of samurai armor, wooden boxes of tea bowls tied together with string. At night in bed Rinn massaged his knotted arms and shoulders.

"You're spoiling me," he said.

"From me you will always receive exactly what you deserve," she said with a laugh, and fitted her body next to his.

In the spring and summer evenings they went for long walks along the waterfront and beside the Nakashima River, looking down over the bridges at the water where, he told her, he had once believed kappas were waiting for him. In August, at O-Bon, the festival of the dead, they lit a candle on a small straw boat for his mother's spirit, which joined thousands of other boats floating in the darkness toward the sea.

In January, Rinn gave birth to a boy, Shoichi. At first they called him Little Buddha, because he was cheerful and bald. Rinn worried that when his hair grew in it would be wavy, Benji that it would be blond, but he was relieved that his son's eyes were black, though too round to be those of a pure Japanese.

Friends brought gifts—a kimono for Shoichi's first-month blessing at the shrine, a samurai doll, a kite for boy's day—and offered congratulations for such an auspicious beginning to the New Year. Mr. Matsumoto sent an even larger gift of money than before, delivered by a representative of the American consulate. *This is part of what I had planned to be an inheritance to you,* he wrote, *but I think it is best that you have it now, when you have greatest need.*

"Haven't the gods smiled on us?" Rinn said, as she sat nursing the baby one night in their room. "From such beginnings to this."

"Yes," Benji said, but when she handed him the baby, warm in his blanket, and he looked down at his son—the miraculous fingers and toes, the delicate blue vein at his temple—he was filled with melancholy as well as tenderness.

As time passed, he sank into an unaccountable sadness that sometimes felt close to despair. Rinn asked what was wrong. "Nothing," he replied, and one morning at breakfast snapped, "Leave me alone."

She jumped from the table, packed Shoichi onto her back, and left without a word. He went to the door and called after her, but she didn't look back.

She'd cheer up, he thought; she'd return in a friendly mood after talking to people in the shops and on the street, showing off Shoichi and exchanging gossip. But that night she was cool, and when they went to bed, with Shoichi between them as usual, she turned away without saying good night.

He went to lie beside her on the tatami and stroked her hair. "I need you," he said. She rolled off her futon onto the floor beside him; they made love without speaking, then he held her so tightly that she wriggled free. "The baby should have his own place to sleep," he said, as she moved away. "That's what's wrong."

"A baby needs his mother," she said. "You don't understand."

"Why wouldn't I understand that?" he shouted.

The baby woke up and began to cry. "Look what you've caused," she said, pulling Shoichi to her.

He flopped down on his futon, tears spilling from his eyes. Shoichi went quiet as Rinn began to nurse him. She shifted herself and the baby closer to Benji. "In Japan," she said, "the baby futon is called the river, between the solid banks of his parents. We are solid together, *ne?*"

He took her hand and kissed it. "Yes," he said, but for a long time after Rinn and the baby fell asleep, he lay curled alone beneath his quilt, listening to the quiet sounds of their breathing, and when he finally slept, jolted awake from a dream he could not recall.

Matsumoto and Son: He stenciled the name on the front window in gold. He cleaned and painted the interior, built cabinets, shelves, and display cases of fine wood. "To my worthy competitor!" Mr. Tsuji said, laughing, when he brought sake to toast the completion of the shop.

"Don't worry," Benji said, "I could never match the Japan Shop." He wouldn't have as many customers, he knew, but he hoped some discriminating tourists would eventually find their way to him. He planned to specialize in antiques and fine arts, particularly woodblock prints of geisha and courtesans.

One afternoon in summer, not long after the formal opening of the shop, Benji looked up from the counter, surprised to see a Japanese woman in Western clothes looking at a display of silk fans. Her hair was cut in a modern style he disapproved of, and she wore a dress that showed her legs.

She moved about the room, inspecting a case of pearls, tea bowls from Kyoto on a shelf, all the while glancing at him. He looked down at his inventory list as she approached the counter.

"Excuse me," she said with a bow that would have been more graceful in kimono. "I understand you specialize in ukiyo-e of the flower and willow world."

"Yes," he said, "paintings and prints by Utamaro, Moronobu, and Kiyonaga, for example. I have no imitations."

She asked to see a selection, and since she seemed an unlikely customer, he brought only a few from the back of the shop and arranged them on the counter. "Here is an unusual Sharaku portrait of a courtesan. The silver background is made of crushed mica," he told her. "Very fine."

"Mmm. Though I am interested only in geisha."

"I see." Why didn't you say so, he thought, but pointed out a portrait of a geisha gazing into a mirror. "One of Utamaro's most interesting, in its use of perspective," he said.

"Mmm-hmm."

Couldn't she speak? These modern women had no manners. "Here is a lovely print of two geisha from the Gion district in Kyoto. That's the Kamo River behind them. And this one is dressed in the style of a Tokyo geisha."

"Very nice," she said. "But not quite what I am looking for."

Fuming—she was wasting his time—he went to the back for more prints and arranged them on a table, pointing out the subtleties of design, composition, and coloration. "These are the most exquisite," he said. "You'll find none better—but of course they are costly."

"I see." She bent over each one, raising and lowering her eyeglasses, then straightened and looked and him. "Have you been proprietor of this shop for a long while?"

"Long enough," he said. A rude question deserved a rude answer.

"But you are not a native of Nagasaki, I believe."

His face went hot. She was insufferable. "I was born here," he said in a level voice, and began to gather the prints. He refrained from asking if she was Japanese.

She tapped the edge of one of the prints, Moromasa's *A Beauty Under a Plum Tree*. "This one interests me," she said. "The figure is reminiscent of a former geisha who was sometimes referred to as Cio-Cio-san."

Benji stared at her, gripping the edge of the table. "How do you know about her?"

She smiled. "Was your name at one time Benjamin Pinkerton?"

"Who are you? Did you know Cio-Cio-san?"

"I believe I have some information that will interest you."

"Please sit down." He gestured toward a low table at one corner of the room. His hands were shaking. "I'll bring tea."

"I would prefer to come to your house. Would that be acceptable? Shall we say two o'clock this afternoon?"

"Yes—please. Let me draw you a map." He fumbled among his papers for a pencil.

"Never mind," she said. "I know where you live."

He closed the shop and sprinted up the hill to tell Rinn. "Finally we will learn something about my mother," he said.

She embraced him. "It's wonderful—and mysterious, *ne*?"

Together they readied the house for the visitor. Rinn set out refreshments: their most flavorful tea, squares of chestnut yokan paste, and some bean cakes; he put his finest Seto vase on the tokonoma shelf. They agreed that Rinn and Mrs. Fukuda would take Shoichi next door so that there would be no distractions during the conversation.

After they left, Benji straightened the shoes in the vestibule and set out a pair of guest slippers on the top step. He left the door open and sat at the table, going over some business papers to calm himself. He wished now that Rinn had stayed to ease the conversation.

The woman arrived promptly at two. "I hope you don't mind that I've brought a companion," she said. Another woman, wearing a bone-colored kimono, stood behind her, looking around the garden. The sunlight through her yellow parasol printed with red plum blossoms cast reddish streaks on the side of her face.

"Of course not," he said, setting out another pair of slippers. "Please come in." The second woman kept her head bowed when she entered.

They sat at the table while he prepared the tea—awkward with everything, the kettle, the cups. Again, he wished for Rinn.

He carried the tray of refreshments to the table, sat down, and poured the tea. The woman in kimono had not raised her head; he wondered if she had some affliction.

"I'm eager to hear your information," he said.

The other woman looked up at him. His heart skipped. Wide-spaced eyes, full lips.

"Are you . . . my aunt?"

"I am your mother." She gave a deep bow.

He laughed; the tea spilled from his cup. He set it down, his hand shaking. "That's impossible. My mother is dead."

"Perhaps she only seemed to be." She gazed straight into his eyes, that gentle, intent expression. He held his breath.

"My mother . . . committed suicide—I saw it."

She rose and came to kneel beside him, her forehead touching the tatami, her arms and hands outstretched before her. "A geisha must learn to perform. Please try to forgive me, dear son."

He looked wildly around the room; the other woman had disappeared. This was a trick. They must have heard he had money.

"I'm not wealthy," he said.

She sat up. "*Sumimasen.* I am stricken in my heart to have caused you grief and shock. And it is a shock to my being to find that you are here. Even with your black hair and man's face, I can recognize you."

"My mother is dead," he shouted.

"Benji-san, do you remember our little game at bedtime that helped you fall asleep? The one who kept the eyes closed for the longest time was the victor. And sometimes I soothed you with a song as well." She began to sing: "*Sakura, sakura, ima saki—ho-ko-ru . . .*" He stared at her; she held her head slightly to one side, as he remembered.

"But I saw you . . ."

"The apparent tragedy was staged for your benefit."

"My benefit?" He jumped up and backed away from her. "I've spent my entire life . . . How could you be so cruel?"

"Dear child, had you remained in Nagasaki, you would have been taken from me, and I feared that you would . . ." She took a handkerchief from her kimono sleeve and wiped away tears. "It was a cruel choice for me, but I could not bear to think . . . I thought how I might flee and take you, but it was hopeless." She looked up at him. "Some girls born to geisha are taken into the okiya, and some others, girls or boys, may be adopted, although—please forgive me for saying so—with your yellow hair . . . I knew that in America you would be well cared for."

"Whipped by my father, plowing for hours, digging up stumps, being called Jap—would you call that good care?"

She covered her face with her hands. "Forgive me. I am deeply sorry."

He paced the room, back and forth to the window, everything a blur. "You could have let me know. If you cared anything about me, you'd have let me know. My whole life—"

"Dear son." She stood beside him, touched his arm; he jerked away. "Every day I have prayed to Inari-san for you, and always I tried to imagine your life. I thought you would forget me—children forget. I hoped this would be the case. When I learned that you were searching for information about me, and saw the monument you have erected, I was very surprised and moved."

"If you wanted me to forget," he said, "why did you leave me that picture?"

"It was Suzuki who put it in your kimono. She told me so only very recently, when she contacted me about the monument in my honor. I had thought it best that you erase your image of your first mother."

"All that time, I tried to imagine you in heaven, thinking of me."

"I was truly thinking of you," she said. "But on this earth."

"How did you do it? That blood . . ."

She looked away. "The blood of a cat."

"My cat? Rice Ball?"

"Please understand that I was desperate at the time. As it happened, your father came suddenly—"

"You killed Rice Ball! Have you no—"

"Dear son—"

"How dare you call me son?" He pushed at the table, teapot and cups clattering to the floor, and began to sob. His whole life had been wrong. By the time Rinn returned, calling out, "What's happened?" his mother was gone.

Keast and Lena had taken what used to be Frank's office for their bedroom. On this hot August Sunday afternoon, a cross breeze from the windows cooled them as they lay on the bed, dozing on and off after a long night during which Lena had given birth to their third child, William, the finest specimen of a boy Keast had ever seen. She'd been late, but that meant he was well developed, with smooth skin and alert eyes. When he'd been cleaned up and Lena reached for him, he caught her finger; he was going to be a Hercules. Keast lay on his side watching the two of them: Lena's eyes closed, her face still flushed from the long labor, her hair loose on the pillow; the baby—finally sleeping now—nestled between her full breasts. William's eyelids fluttered, as if he was dreaming. What could he have to dream about already? Though the passage from one world to another was no small thing.

The sound of children playing drifted up to them. Charlotte was shrieking—Elmer must be pushing her in the swing, probably too high. He ought to go see about it, but he felt so heavy and peaceful, his foot against Lena's, that he could not move.

A racket woke him, children stampeding into the room. "Papa Keast!" Rose shouted. "A man's here with a horse. He gave us jawbreakers and silver dollars. He wants you to come."

"Shh. Your mother's sleeping." He sighed as he pulled himself out of bed. Seemed like veterinarians should have a day of rest, all of God's creatures they tended.

The baby started squalling. Lena murmured something and guided him to her nipple, her eyes still shut. The children went quiet, lining up to watch their little brother, the first real sight they'd had of him.

"Isn't he fine?" Keast arranged the sheet over her other breast, smoothed it over the baby's back.

"The man wants you to come," Elmer said in small voice, his right cheek poked out with the jawbreaker, as if he still had the mumps. He had a funny look—probably been up to something, put a salamander down Rose's shirt or some such. Seemed like twins would get on better.

Keast led them out of the room, tiptoeing, and they went downstairs, Rose and Elmer sliding on the banister, Charlotte holding his hand. Hannah bumped along on her bottom one step at a time; she liked to climb up but not down.

Beyond the gate, a man in a straw hat stood with a horse on either side. Keast reached in his pocket for his glasses.

"By God," he said. "Pinkerton!"

Pinkerton was grinning. "What do you think of this?" he said, tipping his head toward one of the horses.

A black quarter horse, a white blaze on its nose. It couldn't be. As Keast hurried toward him, the horse pricked its ears and nickered.

Kuro. He felt like weeping. He pushed open the gate and embraced him, his face against the strong smooth neck, thinking of Benji, the yelp he'd given when he first saw his new colt. He began to inspect Kuro—his hocks, his fetlocks, his teeth. Other than a harness sore, he appeared to be in pretty good shape.

"Where in tarnation did you find him, Frank?"

Pinkerton took off his hat, rubbed his face, wet with perspiration. He was going bald, and his face sagged like an old man's.

"Darnedest thing," he said. "I was out in DeKalb County, sitting on the porch with a customer, and I saw him go by pulling a cartload of corn. I knew him right away. Paid double his worth, but I'd have paid a millionfold. Old Griffith didn't believe me at first when I said he'd been stolen, but he came right around when I showed him the cash."

"Did Griffith buy him from Moffett? Does he know where S.O.B. is?"

"Bought him at an auction, almost six years ago."

They looked at each other. "Well, that would make sense," Keast said.

Pinkerton bent down to Elmer. "This horse belongs to you now. And to your pretty sister, when you'll let her have a turn."

Elmer and Rose stared up at him. Keast drew them together, arms around their shoulders. "Children, do you remember your father?"

Frank looked dashed when they said nothing. Poor bastard. "You saw him—two years ago, wasn't it, Frank?—at Christmas."

"That's right." Frank squatted beside the children. "I brought you some skates and sleds. Did you like them?"

Keast squeezed Elmer's shoulder.

"Yes, sir," Elmer said. "Thank you for the horse."

"Want to give him a try?" Pinkerton said, standing.

"Yes, sir."

Keast helped Elmer mount Kuro and stared after them as they began loping down Plum River Road. At this distance, the boy on Kuro's back could be Benji.

"At least I've done one good thing in this world," Frank said, looking directly at Keast for the first time. His eyes were bloodshot, but Keast couldn't smell any drink on him.

"How are you, Frank?"

Frank resettled his hat, sighed. "Turns out I'm pretty good at selling plows. Better than I was at using them." He waved a hand in the direction of the farmland that had once been his. "My father . . ." he said, then trailed off.

Keast clapped him on the shoulder. "Come on in the house, Frank. Stay for supper—stay the night. Lena will want to see you and show off her new baby."

Rinn placed the letter on the table after dinner. "From your mother, I believe."

He rose and began to remove dishes from the table. "I've shut her from my mind," he said. In the kitchen, he listened to Rinn opening the envelope.

"She sends her sincerest apologies for her abrupt appearance," she called.

Benji poured hot water from the kettle into the sink and began to soap the dishes. He concentrated on the view of the garden; the peach tree was badly in need of pruning.

Rinn stood in the doorway of the kitchen. "She says, *I am very sorry, dear son, to have upset you in such a thoughtless manner. I am entirely at fault. Please forgive your mother, who loves you so dearly.*"

Benji looked down at his hands, motionless in the water.

"She wants us to visit her in Unzen, where she and her husband, Hiroshi, are proprietors of an inn. They will welcome us, she says, with joy and gratitude. She wishes to have a further opportunity to explain the circumstances to you. Shall we go?"

"I thought you knew how painful it has been . . . always haunted by her so-called death. When I was a child, I even talked to her picture." His voice broke. "I thought about that sword, the blood . . ."

Rinn put her arms around him. "I know you've suffered terribly. But your mother did her best, trying to arrange a good life for you, an education. I wish someone had done the same for me. I studied chamber pots and dirty floors."

"You don't understand."

"Shoichi needs a grandmother. All the effort to find out about her will be a waste if you refuse to see her." She picked up a towel and began to dry a cup. "You're too stubborn."

"So you always like to say."

"Perhaps you're afraid."

He whirled to face her. "My heart is made of courage."

"Let's go, then. Just once."

Rinn accepted his mother's invitation to visit Unzen for a week in August—the best time of year, his mother said, to escape the heat and humidity of Nagasaki. "I can't leave the shop that long," Benji said. He would spend one night, two at the most; Rinn and Shoichi could do what they pleased.

They traveled by jinricksha south of Nagasaki through green hilly countryside, past farms with thatched houses, a watermill, groves of mandarin oranges, fields of tea. Benji looked at the fields, cultivated even on the slopes; most American farmers wouldn't know what to do with a hill, except leave it to pasture. He glanced at Rinn beneath her parasol, Shoichi asleep in her lap, a wide-brimmed hat protecting his delicate skin. When he was plowing in the brutal Illinois sun, he could not have begun to conceive of this moment.

They stopped at a small village for tea in an outdoor garden, then at Mogi boarded a steamer for Obama, crossing the wide inlet toward Unzen. Benji leaned on the railing, looking out at the water, smoking one cigarette after another.

Rinn came to stand beside him. "Even if you hate her, you can put it aside."

"That was easier when she was dead."

The ocean was calm, the boat cutting easily through it. Shoichi's eyes were open now; he was sucking on two fingers and looking from beneath his hat in the direction of the water. Benji thought of himself on the ship with Frank and Kate, in shock from his mother's death. He'd been sick and thrown up at dinner; someone yanked him out of his chair and down to the cabin, where he was sick again.

They spent the night in a waterfront hotel in Obama before continuing to Unzen. Benji had felt queasy all day. "I'm ill," he told Rinn.

She put her hand over his. "It's to be expected. You'll feel better once we arrive."

In mid-morning they reached the inn, a Western-style building set partway up a hill overlooking the town of Unzen. Steam from the hot springs below billowed up in great sulfurous plumes; to divert himself from the odor, Benji concentrated on the vine of sweet-smelling white flowers that ran along the banister of the steps and the porch railings. A foreign couple sat on the porch, the man peering at a bird through opera glasses. Benji and Rinn started up the steps. He would give his mother a brief, formal bow, he decided, no apology for his behavior.

But a maid received them at the door. "Your mother asked me to show you to your quarters." Relieved and irritated, Benji followed her and Rinn along a path up the hill to a Japanese building set in a grove of bamboo.

The maid showed them into a large tatami room with sliding doors that provided views of bamboo and, on the other side, a mossy courtyard garden. "Your mother asks that you make yourselves comfortable. Please refresh yourselves with a bath and a light meal. After you've had time to rest, your mother will come." She bowed her way out of the room.

Benji looked out into the garden, like a stage set with its trickling stream and careful placement of lanterns. "She couldn't even bother to come greet us."

"She's giving us time to adjust," Rinn said. "This is very Japanese."

He didn't answer but sat at a table and smoked while Rinn carried Shoichi around the room, exclaiming over the elegance of the rice paper doors, the scroll in the tokonoma, the flower arrangement there. He closed his eyes, exhausted. While Rinn took Shoichi for a bath, he pulled a futon from the closet and slept.

He woke with a start. The maid was arranging their dishes of food on the table, where Rinn sat waiting, her skin radiant from the bath. There was sashimi, seaweed tied in flat bows, sea urchin, custard for Shoichi. Benji could eat nothing but rice.

After the dishes had been cleared away, Rinn and Shoichi lay down for a nap and he went for a walk, up the hill away from the inn. He sat on a rock in the woods beside the stream, staring at the water, small insects darting above the surface. A raven flapped between the trees and settled nearby, cawing, a rusty, mocking noise. He shouldn't have come; a fool's errand, Grandmother Pinkerton would call it.

A woman in a blue-and-white summer kimono came up the path

toward him, her head bowed. She looked up, and smiled. Her face was luminous. *Okasan*. He looked away from her, into a blur of woods. His heart was racing.

She stopped beside him. "Welcome to Unzen," she said, bowing. "I am grateful that you have come."

"Thank you," he said, his voice too thin. He stood, slightly off balance, and gave an awkward bow.

"Your wife and son are charming. I am very glad to meet them."

"I've been fortunate," he said, "in recent years." Her eyes were not black, but brown flecked with black. He had not remembered that.

She wet her lips and looked at the ground. She was nervous too, he realized.

"It's nice here," he offered.

"Shall we take a walk? We're halfway to a place I want to show you."

They climbed farther up the hill in silence. He looked at a squirrel scuttling across the thick pine-needle floor of the forest, mushrooms at the base of a tree. Here, with his mother.

"You're taller than I imagined," she said.

"In America I was short."

"Did your hair remain light?"

"Yes." He tugged at his forelock. "Dye," he said.

She nodded. "I thought as much."

They turned from the main path to a smaller one, which led to a shrine—a rustic wooden torii, two stone foxes wearing red bibs.

"This is where I came to pray for you all these years."

He stared at the foxes' blank eyes. "What did you pray?"

"That your parents would be kind, that you were healthy."

"He beat me with a whip, a switch . . . whatever was at hand." He was glad to see her wince with pain. "My father's mother was kind. A friend gave me a horse—I used to pretend I was riding to Japan."

She stared at him, her mouth slightly open. He wasn't what she had expected.

He looked at the empty white dishes at the base of the fox statues. "I suppose the squirrels ate the tofu."

"Some creatures ate it since this morning, when I came to pray for your arrival."

A breeze moved through the pines, the sound of one branch sliding against another.

"You might have been beaten in Maruyama too," she said, "and found your food in garbage piles. I had hoped . . ." She pressed a handkerchief to her face. A geisha learns to perform, she had said. But he felt a catch in his chest at the sight of her arm, so thin.

She tucked the handkerchief in her sleeve. "Perhaps we should be going."

They started down the hill.

"It's nice here," he said again.

"Yes, quite tranquil."

"Have you lived here all this time?"

"Almost fourteen years. First we lived in Nagasaki, but my husband did not care to work for his father's business, so he bought this hotel. It suits his temperament."

"I've been wondering . . ." He cleared his throat. "Did you know your husband before the . . . before I left for America?"

"No, I returned to the geisha life. About two years later I met Ichihara-san at a party in Maruyama. His wife had lately died, and he was melancholy. My company gave him comfort, he said, but I was very surprised when he asked not long after our first meeting not just to be my patron but to marry."

"If I had stayed in Japan would he have adopted me?"

"To tell the truth, this might have not have been possible. Perhaps— I am sorry to say—although he is very kind, he might not have cared for another man's son, especially with the mark of a foreigner. This might have been the case with any man, especially a pure Japanese." She paused, knocked a small stone out of the path, then was silent, looking down. "I am deeply grieved to hear of your trouble in America."

He felt a flush of satisfaction.

"Thank you." They walked on in silence. "Do you and Ichihara-san have children?"

"A boy, Natsume, who is artistic like his father. At present he lives with his grandmother in Hagi to study ceramics. The woman you met in Nagasaki—Yoshiko-chan—is Ichihara's daughter by his previous marriage. She lives in Tokyo and is very modern."

They had reached the inn. He looked at the open door, the long, gleaming hall beyond it.

"Does Natsume have black hair?" he asked.

"Yes."

"Not a mongrel, then."

She looked at him steadily. "I have always loved you," she murmured, then walked quickly away from him, down the hill.

Shoichi was asleep when Benji returned to their room. Rinn was at the table with her embroidery. She tucked the needle into the cloth and laid it down. "Did she find you?"

He sat down, poured sake from a ceramic bottle into a small cup. "She claims to love me," he said.

"I believe her. Imagine if I had to give up Shoichi."

Benji looked at the baby, lying on his side. He was still bald as a turnip; would he look like a mongrel too?

He downed one cup of sake, then another. Rinn came to kneel beside him and massaged his neck. Her wavy hair spilled down her back, a black river of silk.

He put his hand inside her loose yukata and buried his face in her hair. She untied her sash, then his, and they lay down on the tatami that smelled of fresh straw, quiet, to keep from waking the baby.

Dinner was served in his mother and Ichihara's apartment, at the other end of the building. Benji and Rinn wore the new kimonos Rinn insisted they have made for this occasion—black silk with the Matsumoto family crest on the shoulders and sleeves.

His mother and Ichihara, a white-haired man with an animated face, greeted them at the door. His mother made the introductions; she looked radiant in a pale yellow kimono.

Ichihara insisted on shaking Benji's hand. "Please addresse me as Hiroshi," he said, "American style."

"Thank you," Benji said with a deep bow, "although I now consider myself Japanese."

"You have made yourself at home in Nagasaki, *ne*? You and your family. Your mother was overjoyed to hear it."

There were toasts and exchanges of gifts. Benji received a gold pen and pencil for his desk; Rinn, a kimono, pale blue with stylized clouds and birds. "I never expected to have such a fine kimono, like a geisha's."

Shoichi helped Rinn tear the paper from his gift.

A multicolored string ball. Benji stared at it.

"Like mine," he said.

"I'm glad you remember," his mother said. "I was hoping you might." She rolled the ball across the tatami, and Shoichi went scrambling after it.

"My ball was lost in a river," he said. "My only souvenir of you. For years I grieved for it."

"Ah." She bowed her head, and for a moment there was silence.

"Please tell us about your life in America," Hiroshi said.

"I was a farm boy, milking cows, plowing. I'll never forget the smell of that black dirt. We lived in the middle of the country—no mountains or trees."

"I thought your father was a wealthy man," his mother said.

Benji laughed.

"Did you have proper schooling?"

"Only in a country schoolhouse." His mother's face fell. "I didn't care so much about education—I only wanted to get to Japan. I left to come here when I was fifteen." Driven away by my father, he almost added, but she was already distressed. He would tell her some other time.

"A long journey for you," Hiroshi said.

"His life hasn't been easy," Rinn said. "But he always persevered."

The meal was elaborate, Shippoku cuisine with many courses: fin soup, pickled Chinese greens, tilefish tempura, beans in sugar syrup. Rinn suggested that Benji tell his mother and Hiroshi about Mr. Matsumoto; his mother leaned forward as he recounted their meeting on the train, the timing of the earthquake, his stays in Denver and California, the curious circumstances of his adoption. "Now he and Matsumoto-san are partners," Rinn said. "Benji-san has a gift for business, and his collection of art is known all over Kyushu."

Benji asked his mother about her samurai family. She laughed. "I may have described such a history to your father, but it is far from true."

"But—all those years . . ." He shook his head. "Was Midori your geisha name?"

"The name my mother gave me." She looked down at her hands. "As a geisha, I was known as Ichiume."

As the dishes were cleared away, she asked Benji to come into the next room, where they knelt beside a small red lacquer chest. "First let me tell you," she said in a low voice, "that I am a mongrel myself. My mother, the child of a Frenchman and a courtesan, had light hair and eyes. She became a courtesan as well, and led a very difficult life. So, you see, I know the difficulties of impure blood. I could not leave you to a similar fate. Ichihara-san does not know the full truth of this," she added. "I was relieved when our son looked pure Japanese."

"This is why I have blond hair," he said. "A history of foreign blood."

"There are many such histories in Nagasaki."

She opened the bottom drawer, took out a package wrapped in rice paper, laid it on the tatami, and carefully unfolded the paper. "Your first blanket," she said, lifting out a dingy white cloth. He held it up; its edges were ragged and there was a hole in one side.

"You liked to chew on it," she said.

"I don't remember." But an image came to him, riding along on her back, the world going up and down. A man in a strange hat asked if he was a big boy.

His mother placed a book before him; on its worn green cover was written, in gold lettering, *America Beautiful.* "From this I tried to picture your life," she said.

He turned through the pages of photographs: the Statue of Liberty, Niagara Falls, the Grand Canyon. There was a stretch of beach with a lighthouse—Cape Cod, perhaps—and a street in a city, two women in bustles looking in a shop window. He paused to study a picture of Japanese men standing in a strawberry field.

"My fortune-teller and I argued about where you could be," she said. "I guessed a city or university, but she believed it was the strawberry farm."

"Your fortune-teller came closest," he said. He closed the book and ran his fingers over the raised lettering. She had thought of him.

He watched as she returned the blanket and the book to the chest.

"I'm sorry for my rude behavior when you came to Nagasaki," he said.

She bowed, her expression grave. *"Daijobu,"* she said in a low voice. "I can understand you. Now please come." Her face brightened. "I have a surprise. . . . I believe I heard her enter."

A white-haired woman with hooded eyes was kneeling beside the table. She stood and bowed when Benji and his mother entered the room.

"Suzuki-chan!" he cried.

"Benji-san." She gave him a shy smile and another bow.

He hugged her, then backed away. "I'm sorry—my American side broke through."

"I see you have grown up," she said.

"I warned her about the hair," his mother put in. She had reseated herself at the table. "Please join us at the table and we'll have more champagne."

Suzuki exclaimed over Shoichi and thanked Rinn for her persistent inquiries about Benji's mother. "Word of your diligence traveled throughout Maruyama." She turned to Benji. "Your mother is sincere in her joy that you have met again. Indeed, I have not seen her in such a state except on the day of your birth . . . and," she added, with a bow toward Hiroshi, "on the occasion of her marriage."

Benji looked at his mother. She was smiling and her head was tilted slightly to one side, just as in the photograph.

"As a fortunate by-product of your search," his mother said, "Suzuki and I have found each other too. She is now our valued assistant at the inn."

For the next few days, his mother and Hiroshi left the management of the hotel to Suzuki and took Benji and Rinn sightseeing. They went to the village of Unzen, where they looked at the shops and summer cottages—the houses were well priced, Hiroshi whispered to Benji—and took a ropeway up to the highest mountain, for a view of the countryside.

One afternoon they went to the source of the hot springs, an area outside the village of Unzen, and walked beside the volcanic mud and bubbling water that stank of sulfur. Rinn covered Shoichi's face with her handkerchief.

"The core of the earth breaks through here," Hiroshi said. "Some Christians were boiled alive in this place, hundreds of years ago," he added in a cheerful tour-guide voice.

"My stepmother is a Christian," Benji said. "Otherwise I wouldn't have been rescued from Maruyama. She was good to me," he added, "much of the time." He felt a sting of guilt; he'd never written to her.

"How did you manage," he asked his mother, "during the years after my father left you with me?"

"I had a friend, Sharpless-san, from the American consulate. Each month he brought an envelope of money, from your father, he said. I learned the truth only in recent years—that the money had been from him. Then I understood that he was rather fond of me." She tried to hide her smile. "He was a loyal Christian, however, with a wife and children."

"Where is Sharpless-san now?"

"In Tokyo, I believe. I've lost touch with him lately."

"Cio-Cio-san, my father called you. Did you love him?"

She shrugged. "I was rather fond of him."

"But I thought . . . and you waited for him . . ."

"That you might have a home." She grasped his hands. "The charade of the suicide was a futile sacrifice. I thought you would succeed in America, but of course I wasn't aware of the harsh circumstances. We have both suffered for my action."

He looked at her, the wide-set eyes he knew so well, her face blazing with life.

"What we imagine never happens, does it?" he said. "But some things are far superior. I could never have imagined Rinn or Shoichi. Or you," he added.

"Thank you," she whispered. She stepped closer to him and he put his arm around her, his hand lightly touching her shoulder, and they stood looking into the distance, at the cool green sweep of mountains dotted here and there with houses and the orange torii of shrines, until Rinn called that it was time to go.

Since 1913 had been a bang-up year for sales, Frank was not surprised to receive a letter of commendation from the president of Wilkes Brothers' Farm Equipment. Mr. Wilkes invited him to Chicago so that they might discuss an expansion of his responsibilities. Would three o'clock on the afternoon of January 11 be convenient?

Frank took the express train to the city in a first-class seat—he could afford it now, he thought—and sat smoking a Cuban cigar as he watched the blur of snow-covered fields. They were putting him up at the Palmer House, so it must be something big. He'd probably be able to buy a house of his own and reunite the children at last. His mother was getting on, too old to look after the younger ones, so he would hire a servant, a mature woman, gray in her hair so the neighbors wouldn't talk. Though God knew he deserved a wife. He felt a flash of resentment at Kate. He was tired of prostitutes, and the children deserved a real mother.

George Wilkes came to greet him in the small antechamber of his office, and they went to sit in what he called the sanctum, an untidy room with papers heaped on the desk and stacks of advertising posters on the floor; on the walls were drawings of farm equipment. A horse-faced man with a thin veneer of cordiality, Wilkes was a former farm boy from the northern part of the state; he understood from personal experience, he said, why customers responded to a man like Tom Pinkerton, who knew what the farmer was up against.

The company was growing, Wilkes said, pushing westward. "We're moving into Nebraska—already have an office set up in Omaha. What would you say to managing that whole operation?" He leaned back in his chair, smiling expectantly.

"You mean all of Nebraska?" Frank said. "Move there?"

"Why, yes. You'd oversee the sales force—a small number at first, but that will change, especially with your being in the field some days yourself. Your home base would be Omaha—fine little city."

Frank had never been to Nebraska. His father had mentioned sod houses, miles of lonesome prairie. "I'd receive a raise, of course," Frank said.

"We'll do the best we can on that score," Wilkes said. "And we can up the percentage on your commission. You'll be comfortable."

Frank thought of Kate, how poorly she'd looked the last time he saw her. "I have a family," he said.

"Good, good." Wilkes patted his desk. "We like to have a strong family man at the helm."

"Do you need a man in Wisconsin?" Frank asked.

Wilkes shook his head. "A man of your potential should jump at the chance of Nebraska. Someday we'll push all the way out to California. You might be our top man in the west. So, Tom," he said, folding his hands on the desk, leaning forward, "how does it sound?"

"Fine, just fine," Frank said, trying to pump enthusiasm into his voice. "Mind if I consider it overnight?" It was a long way from Kate, and he knew his home territory well, customers he could rely on.

"Good idea," Wilkes said, though his smile had faded. "Enjoy your stay at the Palmer—I recommend the prime rib. Maybe after dinner," he added with a wink, "you can find yourself a little entertainment. Let's talk in the morning, then. We need to make a decision soon."

The hotel room would have struck Kate's fancy—a flowered carpet, canopy bed with curtains, fully equipped bath. He'd promised to bring her here, never had. He drew a hot bath, lowered himself into the water. He leaned his head back against the edge of the tub and closed his eyes. Maybe there was an asylum in Omaha.

Or maybe he'd be so far away that he could take a new wife without anyone being the wiser. Of course he couldn't. There were the children to think of. He rubbed his face and arms with a loofah until his skin burned.

While he was dressing, he had a drink, just a small one. He had to be clearheaded to think over Wilkes's proposition.

In the elevator were an elegantly dressed couple, the woman in an evening gown. Every inch of her looked pampered. The man gave him a haughty look. Frank glanced at himself in the mirror, buttoned the jacket of his suit. A string was hanging from one sleeve. When had he turned into a hayseed? He'd always looked sharp in his Navy days. In an office job he could be a more stylish dresser. He wasn't a bad-looking man.

On the way to the restaurant, Frank picked up a newspaper to read at dinner. He was settled into a corner table by an obsequious waiter, ordered the prime rib and a glass of red wine. No harm in a single glass of wine.

He glanced at the headlines—President Wilson in Mexico, a parade on State Street by those damn fool suffragists—thumbed through the paper to look at commodities prices. Wheat was down. He buttered a roll, and turned the page.

A drawing of a Japanese woman sprang out at him. *"Madama Butterfly,"* the advertisement read, *the opera that has captivated the nation.* His stomach lurched as if he were still in the elevator. He'd thought that opera business had died down by now. *Performed in English. 8 o'clock, Auditorium Theatre.*

He folded the paper to hide the advertisement, then glanced around at the other diners. No one was watching.

The waiter brought his food, the beef bloody on the plate. The sight of it made him sick. He sipped at the wine, sour. He thought of the Last Supper, the picture of it in his childhood Sunday-school book. There was a sore beneath his tongue.

He left money on the table and went out. On the street, he asked the doorman for directions to the Auditorium Theatre. "Only three blocks," the man said, pointing. "The tallest building in Chicago."

He started down the sidewalk. It had begun to snow, big wet flakes on wind that blustered from the lake. His feet felt too large to move properly. Maybe the opera was sold out. Cars blared and hooted, the street full of them, shiny black carapaces; on his last visit to Chicago, there had been almost no cars. A new world.

The theater building was ablaze with light; inside, the floors and walls were long sweeps of marble. The only available seats were in the upper balcony, the ticket salesman told him, but the acoustics were excellent even there.

There was an elevator to the balconies, but he took the stairs. His legs felt weak, as if he were ill. An usher led him to his seat. The place was dizzying. In front of the stage were marble arches glittering with lights; box seats seemed to float in space. Thousands of people were talking and laughing. They wouldn't be here except for me, he thought with a little shock. He glanced at the woman beside him: a low-cut white dress, a mole on her breast. On his other side sat a young jackanapes, trying to impress the girl with him. If only they knew. He brushed at his suit and opened the program. Maybe he was wrong. Maybe he had misremembered or dreamed it.

But there it was: Nagasaki, Butterfly. Pinkerton. Sharpless. Suzuki. He straightened, tried to steady himself. The place was too loud. Shut up, he wanted to yell. He yearned for a drink, should have had one more at the hotel. He closed his eyes and waited.

Finally the lights dimmed and there was silence, then a thunder of applause. Music began and the curtain rose on a Japanese house, a man in a naval uniform, another man. The man in the uniform—he looked at the program—was him, Pinkerton. But he was fat and his feet were too small. He began to sing, gesturing like a fool. In English, supposedly, but Frank couldn't understand a word. He turned again to the libretto: Pinkerton and the other man were carrying on about the house, how the doors moved, space shifted however one wanted. The bridal chamber could be anywhere.

There was talk of a wedding. There had no been no wedding. They had it all wrong. It didn't count. He laughed. People in the row ahead turned to look at him.

The American consul Sharpless strode onto stage, to a flourish of the national anthem. Sharpless, too, was portly, nothing like the real man. Amazing they had his name, though. Maybe that Cross woman had corresponded with Kate at some point. Frank followed the duet in his libretto. "Life's not worth living if at every port you can't have a fair maid," Pinkerton sang. "An easygoing gospel," Sharpless replied, "but fatal in the end." The music darkened.

He stared at the singers moving about, bawling at the top of their lungs. What did Sharpless know about life at sea, the boredom, the hungers?

There was another woman onstage now. Butterfly. He'd missed her entrance. She was a handsome woman, but not Japanese. He was relieved to feel nothing, no stirrings. He tried to remember Cio-Cio's face, but it eluded him. He could see her hair, her back, the foot with the little toe curled under.

He scanned the libretto to find his place. Butterfly was telling Pinkerton that she'd become a Christian for his sake. Ridiculous. He glanced at the woman beside him; she was smiling, pleased by this fictitious development.

A love duet. The music was tender for their wedding night. He tried to remember his first night with Butterfly. Of course there hadn't been a wedding. It was at the house, but all their lovemaking had been at the house. He thought of her breasts, her warm legs, her taking his member into his mouth, but that happened many times.

Butterfly turned slightly toward the audience. "They say that in your country . . ." He could hear her plainly, without consulting the libretto. "A man may pierce a butterfly with a pin."

"There is some truth in that," Pinkerton replied. "So you can't escape. See, I hold you as you flutter. Be mine."

Frank thought of the day the butterflies had come to the farmhouse, on the grass and in the trees, in his office. His body went hot. He wiped his face, struggled to remove his jacket.

The curtain swooped shut with a great flourish, and people began to stir. He felt unable to move, as though he were swollen in his seat. Finally he had to rise; the young fellow and his sweetheart wanted to pass. The woman with the mole had already gone. Most of the audience was pouring out into the hall, down the stairs. He let himself be swept along.

In the lobby, people were drinking aperitifs, brandy, whiskey, but he couldn't find the bar. He didn't want to ask; people might think he was desperate. There was a glass of champagne on a ledge. He took it, walked away quickly, and downed it.

He didn't feel well, too light-headed for one drink. He should go. But when the bell rang, he returned with the crowd to the auditorium and took his seat.

He looked at the libretto: *Act II. Inside Butterfly's little house.*

Butterfly and Suzuki were arguing about whether or not Pinkerton would return. Butterfly was certain. She began to sing alone, her voice soaring.

> *One fine day we'll notice*
> *A thread of smoke, arising on the sea*

> *In the far horizon*
> *And then the ship appearing.*
> *The trim white vessel*
> *Glides into the harbor, thunders forth her cannon.*
> *See you; he is coming.*

Her voice rose, swelled with emotion; her face was beautiful with passion.

> *A man is coming,*
> *A little speck in the distance, climbing the hillock.*
> *Can you guess who it is?*
> *Can you guess what he'll say?*
> *He will call "Butterfly" from the distance.*

Frank's eyes filled with tears. All that time, she had been waiting. She had loved him so.

Sharpless and another man reappeared. He closed his eyes and listened to the music, like waves, the way the melody flowed up and down. He thought of the sea, the smell of it, remembered sailing into Nagasaki Bay that first time. It had been a warm June morning. He'd climbed up and down the hills, flowers everywhere, beautiful women, though Cio-Cio-san was the loveliest. A uguisu geisha, Sharpless told him when he introduced her, because like the uguisu bird she had a rapturous voice. She had sung in the house, cooking, cleaning the kitchen; he'd been lulled by the contented sound of her voice. Sometimes she had given him a private concert, plucking on her shamisen.

Onstage, the music and voices grew more intense. Sharpless had a letter from Pinkerton, announcing his imminent return. That much was true; he'd written to ask for Sharpless's help with his business dealings in Nagasaki. It must have been Sharpless who alerted Butterfly. He felt a stab of anger. Sharpless should have been the one to pay.

A blond child was brought onstage. Benji. Butterfly kissed his head. His son. At first he hadn't believed it, but Sharpless had convinced him it was so. Sharpless had called him irresponsible, but how could he have known she'd had a child and that she was waiting?

He fumbled with the program, couldn't find his place, looked back at the stage as people moved about, singing; the voices pounded at him. It wasn't fair. He wasn't the only man—far from it—to have had an arrangement with a geisha.

Butterfly and Suzuki were running about, scattering flowers. Butterfly believed he was coming; she would wait until he came, she and Suzuki and the child.

The three of them knelt. The music changed; there was humming offstage. The light dimmed. It was night, Suzuki and Benji slept, but Butterfly stood, waiting. The humming went on and on.

He thought of his parting from Butterfly when he'd left Nagasaki that first time. Suddenly he could see her clearly, her mournful black eyes, her bent head. She'd looked so forlorn that he told her he would return someday. He'd hoped it was true. He shifted miserably in his seat. He'd wished it so. But—he stared at her on the stage, waiting for him—he had known he planned to leave the Navy. He had made it easier for himself by lying.

The curtain dropped. He was a coward.

He hadn't always been a coward. When he was a child, he'd stood out in the fields to watch tornadoes, the black funnel materializing from the clouds, the long leg of it drifting above the rows of corn. Once a tornado had swept over him, ripping off his hat, then dove down at the barn, dug it up. His spotted pony had been found ten miles away, lying on a road, its eyes white.

He stared numbly at the stage. The curtain had risen. Butterfly was sleeping, Pinkerton and Sharpless looking down at her. "What did I tell you?" Sharpless's refrain. Pinkerton could not bear to see her; he must flee. Farewell. A coward.

There was Kate, looking exactly like Kate, in a blue dress, quiet, kind, modest about her beauty. She took Butterfly's hands, promised to take care of the boy. Of course it hadn't exactly happened like that, but it was true: Kate had taken care of Butterfly's child. His child. The yoke of it had fallen on her. He thought of her in the asylum, glassy-eyed, gone from him, plucking at the bow on the box.

The climax. He held his breath. The child was blindfolded. Butterfly was behind a curtain. A scream—it seemed to come from him—and she rushed forward, falling, reached for the child. Went still.

"Butterfly." His voice offstage. "Butterfly. Butterfly." A voice of grief and recognition.

He had killed her.

A hubbub of bravos and bows and people standing, talking.

The crowd pushed out of the auditorium. He didn't move. His skin burned as if he'd been flayed. He thought of the sycamore tree, stripped of its bark by lightning.

That storm off Brazil, where they'd almost gone down. If he'd died, none of this would have happened. Butterfly would be alive; Kate would have married a gentleman from Galena, lived in the comfort she deserved. Benji wouldn't have suffered.

What had happened to Benji? There was a hard knot in his throat.

He rubbed his hands against the arms of the chair until they chafed. He imagined his hands on fire.

It was all his fault. The lie about coming back.

The foolish return with Kate. He'd always told himself that Kate had talked him into it, but he'd had a few hundred yen to recover from the Mitsubishi shipyard. And he was proud of Kate, wanted to show her off.

Then the note from Butterfly, delivered to his hotel; he and Kate warm in bed.

The horror of her death. He forced away the memory.

He had to take Benji, he'd thought, the sad little fellow, all alone then, his child, his responsibility. Being the big man. But he hadn't calculated the effect on Kate. Those had been scalding years for her, tending to Butterfly's child.

And now she was in that awful place. He shouldn't have allowed it; he hadn't been man enough. He should have sold the farm years ago—he hadn't the gift for farming anyway, he should have admitted that early on—and taken her and the children to live in town. He could have continued with his import/export business. He could have saved her.

The lights went out in the auditorium. He was alone, sitting in the dark. Below, a heavy door slammed shut; the sound reverberated through his body.

He could still save her. He sat upright. If he took the job in Nebraska, he could take her with him. In the home office, with no long weeks on the road, he could care for her, with the help of a good farm woman. At home, in comfort, in peace, her books and music—a piano, she must have a piano—she would return to herself. Darling Kate.

The children would be there: Elmer and Rose at last, and Mary Virginia and Franklin. They could see Mary Virginia into young womanhood, marriage. The little ones would go to city schools, a good education.

He had failed Benji, but he could be a good father to the others. And in Nebraska, neither they nor Kate would hear of this goddamn opera.

It was possible. He could do it. Something like joy rushed through him as he stood and felt his way to the door. He'd celebrate with a drink, and in the morning he'd tell Wilkes and then go for Kate. On his way, he'd buy her some perfume and a new dress.

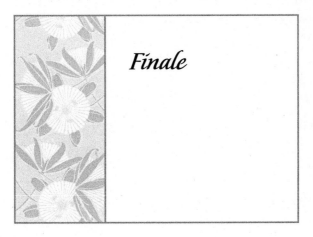

Finale

Suzuki and Butterfly:
Let us sow April here.
Lilies? Violets? . . .

Scatter lilies, roses.

Nagasaki, April 1914

Sharpless was to arrive in an hour, and the house was in turmoil. Benji's mother and Rinn were at odds over particulars of the dinner; Shoichi, to have been bathed and dressed by now, was nowhere to be seen; and baby Yasunari—Matsumoto's namesake—was wailing in Suzuki's arms in the room next to Benji's study.

Benji sat at his desk, his ears plugged with greased cotton as he tried to concentrate on his account books. It was an inconvenient time for company. He was leaving for Kyoto the next day, but his mother said Sharpless had made it quite clear that only this day would be suitable for his visit; he was soon to depart on a diplomatic mission to the United States, and, in the meantime, affairs at the consulate were pressing. Sharpless was also eager to see her, his mother reported: "An angel risen from the dead." Rinn rolled her eyes every time the phrase was mentioned.

The door slid open and his mother looked in. She was wearing an elaborate new wig studded with ornaments and a kimono from her geisha days, which Rinn privately said was too young for her.

"Your wife wonders if Shoichi is with you." She peered around the room.

"He must be playing outside." Benji stood and stretched.

"I'll go find him."

"I hope Sharpless will like my gifts. Did you wrap the Ming vase?"

"Yes," he said, and patted her arm. "Everything will be fine, *Okasan*." For the past month—since Benji's stepsister Yoshiko and her husband had met Sharpless at a dinner party in Tokyo and the conversation turned to "a certain tragic tale"—his mother had talked of nothing but Sharpless in their weekly phone conversations.

He and his mother stepped into the hall, where Suzuki was pacing with Yasunari. "Cutting a tooth," Suzuki murmured. His mother took the baby and, jiggling him against her shoulder, began to hum "Sakura," the same lullaby she'd sung to Benji. Golden light from the window touched the fabric of his mother's kimono and Yasunari's foot.

Benji ran downstairs to the kitchen, which was filled with the odors of hot oil and ginger. Rinn held up one hand. "I've burned my finger."

"I wish you'd agreed to let him take us to a restaurant as he suggested."

"I was quite willing, but a certain other person was not."

"She's nervous—try to be patient. I'm going to get Shoichi."

"I thought you were watching him," she said.

He ducked from the kitchen and went out the front entrance of the house—newly washed, for their guest—down the lane, and up the slope. He found Shoichi at the top of the hill, just where Benji knew he'd be, trying, with little success, to get his kite into the air. "Your mother wants you home. It's time for our visitor."

"I'm winning, Papa-san." A precocious little boy with straight brown hair and tortoiseshell glasses, he was forever pretending—a kite contest now, sometimes a samurai expedition, or an American cowboy hunting down a gold thief.

"Hurry," Benji said, "unless you want a kappa to get you." He made a silly face to show he didn't mean it, but Shoichi squealed and went running down the hill. Benji picked up the kite and rolled the string. Sharpless had given him a kite once, his mother said, with a tiger on it, because it was the year of the tiger. He had no memory of the man.

He lit a cigarette—nothing for him to do at home except be in the way—and looked out over the hill below him, a patchwork of houses and gardens just coming into bloom. The roof of his new house rose above the others; the tile, with its hint of red, had been made by a craftsman in Kyoto. He'd spared no expense on the house—extravagance, perhaps, but it seemed right for him to take his place in Nagasaki with his growing family. They were secure now, thanks to the inheritance from

Matsumoto-san and the connections he'd passed on to Benji, collectors and curators in America and Europe. Sharpless would be impressed by his circumstances, his mother said; she seemed eager to show him off. He glanced at his watch and started down the hill, whistling, to meet the great man.

Sharpless had just arrived and was standing at the edge of the front room with Benji's mother, murmuring as he bent over her. A tall, slightly stooped man with a fringe of gray hair, he was dressed in an American-made suit and a startlingly white shirt; he had brought flowers and a large flat package wrapped in a gray silk furoshiki. There was an air of subdued excitement about him; his blue eyes gleamed as introductions were made and bows exchanged. His voice was a little too loud.

"I never expected to see you again," he said to Benji, "and certainly not your mother," he added, turning to look at her. They bowed to each other once more, deep bows suffused with feeling.

Suzuki brought down the baby—still fussy, but Sharpless pronounced him magnificent—then carried him back upstairs.

Rinn led them to the table beside the open window at the far end of the room; Sharpless was seated in the place of honor, with a view of the tokonoma, Benji's mother to his right.

Benji watched as his mother poured Sharpless's sake and he raised his cup to her. "To Midori-san," he said. "After dinner I have a story for you—for all of you," he added, glancing around the table. "It even bears a title: 'Sharpless's Revenge.' " Throughout the small talk—Hiroshi's regrets that the inn was presently too crowded for him to be away; inquiries after Mrs. Sharpless's health; changes in Nagasaki since Sharpless had left nearly twenty years before—Benji's mother and Sharpless exchanged glances and smiles, in a conversation of their own.

"Now," Sharpless said, after the dishes were cleared away. "My tale." He folded his hands on the table. Benji looked at the starched white cuffs, the gold monogrammed cuff links. There was something careful about his hands, as though he kept them constantly in mind.

"I trust you are all aware of how Midori-san and her son suffered as a consequence of Lieutenant Pinkerton's actions, culminating in the apparent—"

"Yes," Rinn interrupted, glancing at Shoichi. "We know."

Sharpless cleared his throat and continued. "For years, I have suffered from remorse because of my role in the events. There has, of course, been a happy ending"—he paused to smile at Benji's mother, then turned to look at Benji—"but for a long while I thought I had set a tragedy into motion. You see, I was the person to introduce your mother and father and even helped to make the arrangement between them."

"What arrangement?" Shoichi said.

"Shh," Rinn said. "No more questions."

"It often occurred to me," Sharpless said, "that I was the responsible party—having acted as a go-between."

"It wasn't your fault," Benji's mother burst out. "You were only being generous—so like you."

"It is kind of you to say so."

For a few moments, the only sound in the room was that of the small bell outside the window.

"Even at the time of the initial meeting, I had misgivings," Sharpless said. "Pinkerton referred to Cio-Cio-san, as he insisted on calling her, as a pretty little plaything and said he intended to marry an American woman eventually."

"Kate!" Benji said. "Did he already know her?"

"I think not. I chided him for his heartlessness and thought I had made some impression, for when he departed from Nagasaki he vowed to return the next spring."

Sharpless adjusted the cuffs of his sleeves and bent forward. "One evening—this was sometime after Midori-san's apparent . . . when I was suffering from . . . if I may say so"—he glanced at Benji's mother—"grief . . ."

She bowed, hiding a smile.

" . . . I was invited to a dinner party in Higashiyamate, where I happened to be seated beside the wife of a prominent missionary. In the course of our conversation, she revealed that her brother, a writer who lived in Philadelphia, wished to write a story with a Japanese slant, Japan being a country of much international interest at the time.

"As I began the account of poor little Cio-Cio-san and her so-called benefactor, Pinkerton, I could feel the stirring of the woman's interest. She went stock-still when she heard of lovely Cio-Cio waiting all those years with her young son, climbing the hill each day to scan the horizon for his ship—a nice touch, I thought," he said, looking around at them at them with a slight smile. "When I told of the blond wife, the sword, my listener looked as if she might weep. I recall my guilty pleasure in having had such an effect."

"That must be where Haruki heard the story," Benji said to Rinn, "passed on to another missionary."

"Not long afterward," Sharpless went on, "I was transferred to Tokyo at my request—so great was my distress. My wife and I settled in, and I tried to put the horrific event from my mind."

Benji poured himself some sake. Obviously Sharpless was going to draw out his tale as long as possible.

"But only two or three years later I learned that the missionary's brother had indeed published the story—"

"Published?" Benji said. "In America?" He thought of the magazines in the parlor, Kate sorting through them.

"Yes. The story was not quite as I had told it, and it was riddled with errors and flaws with regard to Nagasaki and Japanese culture. However, Butterfly's and Pinkerton's names were intact, just as I had conveyed. Divine Providence, I think of it. Though perhaps he was merely a lazy writer. Nevertheless, I am as much the author of the story as he." He laid one hand on his chest in a melodramatic gesture—a failed attempt at irony, Benji thought. He glanced around the table; everyone else was listening intently. Shoichi looked like a little owl, peering at Sharpless through his glasses.

"However, this is only the beginning of the story's voyage; it next took life in a stage play. Wait—" He held up a hand, cutting off exclamations. "Here is the truly miraculous part: The play was transformed into an opera, *Madama Butterfly*, by the famous Italian composer Giacomo Puccini." He smiled around the table as though he expected applause.

"What is an opera?" Benji's mother said.

"Like a Kabuki play," Sharpless said. "Western style, with more singing."

"But . . . not well known, surely?" Benji asked.

"It is, indeed. *All over the world*," Sharpless said, emphasizing each word. His face broke into a gleeful smile.

Benji felt a flush of rage. "You seem delighted. Please consider the effect on my family." He looked at Shoichi and Rinn.

"What is it, Papa-san?" Shoichi asked.

"Nothing important, little one," Rinn said. "Let's go see Suzuki-chan." She stood, tugging at his hand, and led him from the room.

"None of you needs to worry," Sharpless said. "Japan is one of the few countries where the opera is not known. Of course it would not be popular here. I doubt that it will come to our shores, rife as it is with inaccuracies about Japan. For example, the absurd Yamadori, Cio-Cio's 'suitor.' There is no such name as Yamadori, and furthermore . . ."

They must know about this in Plum River. The shame of it, the humiliation, even worse than the photograph. He pictured Kate, her face bloated from crying, Grandmother Pinkerton coaxing her to eat. Frank— he couldn't imagine what Frank might do.

" . . . the so-called ancestor dolls, the locks on the doors of a Japanese house," Sharpless was saying, "and of course the love of an exquisite, sophisticated geisha for this callow American is implausible." He glanced at Benji's mother; she bowed, modestly lowering her eyes.

"The whole thing is implausible," Benji said. "I can't believe it." The man had concocted the story to charm his mother.

"Neither could I, young man, neither could I." Sharpless shook a finger at him. "But I have proof."

Rinn came back to the room just as Sharpless, with a dramatic gesture, lifted the gray furoshiki off the floor and unwrapped it. "Midori-san," he said, "here is some reparation for what you and your son have suffered." He held up a box of phonograph records. "Famous arias by Puccini. Two are from *Madama Butterfly*. This is a program and libretto for the production I myself saw in New York City." He handed a booklet to Benji.

"Metropolitan Opera House, Grand Opera," he read aloud. *"Madama Butterfly."* A woman who looked vaguely Japanese decorated the cover; she was holding what seemed to be a lute rather than a shamisen.

As Rinn and his mother went in search of the phonograph and arranged it on the table, Benji flipped through the libretto. Pinkerton, Butterfly, Sharpless, Suzuki. Everyone was here. His hands went cold. He looked at the inside cover: *The Only Correct and Authorized Edition . . . Copyright 1906*. It seemed to be authentic. His heart began to pound. "Has this been performed in Chicago?"

"Oh, yes, Chicago to be sure. Everywhere."

Benji stared at Sharpless's arrogant face as he took the record from its case and placed it on the phonograph. "Now, Midori, in this aria, 'One Fine Day'—*'Un bel di vedremo,'* as you will hear in Italian—you are expressing your love for Pinkerton as you wait for his return."

She laughed. "I was waiting for him to pay my debts at the geisha house, as he had promised. And for you to have a father," she added, nodding at Benji.

"A dreadful father," Sharpless said. "A reprehensible cad."

"He wasn't entirely a villain," Benji burst out. "He took me."

"I thought he was unkind," his mother said, frowning. "Cruel."

"Sometimes," Benji said. But he didn't deserve this, he thought.

"Now let me translate beforehand," Sharpless said. "Cio-Cio-san, you are waiting, imagining a wisp of smoke on the horizon, then his ship sailing into the harbor. You hear him coming for you, calling your name. You hope he will call you his baby wife."

"He'd better not," his mother said; everyone but Benji laughed.

"Now," Sharpless said. "Please listen."

"Un bel di vedremo levarsi un fil di fumo . . ." The music washed over them. Benji could hear the longing in the soprano's piercingly beautiful voice.

He thought of Frank lugging around the Japanese–English dictionary, even in the fields, trying to make him feel more at home during those first terrible months. He had a startlingly clear memory of sitting in Frank's lap behind the horses and plow, the warm sweaty smell of him. One of those days when they were in the field, Frank told him his grandfather was a samurai. That had helped him survive, even against Frank.

The music had ended and Sharpless was holding forth again: "Here Pinkerton is expressing his remorse, while I remind him of my warnings."

Frank must have felt more than remorse, Benji thought. Savage guilt, more likely, despair, believing himself responsible for the suicide. And he had been there, Butterfly's child, a constant reminder.

"Pinkerton sings, 'Haunted forever I will be by those reproachful eyes.' One of my prominent lines is, 'Alas, how true I spoke!' "

A passionate male voice poured out into the room, then another, a deeper voice, the two of them striving against each other.

Sharpless scraped the surface of the record as he lifted the needle. The music seemed to vibrate in the silence.

Benji jumped up. "I'm going for a walk."

"Let's all go, shall we?" Sharpless boomed. "To celebrate. I've been hungering for some of Nagasaki's kasutera cake. Shall we visit a coffee shop on the waterfront?"

"If we can talk of other things," Benji said. He waited impatiently during the flurry of getting ready; he hadn't intended a party. Shoichi flew down the steps, wanting cake. Benji would have said no, but Rinn told him to change his shirt first. Finally Shoichi was ready, the women gathered their things, and they set off up the hill.

Sharpless and Benji's mother strode ahead. He and Rinn walked together, swinging Shoichi between them. He looked at Rinn's lively face; how lucky he was.

She looked at him. "This is very strange for you," she said.

"Yes. I can't talk about it yet." He was relieved when Shoichi broke free and Rinn went hurrying to catch him.

He fell farther behind the others, walking slowly up the hill in the dusk. It was a fine evening, the warmth of the April sun lingering in the air. He thought of the light on the meadow at Plum River at this time of day, the white boulders glowing, the cows coming in for milking, their bells clanking. Probably Franklin handled the cows now, and a large share of the farming. He would be fourteen, practically grown. Maybe he had a sweetheart.

Benji thought of the time Franklin gashed his head while they were skating at the Cases' pond and Benji had carried him home, Franklin's breath on his neck. And the time Franklin won at marbles and came running to tell his big brother.

He had abandoned Franklin. And Mary Virginia, with her blond curls and sticky kisses.

He paused at the top of the hill, gazing out over the bay where he'd departed with Frank and Kate almost twenty years ago. He'd spent his childhood with the Plum River family yet had put them from his mind. He'd been absorbed with his life here, the search for his mother's family at first, then Rinn and the children, his shop.

He stared at a large ship in the harbor, a dark shadow against the water.

Revenge. He heard it in Sharpless's voice.

He had taken revenge himself: against Frank, against his loneliness and the unfairness of his life. He'd abandoned them all and as a consequence had lost them—Kate, Grandmother Pinkerton, even Keast. He knew nothing about the family.

And now, this musical drama.

The others waited for him at the foot of the hill, their figures illuminated by the streetlights along the wharf, like characters on a stage.

"You go on," he said, "I'll join you soon." The telegraph office at the

Nagasaki Hotel was always open to send and receive international messages.

The others began to walk along the edge of the water toward the restaurant. "Benji?" Rinn called. He waved her on.

When they had moved away, he turned in the other direction, walking quickly, before he could change his mind, to the hotel. He paused at the bottom of the steps, looking up at the porch—people there admiring the view of the bay, fragments of their speech drifting down to him, English, Japanese, and the clink of ice in their cocktails. He began to move up the stairs, his legs weary, as though pushing through mud, climbing slowly to the brightly lit lobby that waited above him.

Author's Note

The correct translation of Butterfly's name from the Japanese is "Cho-Cho." I have chosen to use the spelling "Cio-Cio" throughout, however, as it has become more familiar to Western readers and opera-goers.

In John Luther Long's story "Madame Butterfly," first published in *The Century* magazine in 1898, Butterfly's name appears as "Cho-Cho." The spelling is preserved in the play adapted from Long's story by David Belasco. This play was the inspiration for Puccini's opera; it is said that Puccini rushed home after a London performance in 1900 and began composing music for the tragic story. Puccini adopted the Italian spelling "Cio-Cio" for his heroine and changed "Madame" to "Madama," presumably because of its Italianate sound, although "Madama" is not an Italian word. "Cio-Cio" has been used in librettos of the opera since Puccini's time, but "Madame" and "Madama" have been used inter-changeably.

The story presented in Puccini's opera was influenced both by Be-lasco's play and by Long's original story. Long claimed to have heard the tale from his missionary sister, who'd traveled to Nagasaki, al-though he also drew upon Pierre Loti's popular novel *Madame Chrysan-thème*. Unlike Long, Belasco, or Puccini, Loti was somewhat familiar with Japanese culture, and his work is more accurate in particular de-tail than is Long's story. Loti lived in Nagasaki's Juzenji neighborhood (where his house is still preserved) with a woman from the Maruyama pleasure district.

In Loti's and Long's stories, Cio-Cio was a teahouse girl (a courtesan); Puccini elevated her to the status of geisha. In my novel, I chose to have her remain a geisha, to be consonant with the opera and with the story that unfolded in my imagination.

Acknowledgments

I am indebted to many people for their assistance with this book. My warmest thanks to:

Andrea Mensch, for the idea.

The late Professor Ineko Kondo, who encouraged me to write the novel.

Laurel Goldman, Christina Askounis, Joe Burgo, Peter Filene, Peggy Payne, and Linda Orr, who were, as always, with me every paragraph, page, and version of the journey.

Nancy Olson and Liz Darhansoff, fairy godmothers.

Caitlin Alexander, brilliant and patient editor, whose guidance did so much to bring the novel into clearer focus.

The Japan Foundation and the North Carolina Arts Council for their generous grants.

Professor Fumiko Fujita, my longtime friend and associate, for introducing me to the Saga-Nagasaki Chapter of the Tsuda College Alumnae Association of Nagasaki, who were of invaluable assistance. I am especially grateful to Suwako Kitamura, Yoshiko Tsuji, Kazuko Ueda, Chizuko Suzuki, and Emi Yui, for help with research, interpreting, guiding, and introducing me to experts in the field, and to Tsuda alumna Shoko Morimitsu, director of Nagasaki Broadcasting Corporation, who also took a lively interest in my project.

Also in Nagasaki, I am grateful to Professor Brian Burke-Gaffney, unofficial historian of Nagasaki and author of a number of books about the city, for answering endless questions and reading the Nagasaki sections of the manuscript. I found his book *Starcrossed: A Biography of Madame Butterfly*, invaluable along with Jan van Rij's *Madame Butterfly: Japonisme, Puccini, and the Search for the Real Cho-Cho-San.* Nagasaki University professor Byundug Jin and the late Tameichi Takefuji also helped me with research, as did the librarians at the International House in Tokyo. I am indebted to Dr. Shin Suzuki, executive director of Nagasaki Municipal Hospital, for extraordinary kindnesses, including walking me through a monsoon rain to a dentist.

My longtime friends Professors Mikako Hoshino and Fumiko Fujita eased the difficulties of travel with their presence and gracious hospitality.

In the United States, librarians at the State Archives in Madison, Wisconsin; the Denver Public Library; and the Galena Historical Society and the Galena Public Library gave invaluable research assistance, as did Roy Dicks, Pete Hendricks, Baker Ward, Chizuko Kojima, Steve Repp, and Ben Dyer. Peter Ruzsa, computer wizard, was very generous with his time.

Hugs to Richard Kollath and Ed McCann for journeying with me across the United States in search of Benji, and to Ed for his careful readings of the manuscript.

About the Author

Angela Davis-Gardner spent a year in Japan as visiting professor at Tokyo's Tsuda College, which inspired her acclaimed novel *Plum Wine,* a Book Sense bestseller and Book Sense Reading Group Pick, a Southern Independent Booksellers Alliance Book Award finalist, and a Kiriyama Prize Notable Book. She is also the author of the internationally acclaimed novels *Felice* and *Forms of Shelter.* An Alumni Distinguished Professor Emerita at North Carolina State University, she lives in Raleigh, North Carolina.

www.angeladavisgardner.com

About the Type

The text of this book was set in Legacy, a typeface family designed by Ronald Arnholm and issued in digital form by ITC in 1992. Both its serifed and unserifed versions are based on an original type created by the French punchcutter Nicholas Jenson in the late fifteenth century. While Legacy tends to differ from Jenson's original in its proportions, it maintains much of the latter's characteristic modulations in stroke.